DEBORAH SWIFT is a *USA TODAY* bestselling author of historical fiction, a genre she loves. As a child, she enjoyed reading the Victorian classics such as *Jane Eyre, Little Women, Lorna Doone* and *Wuthering Heights.* She has been reading historical novels ever since, though she's a bookaholic and reads widely – contemporary and classic fiction.

In the past, Deborah used to work as a set and costume designer for theatre and TV, so enjoys the research aspect of creating historical fiction, something she was familiar with as a scenographer. More details of her research and writing process can be found on her website www.deborahswift.com.

Deborah likes to write about extraordinary characters set against the background of real historical events.

Also by Deborah Swift

Operation Tulip

DEBORAH SWIFT

ONE PLACE. MANY STORIES

HQ
An imprint of HarperCollins*Publishers* Ltd
1 London Bridge Street
London SE1 9GF

www.harpercollins.co.uk

HarperCollins*Publishers*
Macken House, 39/40 Mayor Street Upper,
Dublin 1 D01 C9W8

This paperback edition 2024

2
First published in Great Britain by
HQ, an imprint of HarperCollins*Publishers* Ltd 2024

ISBN: 9780008586904

This book contains FSC™ certified paper and other controlled
sources to ensure responsible forest management.

For more information visit: www.harpercollins.co.uk/green

Printed and Bound in the UK using
100% Renewable Electricity at CPI Group (UK) Ltd

For Josephine

Chapter 1

Amsterdam, Holland
October 1944

Nancy glanced through the slash of rain to where Josef, tall and dark in a belted raincoat, was checking the others were in position. He stooped to tie a shoelace as he came out from the shelter of the weigh-house – one of the oldest buildings in Amsterdam, with its distinctive pointed towers. He looked up briefly and Nancy silently returned his gaze before checking her watch.

She was taut with nerves. 4.25 pm. Obermayer should appear at any moment.

As an agent Nancy often worked solo, but she'd agreed to this mission because she was the only one of her Resistance friends who knew what Obermayer looked like – a short, stout Nazi with an unmistakeable pouchy face. She'd recognise his calculated expression of mild surprise anywhere. It was designed to make you think him merely a bland civil servant, and not the most feared torturer in the Dutch SS.

Time to go. As she walked down the street, she glanced to the news stand to see another of their men reading the headlines on the front of the booth. She'd already seen Wim, sheltering by the tram stop, and Eva was waiting with the van, just around the corner.

Nancy strolled down the road towards the bank where Obermayer was due to meet one of what he called his V-men – informers who infiltrated the Dutch Resistance to sell their secrets to the Nazis. According to her intelligence, Obermayer met the same man every week at 4.30 outside the bank.

All she had to do now was to identify Obermayer by stopping as soon as she saw him, and opening up her handbag – and her comrades would do the rest and bundle him, and any accomplice, into the van. Once they had him, by God, they'd get the name of any traitor and give him what was coming to him. Hence this kidnap. A horrible job, but necessary. As she passed the bank doorway, she clocked a man waiting there.

A sharp intake of breath. Elmo. Oh no. Not one of their own?

A ripple of shock went down her back but she didn't pause her step. Bastard. So he was a double agent, one of the snakes in their midst. And there he was, waiting for Obermayer, cool as you like, smoking and shuffling his feet.

Her heels clacked on the pavement as she walked through the puddles, her head turned away from Elmo, as she hid under the brimmed hat that shaded her eyes. Still, the smell of his foul French tobacco drifted by her face.

No sign of Obermayer. He was late.

Josef and the rest would be tense; it was hard to look as if you were an innocent bystander when you were waiting to kidnap someone.

A heavy-set man walked around the corner and Nancy's heart lurched. She gripped her bag, ready to open it.

Not Obermayer. Her hand relaxed.

She'd got to the end of the row of buildings. She sensed the men's stares of impatience on her back. As if she'd forgotten something, she clapped a hand to her mouth and turned on her heel to return down the street. She walked more briskly now, swerving past other pedestrians, but the noise of footsteps slapping behind her made her stiffen.

A bulk of a man hurried by, beige overcoat flapping. He walked with a slight turnout of the feet, the neck thick as a tree trunk. It was Obermayer, she was certain, but he'd caught her by surprise and she couldn't see his face. She had to be sure.

She speeded her step. He was ahead of her, striding towards Elmo at the bank. She passed a long queue of drab women queuing outside the grocer's on the off-chance of a food delivery.

The man stopped at the bank, which had dripping Nazi flags and a colonnaded portico where Elmo was leaning against a pillar. Obermayer dropped a hand on his shoulder in a familiar way and said something she couldn't hear. Elmo smiled, spat out his cigarette butt, and ground it in the wet with the toe of his shoe.

Seconds later, a young boy leapt out from the queue to snatch up the butt. It provided just the diversion that Nancy needed. She risked a glance up to look directly into the man's face. Obermayer. No mistaking him.

Now! She fumbled with the clasp on her handbag and brought out a handkerchief to wipe her nose, leaving the bag gaping open.

The noise of the van starting up and then a door opening. Her Resistance friends had seen the signal.

Obermayer glanced up at the old gas-powered fish van parked a little further down the road. His lips tightened and his gaze snapped to meet hers. His eyes were grey and knowing.

'Excuse me,' he said swiftly to Elmo, and abruptly, he began to walk away, powering down the street.

He'd smelled a rat, and there was nothing she could do. Should she follow? Already, she was conscious of her men moving on the street, closing in. They had to catch him where they could get him to the van, which was kerb-crawling close behind him. Elmo, the double-crossing swine, had melted away into the bank.

A glimpse of her friend Josef. He had the chloroform bottle in his pocket. He swung out to follow his quarry who was heading briskly for the Apollolaan Hotel, a Nazi stronghold, close to where five canals meet.

But Obermayer didn't get far before Josef leapt at him.

'Gestapo!' Obermayer shouted, trying to summon help as he swung his fists at the men wrestling to pin him down and disarm him. He was still trying to get to his gun, but Wim was trying to crush his hands together.

Josef brought out the bottle of chloroform and the rag and unstoppered it, just as her friend Wim swung his fist to hit the big man. Obermayer reeled, cannoned into Josef and the chloroform bottle shot out of Josef's hand.

A sharp inhalation as the glass shattered. *No. Don't let him get away.*

The pavement glinted with shards of glass and running liquid, as Obermayer lurched out of their grasp.

Nancy ran towards them, uncertain what they could do now, but knowing the plan had failed. Obermayer drew a pistol from his coat and aimed it at Wim.

But before he could fire, two cracks. Eva, who had been in the getaway van, had panicked, drawn out a revolver and fired two shots out of the window.

Obermayer hit the ground like a collapsed building, his head smacking on to the pavement. One bullet had gone through his head, the other his neck.

Shit. The sound of the revolver instantly brought the Greens running. Like lice, they emerged from the side streets and buildings, shouting 'Stop! Stay where you are!'

The Greens were the *Ordnungspolizei*, the Order Police in green uniform who worked for Nazi Germany and were responsible for carrying out Nazi orders. They were tasked with the arrest, execution or deportation of what they called 'Enemies of the Reich'.

Already Nancy's friends were scattering, leaving Obermayer's body as a heap on the pavement. Wim jumped into the van, as Josef set off running and Eva reversed as fast as she could, foot hard on the gas pedal. Nancy was already on the move as she saw Josef dodge between the military trucks that had appeared from nowhere, and hare off alongside the canal. A patrol, alerted by the disturbance, was ready for him and cut off the route. He was surrounded by Wehrmacht helmets within seconds.

In the distance she saw Koos, one of their lookouts, being led away to a truck. She must get out of there. *But slow. Act calm. Nothing to do with me.*

She increased her pace and stepped straight into the chest of one of the Greens.

'Name?'

'Hendrika van Hof.' Her sixth false name.

'Did you see what happened there?'

'No,' Nancy said. 'I just saw trouble. I was going to work, and now I must go another way.'

The man, a grizzled-looking man in his forties, looked her up and down. 'Where d'you work?'

Her cover story was solid now. 'The Prinsengracht Hospital.'

'But that's the other side of the city. What are you doing here on Nieuwmarkt?'

'I needed to buy some press-studs from the market,' she said, smiling pleasantly though light-headed with fear.

'Well, Nurse Van Hof, you want to have dinner with me?'

She blinked. With him? He was old. The thought was repulsive. The question had come out of the blue and she didn't know how to answer.

'I will have to take you in for questioning,' he said. 'Or, you could answer my questions over dinner.'

He had a self-satisfied smugness about him that made her want to punch him, but she knew she had no choice but to agree. All women had no choice but to agree with the police in this war.

And besides, it would look more suspicious if she turned down a free dinner. Not now northern Holland was cut off from their food supply lines. 'That would be very nice,' she said.

'Tomorrow night at seven o'clock. Hotel de Gerstekorrel, near Dam Square. Okay?'

'Thank you.'

'And I'll need your papers.'

In case I run away. She'd understood. Damn. She'd have to hand them over. She opened her bag for the second time that day and took out the papers. They were forged of course. Would he notice? Sweat gathered under the neck of her coat.

He took them and glanced at them again. 'Aah, Hendrika.' He rolled her name round his tongue. 'I will see you tomorrow.'

'Call me Rika,' she said.

The man puffed himself up, pleased. Ugh. Every power-crazed Dutch creep had allied himself with the Nazis. 'And I am Dirk. Dirk van Meveren. If anyone asks, tell them I have your papers. They will be returned to you tomorrow. I look forward to our dinner.'

Nancy got off the streets as soon as she could. Breathless, she fled to Karel's ironmongery shop, a safe house where their resistance cell usually met. Karel was an old hand; he'd been in the Resistance in Amsterdam since the very beginning, whereas she'd only been in Holland for just over a year. Good going – they expected wireless operators to last only a few months.

She burst into his back room without knocking. 'We failed,' she told him. 'Obermayer is dead.'

'Dead you say.' Karel – old, moustachioed, ground down by years of war – paced up and down the counter, occasionally slapping a veined hand down on its surface. Of course now there was barely any stock, the Germans had taken it all to repurpose for weaponry or to prevent the Resistance from doing the same, so the place was hung only with brooms and scrubbing brushes behind its wooden shutters.

'Eva and Wim made it, but they got Josef and Koos,' Nancy said, now she had her breath back.

Karel's sixty-year-old face was worn and lined, his cheeks sunken. He leant on the counter, shoulders slumped. 'I can't do this anymore. Though I don't think they'll talk, you can't meet here. Not now.'

It was a blow. Karel's shop had been closed for months and they'd used it as their *de facto* base.

'Koos and Josef?' He seemed to consider the names, weighing it all up.

She nodded. To lose any agent was a disaster. But worse was the knowledge that Josef had been taken. He was not only their most experienced member, but the bravest of the men, the most agile, the one who had all the ideas and who tied the Resistance efforts together. He was the firebrand of their little band of brothers, the leader, and his loss was like pulling out the heart from their resistance.

Nancy shook her head, her heart still pounding. 'What a botch-up. Elmo was there, meeting that butcher, cosying up to the Nazis.'

Karel rested his head between his hands on the counter. She waited as he let out a ragged sigh. 'I can't believe it.'

'I thought there was something about Elmo all along, too eager, too keen to be involved. It didn't sit right.'

Karel looked up. 'Doesn't seem right he's still out there, whereas Josef . . .' Another sigh. 'We'll have to move on,' he said. 'And it'll break my wife's heart to leave this place. My father would turn in his grave. Been here a hundred and fifty years, this shop. Always thought it'd be here for the next generation. But Koos? He's inexperienced. Not sure how long he'll hold out. Could blab at any moment.' He gestured angrily around the room, at the empty fireplace, the bare shelves, the sad-looking tins of metal polish, and the few remaining boxes of clothes pegs.

'Where will you go?'

'My sister in Brabant? I don't know.'

Nancy shook her head. 'I can't leave. A Green took my papers.'

'What?'

She explained. 'If I don't go to dinner with him, it will look suspicious.'

'You can't. Get out of Amsterdam. If they torture them and anyone talks—'

'How, with no papers?'

'We'll think of something.'

'The Green might look at my pass and ID, and see it's a forgery. And if he does, I'll be walking right into a trap. But equally, if I don't go, he'll have the Gestapo out looking for me straightaway, and he has my photo and my address.'

'Then don't go home.'

'I've no choice. Besides, I need to clear Josef's room of any evidence.'

'You'll miss him.'

She shrugged.

'Oh, I know. You've got a reputation for keeping your distance.'

Had she? She considered a moment. He was right; she'd learnt not to trust anyone. Too many close shaves. And though she liked Josef, there was Tom, back home in England. She ran a hand along the counter. 'Can you try to find out where they took them? D'you think it's the Oranjehotel?'

Karel closed his eyes a moment as if summoning the last of his energy. 'I'm leaving. My bag's already packed upstairs. It's always been ready in case of something like this, but I never thought I'd have the heart to use it. But I've had enough. The shootings, the reprisals. I've nothing left in me, Rika.'

His words peeled her to something raw. It was too close to how she felt. But for the first time, she saw him clearly. This old man, stripped bare of everything he loved, his clothes hanging on a too-thin frame, the dark circles speaking of too much worry and not enough food.

'It's all right, Karel.' She went and rested a hand on his arm. 'You go. It's time to separate. It will be safer that way. We don't know if we'll see our friends again, and we can't know what the Nazis will beat out of them. Better safe than sorry. But you can be proud. You've done so much here, keeping this safe house. Today we got rid of Obermayer, and so some of our resistance men will sleep more soundly in their beds.'

'What about Elmo?'

'We'll leave him running for the moment. Now we know he works for the Gestapo, we can feed him the wrong information. Make sure it works to our advantage. Two can play his game.'

Karel pulled at a thread on his cuff. 'It's playing with fire, if you ask me. Elmo'll sell us all down the river.'

'You've done your bit, Karel.' She patted his arm in reassurance. 'Go get your bag.'

'Take care, Rika. Get out of Amsterdam as soon as you can.'

Nancy let herself into her apartment and closed the door, leaning against it a moment before bounding up the stairs. A black day. Two more of her resistance cell in Nazi hands. Only now did she feel her legs start to tremble. But there was no time to lose, she must clear Josef's room.

Whilst sharing this apartment, she and Josef had kept themselves to themselves, and his door had always been firmly shut to her. Of course he knew Rika was a code-name, and that she had ties back home in England. Meanwhile, she knew he wasn't really called Josef and had lost his girlfriend to a German camp. They respected each other but their personal lives had always been strictly off limits. No complications; that was her rule.

She and Josef were two of the few active members of this cell that were left. So few of them now. The war was supposed to be over, but the Germans had clung on to this part of Holland like an angry toddler with a toy.

Quick. She must stop these senseless thoughts. Going in Josef's room felt like a betrayal. Whatever happened next, he'd never be able to come back.

9

His plaid shirt and a grubby neckerchief dangled on the back of the chair, and a pair of shoes was half pushed under the bed, laces trailing. But she ignored these and went straight to the wardrobe – a big old wooden armoire, and hoisted a compact leather suitcase from the bottom drawer. It was a dead weight. The crystal radio, the way she contacted other networks, and Tom, once a month, with just a few words. No more. Too many was to risk being picked up by the detector vans. She placed it by the door, ready to go.

She ripped through the rest of the room like a burglar, yanking open drawers and cupboards, flinging back the bedcovers, searching out anything incriminating. She scooped up stuff from the bedside table – scribbled locations and places of meetings on scraps of paper. They couldn't tell anyone much, Josef was so careful, but still, best to be thorough.

If the *Moffen* came here, there must be nothing – then if he held out, he could still claim innocence. Not that evidence ever held much sway with the Nazis, but every sliver of hope was worth hanging on to.

A box of matches lived on the shelf above the enamel stove in the kitchen. She struck one, shocked at the flare of sulphur and light in the dimness of the blacked-out room. Soon the papers were just charred flakes in the fireplace.

At the last moment she thought to search through his pockets.

In his jacket her hand touched something cold. A small Molina handgun. More rummaging and she found a cardboard box of bullets. She slid these into her raincoat pocket.

A dash across the corridor for a quick check around her own room. She knew exactly how it was laid out. It was part of the training she'd undertaken back in England with the Special Operations Executive. How far away it all seemed now, the achingly draughty rooms at Arisaig, and her terror of failing when they'd asked her to parachute out of a plane. And yet still, the life-saving instructions her trainers had given her had stuck in her mind. Thank God for them, or she wouldn't be alive.

From them she'd learned she must place everything exactly, so she'd know if anyone else had been here. She surveyed her bedroom. Nightdress neatly folded on the pillow, book precisely angled on the dressing table next to an empty perfume bottle. Nothing had been touched. But now she must leave it all. Leave Rika behind, shedding her as a snake sheds its skin. She had done this so often.

Henrika van Hof would disappear into the Amsterdam fog.

She'd go to Anna, the only person who knew who she really was, and her only friend. Being an agent was a lonely business. She had never mentioned her to anyone, because to do so was a risk to them both. Though Anna was well over sixty-five now – she'd taken Nancy in when she was desperate after the Wehrmacht had shot her previous landlady Mrs Van Hegel. Anna wouldn't ask questions. The only person who would be willing to house a British agent on the run, and her suitcase transmitter.

Nancy picked up the suitcase, feeling the weight of it drag on her arm. She would have to go now, this minute; for being out after dark was always more suspicious. If she were to be stopped by the Stapo it would be the end. But she had to have a means of communication, and she couldn't stay.

Going out there was like being a rabbit surrounded by wolves.

She braced herself for the weight of the suitcase when she heard a noise below. Instantly alert, she raced to the window and looked out. Below, she saw the roof of a green Wehrmacht truck and armed men scrambling out on to the wet pavement.

Had someone blabbed already? Or was it Elmo who had set them on to her?

She couldn't take the risk. Only one way out. The iron fire escape. She dropped the suitcase by the window and thrust up the sash. It was stiff and she had to heave it open. One leg over the window ledge and on to the iron stairs. Heart thudding, she calculated she had a few minutes grace before the men ran round to cut off the back of the houses.

She reached for the suitcase, but it got stuck as she climbed out.

Bloody awkward thing. She wrestled with it a few moments, twisting it this way and that, before letting it thud back to the ground. She'd never carry it down the slippery twisting stairway.

She grabbed the wet railings and half-leapt, half-skittered down the stairs, shoes ringing out as she went. Shouts from above as she jumped off the last tread.

A glance up, two helmeted men were leaning out of her window. *So it was me they were after.*

A snatch of a look down the street. Which way?

She gambled and ran left, just as heavy footsteps ran around the right corner.

A few more seconds' grace.

She shot along the road; feet pounding behind her. They must have orders not to shoot, to take her alive. Skidding around the corner she bumped head first into a civilian, coming the other way. He tried to take hold of her, but she twisted away. Thank goodness his presence in the middle of the pavement also slowed her pursuers.

Up a side alley towards the canal, where she knew a shortcut and a dry dike where she could hide. Her breath was ballooning in her lungs as she dived into the narrow culvert. There was a drainage tunnel here that was dry, and where they had once hid arms and ammunition. She elbowed her way in, and then crouched into the musty tunnel.

Above her head was a curve of red brick and behind her a pipe, now only damp and not flooded. Since the Germans had destroyed many of the lowland drainage systems, floodwater seeped up where it never used to, and dry pipes appeared that used to be channels for water.

From here she could watch feet walking by on the higher footpath, and she gripped tight to Josef's gun in her pocket as she saw men's boots tramp past.

'*Wo ist sie?*'

'*Nichts.*'

They were searching for her. She willed her breath to steady, taking sips of the damp peaty air. Two bicycles passed by, but she kept tight in a ball, hidden from view. She quietly loaded the gun.

After what seemed an eternity, the boots sloshed by through the puddles again. She waited until she thought her legs had gone completely numb before emerging slowly from her hiding place. She peered out first to check no-one was there, then crawled out.

The back of her raincoat was damp and full of mud, her knees and elbows too, and it was growing dark. She must get to Anna's. She walked purposefully down the canal, every sense straining. If anyone asked to see her pass, it would be the end. She'd no papers, and they'd find her gun.

She walked briskly the thirty-five-minute walk away from the city centre. At one point, a German foot patrol was about to approach her, but fortunately a Wehrmacht truck stopped by them, and they went to its window to talk. Head down, heart hammering, Nancy just kept on walking, praying they would not follow her. She was in luck, but she didn't dare look back. To look would have drawn their attention.

At Anna's house she went around the back and gave a soft knock, the three light taps and a heavy one that spelt V for Victory in Morse. The code they all used as friends. Anna opened the door and pulled her inside.

'What took you so long?' she said.

Anna had already got a message from one of her contacts that Josef had been arrested.

'The death of that butcher Obermayer won't go without repercussions,' Anna said, her voice firm despite her age. 'They'll want to make scapegoats of somebody. And that's not good for our cause.' Her lined face creased with worry. 'Reprisals just make us more unpopular.'

Nancy sighed. 'You can't blame them. People can't see what we do, only the times it goes wrong and someone innocent gets hurt. They don't realise who Obermayer was. That he was the man responsible for dismembering almost every resistance cell in Amsterdam.'

'They'll come for you, as soon as someone gives your name. And because you ran.'

'What else could I do?'

A flap of a hand. 'I know all that. But it signals your guilt. You can't stay in Amsterdam, and especially not here.'

'There's still work to do in Amsterdam.'

'With whom? Your cell is finished. It can do nothing useful with its men locked up and its equipment confiscated. You need to join with someone else. We'll have tea, and tomorrow I'll take you to a friend. He'll get you out of Amsterdam and to The Hague. There's a group there that could do with a courier to take messages.'

She sighed. 'I had to leave my transmitter behind.'

A shrug. 'Maybe they have contact with Radio Oranje and can get word back to England about where you are.'

Nancy bit back her disappointment. She'd hoped for more time with her, but she knew Anna was one of the most experienced operatives in Amsterdam, and her advice was golden.

That night she hardly slept. She stood by the window, peering through a crack in the curtain, restless in case anyone had followed her.

Don't be silly, she reassured herself in English. *You saw no-one.*

She dropped the curtain and got into bed again, even the creak of springs making her startle. She was aware as always of how her very presence could bring death to those near her. She'd seen it enough over the years. This was her fourth mission to Holland, and she was only supposed to be a wireless operator, but as soon as she'd arrived in Amsterdam she'd become so much more than that. So few agents were left, so she'd taken on more responsibility. Collecting weapons, delivering messages, liaising with other cells. She'd done it all.

14

Was she jinxed? Josef was supposed to be organising this cell, and for three weeks all had gone to plan, they were about to knock out Obermayer, one of the biggest thorns in their side, but now this.

She'd hoped that with the latest big push from the Allies, the war would be over and within weeks she'd be back with Tom in London, but the Allied operation at Arnhem had failed. They'd been banking on it – the offensive that was whispered as Operation Market Garden.

When the news had come – that Hitler's troops had held the line, that they'd retained control of the ports, she'd cried. She'd been focussed on getting home to Tom, and the relief that the war would soon be over. But things looked increasingly bleak, and there was no way now the British would try to get her out through Nazi lines. The disappointment was hard to bear.

Though the Allies had liberated Maastricht and in the south a sea of orange cloth – the colour of free Holland – was flying everywhere, here, north of the Maas River, they were completely cut off.

Nancy stared at the ceiling, wondering if Tom was thinking of her, and whether he realised she wouldn't be coming home. Now the Amsterdam cell had folded, she'd become such a risk that even Anna was turning her away. She'd never worked in The Hague, but she supposed she'd have to see what she could do. She sighed. Starting again was always the hardest thing to do.

Anna's great skill was, that being over sixty, she could mimic a frail old lady, and Nancy fell into her familiar role of pretending to be her granddaughter. They walked arm in arm, slowly, as Anna put on her limping gait and led her to a small house in a rundown suburb. In reality, Anna was as tough and upright as iron. On the way Anna told her they were going to a safe house she said belonged to someone called Gerard.

'This is Edda,' Anna said to the man who opened the door. Nancy was used to speaking Dutch now, but the sudden new name took her aback.

Edda, thought Nancy. *Another name for me to get used to.* Just for once it would be nice to choose her own name.

The man who filled the doorway beckoned Nancy inside without preamble, and Anna shut the door behind them.

The tiny interior was stuffed with furniture. The conflicting ticks of two cuckoo clocks at odds with each other made Nancy wince. Gerard pointed them to a sofa and bade them sit. There was barely enough room because the sofa was overstuffed with cushions.

A huge giant of a man, he crammed his large frame into the remaining armchair. Nancy found him intimidating with his lowered brows and penetrating stare.

'There's talk of the assassination everywhere,' he said. 'But I heard this morning by radio that they've taken Josef to the Nazi interrogation centre at the Oranjehotel.'

Nancy inwardly shuddered. The 'Orangehotel' was what the Resistance nicknamed the fortress the Nazis used as a prison.

'It's not good news,' Gerard went on. 'It means a public trial and execution. They will be looking to make him an example.'

'I burned his papers,' Nancy said.

Anna smiled. 'See? She's well trained. Can you find a place for her?'

Gerard looked her up and down as if assessing livestock. 'You'll do anything?'

She hesitated. What sort of 'anything' did he mean?

'We need a woman like you; someone pretty, someone not too thin, someone who can decorate a man's arm.'

She was insulted, but had no idea how to respond.

'We need someone to get to know the Nazi officers at the Oranjehotel. In particular the assistant to the SS Oberführer Schneider. Our man's called Detlef Keller. He's in charge of the

16

records – logging information about Resistance prisoners, keeping a tally of who goes in and out, and where to. Our sources in The Hague have been watching him. They say he's lonely and impressionable. That he hangs around the bars looking for a pretty girl. We need inside information from him – not only about what the Germans have gleaned about our networks, but about where they send the prisoners, so we can trace what happens to our operatives, and if possible, intercept the transports.'

'You mean, we're going to try to get our men out?'

'We're considering it.'

'How will I make contact with this Keller?'

'Infiltrate his circle as best you can. We will give you money, enough to furnish an apartment, and give you a decent wardrobe. He's a drinker, and often socialises with others in the Wehrmacht Command.'

She was wary. 'Has it been tried before?'

'Once, but not with Keller. The last girl we had in mind didn't even make it as far as signing the lease on the apartment. She got picked up because she got careless with her cover story. Then when they arrested her, she crumbled.' His voice was full of disgust.

'I'm not the crumbling type,' she said, raising her chin.

He laughed then, a great belly laugh. Nancy was surprised how much it changed him.

'She'll do,' he said to Anna. He turned to Nancy. 'A rich widow, that's what we have in mind. Someone looking for a good time and a replacement husband, one preferably high up in the Party.'

A woman that sounded despicable. 'You're really going to try to get them out?'

'We'll try. Josef at least. Without him, the Amsterdam cell will collapse. We need him and his prospects are bleak.'

She took it in, that Koos was considered less valuable than Josef. The thought hurt in a way she couldn't dispel. But if they could save one . . . 'I'd like to help. Josef's a good friend, and he covered my back too many times to count.'

17

'If you think you're up to it. It will take a cool head and a quick mind.'

'You think I don't know that?' she sparked back at him. 'I've been in Holland on and off for more than a year. My life has been on the line often enough.'

'Then you can try. You can stay with my brother whilst we construct a cover story and until you find an apartment.'

Chapter 2

Baker Street, London

Tom Lockwood put the newspaper down on his desk, took off his glasses to rub his eyes, then put his head in his hands. So the rumours were true. Operation Market Garden had failed. Monty's tanks had got stuck in mud and instead of a liberated Holland, they were now faced with half a country cut off completely from foreign aid. What would Gerbrandy, the Dutch Prime Minister, do now?

Tom chewed his pencil. No-one could possibly understand just how desperately he'd been looking forward to Nancy coming home, and to the end of this whole damn war. A few weeks ago, he could almost touch it.

And what would liberating only half of Holland mean for his job here at Baker Street? Would N Section be training any more men? He enjoyed his work – there was something satisfying in bashing the mysteries of codes and ciphers into the brains of new agents.

Just then his telephone rang.

Neil's familiar voice down the crackly line. 'Have you heard anything?' He meant about Nancy of course, though he couldn't say it. Neil was Nancy's brother and they were both supposed to think Nancy was working as a nurse with the First Aid Nursing Yeomanry, or FANYs. They weren't supposed to know she was an agent in occupied Holland.

'No, nothing,' Tom replied. 'Just what I read in the paper.'

'Lilli and I listened to Radio Oranje last night, like I always do. It's horrendous. The port of Rotterdam is in ruins and the Germans are destroying anything the Dutch have built, out of sheer spite. Generations of trade reduced to rubble! Not just that, but can you believe they're bombing and destroying pumping stations? At this rate coastal areas will soon be back under water. They're evacuating the coastal towns but there's no way people can get out of the occupied zone, they've just nowhere to go.' His voice cracked. 'Most of them are too scared to do anything but hide.'

Tom flipped the paper over, one ear glued to the phone. 'I've got *The Standard* in front of me and it says here they've no electricity or fuel. No trams, no telephones. We have to do something. I can't bear to think of how bad it must be.'

'What? We can't do anything.'

'I don't know.' He lowered his voice. 'Get Nancy out somehow.'

'But how can we do that? I'm still here at the radio unit at Wavendon, and you can't do anything with Beauclerk. You know how he has to okay every last little thing.'

Tom pictured his boss, worn ragged by the war. Beauclerk was a nervous wreck, but he'd some sympathy for the man. Though still heading the offices at Baker Street, he was obviously unwell, grey in the face and showing signs of Parkinson's disease. 'I don't know. Can you and Lilli get up to London?' Lilli was Neil's wife.

'Maybe, next weekend, if we can get a train.'

'Come to my flat then, and in the meantime, I'll see what I can find out.'

Tom loped up the long flight of stairs to the offices and knocked on Beauclerk's door. A grunt of 'Enter' from his boss. Beauclerk was leaning on the desk, poring over the same latest edition of the *Evening Standard*, a cold cup of coffee at his elbow. The picture of the king on the wall behind him had been replaced with one of Churchill, complete with brooding, intent expression, and cigar in hand.

In contrast, the war hadn't treated Beauclerk well, his face was drooping, worn and greyish, like old lined concrete.

A sigh. 'What is it now?' Beauclerk's voice had a resigned tone. He clutched one arm to his waistcoat to stop it shaking. His Parkinson's disease must be getting worse.

'I saw the papers. What are "N" Section doing about the agents in the North?' Tom asked. 'Are they being evacuated?'

A sigh. 'You know perfectly well I can't tell you that.'

'Which means they aren't.'

'Their intelligence is still useful. And the place will fall eventually. Has to.'

'Eventually. When they're all dead of starvation. You've read it?' Tom pointed to *The Standard*.

'Look, I can't do anything. I know it's bloody, but I can't. I should throw you out of my office with a flea in your ear for even asking.'

'You won't though. Because you know I'm one of the few people you can trust. That you can tell the truth to. And that counts for a lot in this mad old game we're in.'

Beauclerk made a face and stirred his cold coffee. Tom watched the milky skin congeal around the spoon.

'It's plain enough we can't get troops over the Maas River,' Beauclerk said. 'The Germans have bedded in. The coastal ports are sealed. No-one can get in or out. We've stopped all agent drops. Anti-aircraft guns line the banks of every estuary and canal, so there's no way we can fly anyone in or out.'

'So our agents'll just be left to rot with no supplies, no ammunition, and no possible way out.'

'I'm sorry Tom, but I can't do anything. And I suppose now's as good a time as any to tell you – I'm retiring.' He shrugged. 'I'm an old horse and they're putting me out to grass. Ill health.'

'When?' Tom reeled. Baker Street 'N' Section without Beauclerk was unthinkable.

'End of next week. Last of the month. It'll be Paterson's problem then, not mine.'

'Paterson? Rodney Paterson?' Tom couldn't believe it. 'But he's hopeless. He's just a jumped-up yes man!'

'Whatever you think of him, he's my replacement. He's tasked with winding down my section of the Political Warfare Executive. And you know him, he always likes to do things by the book.'

Tom groaned. 'Everything he does is glacial. It's a catastrophe over there! Someone will have to do something – not just for our agents, but the whole of Holland. What does Queen Wilhelmina think of the fact you're backing off?'

'Not much. But then you could hardly expect her to be dancing a jig. She's urging England to act, but we can't do anything without more military support. We're petitioning the US, but so far, no luck.'

'If Paterson starts negotiating, we'll all be dead and gone by the time he's got out his pen. Shit. What a mess.'

'Wish I could do more to help, but my hands are tied—'

Tom was already interrupting. 'No you don't. I know you – you'll be sat in the Gentleman's Club in the Cavendish reading the paper with not a care in the world, whilst Nancy's still stuck out there.'

'Insults won't help, Tom. And you're not stupid, we can never let the personal drive our decisions, you know that.'

Beauclerk knew Nancy was in Holland, damn him. 'You always bent the rules for me a bit before, and I'm asking you to bend them now.'

'It's too late, Tom. I'm leaving, and I can't do anything, can't sign anything anymore. Only the debriefing documents, that's all. You'll have to ask Paterson. Close the door on your way out.'

Tom took one last look at him, at the set of his face, and realised it was no use. Angry, he slammed his way out of the room.

He'd got halfway down the corridor when he turned back. He pushed open the door without knocking. 'Sorry, sir,' he said. 'We go back a long way, and you deserve your retirement. I wish you all the best.' He held out his hand across the desk.

Surprised, Beauclerk lifted his shaky hand and Tom grabbed it to pump it up and down.

Beauclerk's eyes were suddenly watery. 'Bloody Lockwood,' he said. 'I sure as hell hope Paterson can cope with you, because I never could.'

'Okay,' Tom said to Neil. 'I've got a plan.'

That weekend Neil and Tom were sitting on the floor amid piles of books because Tom's bedsitting room was so cramped and sparsely furnished that there was no sofa. 'Oh no,' Neil said. 'Not another of your plans. Remember the last one?'

'Less of that!' Tom said. 'At least we warned Nancy, even if it didn't exactly go the way we wanted. And my plan this time's really simple. We just go to Holland, find a way to get her out.'

Lilli, pregnant and lolling on the only armchair, rolled her eyes.

Tom continued, 'Wait while I explain. Look, the PWE is winding the Netherlands section down. They know there's no point in sending more agents to Holland, not when half of it's already under Allied control. And especially now they know the resistance lines in the North are compromised.'

Neil was about to interrupt but Tom held up his hand. 'Bear with me. The Allies are bedded down in Holland, south of the Maas river. So we can get as far as there, no problem. But I've done a bit of digging – about what our agents are up to via a friend who works for Prince Bernhard – you know, the Government-in-exile – and it turns out there's a resistance cell called Group Albrecht. They're still in operation and based in Biesbosch. Hold on, whilst I get the map.'

Tom unfolded a map of Holland which was already marked with scrawled ink dots.

'What are these?' Neil asked, pointing.

'The places where I found out Nancy was,' Tom said sheepishly. 'I think she's here in Amsterdam right now.'

'You big softie,' Neil said. 'Is that what all these are about?' He pointed to the language books piled up on the floor.

'My Dutch isn't so bad now. And it brings me closer to her.' Tom hunkered down to point at the map. 'Anyway, here near Dordrecht – see this? This is marsh – mostly flooded now, but it's a kind of watery labyrinth, one the Germans are reluctant to tackle. But this Group Albrecht apparently know the safe routes through the maze, and are making daily crossings, bringing people out. Folk who need medical attention – diabetics who need insulin, downed British airmen, people like that. But if they can get people out, they can get people in.'

A snort from Lilli. 'You think Neil should join that?' she asked. 'Don't forget he's got a bad leg. He can't do strenuous things. And besides, he's still working for Delmer at the radio station.' Lilli was forthright as usual.

'But for how long? People from the radio station are looking for new jobs already,' Neil said. 'Max is going to the BBC in Shepherd's Bush and Ron's already gone to that new BBC service they're setting up in Manchester.'

'But you said you didn't want to move from Milton Bryan with me expecting,' Lilli said, patting her stomach. 'And now you want to go flying off to Holland? Put yourself in a war zone?' She shook her head. 'You've lost your mind.'

Neil reached to put an arm around her shoulders. 'No, I'm just out of my mind with worry about Nancy. Darling, don't forget, I've got Dutch blood. One day it might come out to Mother that Nancy's over there in Holland and not in Birmingham, and I'd never be forgiven if anything happened to her – not if Mother found out I knew and did nothing. God only knows what Nancy's dealing with. We can't just sit back while people die.'

'It's winter,' Tom added. 'They're completely cut off, and they're in an occupied country.'

Lilli looked stricken. 'You're not going. You've no idea, have you? Unless you've seen it, you don't know what the Nazis are like. It's like a crusade, a religious crusade, and just as bloody. They'll be worse, crushed up there like cornered rats.' She pushed Neil away. 'What if you don't come back?'

Tom was suddenly very aware of where Lilli had come from, that she too was a refugee, and would be alone here in England if Neil was to go with him.

Neil turned to Lilli. 'It's bad if the Germans have control of all the ports. The papers say the railway workers went on strike, to stop the Nazis transporting Jews, and since then the Germans are stopping all supplies getting in. So there's no food, no fuel. The Germans are deliberately starving civilians as punishment.'

'It's not Germans,' Lilli burst out. 'How dare you! Of course we care if people starve. It's Nazis. We're not all the same.'

There was an awkward silence. Neil's face had closed into a tight, worried expression. He reached out to Lilli's hand again but she pulled it away and turned her face to look out of the window.

'Look Tom,' Neil said quietly, 'I'm not sure I can leave Lilli right now. I know there's Nancy . . . but we've got our baby's future to think of. If anything happened to me—'

Neil looked torn, and Tom felt for him. 'Okay, okay. I understand. It's just you're the only one I can trust.'

'Look, the only thing I can think of is that I'll see if I can get transferred to a station more directly in contact with the Dutch lines. I'll write to the BBC, see if I can get in with Radio Oranje in London. After all, I can speak Dutch and German.'

Tom knew how hard that would be for Neil. He'd left the Baker Street office under a cloud, having got caught up in a British Fascist plot, and he'd been sent, as a sort of punishment, to a dull desk job with some tin-pot radio outfit in Milton Bryan in Bedfordshire.

'London?' Lilli spoke the word with venom. 'We're comfortable where we are, aren't we? Why would we want to move to London with all that smoke and bomb damage and nowhere for children to play?'

'We'll talk about it later, darling.' Neil said. 'Tell Tom about that film we saw last week, *Perfect Strangers.*'

'You tell him. I'm not. Besides, I don't want that to happen to us,' Lilli said.

'What?' Tom asked, aware that Neil's attempt to change the conversation had somehow misfired, and that Lilli still seemed upset.

'This married couple in the film, their marriage fell apart because of the war.'

When they'd gone, Tom stared down at the map, tracing the river frontier in his mind's eye. He was disappointed but he could see that hoping Neil would join him was unrealistic. It was just daunting, the idea of jumping into it alone. And most of it was because he was just so desperate to see Nancy again; it had been more than nine months since she'd last been home, and after those few precious days he missed her like having a permanent hole in his chest.

He went over to the curling photograph of her propped up on his mantelpiece. It was a terrible shot, taken on a windy day on Primrose Hill, last time she'd been on leave. Her hair was blowing over her face and he'd somehow clicked too soon, so it was all blurry. But it was Nancy all right, her smile underneath it all, and it brought it back, the moment she had to go. How they'd both tried to be stupidly brave at the station, but he'd ended up running after the train like a kid, to catch the last possible glimpse of her.

He took off his glasses and rubbed his eyes. Baker Street were doing nothing to get her out, just leaving her to rot. The thought that they'd just let her down, abandon her after all she'd done, well, it made him want to spit.

He slumped back into his chair and stared at the map again, at the winding coils of river and canals that criss-crossed the country, at all the places she'd been. The idea that you could actually get into Holland now through the Allied Lines wouldn't let go. What was to stop him going there and getting her out? Since no more agents were being recruited, his previous vital work training them had dried up, and now it was just endless writing up records. Anything would be better than doing more of Beauclerk's soul-destroying paperwork. Especially Paterson's even duller paperwork.

Oh Nancy, I miss you so much.

The next day Neil called him at his office. 'Sorry, Tom, I just can't come with you. We had another row about it last night. It's too much to ask of Lilli. Partly it's her, and partly it's my mother. Mother's not been the same since Father died and she really doesn't need to be worrying herself sick over where I am on top of it all. She's already almost frantic wondering why Nancy hardly ever writes.'

'It's all right, old chap,' Tom said. 'I know it wasn't the brightest idea.'

'I still want to do something,' Neil said. 'So I've been on the blower this morning trying to get a job with Radio Oranje. So far, they're not biting. And Delmer's not happy, he wants to keep the team at Milton Bryan together until the end, and he got really ratty, telling us we're all jumping ship. It was bloody.'

'Sorry. It's my fault. You'd best just stay put.'

'What about you?' Neil asked. 'Will you give notice, or what?'

'I don't know. I'll need to talk to the new head of our section – Beauclerk's retiring.'

'Who is it?'

'Rodney Paterson.'

A groan. 'Oh God. Good luck with that,' Neil said.

Chapter 3

The Hague
November 1944

Nancy headed down Marktstraat from the station, towards a block of apartments mostly inhabited, so Gerard had told her, by well-to-do Nazi sympathisers. He had told her to meet the manager and estate agent there, a Herr Brouwer, who would show her some apartments.

Apparently the whole top floor of the block was taken up by high-up SS officers of the Gestapo, and the rest by other officials of the Party, wealthy Nazi sympathisers, or the *Sicherheitsdienst* – the German security service. She glanced in an empty shop window, and didn't recognise herself in the new black suit under a burgundy-coloured coat with a sleek fox-fur collar. Gerard had supplied her with a black felt hat with a brim. Fashionable widow clothes. She had styled her hair with rollers the night before, and Gerard had even handed her a lipstick.

'The Nazi women are all painted,' he'd said. 'You need powder and a look of artificiality.' Never mind the artificial look, she felt artificial on the inside. Even going into the lobby was going to take nerves of steel.

Her navy leather handbag had new identity papers, and she'd been given the name Danique Koopman. So now she was Danique. Well, perhaps it was classier than Rika. Her supposed husband, Anton, who'd died of heart trouble, had been an industrialist owner of a foundry in Nijmegen. American bombers had destroyed the town one afternoon in February – awful, they mistook it for German territory. Thousands dead, wounded or missing. Everyone in the Resistance had felt it as a body-blow, and for many Dutch, this was the worst day of the war. How could it happen? How could their beautiful medieval town be crushed to mere rubble by their own side?

As she approached the apartment block, she paused and inhaled sharply, her hand on her bag. Nearly there. She took a moment more to consider her new identity and remind herself of plausible answers to possible questions about why she was in The Hague.

The ID photograph of Danique Koopman had been rigged with her own photograph by a forger called Greta. Nancy had studied the dossier of information about Frau Koopman, but it didn't ease her nerves. Danique's husband had been a big supporter and donor to the Nazi party, and he'd left her comfortably off. Danique herself had disappeared in the slew of bombs over Nijmegen, and they assumed her to be dead. No record of her survival had ever been found. Even so, after years of doing such roles, this one felt particularly shaky. It was unlike any other role she'd attempted to take on in the whole time she'd been in Holland.

It also made her squeamishly uncomfortable because of Tom.

What would he think? His smiling face appeared in her thoughts, the way he always looked at her with a mixture of admiration and concern.

She continued towards the apartments. Now, not only was she aiming to get close to a Nazi administrator, but she was thinking about the Oranjehotel, a name that conjured evil shadows.

It was notorious – a prison where agents were regularly tortured and executed.

As she swung in through the revolving doors of the apartment lobby, she pulled her shoulders back and put on an imperious smile.

'Ah, Frau Koopman, very nice to meet you.' This must be Brouwer, the manager, coming out from behind the reception desk. She guessed him to be in his early forties, thin hair already balding. Immaculate in a shiny suit and tie, a clipboard under his arm, he'd emerged from a small room off the lobby. He gave her a small formal bow. 'We will use the elevator to reach the fourth floor.' He held out an arm to gesture her ahead, and she made a barely perceptible nod of acknowledgement.

Inside the lift, she stood tall, but didn't attempt small talk. She pressed her lips together feeling the unaccustomed slide of the lipstick. At the second floor the lift bell pinged and the door swung open. A tall man in Nazi uniform pulled open the metal cage and stepped in. She moved as far to the back of the lift as she could.

'Good morning.' His eyes met hers and he gave a brief apologetic smile.

'*Heil Hitler!*' shot back Brouwer.

The new arrival gave him a look of impatience. A quick assessment of the insignia on his uniform told Nancy he was a high-up officer of the *Sicherheitsdienst* (SD). It didn't make her feel any better. She studied his back as the lift cranked up to the fourth floor. The high stand collar with his hair half-shaved above it. He carried his cap, slapping it mindlessly against his thigh. Being this close to him caused Nancy's belly to tighten into a hard knot.

The lift clunked to a halt and the German pulled open the cage and opened the door for them both to get out. 'After you,' he said.

'Thank you,' Nancy replied, stepping out.

The SD officer went ahead of the manager, and she watched him stroll down the corridor and unlock a door at the front of the building, before looking back to stare at her.

'Apartment eighteen is at this end,' Brouwer said. 'This way.'

She was having second thoughts. Having a high-up Nazi as this close a neighbour was unsettling. Perhaps there was another floor she could choose. She'd look at the apartment, and then suggest it was too large.

The apartment was indeed vast. It looked out over Wagenstraat, a shopping area in the hub of the city. From the window she saw shops with lines of people standing or sitting on the pavement, as well as buildings that had been boarded up. Today a sea fret had drifted in from the coast and the city was shrouded in fog.

Her heels echoed on the parquet wood floor as she examined the living space which had been furnished in luxury by someone with solid conservative taste. There was a three-piece suite and a standard lamp with a parchment shade. A few oil paintings of winter canals and the inevitable windmill were displayed on the walls.

'It's rather too big for one,' she said. 'Is there somewhere smaller you can show me? On another floor?'

'No,' Brouwer said. 'There is nowhere else. And besides, this is the one Gerard picked out.'

She startled and gave him a close look. 'You're . . .?'

'You can call me Steef. I'm a friend. I manage the building here, and I try to feedback what intelligence I can.'

She appraised him anew. A neat, dapper man, so unremarkable he had an air of anonymity. It was hard to believe he could be part of the Dutch Resistance.

He smiled. 'I advise you to take the apartment, Frau Koopman. It is closest to Herr Detlef Keller, the man who was just in the lift. And I believe you and he are to become close friends.'

Chapter 4

Nancy had been in the apartment for a month, but was no closer to meeting Keller, although she'd gathered information from Steef on the prison at Scheveningen where Keller worked. No-one had told her the prison was run by SS men, and the thought was daunting. It apparently housed over a thousand detainees, many of them Jews, political prisoners or resistance workers, who would then be transported to camps or executed in the dunes behind the prison.

Josef was still alive, thank God. Steef had heard through the network that he was to go to trial, if he survived that long. Apparently the date of the trial could take months whilst they beat the detainee for information and located their contacts. That was bad news, and something they should all be aware of – that Josef might crack at any moment. Josef was a founder member of the Resistance Council, the *Raad van Verzet* or RVV. And when he went to trial, the verdict would almost certainly be 'guilty' and a sentence of execution.

Nancy missed her old friends in Amsterdam; the people she knew and trusted. Starting afresh again demanded all her reserves, though so far everything had run smoothly. Steef had supplied her with a whole wardrobe of clothes and a good stock of candles because gas and electricity were intermittent. Coal he could not give her, because even the Resistance couldn't get any.

Steef urged her to economise on the candles as best she could. 'Our supply lines are busted,' he said. 'I don't know when we'll get more. But you'll definitely need this. Keep it safe; it was hard to get.' He handed her a box, and a brown phial of liquid.

She opened it. It was a contraceptive sponge in a net bag. Heat rose to the roots of her hair.

'Standard issue,' he said. 'The phial is quinine sulphate, a spermicidal liquid. All our female agents who do this kind of work are issued with it.'

This kind of work? His matter-of-fact manner couldn't erase the idea that she was actually being asked to sleep with a Nazi. *No. She'd never do that to Tom.* She shut the box. 'Could you get me a transmitter?' she asked. 'I had to leave mine behind.'

'Unlikely. Besides why would you need one? Having anything like that in this apartment would be far too much of a risk.'

'But surely the best place to transmit from would be right inside an apartment like this; a place crawling with Nazis?'

'But what use would it be? This is a task that doesn't require any contact with London.'

She couldn't tell him she wanted the transmitter to keep in touch with Tom. She improvised. 'I was the main contact for news from Amsterdam – about supply drops and so on. We need something like that in The Hague. It's ridiculous us having no contact with our Allies out there. Even Gerard thinks so.'

He frowned. 'I'll see what I can do, but it will have to be well hidden and for emergency use only.'

'Thank you Steef, I promise I'll use it wisely.'

After Steef had gone she got out the wooden box again and opened the bag with the sponge. She was filled with misgivings. It wouldn't come to that, surely?

* * *

33

The apartment was too big for just one person, and she missed the reassurance of Josef or another resistance worker being next door. But worse was having no contact with England. It made her feel disconnected. She wondered what her brother Neil would be doing and whether he was enjoying married life. He'd got married last year and she'd missed his wedding, and it still pained her that the SOE hadn't been able to get her home on leave.

At least England was still free. From the window she saw the dreaded Nazis come and go, the SS in their distinctive cavalry trousers and boots, and the Wehrmacht, trussed up in greatcoats and helmets. None of them looked as thin or shivering as the resident Dutch. The winter cold had set in, with a chill that pinched like a vice, and an icy drizzle that soaked through her clothes. With the supply lines cut by the Germans, if she wanted to eat, she had to queue.

She braved the weather and headed to the shops, her canvas bag over her arm. Everything looked grey except for the damp slashes of red with the Nazi emblem that hung from the town hall and every civic building.

A yellow notice pasted on the outside of a shop window caught her attention. Printed in German and Dutch, it demanded that every family must hand in blankets and clothing to the value of more than seventy guilders. She peered at the price list. They couldn't be serious?

Winter coat 50

Raincoat 30

Blankets 35

So the list went on. Even underpants were listed at five guilders! And the notice said a certificate of receipt would be issued, for the authorities would conduct a house search to check people had donated.

It was beyond cruel that the Germans were demanding that people with no fuel or electricity should give up their warm clothes. Would the Nazis come to her? She guessed not, as she was resident in the Nazi building, and supposedly a member of the NSB – the Dutch equivalent of the Nazi party.

As she was reading, a hand suddenly reached out from behind her and snatched at the paper, ripping it from the wall.

She whipped round. An old woman was there, thrusting the paper under a woollen shawl in her basket. A basket already full of balls of crumpled yellow paper.

'Is it real?' Nancy burst out. 'I can't believe they'd do this. What's it for, this collection?'

'They're saying it's for poor German soldiers. Huh. Those bastards, the ones that lost everything scarpering from France and Belgium. Let them freeze their balls off, that's what I say. They brought it on themselves. We're giving them nothing.'

'I'll help you. I'll do Vlamingstraat and we'll work outwards from there.'

The woman looked her up and down, but then whispered, 'Your family won't like it. My husband didn't. He thinks we should obey the proclamation. That I'll only make trouble for us if I refuse, that the Gestapo'll come to the house and take all our things anyway. But he'll be the first to complain if there's no blankets on his bed.' She threw up her hands. 'It's an excuse anyway. He means he's scared in case they come and he gets rounded up in one of their *razzias* and shipped east.'

'Is he hiding?'

The woman narrowed her eyes, realising, Nancy guessed, that she'd given too much away.

'I'm saying nothing.'

So he was an *onderduiker* – in hiding, like so many other men. 'I understand,' Nancy reassured her. 'I mean it. I'll do that section.' She pointed.

'Then watch they don't see you. The Greens will arrest you for just walking down the street and looking at them wrong.'

The woman glanced right and left and hurried away. Nancy was glad to have something to do. She'd tried to see what times

Keller came and went, but his car must go to the side entrance. Even keeping watch, and hanging round the lift doors, she saw no sign of him.

The yellow posters were everywhere, pasted over previous ragged proclamations, but she had to be careful about ripping them down because The Hague was full of police, not only the Dutch Greens but also the *Sicherheitspolizei*, the senior SS security police, in grey. It seemed unbelievable that the other half of Holland was free, whilst The Hague was still in this Nazi stranglehold.

Her bag filled with damp yellow paper. No point looking for a street litter bin, they'd all been taken away – along with the tram lines and railway tracks – to make the metal into German weapons. Still, this stuff would burn, and give her a few minutes' warmth.

When she got back to the apartment block there was nobody about, not even Steef, who usually came out to speak if he saw her pass. Steef lived in a small ill-furnished cupboard-like suite near the reception. It had a connecting door to the lobby and to an area to store luggage and cleaning equipment.

She pressed the button to call the lift. But it seemed to be stuck between floors two and three. Damn, no electricity again. She'd have to take the stairs. She'd got only halfway up when she heard feet coming down and stood to one side to let the person pass.

It was Keller, but this time his cap was on, shadowing his face. Only his jaw was visible and the flash of his eyes. 'I don't believe we've been introduced,' he said, stopping on the step above her. 'Detlef Keller. I'm a neighbour.'

'Pleased to meet you, Herr Keller,' she said, her heart thumping. 'Danique Koopman.' She moved so that her bag full of crumpled papers was pressed between her skirt and the wall.

'Brouwer tells me you've just moved in to number eighteen. How are you settling in?' He was still blocking her path, and her pulse pounded wildly at her throat.

'Very well, thank you.' She realised she would have to offer more to sound natural. 'But I hadn't realised this part of the city would have so little to buy. The days of a good wine and a piece of fine steak are over, I fear.' That came out wrong. It seemed like fishing, and he knew it.

He smiled, 'Then we shall have to do something about that, Frau Koopman. Perhaps you might wish to dine with me one night?'

It was moving too quickly. She beat a hasty withdrawal. 'Oh, I didn't mean to imply . . . oh, I do beg your pardon. I didn't think . . .'

'It was a genuine offer. It would be pleasant to get to know each other as neighbours, don't you think?'

'Yes, of course. It's just . . . well, I was widowed last year and I'm still not used to the idea of . . . of dining with someone else.' Oh no, that had come out even more awkward.

He was smiling at her now as if he found her amusing. 'Then perhaps we could take a coffee in the morning. I breakfast at the Blue Café on Torenstraat every morning. You could join me there and I'll tell you all the best places to get what you need.'

'Oh, that sounds wonderful. Thank you.'

'Is that bag heavy? I can carry it up for you.'

'No,' she squeaked, inwardly panicked. 'It's not heavy, just a little bread. The lift was stuck you see—'

'Yes, the electricity's just come on again, but the lift's still not working. I was on the way to get Brouwer to fix it.' He stood aside then and let her pass. 'So nice to meet you, Frau Koopman. *Tot ziens.*'

His Dutch pronunciation was execrable, but she was so glad of his goodbye it was all she could do not to run up the stairs. As soon as she got inside her apartment she burned the papers, pushing them into the fireplace with a poker until only ashes remained.

Only then did she flop down on the sofa.

She wasn't sure she could do this. Being a courier and a wireless op was one thing, she never had close contact with any Nazi. But to be in this apartment right under the nose of all the most notorious Nazis of The Hague was quite another.

It was also draining. Her reserves of energy were low after eighteen months of stress and worry, and years of wartime rations. She couldn't face cooking, so she ate the slither of black bread and hard cheese that were all she'd been able to buy in the local store.

In the evening she was dozing, when there was a soft knock on the door. The Morse 'V' knock that meant a friend. Warily she opened it, worried, even so, that it could be Keller. But it was Steef, and she beckoned him in.

'They're demanding everyone hands in their winter clothes,' she said to him. 'I just ripped down maybe a hundred notices.'

'I know,' he said. 'But we're onto it. We've got hold of a few German exchange certificates and we're printing them off by the thousand. We have a woman in Bezuidenhout who prints stuff for us. So the Nazis won't know who's given up their clothing and who hasn't.'

'Who's the "we"?' she asked. 'Are you with The LKP?' She named one of the Resistance organisations.

'No. The CS6. The LKP don't do anything except sit around on their backsides and argue. They used to do assassinations, proper sabotage, but now it's mostly sorting out people in hiding, making them fake ration cards and so on. The CS6 is a bit more proactive. I came to ask you if you'd help us while Keller's out at work – by pushing the fake clothing certificates through people's doors, or putting them in their mailboxes.'

'All right. Will you drop them off here?'

He gave a splutter of a laugh. 'You're joking. No. This is Nazi Central. Meet me outside the tower of Sint-Jacobskerk, and I'll pass them over. Shall we say two o'clock? Bring a bag. By the way, we heard yesterday that Josef is still in the Oranjehotel awaiting trial. He's too valuable for us to leave there, not if there's any way on earth we can get him out. The Amsterdam resistance food lines are starting to disintegrate without him.'

She took a deep breath. 'I met Keller this morning on the stairs.'

'And?'

'I'm not sure I'm the woman for this.'

'Don't go soft on me now! You're the only woman who's eye-catching enough to snag a Nazi. And the only agent who has survived long enough to really know what she's up against. You know they call you the cat with nine lives? Well, we need you. We've invested in you – all those clothes, the rental on the apartment. The war's not over and there are still lives worth saving.'

She was quiet a moment before she said, 'Keller asked me to go for breakfast with him.'

'Then for heaven's sake go! What are you waiting for? Accept his invitation and then come on to meet me afterwards. You'll need an excuse for going door to door, so we're printing a few leaflets of church services. How are you at looking devout?'

'About as good as looking like a Nazi whore. What if I mess up?'

'You won't. You know what the penalty is.'

She was silent.

'Two o'clock then?'

'Steef?'

He looked up.

'Any news on the transmitter?'

A sigh. 'Gerard's sorting something. Might be a week or so.'

The next day Nancy dressed carefully in a black blouse and skirt, but with a different hat and coat. She needed to look wealthy, like she would look right on the arm of a high-up German. She'd studied how the *Moffenmeiden* – German collaborators – dressed, and they were well-coiffured with immaculate nails under their leather gloves, and a fashionable air that few other women could afford.

Tom wouldn't even recognise her. She pictured his face and it brought her a flash of pain just to think of it. What was she doing here, when she could be safe at home with Tom in London? But she knew why; it was too hard to get her out. Besides, once you had seen the oppression of a whole proud people like the Dutch, you couldn't possibly stand by and do nothing. She'd seen too many deaths to do nothing.

Still, she'd be able to contact Tom soon. Their fragile line of communication was like thread that sewed them together, and without it, everything seemed to lose its point.

She'd studied her false identity for hours last night until her eyes protested at reading old Dutch society magazines by the flickering light of one candle. Frau Koopman had apparently liked to shop, and had a passion for golf. Neither of which were possible in war-torn The Hague. Methodically, Nancy checked her bag for her papers and her cash, her way of countering the fear that was rising inside her in a cold wave. The lift was operational now, and two more Nazi uniformed SS men were already in it from the floor above. Nancy looked at her shoes, although one of the men, the one with bad body odour, tried to make conversation.

She was relieved to get out and be on her way and walked smartly down the street to Torenstraat to the only coffee house in the area which was still serving. Of course it was the haunt only of Germans and their sympathisers. She paused to take a deep breath and try to calm down. The place was full, and the smell of pastry and warm bread was intoxicating. Her mouth watered. Perhaps they could even get real coffee here.

In the corner Keller lifted a hand to her, and then as soon as she had sat down, he summoned the waiter.

'Coffee and bread for the lady,' he said.

She took her time taking off her gloves so she had a moment to get a proper look at him. He was younger than she'd thought, with schoolboy features set very close together under a widow's peak. His neck had a shaving rash over his too-tight black collar.

'Cold today, isn't it?' he said over the clatter of the room. 'But it's always warm in here. I have a half-hour before my man arrives, he will drive me to work. What will you do with your day?'

'Queue,' she said, with a smile. 'When I moved here, I was unable to bring any of my staff with me.'

'Then I know a woman who is a good maid of all work. She is a janitor for many of our apartments. Shall I write down her address, or ask her to call on you?'

'I'll take her address,' Nancy said, having no intention whatsoever of employing someone who had the Nazis' ears. 'I'm often out at the shops. Everything takes such an age now we have to queue.'

Keller whipped out a fountain pen and waved it at her with a raise of the eyebrows, whilst she fished in her handbag for a piece of paper.

'Sorry,' she said, bringing out an old laundry receipt, planted there helpfully by Steef. 'I left my address book at home.'

He wrote out the woman's name and address on the back of the receipt in a childish hand, but she thanked him profusely and stowed it away. It would be good if the Resistance could get hold of this woman and interrogate her. No lead was ever wasted.

The coffee arrived, and yes, it was mostly acorn, but the bread came with a spoonful of yellow apricot preserve. Though she was ravenous, she tried to eat it politely, dabbing at her mouth with a napkin.

There was a little more small talk in which Keller took over, and told her he was originally from Dortmund, and had an elder brother also in the *Sicherheitsdienst*. As he was talking, the door opened and another painfully young officer gave him the eye.

'My chauffeur,' Keller said. 'Damn, he's early. But I am free on Saturday evening if you would like to go dancing. We could eat first at Schlemmers.'

Schlemmers was a restaurant catering only for German officers. She summoned an enthusiastic smile. 'Lovely.'

'I'll pick you up at seven. Apartment eighteen, is that correct?'

'That's right,' she said. 'Eighteen. Knock loudly because I sometimes play my gramophone.' She meant, *knock loudly so I know it's you, and not Steef or any other friend.*

'It's been most pleasant to breakfast together,' he said, standing up and summoning the waiter. 'My apologies I have to leave so soon. Perhaps we could do it again one morning, but I will see you in any case on Saturday.' His formal manner was somewhat grating. He was trying hard, but she couldn't imagine ever relaxing with such a man.

He put his cap on and tugged it down hard, before thrusting some of the horrible tinny occupation coins at the waiter and strolling out. Once he'd gone she let out her breath, but was aware that several other men in uniform were staring at her. Anxious not to appear in a hurry, she toyed with her teaspoon for a moment or two and pretended to read the menu.

She put on her gloves again and strolled slowly out, even though all the eyes in the café seemed to be watching her.

Once out on the pavement she went around the corner and leant up against the brick wall to catch her breath. She felt the way she did when she first parachuted out of an aircraft eighteen months ago, shaky with adrenalin, or perhaps with the unexpected sugar.

She'd found out nothing, yet every time she agreed to meet this man, her life would be at risk. She thought she'd understood this before she met him, but the reality of actually doing it had only just hit home. *God, let this war be over soon.*

'All right?' Steef asked.

'Yes. But I didn't find out anything important.'

She was talking to Steef outside the church as he handed her a wodge of leaflets, along with a few church bulletins to go on the top of the pile. The wind was strong, so she had to press them down in her basket.

Now even the weather was conspiring with the Nazis to batter the Dutch. The Hague had a discarded air about it, no longer a city of pride. Nevertheless, she did all the streets on Steef's list, unsurprised at how few people were outside. In vindictive revenge against their defeat in lower Holland, the Germans had rounded up any man over sixteen for work in their factories, and so the only men left in the city were Germans, men in service to them like Steef, or *onderduikers* – divers – men who were in hiding from the raids.

At the sound of heavy marching boots she automatically froze inside. In one street she heard men's shouts to open up! '*Aufmachen! Aufmachen!*'

A patrol stopped her, and she told them she was on Church missionary work, showing them the top pamphlet. They sneered at it, but the rain was so heavy, bouncing off their helmets, that they were in a hurry to let her go.

Her delivery over, she hurried back past the shuttered shops, but there was a commotion and the sound of breaking glass ahead and she hesitated, wary to go on. Down the street a group of women and children had smashed open the shutters of a shop and were climbing in through the window. The sign in Dutch read 'pharmacy' and people were scurrying out laden with boxes, bottles, anything they could loot.

The growl of an engine and a squeal of brakes. Nancy dodged down a side street.

Wehrmacht. It wouldn't do to be caught, not here in front of this looted shop. As she pressed herself to the wall, a stream of ragged people ran past the end of the alley, their booty clutched in their arms. But almost immediately two shots rang out.

She waited until the streets were silent before creeping out onto the main road.

Two women lay there, both shot in the head. One had a placard with 'I am a looter' hastily scrawled on it in shaky Dutch. A woman leant out of a window from a neighbouring shop and said; 'They made her write it herself before they shot her.'

Nancy didn't stay. The pavement crunched, and the stink of indigestion medicine oozed from broken bottles. When she got home, soaked and bedraggled, she just prayed that Keller would be nowhere in sight. She crept along the corridor and let herself into her apartment with relief.

The next day Steef came by her door to tell her the Resistance printing ruse had worked, and with so many fake certificates for garments, the Germans had abandoned collecting donated clothes altogether. Instead they'd taken to bashing on doors wherever they felt like it and stealing what they wanted.

Of course, here in the apartment she'd be safe. Everyone knew it as a Nazi warren, and Dutch people gave it a wide berth. Thinking of clothes, she would need something to go dancing in. She went to her wardrobe and picked out a skirt of good material and a blouse. Not dressy enough, but perhaps she could exchange this.

Later Nancy headed for the main market square. As usual crowds of women lined the wet pavements holding out items to sell. Black market goods mostly, a small piece of cheese, a single dried apple, a knob of butter. But many of the women were trying to sell aspirin and cough mixture on the black market. She could guess where *that* had come from.

She pushed her way through, past women calling out, 'Cheap! Good price!' until she came to the trestles at the end of the square. There, pinch-faced women picked their way through old heaps of clothing, squabbling over the warm things with the most wear left in them.

Nancy saw a flash of silky blue material, and pounced on it. She dragged it from the pile and shook it out. Everything smelled of mothballs and damp. The dress was a little large, but she'd be able to take it in, and the extra material could be used to make a hair decoration or shoe bows. The silk was good, and it reminded her painfully of the silk she'd worn in the days when she was in London, and of Tom, and the 'silk code' they'd invented together. She was still using her silk code, the slip of silk sewn into her underwear and printed with a grid. It was the best way to transmit coded information back to England.

She didn't do any coding or transmitting now, she thought ruefully, now she was to be . . . what? There was no easy label for what she did now. An informant, yes, perhaps she was that. A sharp elbow jolted her from her thoughts as a woman pushed by. Several elderly but fierce women stood guard over the stall, with more standing by in case of trouble.

'Will you take these, for this?' She dragged the skirt and blouse from her bag. Immediately she was surrounded by clawing hands.

'Straight swap?' a burly woman in a hairnet asked, whipping them into her arms.

'Yes, please,' Nancy said.

The women whispered behind her back, calling her a Nazi whore.

The words stung deep in her heart, but she thrust the blue silk into her bag and clutched it tight to her chest. Just as well, for while they were talking, a thin young woman reached a bony arm past her to grab something from the table.

The woman in the hairnet set on her, beating her on the head. 'No pilfering!'

Nancy dodged away, through the crowd of women.

She spent the rest of the day sewing, trying on the dress and sewing again. Keeping her hands busy kept the frightening thoughts of what she had to do at bay. The dress wasn't perfect, but it would do. She'd lost weight, she knew. The diet for the local Dutch had become mostly beets and green leaves, with the occasional potato, gristly sausage or adulterated bread. She prayed the Allies would break through soon, and stop this misery. It was hell to know there was food being brought in to the rest of Holland, but they'd leave the folk in the North to starve.

She wondered what the men in the other apartments were eating.

No, don't think of it. Her stomach was already growling with hunger.

Chapter 5

London
December 1944

'There's someone I want you to meet!' Neil's voice down the phone was excited.

Tom clamped the phone receiver to his ear and got a pencil ready. 'What about?'

'Just say you'll meet us. Tomorrow, I'll come up to London. His name's Pavel Aaldenburg and he's Dutch. We've had the most belting idea!'

They arranged to meet at lunchtime at the Lyons' Corner House, where Tom knew it was always busy and noisy and no-one would pay them any attention.

When he arrived at the door, Tom told the Nippy, 'I'm meeting someone, he's booked a table – name of Callaghan.' She led him through the tables to a place at the far corner where Neil was already waiting, along with a tall, lanky-looking man, in a flat cap. This must be Pavel.

Neil waved and the other man looked up, and a smile lit up his broad open face.

'Can I order first, before we talk? I'm starving,' Tom said. He didn't go for Shepherd's Pie this time because it always reminded him of Nancy. That's how they'd first got together – here in the Lyons' Corner House over Shepherd's Pie. He ordered sausages and mash instead.

'That sounds good. I'll have the same. A man needs his sausage.' Pavel winked at the young waitress in her black and white uniform, and the girl, grasping the innuendo, turned scarlet.

Tom, seeing her misery, said, 'And tea please. We'll take a pot of tea for three.' He handed her back the menus.

Once the waitress had gone, Neil said. 'Pavel and I have cooked up a plan.'

The other man grinned.

'Tell him,' Neil said.

'I'm a photographer,' Pavel said. 'And I've got an idea for a commission. I want to get behind the lines in occupied Holland – do a piece on the two sides of Holland, something to try to get the Americans to do something. An opinion piece if you like.'

'That's a cracking idea,' Tom said. 'Churchill's been trying for ages to get the Americans to bite.'

'Pictures would sell the story,' Pavel said. 'But I need an assistant, someone who can keep me in touch with England via wireless. And someone who can write decent copy.'

Tom knew immediately what they were asking. 'Who's organising this? Is it the BBC?'

Pavel shrugged. 'No-one. I'm a freelancer. Once I have the material, I'll sell it, no problem.'

'You mean, we'll just do it ourselves?' Tom was doubtful.

Neil was almost fizzing in his seat. 'It's perfect, Tom, isn't it? I'll be your contact here in England and we'll stay in touch by radio. Lilli has said she'd make us both radio sets. You know, her father worked for Blaupunkt, so she'll supply you with an unofficial transmitter, and we can use your coding method. You'll be in charge of getting on a frequency and making the

47

transmissions, and of finding a way of getting the copy and photographs out.'

Pavel leant forwards. 'I know nothing about coding or radio, but I guess being Dutch will help. I've got contacts in the North.'

'It'll be harder, with two of us,' Tom said, stalling. He was uncertain of Pavel Aaldenburg and unwilling to team with someone he didn't know.

'It'll be perfect,' Neil said. 'Between us all, we should be able to get you there and get the story out, and once we do, the Yanks'll be clamouring to help.'

Pavel agreed. 'A first-hand report, and pictures, that'll do the trick. Fly-on-the-wall stuff, showing how bad it really is. Otherwise it's all too easy to ignore. But a splash across the papers – the public outrage will mean they'll have to do something.'

'It will take planning, and I need to think about it. Going into an occupied zone is a life-risking activity.' Tom paused as the waitress delivered his food. He'd grown cautious, it had dawned on him that going off into occupied territory with someone he hardly knew might not be the wisest idea. It was just the sort of thing he was always advising agents not to do. 'I can't just up and go without giving it serious thought – there's my job for a start.'

Neil slapped his hand on the table. 'Oh Tom, for pity's sake! A month ago you were the one who wanted us to go straight to Biesbosch and crawl through swamps to get there.'

He was right. But the prospect of doing it with someone he knew and trusted was different from doing it with someone he'd only just set eyes on.

'Well, you get the passes sorted and the funding, and we're on.' Tom was playing for time, because he didn't like to put a dampener on Neil's big plan.

'Good man!' Pavel thumped the table. 'I'll need to make up a resumé for you. Don't suppose you've any journalism experience?'

'None whatsoever.' He hoped this would put Pavel off.

'Good. Then we can just make it up.'

Chapter 6

The Hague

On Saturday, the knock at the door came when Nancy was least expecting it. Steef had only just left and she was still applying her make-up in the mirror. It made her almost shoot up from her chair. Earlier she'd tidied the apartment and even got Steef to supply a picture of Koopman. She'd framed it in a second-hand frame, and tried to get used to the idea that he was her deceased husband.

The knock again. So he was impatient.

In a panic she rushed to the door to let him in.

'Oberstleutnant Keller! Do come in.' Of course he was in uniform. Did they never take them off? She supposed it was to maintain power and control.

'Frau Koopman. You look stunning.'

She felt her face grow hot at the compliment as he strolled in, his gaze sweeping the room. Perhaps he was comparing it with his own apartment.

'I thought for a moment you hadn't heard me and must be playing your gramophone,' he said.

Of course, there was no sign of one. 'What a fool,' she said. 'Of course my gramophone was left behind in Nijmegen. I forget I no longer have it.'

'A shame. I have a good one, you may come to hear it any time.'

'I'll just fetch my coat,' she said, hurrying to the bedroom. *Calm down*, she told herself. *Go slow. You nearly gave yourself away. Just watch everything you say.* She unhooked her coat from the hanger in the wardrobe and put it over her arm. When she got back to the living room, he was staring out of the window.

He turned. 'Let me help you.' He approached and she let him help her into the sleeves.

Strangely, he was all fingers and thumbs. It struck her that perhaps he was nervous too. When he was close, she caught the slight smell of metal polish and she wondered if he'd polished his insignia just for her. He ran a fingertip under her hair to free it from her collar, and the touch of his finger on her neck made an unpleasant tremor shoot up her back.

'Cold?' he asked. 'It will be warm in the restaurant.'

He held the door for her in a rather ostentatious way, and they descended in the lift.

As they walked out of the door, he hooked his arm in hers as if to take ownership. 'You must call me Detlef,' he said.

'Danique,' she replied. But she could almost feel all the eyes of the street staring at her as she went. It was a cold night, but still the warmth of his arm was an unpleasant reminder that she would have to dance with him.

Dinner was somewhat strained but she managed to smile and look interested and not appalled by Keller's conversation about his childhood in the *HitlerJugend*. The dance hall was in the grand Hotel des Indes, which she'd only ever viewed from the outside. She'd always avoided its impressive white façade because it was now number one home to the Wehrmacht High Command.

Keller whisked her in through the sumptuously furnished lobby, all pot plants and chandeliers, and into the ballroom. The grey-green uniforms, and the grey of the SD were everywhere, along with the navy of the *Staatspolitie* – the Nazi-converted police.

They found a table at the edge of the floor and an elderly waiter offered them beer. She ordered soda water as she needed to stay sober. It still came as a shock when Keller gestured to her to get up, and she found herself tightly clamped against his chest.

His dancing was terrible. 'I apologize,' he said, 'my dancing needs more practise. But is fun, no?'

She gritted her teeth and tried to relax. At least he'd admitted to his two left feet.

At long last the band took a break and he steered her to their table in the corner. The room was filled with other soldiers and their Dutch *Moffenmeiden,* all dressed to impress, and she looked at them with disdain. Until she realised that she was very definitely one of them now. Who knew what hard choices those other women were making?

'Tell me about your work,' she said to Keller, in an effort to open the conversation.

'It is very dull. I am an administrator at the Scheveningen Prison. Someone has to do it.' He shrugged. 'It is not a pleasant job, to deal with criminals all day, but at least I am in the office and have few dealings with them.'

'Do many staff work there?'

'More than fifty men if you include the guards and the gatemen. But in my office only three. There is a clerk and me, and then the boss Schneider. He's always on our case. His office is connected to ours by a door so he can crack the whip. He likes his paperwork. For him, everything must be in order.'

'It sounds like a lot of responsibility.'

He wagged his head as if to say *not so much.* 'Of course the orders to Schneider come mostly from the judiciary, or higher command. And my job is to be sure the prisoners go to the right place after sentencing, and keep the records.'

She knew what that meant, execution, work camps, or death camps. But she decided not to pursue it for now.

'So what did you do before you joined the army?'

'Nothing. I was at school.'

So young! Even younger than she thought, and yet now holding all these lives in his hands?

'I'm lucky to have ended up behind a desk. I think because I am a mathematician. I was planning to study Mathematics at Frankfurt University.'

'Perhaps you will be able to go back to your studies when the war ends.'

He laughed, a high-pitched guffaw. 'No. Not now, I'm sure the Party have other plans for me.'

She'd underestimated him, she'd thought these men to be bullies without brains; she hadn't thought to be dealing with an intellectual. He'd be very surprised if he knew she'd been trained in the Tom Lockwood method of mathematical coding.

'Let's dance,' he said as the band began again. 'This is one of my favourites.'

She stood and allowed him to take her by the arm and lead her back on to the floor. It was a waltz, and he was passable because the steps were simple. His hot hands pressed her towards his chest so that she felt as though she was almost suffocating in her blue silk dress.

At the end of the number, she stepped away, but another man, taller, stepped in.

'May I?' he said, in perfect Dutch.

She just had time to register the fact he was in a black SS uniform, and that Keller was looking distinctly uncomfortable.

The new man took her in a waltz hold and whisked her away. 'You dance well,' he said. 'I saw you from the other side of the room. How do you know Keller?'

'He's a neighbour,' she said, meeting his eyes for the first time. His were slate grey, flecked with bronze. 'We live in the same apartment block.'

'Then you're my neighbour too. I live on the top floor.'

The top floor. Where Steef had said only high-up Nazis lived. The crème de la crème of the Party. She had no time to take this in as he steered her into an intricate corner turn.

'By the way, I'm Fritz. What's your name?' She told him and he repeated it. 'Danique. Very pretty. Will you promise the next dance to me too?'

'I don't think I can. I feel a little awkward because I came with Oberstleutnant Keller. He accompanied me here from the apartment.'

'Don't worry about Keller, he'll get over it.' He glanced to where she caught a glimpse of Keller looking disgruntled and staring into his beer. 'And besides, he's paid to do as I tell him.'

So he was higher in the pecking order than Keller. For the next few dances, she was swept around the floor by this new man, Fritz, before she could finally go back to her table. Before she went, Fritz said, 'Which number is your apartment?'

She didn't dare lie. 'Eighteen,' she said.

'Then I'll be in touch.' He smiled, gave a short bow and went to join a few other SS uniformed men at a table at the far side of the room.

'I'm terribly sorry,' she said to Keller. 'He was insistent, and said you wouldn't mind.'

'You should have refused,' he said petulantly. 'You were my date for the evening. I hate that about Schneider, always muscling in where he's not wanted.'

'I'm here now,' she said. She noticed the jug of beer was now empty, and Keller was sweating.

'But Fritz always gets what he wants. The boss's . . . perks.' He used the German word, *Nebenleistungen*, but she understood him perfectly. Her German had improved since being forced to live under their occupation.

'He's your boss?'

'Not just my boss. Now the director of the prison is away,

Schneider rules over everything, oversees every last detail.' He made a face. 'What he says, goes.'

Hell. She remembered what Steef had said, SS Oberführer Schneider of the Oranjehotel. She'd gone out to catch a fish, and had caught the attention of a bigger fish by mistake.

She turned to Keller again, in some sympathy. 'I'm sorry if I offended you,' she said to Keller. 'It's just difficult to know how to refuse high-up officers without causing offence.'

Keller grunted a reluctant acknowledgement and then stood. Roughly he dragged her back on the floor and proceeded to trample over her feet. Oh, to be dancing with Tom again at the Hammersmith Palais.

She caught Keller flashing a triumphant look at Fritz, who was watching them through narrowed eyes as they sped past.

The second time they went by, Fritz stood again and caught Keller by the arm. 'You're trampling the lady's feet,' he said in German.

'I was not,' Keller said, by now slightly the worse for drink. 'Was I?' He turned to Nancy. Nancy's features turned to stone. There was no way she could answer.

'Leave her be, now,' Fritz said.

'I will not, you've no right to—'

'You're upsetting the lady.'

Keller drew back a fist to punch Fritz in the jaw, but Fritz shot up his arm and parried it, as if batting away a fly.

More men stood up in anticipation of a fight, and all Nancy could do was try to back away.

'Assaulting an SS superior is an offence,' Fritz said icily, gripping Keller's arm.

'I'm off duty, aren't I?' Keller yelled into his face. 'I'm not one of the damn Dutch, you can't tell me what to do.' But he saw he was outnumbered and ripped his arm away, before storming off, leaving Nancy abandoned to his rival. Nancy swallowed. She'd understood the whole exchange and it had rocked her nerve.

'Are you alright?' Fritz asked her, now speaking in Dutch.

'I'm fine, just a little shaken.'

'I'm not surprised,' he said. His Dutch was excellent, only lightly accented. 'He's got a temper, young Keller. Great brain, but needs to control his anger. And he can't hold his drink. Don't worry, he will be disciplined for his behaviour tomorrow. And I will take you home in my car.'

'Thank you,' she said. What else could she say? Yet her mind was throbbing with foreboding. She'd made an enemy of Keller who she was supposed to be getting to know, and then accidentally found herself in the company of the most ruthless man in The Hague.

In the lobby, an armed man who looked like a valet fell into step beside them. Schneider acknowledged him with a nod – some sort of bodyguard? Just outside the hotel a chauffeur was waiting by the idling car which was belching out exhaust smoke into the cold air. He jumped to open the car doors. It was only a short distance to her apartment, but it seemed Fritz never walked. Probably because he would certainly be a target for the Resistance if they could get a shot at him.

On the way home, the valet climbed in the front and Fritz seemed relaxed as he sat back in the leather comfort of the backseat of the car. He was not what she was expecting. He had the easy manner of a person used to getting his own way. He was good-looking in the severe German manner, with straight forehead and a slightly arrogant tilt of the chin. His wiry blond hair was tamed by a very short cut, but sprung up from his head like sheep's wool.

'I would like to take you dancing again,' he pronounced. 'But dinner first in my apartment. Not in a restaurant; the food in Holland is terrible. I'll have my chef prepare something.'

Again, he expected her to just fall in with his plans. 'I will look in my diary,' she said, desperate to play for time. 'Which day did you have in mind?'

The car pulled to a stop and the valet and chauffeur jumped out to open the doors.

'Saturday night again?' he asked. 'Shall we say six-thirty? I'll make sure Keller doesn't bother you. I'm in apartment number two on the top floor.'

'I'll check my diary and leave you a note in your mailbox,' she said. It was only an ounce of her own control, but she wanted to assert it somehow. 'Though I feel I have to tell you – I'm a little out of practise with dinner dates. I'm recently widowed, you see.'

'I'm sorry to hear about your loss. Was your husband fighting?'

'No. Anton had a weak heart. It was a shock to lose him, and even harder in wartime when everything is difficult, even funeral flowers. I can't help feeling I'm still not quite ready for the social whirl.'

'Then how would a quiet dinner suit? We don't have to dance. What about Sunday evening instead?'

'That would be lovely. Since Anton died,' she improvised, 'I've missed conversation over dinner.' Conversation she could manage. The other . . . would only make her think of Tom.

The valet accompanied them in the lift. He was a boulder-like man who never smiled and whose eyes roamed everywhere. The *wolfsangel* rune on his collar identified him as an ex-Dutch army man. *Another one gone bad,* she thought. His hand was on his gun the whole time they were in the lift and it filled Nancy with discomfort.

At the fourth floor the lift stopped and the valet opened the doors. Fritz grasped her hand and brought it to his lips. A brush across the back of the hand. 'So sorry for tonight's scene. I look forward very much to our dinner next week. Goodnight, Danique.'

'Goodnight, Fritz,' she said. 'Thank you for bringing me home.'

The valet pressed the button and she watched the metal box sail upwards, and listened for the clank and rattle of the lift doors on the floor above before she could finally let out her breath.

She glanced down the corridor to where Keller had his apartment. She must make sure she didn't bump into him again, or life would get very awkward. She had been supposed to make a friend of him, not an enemy. And how would she survive dinner with Oberführer Fritz Schneider without giving herself away?

Chapter 7

Bedfordshire, England

'The den's this way,' Neil said.

Tom had travelled to Milton Bryan by train to meet up with Neil and Lilli in their new married quarters. It wasn't much of a house, a brick built 1930s semi with a small garden. He was led into a cramped back room, probably once the dining room, where Lilli, now even heavier, was leaning over a desk. The room had the metallic tang of solder and hot wire, and burning dust from an electric light hung low over where she was working. An upright paraffin heater was the only heat.

There was hardly any room to move, for the place was jammed with tables covered in bits of old radio. Lilli didn't look up, but kept her eyes fixed on the radio she was re-wiring. 'Just give me a minute,' she said.

Tom took the chance to prowl around the room, squeezing past all the tables. A plan chest with drawers marked with components for radios, neatly labelled 'capacitors' and 'antennae'. On one wall were shelves stacked with dog-eared cardboard boxes. He peered in them to see second-hand parts – valves, coiling tubes and headphones.

Under the blacked-out window stood an empty field layout of the battle of Waterloo, and shoe boxes marked *French*, *British* and *Prussian*. It was typical Neil.

'Given up playing war games, I see,' Tom said.

'Ha, ha.' Neil was good-natured about the jibe. 'Chance would be a fine thing. No. Lilli just got fed up of the dusting. Too many lead soldiers. Far too fiddly.'

'Nearly done,' came Lilli's voice. 'It was just a repair.' Lilli's father was an engineer and she had learned all about radio from an early age.

She stood up now to stretch her back, her belly straining at the front of her dress. 'It's all ready for you.' She bent over to reach under the desk to drag out a small brown suitcase. 'You know it's strictly illegal,' she said. 'Not only this—' she pointed at it, 'but to find a frequency.'

'I know,' said Tom. 'And I'm very grateful.'

Neil jangled car keys in front of him. 'I'm going to drive the receiver to the car park of the Red Lion, try to pick you up from there. Lilli will take you through how it works. If we don't get through, we might have to tweak it.'

When Neil had gone, Lilli pushed aside a radio casing and put the suitcase on the table in front of him.

She looked up. 'I hope you know what you're doing. I don't want Neil getting in any trouble.'

'I'll be in touch once I'm in the Allied zone. And Pavel has a permit to take photographs.'

'You're not listening. All illegal frequencies are checked out by the Voluntary Interceptors, in case they're German spies. And me being German . . . well. We can't take unnecessary risks.'

'I know. I used to work at the interception centre in Barnet. We'll be careful, I promise.'

'And you'll only transmit this side of the Allied line?' Her dark-eyed gaze probed his.

This was what he and Neil had agreed to tell her. But she was not stupid, and now as her eyes met his, he felt his insides squirm. He knew that the whole point was to have communication from behind enemy lines and so did she.

She watched his discomfort with an expression of disgust, before opening up the case. 'Men,' she muttered. 'Always want to be heroes.' She began unpacking, but then stepped away, rubbed her hands down her sides and across her belly. 'You unpack it. It's what you'll have to do when you get there. If you ever do. And even more important, to repack it at speed if you need to run.'

He began to lay out the equipment in an atmosphere of ice. After about five minutes it was all set up.

'Aerial?' he asked.

Lilli pointed to where the end was hung out of the barely open window.

He was vaguely aware that he was frightened of Lilli. Of her strength, and the fact she was somehow more than herself now she was pregnant. A tiger-like feeling of protecting her young.

He slipped on the headphones to escape the sensation, plugged in the aerial, and looked at the crib sheet and frequency Neil had scribbled down. The matching crystal marked with that, he set into its socket.

A few moments later, all he was aware of was the static in his ears as his fingers turned the dial to 'receive', listening for the agreed call signal from Neil.

'I can't get anything,' Tom said.

'Give him a chance. Maybe he hasn't got parked up yet,' she said.

But just as she spoke, the unmistakeable sound of Morse. Neil's call sign.

Tom's Morse skills were ingrained after years of training. He grabbed a pencil, and scribbled down the message.

TWO PINTS ORDERED STOP PICK YOU UP IN TEN STOP OVER

A flick of the dial to transmit, and the lights went out. Tom

hammered away on the Morse button. His call signal first, then
OK STOP DRINKS ON ME STOP OVER

He removed the headphones.

'Well?' Lilli said.

'He'll pick me up in ten minutes for a pint.'

She nodded. 'It's a robust set. All official parts. Neil bribed someone at Waddon Hall, the Baker Street supplier.'

'Thank you. You know that without it, the whole thing would be impossible?'

'Without it, Neil would have wanted to go with you. He's in shreds about Nancy, and it was the only way I could get him to stay here. But I have to be honest – I don't like it, because it's a risk to us both – a risk we wouldn't be taking at all if it wasn't for you and your damn-fool ideas.'

There was nothing he could say in reply to that, even though it was actually Neil's idea, so he kept his thoughts to himself. 'We have to get Nancy out, you do see that?'

'Of course. What do you think I'm made of? Stone?' Her voice held a trace of tears. 'But I know what it's like to lose someone. And with the baby coming . . . well I just couldn't bear the thought of losing Neil.'

He softened. 'Any news of your father?' Lilli's father was missing, arrested in Berlin by the Nazis before she came to England.

A shake of the head. Her lips pressed together as if to stop the words, and her hands clasped tight across her stomach.

'Shall I retrieve the aerial?' He didn't wait for an answer but began reeling it in. When it was done he re-assembled the transmitter into its suitcase just as there was a pip from outside.

'That was quick.' He turned to Lilli. 'Good luck with the baby,' he said. 'I hope we'll be back in time to wet its head.'

She paused, and there was a moment when she seemed to realise this might be their last meeting, and she pulled him awkwardly into a hug, her bump pressing into his stomach. 'Take care,' she said. 'Come back safe, for Neil's sake.'

'I will.' He clicked the suitcase shut and locked it.

'Remember,' Lilli said, 'keep the transmitter for emergency use only.'

The Red Lion in Milton Bryan was quiet as it was a Saturday afternoon and most people were at home keeping out of the chill. The pub lounge felt cold; Tom and Neil were the only two men in the so-called 'snug', except for the landlord who was up and down to the cellar. Both of them stayed in their overcoats to ward off the damp.

'Worked like a charm,' Tom said. 'Though it's a long time since I had to do any transmitting.'

'Like you said, we'll use the silk code, the one you invented at Baker Street, but our own version. Here.' Neil handed Tom a silk handkerchief. 'From my father's things after he died. Will it do? Is there enough room to print the number code?'

Tom felt the material. 'Ideal. And it will be big enough to make cyphers for all three of us. But don't you want to keep it?'

A shrug. 'Father'd be over the moon to see it used this way. I'd be doing something right for once. Just as long as you can get Nancy out, that's the main thing. Now Father's gone, Mother couldn't stand it if anything happened to Nancy. It sounds like hell out there and I worry about her every day.'

'What about Pavel? Is he ready? He's got all his equipment and our passes ready?'

'Saw him last night, and he's all set. He's got your papers too. You just have to act like a journalist – look like you're making notes or something. You'll see; we'll be a great team, you and Pavel and me.'

'How did you get to know Pavel?'

'Met him through the Sunday amateur football league. I'm score-keeper and groundsman. Lilli thought I should get out more, and she does the teas. Pavel's a great player, can't half run.'

'So why's he in England and not in Holland?'

'Came over with Queen Wilhelmina, to cover their exile, and he was supposed to go back, but it turns out the Dutch were keen for more photographs of their royal family. Pavel saw which side his bread was buttered and cashed in on the demand. But now the southern part's free, there's less interest. People have other concerns now, like stopping the in-fighting between those who went along with the Nazi occupation and those who didn't. And to be honest, I think Pavel's a bit bored. He says British girls are too stiff and humourless.'

'Cheek. Nancy's got a great sense of humour.'

'I guess no-one's got much to laugh at right now. We're all sick to death of this war.'

'Must be hard for you though, isn't it, being married to a German?'

'She's a refugee.' Neil was emphatic. 'Not the same thing. And yes, she gets some stick, but a lot less now she's Mrs Callaghan.'

Silence as they supped their pints. Tom leant in and lowered his voice. 'You know she asked me if we'd be transmitting from behind enemy lines.'

Neil put down his pint. 'And what did you say?'

'I denied it. Of course. But it made me feel like a cad. She saw through it straight away.'

Neil sighed. 'Yes, she's sharp as needles. She's worried they'll arrest us, and what would happen to the baby if they did. Just last night I woke up and thought, I can't let you do this, and I was going to call the whole thing off. But then I thought of how there's no plan to feed anyone in Holland, and the powers that be are simply ignoring it and hoping it will go away. Nancy's always been my little sister and from what I can see, she's had more than her quota of narrow escapes already.'

Tom was nodding along. 'I can't sit here in London any more. Every time Nancy comes home on leave it makes me feel more useless. I've got to do something.'

'At least we know where she is,' Neil said. 'Most families don't – they've no clue their relatives are even abroad. We're lucky.'

'Really? Sometimes I think it would be better if I didn't know. Then I'd just get her postcards like Mother does, and think she was in a nice safe nursing ward with the FANYs somewhere. Then I could get rid of this constant niggling worry.'

Neil gave a grunt of acknowledgement.

Tom took a sup of his pint and shivered. He'd had enough of waiting for the war to end. It wasn't just the chill of the pub with its worn-out bench seats, but he saw that the turn-ups of Neil's trousers were frayed, and his overcoat patched badly at the elbows. That was the pair of them, like everyone else in England – frayed at the edges and badly patched up.

'Here's to the mission,' Neil said raising his glass. 'What shall we call it?'

'I don't know. Something to symbolize Holland I suppose. How about *Operation Tulip*?'

Neil laughed. 'Sounds ridiculous.'

'Just like the war then,' Tom said. 'People killing each other over scraps of land. And in Baker Street, it's all reduced to paperwork. Drives me nuts. Acres of it – shelves full of reports, files, memos, all of it top secret, all of it shipped to a special vault under lock and key.'

'It all counts, Tom.'

A sigh. 'I know. And I didn't mean . . .'

'To Operation Tulip.' They raised their glasses and drank.

Chapter 8

The Hague

'You've got to accept Schneider's dinner invitation,' Steef told Nancy, 'or it will blow your cover.'

They were sitting in her apartment, both huddling in their coats because the December weather was so cutting they could see their breath, and there was no fuel. She noticed, now she looked more closely, that Steef's suit hung on him, the pants held up by braces.

'If I'm to do it, I need to know what to ask.'

'Exactly the same as if you were working with Keller. Schneider's a different character, because though he has a thing for the ladies, according to our intelligence he switches women frequently.'

'Sounds charming.' She pointed to the flowers that had arrived that morning, hothouse Christmas roses in fancy cellophane, and laughed. 'He sent me these this morning. Where the hell did he get them? How the other half live, eh?'

'Don't laugh about it because we're in a dire situation. Without Josef to negotiate with the South, the Resistance in Amsterdam is separating into different factions. The communists hate the LKP fighters, the LKP fighters don't trust the partisans, and nothing gets done, so our people continue to suffer.' He gave a deep sigh. 'You're our last hope. The main thing is to ask for a tour. See if you can somehow get inside the prison. Our plan then will be to try to get Josef out. But we can do nothing without intelligence, and so far, no-one fit to talk sense has gone in and then come out again.'

'It will take time to build Schneider's trust.'

'Time's something we don't have. He may tire of you, and besides the trial could be soon, and after that the chances will be zero.'

'So how long have we got?'

'I'm guessing a month max. Depends on if he talks. Could be sooner.'

She stood up and paced the floor. She had two options – one was just to let go of the apartment and disappear. That was the safest way. At least she'd stand a chance of getting home to Tom. But then the Resistance in Holland would be leaderless, and there would be no-one to look out for the ordinary folk. The ones that were already scrounging in dustbins for food and fuel, and who had no other source of help.

'Come by on Sunday morning, and I'll tell you what I've got.' It was her agreement. But also she needed Steef to be there when she returned, someone to know she was still breathing.

On the night of the dinner date, Nancy came out of her apartment to go to Schneider's. She locked up, then turned to see Keller coming out of his door. Nancy's heart jumped a beat. He'd also be going to the lift, so there was no way to avoid him. She gave him a pleasant 'Good evening' as she strode by.

He didn't follow, but his words did, harsh and accusing. 'There's a word for women like you.'

She opened the lift grill and the door and stepped inside, relieved to close the doors on him. Her mouth was dry as she ascended in the lift to the top floor. After she got out, she saw the call light go on for the ground floor. That was probably Keller going downstairs. She wished to heaven he lived somewhere else.

The top floor housed only two apartments and several offices where the doors were propped open with a wedge, and men in SS uniform or plain clothes were still working under lamps at typewriters or paperwork. They glanced at her without interest as she walked by, giving the impression that women must often pass this way.

Passing one of the offices, she glanced in and her heart almost stopped. It was Elmo. The man from the Amsterdam network that they knew to be a traitor. At the sound of her heels he looked up, and seemed about to speak, but she hurried by, though she'd caught sight of the puzzled look on his face. Her mind was racing. Elmo had seen her. And he had to know who she was, though she realised she must look completely different with all the make-up, her hair in a chignon, and dressed in these fashionable fitted clothes.

She paced down the corridor before he could get a closer look, peering at the doors, terrified he'd come after her. Number six, number four. Number two. She rapped a bit too loud, then stepped from foot to foot, impatient to be out of Elmo's view.

She had a moment's vivid apprehension. This was it. She was about to go from the frying pan and into the fire.

Please answer. Her heartbeat was too fast – she could feel the blood pulsing at her neck.

Fritz's valet appeared and let her in. He gave her no greeting, simply opened the door wide and she stepped inside.

The apartment was so bright with lamps that she was momentarily dazzled. Fritz was coming towards her; and all at once she realised where she was, and it set off the twisting in her stomach. He was dressed in a civilian suit and tie, with shoes polished to a glassy shine, and his hair well-oiled. 'Danique, how lovely!'

'Thank you for the flowers,' she said. She had to put Elmo behind her.

'My pleasure.'

'I didn't know you could still get flowers like that. I thought perhaps the growers had eaten them all.'

He laughed and wagged a finger. 'Don't be naughty.' He indicated she should sit down, and she navigated her way past some small tables to an armchair. 'Small pleasures are the best, are they not?'

'Absolutely. The smell of real coffee or hot bread.'

'I hope you're hungry, the chef has prepared dinner for us. Make yourself comfortable while I make our drinks.'

He went into the kitchen, and she had a chance to examine her surroundings. The room was bigger than hers and electric lamps glared from every wall. A fire was lit, and she realised suddenly she was warm. She took off her jacket as she scanned the vast parquet floor which was stacked with furniture or boxes. It was as if she'd arrived in an antique shop. No, not an antique shop – a museum storeroom. Oil paintings of all types were resting against the walls, one gilded frame leaning over another. An exquisite marquetry table sat near her elbow and Fritz placed a tumbler of liqueur on it when he returned with the drinks.

Towards the blacked-out window a dining table was set up with shining cutlery and glasses for two. 'Tell me about yourself,' he said, settling on a chair opposite. 'How you came to live in The Hague.'

The nightmare question. She trotted out her cover story, aiming for a natural way of speaking. 'So you see,' she finished, 'I couldn't bear to stay in Nijmegen any more with Anton gone, and when I heard the French and English were coming – well, I knew things would get bad for me. Other members of the National Socialist Party told me it would be safer in the North. So that was it – I packed up a few of my most precious things, and fled here, where I could be sure of meeting others of my persuasion.'

'You were wise to do so. Their occupation will be short-lived. Our forces will soon overcome theirs.'

She hoped to heaven he was wrong. She looked towards the door, where the valet had taken a chair and was sitting staring at them with a fixed expression, watching and listening to her every move.

'And what do you do, here in The Hague, Fritz?' she asked, putting on a smile. 'Keller said you are his boss at Sheveningen.'

'I don't like to talk about my work. It is not very pleasant. Once the Reich is fully in control, such a prison will no longer be necessary.' He took a gulp of his whisky and she followed suit. The hit of the liqueur made her sit bolt upright. *Don't get drunk.*

This was going to be harder than she thought if he wouldn't volunteer anything.

'What did you do before the war?' she asked.

'I was a policeman,' he said. 'Many of us in the SS were. It is not so different. Our training taught us to spot those who lie and cheat, and those with something to hide. So it was a useful experience. And of course patrolling our community. I was a sergeant when I left, but now I've moved up the ranks, though sometimes I wish I hadn't.'

'Oh? Why's that?'

'Back then there were so few crimes,' he said wistfully. 'Arnstadt was a small town. Some petty robbery, youths mainly, for the fun of it. Thefts of garden tools. But it stopped once they were in the *HitlerJugend*.'

'It sounds nice, this small-town life.'

'To be honest, it was a little dull. I felt I was wasted there. Once Hitler came to power, policing became much more of a career. It was exciting to see the movement grow.'

It was power, she thought. The growth of men's power. None of it filtered down to the women unless they were on the arm of one of these men.

'So when did you move to The Hague?' she asked, between tentative sips of liqueur.

'I was sent here to quell some unrest. The revolution had started you see, towards a more unified Germany, and the undesirables didn't like it. But also, there was a lot more for the police to do. New orders – policing those that were being deported. Clamping down on subversive behaviour. True, there were some things I disagreed with – too many deportations, the amount of paperwork for that – unbelievable. But in the end you had to be either for or against, and I could see the good it was doing for our nation and I wanted a part of it. Trouble with war is, the job is twenty-four hours.'

'Will you go back to policing at the end of the war?'

'I doubt it. I won't stay in Holland – too cold and damp, and I miss Germany. Here, there is too much in the way of our reforms. Every last thing is a struggle, and I'm tired of fighting people. When I retire, I'm hoping to set up some sort of art business.'

'Ah. I noticed all the paintings.'

'I'm a bit of a collector,' he said, 'I want to take these home where they'll be appreciated.'

'I love art,' she improvised, 'and so did my husband, but such a shame – our collection was lost in the bombing.'

'That's precisely why I've gathered these things here. It was hard to get them out. I needed many men at the museums to move them – ah, what a hustle that was.'

'Which are your favourites?'

'Anything very old. Can't bear this new stuff with bits of newsprint stuck to it, or random sploshes. Or nudes with square faces.' He made an expression of disgust. 'No. I like a good painting of horses or a landscape of lakes and mountains, something inspiring—'

The soft noise of a gong interrupted him.

'*Ach, gut*. Dinner is ready. Do come and take a seat.'

She sat down opposite him, and though she was facing the window there was no view because of the blackout, so she had no choice but to look at Fritz. He raised his eyebrows and smiled at her as he tucked his napkin into his collar. His face was broad across the forehead with a nose that could once have been broken. He would have been handsome had she not been so determined to hate him.

She smiled back at him, then took the ladylike option and smoothed the napkin across her lap.

The chef, who was also, it seemed, their waiter, brought them a soup. It was so delicious she was almost in tears that she couldn't share it. She hadn't had food like this for years. She was aghast to see he left half of his in the bottom of the bowl.

'I don't care much for this,' he said, slapping down his napkin.

'I suppose I'm used to it,' Nancy said. It was *snert*, the traditional Dutch split-pea soup. 'My mother used to make it.'

'Ah, home cooking! Now you're talking. My mother made the most marvellous *labskaus* – meat and beetroot stew. When I get home, that's the first thing I'll ask for.'

She concealed her amusement. Even a Stapo man like him hankered for his mother's cooking, it was rather sweet. They talked a little more about his mother, who was still living in Heidelberg.

More courses followed, but Nancy could eat little. The soup had filled her stomach, which had shrunk so much it couldn't cope with more. Fritz ploughed his way through a pork cutlet, and even a strudel dessert. Oh, to be able to whip her portion off the plate and take it home!

The valet sat impassively by the door ignoring their talk. She wondered whether he and the chef would polish off the leftovers when she left. But later she realised he never got the chance, because when the meal was finished Fritz said, 'How about a little stroll? After dinner I always like to go outside and get some air.'

He walked her alongside the canal, which had now been filled in and become a road. They hadn't gone far when she realised they were being followed. His valet, who she now was certain was some sort of bodyguard, was in the shadows just behind them. So no chance of an assassination at close quarters, then.

Fritz stopped by the canal bridge and reached down, and she thought he might want to kiss her. But instead, he placed a hand on her shoulder. 'You look very beautiful in this light, Danique.'

She shook her head, unsure what to say. Her only thought was not of Fritz, but of Tom.

Fritz let go of her shoulder and took her arm. 'It's a shame that war turns everything ugly. I hate that it destroys great buildings, the ones men have taken centuries to complete.'

'And not just buildings,' she said. 'So many men lost to this war machine. And civilians; those who are just casualties of it all. Such a waste.'

He ruminated a moment. 'Did you have a garden?' he asked.

'Yes, once. Why?'

'Because that's how I see war. Like the war on weeds. You have to eliminate the things that would destroy the beauty of the garden, like the weeds that want to take over everything. Those need to be rooted out, so there's more room for other more desirable things to flourish.' She understood they were not talking of weeds and it made her cringe.

'But don't you think the most beautiful places are the places where nature has been allowed to do what she does, without interference from man?'

He stopped, gazed out over the canal. 'You think? We had a beautiful forest near us, and I loved to go there as a boy. And yes, I remember the beaches, the sound of the sea. So yes, I do agree. But cities; well they are another thing. If we are to be organised, to be productive, then we have to have systems. Like the factories that make things. Nature has its own systems, don't you agree? The hawk preys on the mouse, and we think nothing of it.'

'It self-regulates. But we never look at it from the point of view of the mouse.'

He laughed. 'Too true.'

She shivered, for it was cold, and in her blue silk, she had not dressed warmly enough.

'Come on,' he said, turning her around to walk back. 'Enough of politics. We'll go back to my apartment,' he said. 'We can continue our conversation there, and have a nightcap. I'd like you to look through my paintings, perhaps choose one for your apartment, as you have lost so much.'

'Oh, I couldn't do that,' she said. She thought of all the people whose houses had been plundered for his 'collection'.

'I insist. I have many, and it will please me to think of you enjoying it.'

'Mesman,' he called. The valet emerged from the shadow of a building. 'Get Bakker to bring the car,' he said in German. 'We're ready to go home.'

The German language reminded her with sudden clarity that Fritz was the enemy. And also that he could just demand that a car be fetched whenever he wanted one.

Once inside the car, his hand rested disturbingly on her leg and on one occasion slid languidly over the silk, up and down her thigh, until he withdrew it.

The fact he might make a pass at her made her recoil from him, but at the same time she knew that was the way it had to go, if she wanted to get more information out of him. But she wouldn't make it easy; she'd get her information first, and she'd delay that moment as long as she could. How could she think like this? On the way home she wondered if this assignment was turning her into someone she didn't recognise; someone hard and calculating.

In the apartment she was obliged to listen as he brought out painting after painting. It was obvious that in his own eyes he was quite a connoisseur. She'd endured an hour of explanations, opinions on which painting had the most value, lectures on which artist was a pupil of an earlier master and so forth.

In the end he asked her to choose something, and she pointed jokingly to a landscape on the wall. One he said he particularly liked. It was an almost empty view of distant mountains with a fine mist over trees.

Surprisingly, he didn't demur. 'Ha! I knew you'd choose that one! We have the same taste. I know it. It will give me the greatest pleasure to think of that hanging on your wall. And every time you look at it, you will think of me.'

No. Every time I look at it, I will think how much the Nazis have taken from the Dutch people.

'Thank you, Fritz, but I couldn't. I wasn't serious.'

'I insist!' He strode over to unhook it.

She thanked him profusely. 'It will look fine above the fire-place, if you're sure. Have you got any paintings in the office where you work?'

He looked at her as if she had said something unbelievable. 'Where I work? No. There are no paintings there.'

'Why not? Anton had paintings in his office. You could have something of beauty there, couldn't you?'

'Perhaps.' His expression showed he had never considered the idea at all. 'I suppose I could take a painting, or a sculpture or two.' His face lit up with enthusiasm. 'It's a good idea. I suppose I didn't think of it because the man who had the office before me hadn't thought of it either. But now – yes, why not? I'll choose something to lift the spirits.'

'I'd like to see your office, see where paintings could go.'

'No, you wouldn't. It's an ugly place, no place for a beautiful woman like you.'

She let her eyes sparkle. 'I'd like to see the lion in his lair.'

He smiled, enjoying the flattery. 'Perhaps one day, when I have my paintings there. You are the only person to suggest such a thing. But perhaps you are right, maybe it needs a woman's touch.'

'And afterwards, I'll come and inspect it, see if it meets my approval.'

74

He laughed. 'I'll hold you to that.' His manner was joking and intimate. She realised they were in danger of becoming friends.

But that's what you want, isn't it? 'It's getting late,' she said, looking at her watch.

'Mesman will escort you down. I've really enjoyed this evening; just to talk. It's such a relief to talk. Most women, well to be frank, they want something.' He raised his arms in a shrug. 'We'll see each other again, yes? I'm free tomorrow evening.'

'I'll check my diary.' She'd discovered nothing, but she knew that to fawn over him would make her seem less desirable.

Escaping his apartment was like being released from a strait-jacket, despite Mesman leading the way. By now the office doors were closed and the corridor empty. Even the lift felt spacious. But from what Steef had said, Schneider liked a good chase, and she intended to give him one.

Fritz paced the room once Danique had gone. Before she left, he'd given her a painting. Why had he done that? It had been his favourite. Already he missed it.

It was an impulse, because she was attractive, with those large doe-like eyes and straight nose. Good legs too. He'd enjoyed the evening, and it had been refreshing to actually have a decent conversation. The other Dutch women in The Hague were all just greedy whores. But Danique had a touch of refinement and maturity. Probably because she was already won over to the National Socialist cause. Her husband had been a friend of Goering after all, so they must share the same interests, the same ambition for the new world coming.

He found the way she crossed her legs, her modesty appealing. She was grieving her husband and idly, he wondered what this Anton had been like in bed.

He'd like to give him a run for his money.

Ah yes, he'd like to see more of Danique. He glanced at his watch. Not too late.

He reached for the telephone, and when it was answered, spoke rapidly in German.

'*Ja,* Dobermann. I need some intelligence. Everything you can find out about a Dutch couple from Nijmegen. Members of the NSB, Anton and Danique Koopman. Who they know, what their business interests are, bank accounts, their links to Germany.'

Chapter 9

The next morning Nancy awoke in that no man's land between waking and sleeping, where memories are jumbled and shrouded in fog. Until she remembered that the dry mouth was because Schneider had given her brandy with her coffee.

She dressed quickly and hurried down the stairs to the lobby.

'We have to do something about Elmo,' she said to Steef. 'I saw him last night on the top floor.'

'What, here?' Steef leant forwards over the reception desk and his eyes scoured the lobby.

'Yes, here! Talking to one of the Gestapo in the offices upstairs.'

'Did he see you?' He beckoned her into his office out of the lobby.

'Yes, but I think he couldn't place me. I look so different from before. But he might remember who I really am at any moment, and then I'd be sunk.'

'Then we'll have to eliminate him. I'll get someone to see to it.'

She pressed her lips together. She understood what it meant, but even after years of being an agent she'd never been wholly comfortable with the idea of taking another life. Not in cold blood. Face to face in combat, then yes. But not planned assassination, and not of someone she had worked with.

She changed the subject, keeping her voice low. 'Schneider won't talk about his work, I can't get him to open up, he's cagey about anything to do with the Oranjehotel.'

'Then you must pressure him more. Use your womanly wiles.'

'Oh. it's alright for you to say that, but it's just not that easy.' She shook her head at him. 'Too much pressure and he'll smell a rat. Not enough, and we won't get anything. And besides, I have a man back home and it just tears me up doing this.'

'You think we're not all doing unconscionable things?' His eyes grew hard and bright. 'I live this life because I have a wife and child, and I want them to see freedom. Do you think I don't think of them going hungry every minute whilst I bow and scrape to men like Schneider?'

She swallowed at his obvious distress. 'I didn't know—'

'Understand this. We're up against the wire. People will starve to death because of your "conscience".' He spat out the word. 'Look, we've set up a soup kitchen in the centre of town and we desperately need more supplies. We need the resistance factions to consolidate and work together to sort out canal routes, road routes, any way of getting food from the South. We need someone with authority, someone who knows all the factions and can co-ordinate them in a food effort, and Josef is the only one who talks with them all and is tough enough. The Resistance is all we have. The only way to magic food into people's mouths.' He pushed her back out of the door. 'Do what you came here to do.'

He paused as a Gestapo officer came by on his way to the lift. Nancy gave him a polite nod.

When the officer was out of earshot, she leant in towards Steef. 'It will take time, I can't do miracles overnight.'

'When are you seeing him again?'

78

'Soon. I haven't confirmed the date. At least I might get fed. Though I fear I will have to get in bed with him to earn it.'

'Then you aren't the only one. Think you're so different? There are women all over Holland doing the same, and for a single slice of bread.'

She lowered her gaze, unwilling to let him see how much the words had pierced her.

'Drop by to see me the next day. Coming to your apartment is a risk. I have to be on the other end of the bell in the janitor's room when they call. Too long an absence and they'll start asking questions, or worse, move me to a German armaments factory.'

Later she dropped a note into Fritz's mailbox agreeing to dinner at his convenience. Steef's words haunted her. She felt she was somehow letting him and his family down.

To ease this tight feeling she concentrated on the certificate mail drops – there were still more to do, and she knew, if nothing else, in this bitter weather, they might go to light a fire. The leaflets she was delivering were resistance propaganda. Steef had told her how some Dutchmen had given themselves up to go to Germany, thinking they'd be better fed. But the word was that many died there, from overwork, undernourishment and disease.

A thin friend of Steef's, a man called Albie with a heavy moustache, and cap pulled down to his eyes, met her at the church to collect the mail drop. She supposed him to be about forty though he looked much older, and he could barely stand still whilst he pushed the pile of papers into her hands.

Today's leaflet said simply, *Don't think the Hun will do anything but cheat you and beat you.* Another to stop the loss of any remaining Dutch men to the German machine.

She walked fast to alleviate her hunger. She'd had no breakfast and though it was Saturday, there was no bread to be had. The same desperate women hung round the square offering looted goods in exchange for food. An icy sleet was falling, yet still they stood there – hope the only thing holding them up.

Now the weather was colder, the streets had been scoured clean of litter. All Nazi proclamations or propaganda had been torn away, window shutters had disappeared from every house, and no cardboard or loose wood remained anywhere, all gone into people's stoves.

Nancy was glad of her warm coat with its fur-trimmed collar and elegant wool gloves. She suspected that like most second-hand clothes they had belonged to deported Jews and the Resistance had somehow managed to get to them before the Germans did.

At midday she passed the queue for soup and a woman spat at her. 'NSB!' she yelled. The initials for the collaborators.

More yells and insults followed, '*Hoer!*' '*Moffenmeid!*'

Nancy rushed by with her head down. Dressed like this, if she was to eat, it would obviously have to be with the Germans. She couldn't wear the worn-out clothes ordinary women wore – to risk being seen in old clothes by Schneider, or indeed the other Nazis from her block, would raise the question of who she was. She must keep up the pretence of being a Nazi collaborator, no matter how much it chafed.

Passing the back of her building on the way home, she noticed a trio of small girls, clad only in skirts and knitted jumpers, more darn than whole, their shoes more hole than shoe. Faces filthy, and blue with cold, they were raking through every dustbin. The biggest girl, her fair hair tied up in a grimy ribbon, was hanging on to the waist of the smallest as she leant in. Sleet had turned to snow.

As Nancy walked by, a scrawny rat scuttled out from behind the bins. A shout of excitement, and the children pounced on it corralling it from one place to the next, until finally, the fair-haired girl grasped hold of it. She screamed as it sank its teeth into her arm, but the other two bludgeoned it on the head with a dustbin lid until it gave up.

The sight made Nancy want to laugh, but at the same time cry. Over time the cats and dogs had disappeared. Most vermin had fled to the country in search of food, this rat was brave, but not as brave as those girls.

The children saw her staring, and with scared eyes, they scooted off, the biggest girl clutching her grisly treasure to her chest. Instantly, a gang of bigger boys shot out from nowhere to attack them.

'Hey!' Nancy yelled, waving her arms, trying to scare them away.

'What's she got?' The four bigger boys in ragged jumpers tried to wrestle the prize from the girl's arms. She clung on, while the other two girls kicked and scratched.

Nancy rushed in to drag them away. The bigger boys turned vicious, pummelling her, raining blows on her back, until one of the boys wrenched the rat away.

'Mama'll be pleased,' piped up the youngest boy, swinging it by its tail.

'You little bastards,' Nancy said, as the boys dodged out of her reach.

'Keep your gang off our patch,' the big boy yelled at the girl. 'Or we'll tell the Nazis you're Jews.'

The girls scarpered, skidding down the street like lightning.

She'd been helpless, Nancy realised. She was supposed to be fighting the Nazis, yet she'd been helpless against a bunch of kids. Nancy leant against the building. It had shaken her; that being a bully or being a coward had now become the only way to survive. What was the world coming to, when children would fight over a rat?

She went in through the revolving door, still feeling the fists of those boys. She used the stairs every time now and prayed she wouldn't meet Keller. She had a dread of the lift getting stuck between floors when the electric went off.

When she got back to the apartment she shook the snow off her coat, took off the pinching shoes, and rubbed her sore feet.

She was tired. Lack of food meant lack of energy and she would need it all for this assignment.

Steef's words made more sense now. She'd re-double her efforts to get inside the prison and do her part to get Josef out. There was power in working together, in coordinating your efforts like those children did.

Those poor girls. She'd take a bigger handbag when she went to dinner with Fritz, see if she could bring a little food home, and give some to those girls.

A few days later, Fritz was in his office when the telephone call came from Dobermann of German intelligence. Fritz pressed the receiver to his ear. He hadn't been able to stop thinking about Danique, and couldn't wait to see her again.

Dobermann rattled off details of Anton Koopman's business interests, and reiterated that his factory had been producing shell cases for Germany.

'And they are members of the NSB?'

Dobermann confirmed that Anton and Danique Koopman were indeed members of the NSB, but that Anton was dead. A heart attack, back in 1943.

Fritz leant back in his chair, relieved. He couldn't stop smiling.

'And you've seen the death certificate?'

'Yes. He's definitely dead.'

'What about his wife?'

'We don't know. Their house was destroyed in the bombing. Completely obliterated. I don't know where the wife is now. But I checked her bank account, and though it was quiet for a few months, there have been some recent transactions, so she definitely survived.'

'Where? Here in The Hague?'

'No. The last one a few weeks ago in Nijmegen. A large amount. And her pearls, taken from the vault. The clerk remembers her.'

'What? What does he remember?' He wanted every detail.

'She was impatient with him. A little rude. But a very attractive woman. Well-dressed, good shoes and handbag.'

Fritz smiled. 'Thank you. Keep a check on her bank account would you, and any transactions. Call me in a week if there's anything new. And get that clerk removed, he obviously can't recognise class when he sees it.'

After he'd put the receiver down, Fritz sat back in his chair and stretched. He had a good feeling about Danique. Of course his wife at home need never know. He'd write to Stella as he usually did, get news of his sons, but it would be pleasant to share his life again.

Faintly, in the background, he heard screams from the interrogation cells in the yard. He went over to the Swiss Maestrophone in the corner and put a disc on the turntable, lowering the needle until the crackle faded and the strains of a waltz filled the air.

He remembered the feel of Danique in his arms, the softness of her skin when they danced at the Hotel des Indes. He couldn't wait for the weekend to come. Something to take his mind off the clank of prison doors and the stink of unwashed men.

And he must find her a special Christmas gift. He'd missed what the Dutch called *sinterklaasavond*, St Nicholas Eve, on 5 December. But perhaps he could rustle up something for Christmas Day. He felt guilty, for Hitler didn't hold with all that Christian stuff. But it would be a good excuse to please Danique.

Chapter 10

'How have you spent your day?' Fritz asked Nancy, as she settled down on the sofa. A copy of the SS paper *Das Schwarze Korps* lay next to him. Fritz was a charming host, so long as you could stomach what he did for a living. Impossible, as he was still in uniform.

She'd anticipated his question. 'I'm afraid it was mostly sleeping. I'm so tired these days, the way the war drags on, and I was woken last night by the siren again and had to go to the shelter. Where do you go when it goes off?'

'The German shelter near the station.'

'What about the daytime?'

'Nowhere. Not in Scheveningen. The British wouldn't bomb the place where all their resistance men are held.'

'True. No alarms today, then?'

'No. The usual sort of day. And I have to say, like you, I'm a little jaded. The lack of time off, well, the shifts get wearing after a while.'

'Is it very dull?'

He rubbed the back of his neck. 'At first I thought it was interesting, but now I've heard it all before. The denials, the bluster, the protestations. The amount of violence it takes for them to talk. You see, we're dealing with men with little moral compass. They'll lie and try to deceive us, thinking they'll be able to bluster their way out and go free. Fools. They're always in there for a reason. I trust those who made the arrests. But a whole day of listening to it all gives me a headache.'

'Poor Fritz. It sounds unbearable. Can't you resign?'

'You don't know how often I've thought of it,' he replied, 'but sticking with it is the best option right now. If I don't do this, then I'll have to serve somewhere else. All German men must serve the Reich. If I didn't stay at the prison, I would have to be Kommandant at one of the camps. Or Russia. And trust me, the Wehrmacht on the Russian Front in the depths of winter is not a good choice.'

'A lot of stress, eh? Dealing with dangerous men, fanatics who want to bring the Party down.' Was she fishing too much? She put on an innocent face.

He turned to look at her. 'I'm well guarded. Mesman is always nearby, and he knows the situation. All high-up officers have protection.'

'Very wise,' she said.

He crossed his long legs in their black boots and cavalry trousers. 'Tell me about your husband's business. He was in the manufacture of lamp posts and street furniture, I believe?'

A ripple of apprehension went up her back. She hadn't told him that, so he must have got his men on to checking her out. *Take care, Nancy.*

'I'm afraid I didn't have much to do with the foundry or the factory,' she said. 'But the situation in Europe worried Anton and as soon as the Dutch occupation began, he agreed a sum with Goering. To turn the whole lot over to the Reich for arms manufacture. He'd been a party donor for years, you see.'

85

'A good thought. It's a shame the factory's no longer in our hands. I hate to think of those English dogs having use of it.'

'Anton's timing was always impeccable,' Nancy said. 'You could even say he died just in time. And I'm glad of his money now, because if he hadn't sold, there'd be nothing to keep me afloat. Not after the bombing.'

'He sounds like a good husband,' Fritz said.

'The best.' She attempted a choke in her voice, desperate to get away from the fact Fritz was quizzing her instead of vice versa.

Fritz rested a hand on her shoulder, and with a murmur of sympathy went to pour more drinks. She asked for soda water this time, and vowed to stay off the brandy.

By now, she was waiting for the dinner bell. They sat in the same places as before, and this familiarity made her deeply uncomfortable. When the chef served the soup today it was the same soup as the day before, re-heated. *So*, she thought, *even Germans have to make compromises.*

Fritz threw down his napkin immediately. 'I told them I disliked this soup. I'll have to have a word in the kitchen.'

Raised voices drifted through the closed door but whilst Fritz was gone Nancy hurriedly tore a chunk off the bread, and put the other wedge of bread into her bag. She started eating the soup, for her stomach was rumbling.

When he returned, she apologised, 'I'm sorry, Fritz. I couldn't resist starting.'

'I'm glad you've an appetite,' he said, smiling. 'I can't bear women who pick at their food. And it's so good to have company, someone who'll talk about the arts, the finer things in life.'

He'd assigned her a role, and she took it. 'Tonight, let's choose some things for your office. There's no reason why it should have to be as bare as the cells.' She was intent on getting inside his office somehow.

Fritz toyed with his food, leaving the bowl full until the chef came to take it all away. She could only remember a few Dutch artists, and soon ran out of conversation about paintings, but Fritz seemed more than happy to take over, lecturing her with long explanations of German masters. She smiled politely, though her mind was racing, thinking ahead and hoping he wouldn't try to seduce her.

All his talk of priceless art, whilst there were people outside his window who couldn't eat. She watched the way he cut his pastry into neat squares and ate from his plate in an ordered way, finishing the pie before tackling the potatoes. The greens, he pushed to the side.

She quelled the urge to scrape them from his plate.

'Do you need extra rations?' he asked, suddenly, looking up from his last forkful. 'I hadn't thought . . . I can arrange for you to have extra coupons. Perhaps you might like to cook for me one night. A sort of Christmas celebration? There will be electricity on Friday night because that is the night we have to send telegrams.'

'Oh, I'd love that,' she said. 'Anton used to enjoy my home-cooked stews. But I don't know where I can get good ingredients now.'

'Take your coupons to the stores master at the Hotel des Indes. He has a cellar of good provisions. Tell him I sent you and he will give you what you need. I'll write you an authorisation.'

'Oh, how wonderful to cook again, Fritz! And to have someone to enjoy it.' Her mind fluttered around Tom. How she would love to cook for him instead. She dragged her attention back to the man in front of her. 'When I've seen what I can get, then I'll send you an invitation.'

'Friday? You'll need to look in your diary,' he said, raising an eyebrow.

'Yes, I will!' They both laughed. She was glad he had a sense of humour, but the darkness beneath made it bitter just the same.

The rest of the evening Fritz regaled her with his opinions on what he called 'the Bolshevik threat', whilst all the time edging nearer to her on the sofa.

'The Russian citizens are totally deceived by the corrupt Soviet leadership,' he said, patting her knee with a hot hand. 'They abuse the population – see them only as fodder for their own purposes, controlling them through fear.' His hand strayed further up. 'The leaders have no moral compass. The average citizen is simply a tool in the hands of a thoroughly corrupt leadership, intent on spreading red propaganda.'

'Awful.' She moved away, smoothed her skirt back over her knees. She stared at him with what she hoped was an expression of deep interest, and let him talk on and on, oblivious to the irony of what he was saying.

At the end of it, he seized her hand again and kneaded it. 'You are so understanding, Danique. I have missed good conversation.'

As long as it's one-sided.

She smiled, relieved he didn't make a pass at her. His brief looks at her legs and bosom made her sure that eventually he would, but he was biding his time. She kept up the pretence of grieving widow, though she knew it would displease Steef. The thought of the small box with its sponge made her shudder.

As early as she dared, Nancy said her farewells and left Fritz's apartment. She feared to go earlier, because she had to convince him she liked his company. If only she could get a chance to snoop around his apartment! As it was, Mesman was always there, a quiet, disconcerting presence sitting in the corner with one hand resting on his holster, the gun always visible.

What had she learnt? That Fritz had made checks on her. The thought itched, because despite his assurances, it meant he didn't entirely trust her.

The next morning she hurried down to try to see Steef, to fill him in on anything she'd gleaned from Fritz, though in truth it was precious little. When she arrived, he was on the telephone calling a car for one of the men from the top floor.

After he put the phone down, he leaned over the counter.

'Got something for you.' He beckoned her around the desk and pointed. Sitting on the floor was a small brown suitcase.

'Is that what I think it is?'

He grinned. 'A little Christmas present. Take it straight upstairs. SS Unteroffizier Hass is coming down for his car any minute.'

She picked up the case, as ever surprised by the weight of the transmitter. Should she get the lift? No, she might meet Keller coming down. She lugged the case to the stairs and began to climb.

A tap of feet hurrying down. She stood aside to let the SS officer pass.

He smiled at her. 'That looks heavy,' he said. 'I'll carry it up for you.'

'No, it's alright,' she said, flustered. 'I'm nearly there.'

'Frau Koopman, isn't it? From number eighteen? Fritz has been telling me about you. That you've just moved in.' He was wrestling the handle from her hand.

She had no choice but to follow him.

'What've you got in here? You should have taken the lift.'

'Books,' she blurted, thinking quickly. 'I like to study.'

He put the case down outside her door and gave her the '*Sieg Heil.*'

Her palms were sticky at the thought he could have searched her case. A close call.

Back in her apartment she locked her door, unpacked the transmitter, then rigged up the aerial out of the boxroom window at the back of the apartment. She tucked the end of the wire behind the blind so it was hardly visible, because after all these years, she knew every transmission was a risk.

Once it was all set up, she took a deep breath and began to count down the hours and minutes to transmission. Fritz would be at work by now, and so would most of the men, only those in the offices on the top floor would be in. Eleven o'clock English time, Mondays, Wednesdays and Saturdays only. Today was Monday. Now was an ideal time to transmit to Tom.

Please, let him be there.

For the last few years she had kept in touch with Tom via their secret code – a code only they understood. It was a private joke. If she was alright she would transmit just two words, 'Shepherd's Pie'. This was the meal they'd first shared at Lyons' Corner House in London. If she needed help or was in trouble she'd agreed to transmit the word 'Bacon', as in 'save my bacon'.

Of course the word would never be used. It was a little joke, because if she was really in trouble there'd be no way to send any kind of message. On a few occasions he'd not received her message and she had spent weeks worrying because a reply did not arrive. But today the one-word reply arrived almost immediately. The reply read, 'Sauce'.

The sight of that one word, with its cheery double entendre, filled Nancy with elation.

'Sauce' back to you, you lovely man, she thought.

The fact that somewhere in England Tom was thinking of her and listening out for her message was like an injection of sunshine.

Oh Tom, she thought. A wave of longing almost took her breath away. It astonished her, that even when so much was destroyed, when death literally stalked every corner, that she could still feel this surge of life ripple through her veins.

The desire she felt for Tom was matched by the disgust she felt for Fritz.

Oh God, let the Allies come soon.

Chapter 11

The next day Nancy continued to deliver more leaflets dissuading men from going to Germany, and left Fritz a note to say she could see him on Friday. By evening there was an envelope in her pigeonhole by reception.

A thin slip of paper, and some heavier foolscap. She unfolded the thin slip.

Looking forward to Friday night. I'll bring wine. Wear your pearls. Fritz.

The foolscap was a paper covered in red and black official stamps. Written authorisation to go to the Wehrmacht hotel for provisions, and a strip of Nazi army food coupons. Damn, the authorisation was date stamped. Only for Friday. She supposed to prevent her using it for any black market trade. Was Fritz mean-minded, or did he just not trust her?

And what did he mean, *Wear your pearls?* Did he just mean she should dress up? She didn't own any pearls, and the jewellery Steef had given her was only a few fake gold brooches. Still, she'd pin one on, if he liked her to wear jewellery. Usually her only necklace was the St Christopher medal that she wore round her neck under her blouse. It had been a gift from Tom before she flew back to Holland – St Christopher, patron saint of travellers.

She put the coupons and authorisation in her handbag. Maybe a good meal would persuade Fritz to tell her more. Nobody told you when you began this spying game, how frustrating the waiting was. She set off with her basket over her arm to queue, angry that there was food she couldn't get at until the end of the week. Her own cupboard was bare. Steef had initially supplied her with a few dried beans, Gouda cheese, a pound of flour, a pinch of salt and pepper, and some ground linseed oil he'd got from a relative in the country, but now that was gone.

Suddenly she had an idea. She knew where the printer was – Greta, at Maystraat 18 in the Bezuidenhout. Nancy'd been there once before to drop off some leaflets. Perhaps she could get more authorisations and coupons forged.

Nancy hunched against the rain and hurried to Greta's and down the steps to the front door, a bag of washing clutched to her chest. Supposedly Greta took in laundry. It was a good cover.

She had to knock twice before Greta came, sticking her head out as if sniffing the air, her face full of suspicion. She was a hard-faced woman in her forties with startling ginger hair under a tightly-tied headscarf. Nancy thrust the parcel at her and gave the passcode which was, 'It's only shirts today.'

'Yes, yes. No need for that. I'm not so old I don't remember a face.' Greta let her in and led her into the kitchen, a place crammed with shelves of blue and white Delft crockery. The actual printing press was hidden in a bomb shelter in the garden. In Holland you had to be careful of rising water levels so she'd set up the press on flagstones to keep it from sinking.

Nancy took out the authorisation that Schneider had given her for the stores at the Hotel des Indes, and the extra ration cards and spread them out on the long kitchen table.

'Any chance you can make more of these?' she asked, pointing at the authorisation. 'Signed, but with different dates? Say a week or two apart?'

Greta pulled the paper towards her. 'Easy enough. But might take a while. I have a backlog.' She was staring at the slip. 'Have they got flour there then, and bread?'

Something about the way she stared made Nancy uneasy. She realised she had probably given away more information than she should.

'Not much,' Nancy said. 'But I'd thought to go back and get some supplies for the central kitchen. I can't do it too often, or they'd notice. But every little helps, right?'

Greta nodded, and put it aside. 'I'll send a message when it's ready. The ration coupons – they're useless now there's no rations. The Germans can eat, but not the Dutch people.' She shot Nancy a disapproving look. 'Our shops are empty, so ration tickets are only good for the fire.' She turned away and picked up a stash of leaflets. 'These are to go to Steef.'

They were more of the leaflets dissuading men from going to German factories.

Fit to fight back, not fit for the factories!

Nancy concealed them in the false lining of her bag along with the ration tickets. She felt nervous now about leaving the authorisation slip with Greta, but it was too late to take it back. Something about Greta's pugnacious attitude made her a person not to cross.

When she returned to the back of the building the three scavenging girls were foraging again in the dustbins. Remembering the scrap of bread in her handbag she called out to them.

'Hey!' They looked up, startled, preparing to run.

She opened her handbag, took out the bread and placed it very definitely on the lid of a dustbin.

'Quick!' she said, 'Before those boys get it.'

She backed away and the eldest girl swooped in. Within a moment she'd split it into three and it was down their throats. They looked up hopefully, like dogs waiting for a treat.

'No more,' she said. 'But come back on Friday.'

They said nothing, just stared with that hollow-eyed look of disbelief.

At last Friday came. Today she could buy proper provisions. The thought made her realise just how much food was a preoccupation.

She went as early as she dare. The hotel was quite a different place in the daylight. The red swastikas hung damply in the drizzle and the place seemed more rundown in the harsh light of day. No Christmas garlands or sign of festivity were to be seen. The paintwork was grubby and scuffed, the windows dirty. No-one had time for cleaning in wartime.

At the reception desk she asked for Herr Karlauf as she'd been instructed, and a uniformed man appeared. He took the note and asked her to follow him.

Down the servant stairs and into the basement under the hotel. Behind the locked metal door, the sight astounded her. A pile of tins of powdered milk as high as her shoulder, more tins of meat and fish, and sacks of cereal and flour piled one on top of the other.

One wall had a flitch of ham hanging there and a shelf with two dead chickens under fly covers. There were even eggs in a basket, reminding her of collecting eggs with her mother and brother when she was a child, and brought a sudden unexpected lump to her throat.

Her shopping list suddenly seemed so small when confronted with this mountain of food. Despite herself, her mouth watered and her belly rumbled. She recovered herself and got out her list and her coupons under the store master's eyes, then stacked a few things on the shelf to the side for him to check. He checked off a pound bag of flour, baking powder in a twist of paper, as well as two eggs and some ham, not to mention a pot of lard and some potatoes.

'All in order, Frau Koopman,' he said. 'Oberführer Schneider's been quite generous this time. He must like you.'

His implication and the way he looked at her with such disdain made her boil with rage. 'We are friends,' she said firmly.

'So were the others.'

Bastard of a man. She glared icily and picking up her basket, went back upstairs into the light.

Away from the hotel, the prospect of cooking cheered her, even if it was for Schneider. She wished she could get extra wine – it would be useful to get him drunk.

On the way back she passed barefoot children digging up the wooden tram sleepers for fuel. No doubt their parents were 'divers' or just too afraid to come outside.

The ragged girls were at the back of the building waiting hopefully. She took out two potatoes from her hoard and stood there waiting to hand them over. The girls came closer. She wanted to talk to them, find out where they lived, how come no-one was looking out for them.

She waited as they came closer. The elder one's hair was matted and looked like it had never seen a comb. The younger ones held back, one holding a dustbin lid.

'I've some potatoes,' she said.

Everything happened so quickly she couldn't make sense of it.

One minute she was holding the basket, the next something hard and sharp and metallic hit her in the face. A yell and clawing hands as the basket was torn away.

The sound of running feet. The girls ran off, the older one clutching the basket.

'Stop!' She set off in frantic pursuit. Eyes watering. The girls were smaller but wiry, they shot down a side street and she saw their heels disappear around a corner.

Outraged, tears stinging her eyes with rage, she blundered after them. For about twenty minutes she searched for them, but not a trace of them.

Stupid, stupid. She'd thought to tame them like wild animals, forgetting that wild animals bite. She was conspicuous in a way she'd never been when she was one of them. And now she realised it also made her vulnerable. If children could steal from you outside your own apartment, they could also mug you and take anything you possessed.

Anger competed with anxiety. Now what was she to do? She'd no food, and Fritz was coming for dinner. What could she tell him? There was only one way, and that was to tell him the truth. He'd be expecting a good dinner. Perhaps she could offer to take him out after work?

As she went into the apartment she kept an eye out for Keller. She hadn't seen him in the last few days, but the fact that she might, always set her heart pounding.

And now she was not only afraid of the Nazis, but also of her own people.

Chapter 12

Nancy had written Fritz a message and left it in his pigeon-hole saying she couldn't cook, and asking him to call on her. She didn't dare go back to the Hotel des Indes again – they might accuse her of profiteering. Instead, she hunted around her apartment to check nothing incriminating was on show. The transmitter was a problem, but she stowed it at the back of the wardrobe with a selection of shoes on top, as if it were part of her luggage.

But still, as dusk fell and she waited for Fritz, she grew more and more restless with nerves. She'd dressed in the blue silk she'd bought from the market, but she was so thin now, it gaped at the neck. Wary of showing too much cleavage she was relieved to find a decorative flower brooch on a blouse Steef had supplied, so she used this to fasten the front securely together. She had no pearls, so this would have to do.

At just after seven she already had that trembly feeling as if she were about to sit an examination.

A rap on the door.

She jumped. Steef. Not the knock of Fritz, whose hand was heavier. She ran to the door

'Not now!' she said, peering through the door. 'I'm expecting Fritz any moment. I asked him to call in on his way home, and it would look bad if he found you in my apartment.'

'Just a few minutes.' He pressed his way in.

'You'll have to be quick.' She didn't ask him to sit. 'What is it?'

'Trouble from the *Militair Gezag*, the military in charge of the liberated south. Queen Wilhelmina wants to take back control – wants to ship her government back into the free zone.'

'So? That's good, isn't it?' She tried to hurry him.

'The MG are refusing. They say her arrival will cause chaos because there's still so much clearing up to do, and that everything's broken. Law and order's still not restored. But oh no, the fossilized bureaucrats in London want to bring back the monarchy!'

'Will the queen listen to them?'

'Who knows? But if she doesn't come and the MG keep control, Holland'll be a military state again. To maintain order the MG are keeping key staff, even – God help us – men who collaborated with the Nazis. Collaborators should be punished, not just moved sideways into peacekeeping roles.' Steef was getting aerated now, his face red with heat.

'Awful. Look, Steef, you have to go, I'm expecting—'

'Can't they see, we'll never agree to be ruled by another bunch of heavy-handed police, or any Nazi-like force, not now, not ever.'

'So why does that affect us here?'

'If we don't do something to stop the MG, the government will let them take control. They hate the Resistance because we don't tow their line. It'll be the Nazis in the South all over again. We'll have no access to supplies, because they'll feed their own and we'll be the poor relation.'

'So what can we do? It's out of our control. Steef, you need to go.'

Steef took hold of her arm. 'We need Josef. They'll talk to him. We need a hard negotiator with the right contacts. I tried to telephone the MG command but they won't even talk to me.' She wrestled free, but he carried on talking. 'What'll happen to us all if we can't get supplies from the South anymore? Our rations are already down to two pieces of bread with a few beets. It's not enough for survival, not enough to fuel any kind of resistance. If we can't eat, we can't resist. You need to get into the prison. Do whatever you have to do, but you have to find a way to—'

His words were interrupted by a hard rap on the door.

Fritz.

She stood stock still. Steef shot her a look. It would look strange for him to be in here, but she had no option but to make an excuse. She threw Steef a sharp glance of recrimination and went towards the door. 'Coming.'

As she passed she hissed into Steef's ear, 'You're here to mend a tap in the bathroom. Get in there now and take a look.'

She pinned on a smile, but was dreading the conversation with Fritz about losing the food, especially with Steef there in the bathroom. When she opened the door, Fritz reached to kiss her on both cheeks. He was immaculately dressed in civilian clothes and smelled of the pungent hair oil he always favoured.

Fritz turned on the doorstep and spoke to Mesman who was at his shoulder as usual, 'Wait outside.'

'Sorry,' Nancy said. 'I've got trouble with the tap in the bathroom. Herr Brouwer's just having a look.'

At that moment Steef emerged. 'It's just a washer,' he said. 'I'll come tomorrow and fix it.'

'No need,' Fritz said. 'I can do that for her.'

Steef gave a nod. His face had turned bland, impassive. 'Very well, sir.' He must know it was an order. Everything with the Nazis was an order, even the most pleasant suggestion. Nancy watched Steef bow his way out. There was nothing he could do but go, and now she'd have to explain an imaginary leak.

'It's not your day, is it?' Fritz said. 'I got your note. So there's a problem with dinner, never mind, we can dine out. Couldn't you get to the hotel?'

She explained briefly about the children who'd stolen her supplies.

'We try to control it,' he said, 'but these children, they're like vermin. Get everywhere and into everything. Some of them tried to loot the bread delivery yesterday, one distracted the driver whilst a mob of women and children crowbarred the van open at the back.'

'They must be pretty desperate to do that.'

'Ach, you and your kind heart! But we can't feed them, you know, and not just because of the shortages.' He sat down and rubbed his hands up and down his thighs. 'There are too many people who wish us ill, now the South has been lost. If we feed them, we feed an army. And it will only lead to bloodshed in the end. Better they be hungry and docile until the Reich wins back the South. Less trouble for us all.'

Docile? She'd give him docile. She bit back a retort. Instead, she stood. 'Shall we go and find a restaurant? I'll get my coat.'

'There's no hurry,' he said. 'How about we have a drink here first? I've had a ghastly day and I just need half an hour to brush it off.'

She steeled herself to be pleasant, and went behind him so he wouldn't be able to put a hand up her skirt. 'Was it that bad?' she said, standing behind him to massage his shoulders. She kneaded briskly even though she didn't really want to touch him.

'Oh, you've got magic fingers,' he said, groaning.

She kept on squeezing with her fingers.

'One of our men, Obermayer, was shot dead by partisans in Amsterdam, and we're holding the perpetrator,' he continued. 'I had to interview him and it took much longer than I thought. A surly, violent man, one with no cultural interests, only a misplaced sense of Nationalism.'

100

Josef, it had to be. No cultural interests? He had been a musician once, before the war. After the conversation with Steef, Josef's name struck her like a knife in the guts. 'I can never understand when people don't celebrate our culture,' she said lightly, to cover her emotion. 'We have a long history of beautiful works of art, here in Holland – right back to Vermeer.'

'Our shared culture. Hitler's view is that the Netherlands has always belonged to the Aryan race. Many Dutch feel the same; as you do, close to their German brothers, yes? But I suppose when society is changing there will always be dissent.'

She stilled her hands a moment. It was fine to talk about dissent when you were the oppressor; quite different if you looked on it from another angle. She saw the bristles on the back of his neck above his uniform collar and it enraged her. 'Come on,' she said, unwilling to touch him again. 'I'm hungry.'

He sighed. 'I need to use your bathroom. I'll take a look at the tap whilst I'm there.'

'Of course. Down the corridor, first on the left.'

She watched Fritz stride off, but heard the click of the bedroom door. The cheek of it, he was having a look in her bedroom. She didn't dare say anything. She just gripped her fists tight, praying he wouldn't find the transmitter.

She heard the door click shut again, followed by the creak of the door to the boxroom where she kept her cleaning equipment and iron and ironing board. Seeming satisfied he'd snooped enough, she caught a glimpse of him going into the bathroom. She knew he'd find nothing wrong in there, except that the tap was working perfectly.

The toilet flushed and a few moments later Fritz was back. 'Yes, there's a problem,' he said. 'The washer needs changing. I'll come by tomorrow after work and sort it out for you.'

'Thank you.' There was no problem. He just wanted an excuse to see her, or maybe to snoop in her apartment.

'You will have to have a maid,' he said. 'We can't risk you

going out shopping alone again. I'll find you someone suitable. Someone reliable and trustworthy. You have space in the small room at the back.'

'Oh, but that's hardly necessary, I don't think—'

'I have the perfect woman in mind. And there'll be no more trouble around the back of these apartments. I'll get someone to clear it up.'

She barely noticed the end of the sentence because she was still wondering how to get out of having a live-in maid. Someone in Fritz's pay would no doubt be a Nazi, and spy on her.

He helped her into her coat, and she was grateful for its warmth. Everywhere was cold, the damp winter air penetrated right through her clothes.

'You are not wearing your pearls,' he said suddenly.

Why was he so obsessed with pearls? She laughed it off. 'I did have a set of pearls but now I find them rather old-fashioned, so I sold them when I moved to The Hague.'

'A shame. I have always liked the look of them against a woman's skin.'

He was staring at her as if she should say more. She stepped out into the corridor anxious to be moving.

'Don't forget to lock up,' Fritz said.

She already had her keys out. It seemed that now he was going to rule her life.

But as they walked down the stairs, with Mesman like a shadow behind them, she knew that actually she felt quite relieved. She was tired, and after more than a year of running and hiding, it was actually dangerously pleasant to have the Nazi party take care of you.

'Unteroffizier Hass tells me you're studying,' he said.

'Studying?' It took her a moment to realise what he was talking about. The man on the stairs.

'Yes. He carried your books up for you.'

What the hell could she be studying? Something the Nazi party would approve of. 'I have too little to do now Anton's gone. So I sew and knit. Read books on crafts. It's not really studying, just an interest.'

He squeezed her arm. It seemed to have been enough, and he obviously had no interest in it. But now she'd have to somehow get these books. Her mind raced.

They walked to *'t Goude Hooft*, a restaurant filled with a sea of grey-green uniforms with the occasional black-clad SS officer, and a few couples in civilian clothes.

'Good to walk, isn't it?' she said. 'It clears the head. Especially if you've had a bad day.'

'I can't tell you how bad. It's worse now, because everything's in disorder. Hitler doesn't understand what it means, that we lost half the country. Some of the hubs of our operations were there, and we lost so many good men. Our deportation routes have collapsed. Nothing is working the same. And since these damned railwaymen's strikes, we can't even get supplies for the prison.'

They sat down. 'Is there anything I can do to help?' She had a flash of inspiration. 'I'm so bored at home all day, when with Anton I used to be at the hub of a business. Accounts, answering the phone, that sort of thing.'

It was a long shot, but worth a try.

A vigorous shake of the head. 'The prison's full of the worst type of people.'

'I understand. You don't want us women in your way.' She laughed it off. 'Perhaps I can find something else to occupy me, some voluntary work for the Party.' She hoped she had sowed the seed of an idea, at least.

'Let's order.' He was changing the subject, and she knew she shouldn't appear too keen to work at the prison. As if it really didn't matter, whilst knowing it desperately did.

Just as she was looking at the menu, a voice made her look up.

'Fritz!' A man slapped him on the shoulder. 'Can we join you?'

Fritz looked less than pleased, but said, 'Please do.'

'You've met my wife, Helene?'

Nancy gave the woman a smile, and it was returned, though Helene's eyes were calculating, assessing her clothes and by that, her rank and her worth. Helene was wearing a patterned blouse under a matching jacket and skirt, and her hair was so immaculately coiffured as to be almost rigid.

'This is my neighbour, Danique,' Fritz said. 'She's new to The Hague, fled from Nijmegen when the invaders came.'

The man now sitting opposite gave her a warmer smile than his wife had. 'Gottfried,' he said, introducing himself. He was a balding, middle-aged man, with pale, almost white skin. He spread-eagled himself on the chair as if he lived there, his pronounced belly straining at his suit trousers. The regulation Nazi haircut meant he was naked above the ears until the sudden shelf of hair halfway up his head.

'Good to meet you, Danique.' His Dutch was heavily accented. 'If you're new in town, Helene will no doubt introduce you to the ladies.'

Helene fiddled with her empty glass. 'The wives meet in the Bloemen Café every Tuesday afternoon for charity work. You must come.' The invitation was without warmth. By 'wives' she no doubt meant Dutch Nazi collaborators. The real wives of these men were probably still at home in Germany.

'I'd love to,' Nancy said coolly. 'What sort of charitable things do you do there?'

'We parcel up blankets and clothes to send to the front. If you come, wear an apron, some of the things we have to pack have come from houses that have been requisitioned. They're not that clean.' She said this as if it was the fault of the people they'd stolen the items from. 'Mind you, anywhere on the Russian border the men'd be grateful for it.'

'We're not beaten yet,' Gottfried said. 'A temporary setback, because of the winter weather. In the spring, it will look different, you'll see.'

Did they really believe this? Surely not. It was obvious to all that Hitler's grand plan was failing, now that the Russians were moving slowly to the West.

Gottfried summoned the waiter and they ordered. Before she could speak, Fritz ordered for her, and Gottfried did the same for Helene. It was as if the women were allowed no voice.

When the food came, the men talked in German whilst the women passed plates and smiled at their attempt at jests.

Without warning, Gottfried reverted to Dutch. 'Did I hear right? You come from my home stamping ground of Nijmegen?'

Nancy was momentarily stunned. She felt her pulse throb behind her ear.

He hadn't stopped talking. 'Oh, yes, I was a . . . what you say? Ah, an undergraduate there – at the Catholic University. It was just over the border from Germany then. In hot weather we used to swim in the Waal. Ah, such happy days. Where did you live, Danique?'

A sudden sweat. She couldn't remember where she was supposed to live.

'Near the old city wall.' She said the first landmark that came into her head. 'But I left in September. I nearly left earlier, in February, because of the American bombs. My husband, Anton, was already dead by then and I had no reason to stay. But it took me a while to get up the courage and decide where I wanted to go.' She was gabbling. She took a breath, held up her palms. 'It was all so confusing, with the borders moving all the time and never knowing where one would be safe.'

'So I hear. But you got out just in time. The Luftwaffe's taken to bombing Nijmegen to give the British a taste of their own medicine. Sadly, the place is more ruin than town now.'

'Rembrandtstraat, that's where I lived.' She couldn't help blurting it out, now she remembered. She flushed, realising it must look odd, but Gottfried didn't notice. He was too busy unpeeling a cigar.

'Oh, I know it well,' he said. 'Do you remember the little bookshop on Erdenstraat?

'I'm afraid I'm not much of a reader.' *A lie.* 'Except craft books,' she added hurriedly. But she was on shaky ground. She had only the most basic knowledge of Nijmegen. 'Life was always too busy for reading,' she said. 'Up until the war, I used to do the business bookkeeping for my husband.'

'Well, anyway, you're well out of it,' Gottfried said. 'They've put our man, Mayor van Lockhorst, out of office, and replaced him with one of their communist fanatics. Like you, he fled north. Groeningen, I believe.'

'Yes, it was a quite an exodus,' Nancy said, imagining how it might have been. 'Trains were terrible, so much disruption, and everything so difficult to arrange.'

They nodded along with her and it helped ease the disquiet in the pit of her stomach. She felt as though she was sitting on hot coals.

The meal was food she could never have imagined still existed in The Hague. A veal cutlet with potatoes and French beans. There was no possible way of stealing any though. She watched Helene devour hers whilst the men were still talking. Helene blotted her lipstick carefully as she wiped a smear of grease from her chin onto her napkin.

When her plate was empty, Nancy floundered trying to find conversation to make with Helene. She should have had a lot in common with her, but she had nothing, and the gaping hole of knowledge about these women and the sort of lives they lived, loomed large. Helene too, seemed not at all interested in talking with her. They sat in awkward silence, with Helene half-turned away.

Gottfried lit his cigar and puffed a cloud of foul-smelling smoke over the table. He seemed to be staring into space. Abruptly, he turned to her. 'You said you used to do book-keeping?'

She blinked. What? 'Yes, though I'm probably rusty.' She hedged, not knowing what was coming. 'It's more than a year though, since I've done anything like that.'

106

'We need someone like you to keep a record of our stores. Our previous bookkeeper ... well, let's just say we found her unsuitable.'

Fritz looked discomfited. 'Now, wait a minute Gottfried, I'm not sure Danique is looking for a position—'

'No, Fritz,' Nancy interrupted, 'it's quite all right, I'm open to productive ways to fill my time.' She gave Gottfried a sparkling smile. 'My husband left me well provided for, but perhaps I would be of more use to the Party in Gottfried's department than doing voluntary work with Helene.'

Helene gave her a sour look.

Gottfried smiled like a cat who had got the cream. 'I'll look into it, and I'll arrange for you to come for an interview next week. A mere formality of course, and to take a tour, see what's involved.'

Fritz gripped her arm too tightly and leaned towards her to whisper, 'Are you sure?'

She turned to him. 'I'm happy to see what it involves, and then I can make my decision.' With any luck she'd be able to get inside the prison, get the information she needed and then disappear.

The rest of the evening passed slowly. Fritz was obviously irritated that she might consider working for Gottfried. She hadn't thought of Fritz as a man who sulked, but now that fact was uncomfortably apparent. Probably because earlier, he himself had turned her down.

Fritz summoned the waiter for the bill, and the two men paid.

'I'll see you on Tuesday at the Bloemen Café then, Danique.' Helene air-kissed Nancy on the cheeks. 'That's if you are not otherwise engaged.'

'Lovely,' Nancy said, having no intention whatsoever of going anywhere near it.

'And I'll send you an appointment by courier,' Gottfried said, fixing his eyes on Nancy's cleavage. 'It's been a most pleasant evening, Fritz.'

'Hasn't it,' Fritz said grimly, as the couple got up to leave.

As soon as they'd gone, Fritz turned to her. 'You don't want to work for that terrible man. He'll work you to the bone, and I'm pretty sure his last book-keeper left because he became too familiar, and when she made a fuss, he had her deported.'

'But I thought you were friends?'

'He's a man with influence, yes, so I have to pay him lip service.'

'But isn't he of lower rank to you?'

'Yes. But that doesn't stop him throwing his weight about. Gottfried Glaser controls the stores at the prison. Not a single pencil or paperclip gets signed off unless it's been agreed by him. We all must curry favour with him, otherwise our departments simply can't function. He's not above depriving your office of typewriter ribbon if it suits him. Even mine. The man's got a power complex.'

'Then I'll have to go for an interview for your sake, to keep him sweet. Don't worry, I can always say it's not for me, and turn it down.'

'You don't know Gottfried. He'll bully you into it if he can.'

'I'm not a woman who's easily bullied, Fritz.'

Chapter 13

Allied Zone, Holland

What a way to spend a Christmas holiday, thought Tom as he clung to the ship's rail, willing his stomach contents to subside. A constant slash of wind and rain made him squint into the grey distance, hoping for an end to the torture and the sight of Holland. The requisitioned troopship was full of trucks, and soldiers on their way to rebuild the infrastructure lost to the Nazis.

'We'll be clearing the roads of mines,' one of the soldiers told him. 'Hope I don't get blown into the New Year.' He gave a hoarse ironic laugh.

Pavel groaned and hung over the side, spitting into the sea. The horizontal rain and huge crashing waves didn't let up, and Tom was glad of his warm underclothing. He thought momentarily of the silk code sewn under the label of his vest, and wondered how many agents in Holland were still using one exactly like it. Nancy would be, at least. And soon he'd be transmitting to her from her home airwaves.

He and Pavel were both dressed in civilian clothes with mackintoshes over the top. City clothes that were supposed to make them look like journalists, but were completely unsuited for this gale. Ridiculously, Tom had brought his book with him, *The Good Earth* by Pearl Buck. He could never bear to be without something to read, but his hopes of reading it had been immediately dashed as soon as he boarded the naval tanker full of British troops.

After the sea crossing they were asked to show their papers to the English army officer at the port. Tom strode up, though he felt his belly tighten as the officer in charge checked them over.

They searched through Pavel's luggage, and examined his passport. Pavel's papers had been supplied by the Dutch War Office to say he was a photographer on an official mission. Tom mentally crossed his fingers. His papers stating he was a journalist were forged – printed at the SOE offices in Baker Street. The print department was used to Tom asking for papers for agents in occupied territories and didn't think it unusual when he put in a request for these, though at the time he'd felt his conscience prick.

When his papers were handed back to him, Tom let out his breath.

'Sorry, sir, but you can't keep this,' the man said staring at the open case before him.

It was the transmitter.

'What?' This was something Tom had never considered.

'I'm afraid I'll have to take this. All transmitting equipment is to be requisitioned and only issued when necessary.'

'But it's my personal set,' Tom said, 'made especially for me, so I can send reports back to England.'

'I'm afraid all transmissions are strictly monitored, as is all correspondence. Dutch orders.' He smiled in a puffed-up sort of way. 'Of course you can write your reports here, but you can't send them. Not until you're back in England.'

'But that's ridiculous! What's the point of sending journalists here if they can't report?'

'Search me. I'm just doing my job. Not my rules, sunshine.' And he shut the case and stacked it behind him, out of Tom's reach.

Pavel had watched this unfolding but said nothing until they were out of earshot of the customs men. 'Why'd he take your kit?'

'He was just being a bastard,' Tom said, 'throwing his weight around. But there wasn't anything I could do. I'll have to try to get news through to Neil by phone somehow. It won't be a problem here in the Allied zone, but what will we do once we cross the line?'

Pavel ignored him, and stamped on the ground. 'God, it's good to be back on home soil.' He bent down to put his two hands down to the pavement.

It was oddly touching, and Tom stepped away until Pavel stood up again, his face pink. At least he still had his camera. Tom had watched him pack his box in England – lenses and a small Leica, along with a bigger Contax camera and rolls of film packaged in cellophane and rubber to keep them dry.

They both paused to get their first look at Holland. From here the town of Middelburg was only visible as a blur through the drizzle, and the ground still swam with puddles of oily water.

As they grew closer, lugging their bags towards the town, Tom slowed, unable to believe that any city could be so flattened. London was bad enough, but Middleburg – it was a wasteland. He'd heard it was a historic medieval town, but this was a place crushed into oblivion. The grey skies and freezing briny wind didn't help.

Pavel stopped to stare at a giant pile of bricks and splintered wood. 'I can't believe it. The Gouden Sonne used to stand just here,' he said, pointing, his face white with shock. 'It was a famous restaurant, built in 1665.' His jaw was working, holding back emotion. 'I can't take it in – how something that stood for hundreds of years can just be gone.'

Tom gazed about. Though the roads had cleared, he was wading through centuries of hand-carved care and labour, all reduced to heaps of useless debris. How many years to rebuild it all? Tom balled his fists. He had the urge to take hold of a German by the throat and shake him for the senselessness of it all.

'Bastards,' Pavel said. He slumped on a fallen stone amongst the rubble. 'It seems disrespectful to try to make propaganda out of *this*.' He gestured at the blackened boulders, at the dripping church with no glass in its arched windows. Its distorted wooden beams had been incinerated to charcoal, and the iron girders of the porch twisted by fire into grotesque snakes.

Tom was sober. They were there in Middelburg only to make contact with England and so he could make a report of it and Pavel could take photographs. Photographs to persuade the Yanks to do something about Holland. Now he had no transmitter and Pavel seemed too stunned to get out his camera.

'And the war's still going on in the North,' Tom said.

The reality had bitten; that once they got into the occupied zone, they would face live bombs. That all movement would be much harder. And they were supposed to travel on by boat, up the canals. Fat chance! Back in England Pavel reckoned the journey to Biesbos would take a week, and they should get through to the German side a few days after. Now that idea seemed ludicrously optimistic.

Tom summoned some energy and turned to Pavel. 'You'd better take some pictures. That's what we're here for, isn't it?'

'Then you'd better write something, Mr Journalist.'

Pavel reluctantly took out his big camera.

Tom watched, perched on a broken wall, surprised at how quickly Pavel took his shots, kneeling or reaching to get different angles. He'd expected cumbersome equipment and long exposure times, but Pavel was nimble and the click of the shutter rapid.

Tom took his reporter's notebook out of his pocket and scribbled as fast as he could, trying to record what was in front of him. The details, the way the graveyard had turned into toppled masonry, its broken headstones scratched with swastikas.

Was it like this in Amsterdam? What was Nancy doing? He didn't care, as long as he could see her face again. The thought she might be in a city ruined like this, filled him with urgency. *I'll get to you, somehow,* he thought.

Later that day Pavel had managed to talk to some Dutch bargees and secure a passage up the canal. They'd be following the front line almost all the way via canals and backwaters.

Dreissen, the skipper, was a laconic old fellow, who had muffled himself in a ragged oilskin jumper. Underneath his hat a grimy red scarf was wrapped around his ears. By three-thirty and with their help, he'd loaded the barge with provisions and, because of the waning light, he was anxious to leave.

Tom thought regretfully of Neil, who would be sitting patiently in his sitting room at four o'clock waiting for the radio call from him that would never come. Thank God Neil hadn't travelled with him, was all Tom could think; the idea of him negotiating this landscape with his stick was almost laughable.

Tom had imagined the barge to be something picturesque, but it was an old metal hulk that stank of diesel and damp. Dreissen's job was to deliver aid supplies between the port and the villages along the canal, the artery that fed the countryside. He'd demanded, and counted, payment in guilders from Pavel before letting them aboard. Also on board was Dreissen's daughter, Liese, who watched them covertly through cat-like eyes.

Pavel's camera soon elicited Liese's interest. She was about eighteen years old, Tom guessed, dark-haired and slim, with that 'couldn't care less' attitude affected by the young. Pavel humoured her a little, offering to take her picture, and before long a little flirtation of eyes and looks was going on. Tom's jaw tightened as he saw Dreissen watching the unfolding pantomime with disapproving eyes.

Now Pavel had his eye to the lens he couldn't seem to stop taking pictures of Liese, and Tom had to keep Dreissen's attention on the navigation by plying him with English cigarettes. As the sun sank lower in the sky, Tom blew on his rain-frozen hands and turned up his collar against the squally air. It was already cold enough to drop below zero.

Pavel jumped off to take pictures every time they stopped at a lock. And even more regularly when there was a need to help.

They hadn't gone far when the boat shuddered to a stop.

'What is it?' Tom asked in Dutch.

'Canal blocked,' Liese replied.

'Yes, sorry,' Pavel added. 'Apparently we can only go about fifteen miles before we'll have to change boats. The Germans blew up one of the canal basins, made it inaccessible.'

'Why didn't you tell me?'

'And turn down a lift?'

It should have been obvious that many of the canals were blown up, or filled with debris from shelling. Tom sighed, and asked Pavel in English, 'What will we do?'

'Don't know. We'll just have to see how bad it is. See if someone else will take us on.'

Meanwhile, Dreissen and Tom laboured to haul the boat off the debris that was fouling the bottom of the canal. No doubt that was why Dreissen had taken them on board; to help move junk and speed his progress. Tom was forced to wade into the freezing filthy water to pull out what turned out to be a discarded camouflage net entangled in the propeller.

Further up, he had to tow the barge around the remains of a tank, half-submerged down the bank. His hands blistered as he hauled the rope of the vessel around the already rusting hulk.

Tom cursed Pavel and his camera every time they had to wait for him to catch up, and Dreissen grew more and more tight-lipped at Pavel's smirks and asides to Liese. Tom couldn't blame him. He was pretty pissed off with Pavel himself.

When they stopped to refuel, Tom asked him, 'Do you really need to take so many photographs?'

'Of course,' Pavel said. 'That's why I'm here, isn't it? Out of hundreds, there will only be one or two good ones.'

'It's just Dreissen needs help with unloading, and I can see he's annoyed when you're snapping away instead of helping.'

'But my work is to document it all. Not to be a dock worker. Anyone can lug sacks, but not everyone has the eye.'

Tom reined in his indignation. 'I don't think he sees it that way, and we need to keep him on our side.'

'Pah. In a hundred years, he'll be forgotten, but my pictures will live on.'

Tom was silent. Posterity was all very well, but they didn't need to upset Dreissen or they'd have no lift. Dreissen's surly manner was like a powder keg waiting to explode. The poor chap had probably had to protect Liese from the Boche long enough, but now he had to protect her from one of his own.

When darkness fell they moored in a long stretch of water surrounded by flat countryside. They were to sleep on deck, Dreissen and Liese below.

'Best get some kip,' Tom said.

'Bloody cold,' grumbled Pavel, as he dragged his blanket further up to his chin. 'Must be about minus two.'

The coarse blankets did little to keep out the freezing dampness of the air, which seeped through Tom's clothes right to the bone. He rubbed his eyes, for he'd taken off his spectacles for safe keeping and stowed them in his pocket. He had good long-distance vision, just close-up stuff was a problem. He'd try to do without them. In the dark the lone cries of geese were plaintive, like mourners at a wake.

Tom shifted to try to get comfortable. He was restless and couldn't sleep. The whole idea of reporting back to Britain now seemed the very least of their problems.

But now he was here in Holland there was no way he'd go back to England without seeing Nancy. No matter what sort of a nightmare it turned out to be. He was here now, wasn't he?

He had to hold on to one idea; if they could get in, she could get out. Then at least they'd be together.

Surely now she'd want to come home. If he could only get her over the border into the South, she'd be safe and this awful nagging pain in his chest would stop.

Chapter 14

The next day Tom woke up stiff and disorientated, with hands so numb he couldn't feel them. He bashed them against his legs to get the blood flowing, and lifted a hand to Dreissen who was steering from the back.

In the grey mist, the barge slid along through flakes of ice. Occasionally they were stopped and had to show their passes to British and Canadian troops. Dreissen ignored it all and carried on, taciturn and scowling under the *phut phut* of the motor. They travelled a stuttering passage through fields strewn with dead vehicles and ruined trees. It was as if they'd arrived in a kind of no-man's land.

The blockages in the canal became more frequent, and as they passed through a small town they got to a lock that was completely broken, the sluice gates leering into the water, bloated bodies bobbing against the banks. Tom turned his head away. He couldn't tell if they were civilians or soldiers, their corpses blocking the gates. He guessed German, as they were still floating there.

This must be why they were banned from travelling further.

But at the sight of the boat, figures emerged from the dusky gloom, old men in caps and jackets tied together with string, chapped-nosed housewives in clogs, and silent skinny children gawping. The boat's motor stilled, and suddenly there was frantic activity, with Dreissen hoisting the supplies from the hold and tossing them out to those waiting on the bank.

Big smiles and excited chatter. Someone fetched a horse and wagon, and Tom scrambled to help load it, wishing them a good day in Dutch. A grey-haired woman kissed him roundly on both cheeks. Tom couldn't help thinking, if these poor folk were the liberated people, what were the others like across the river?

The people insisted they go to the village where they were taken straight to an old hostelry, very down at heel, and with bullet holes pocking the outside walls. There was nothing to drink behind the counter, but a toothless old man brought out a colourless spirit and carefully measured it into dusty glasses.

Pavel swigged his back and then coughed, eyes watering.

'What is it?' Tom asked.

'Some sort of hooch. Made from beets I suppose. Awful stuff, but you have to drink it. Besides it'll keep out the cold.'

The old guy was signalling at him to drink, waving his hands with a gummy grin.

After that, things got bleary. Someone got out a fiddle and accordion, and dancing began. Liese grabbed Pavel by both hands and soon they were doing a wild polka. Tom and Pavel were treated like heroes and there was much laughing and jesting, and what seemed to be jokes about both the Germans, and the British – judging by the sideways looks that kept coming Tom's way.

They refilled his glass, and Tom guessed he had two or three of these shots of what tasted like meths before he began to feel like his arms were made out of cotton wool.

'Just going for a piss,' Pavel said. His face was flushed and shiny with sweat.

Tom nodded and tried to stay awake. At one point a plate of pea soup was put in front of him, and at some later point he realised that though Dreissen was still at a table surrounded by locals, there was no sign of Pavel or Liese.

'You stay here,' the toothless man said, approaching him and clapping him on the shoulder. 'Room upstairs for you and your friend, yes?' He pointed.

Unsteadily, he followed him up the back stairs to a small room in the eaves of the house. The room was unfurnished except for what appeared to be two old straw and fleece-stuffed mattresses. But Tom's head was spinning and he couldn't have cared. All he wanted to do was lie down before he fell down.

He lay down fully clothed in coat and shoes and let the room slowly spin to a stop.

Shouting and a commotion outside his window. Daylight already. Tom squinted out but couldn't see anything, so he hurried bleary-eyed down the uneven steps, to find out what was going on.

When he emerged into the square outside, a fight was already in progress. What the devil? He cast a sidelong glance at Liese who was leaning forwards over a fence, screaming like a harpy. It took seconds for him to realise the men locked in an ungainly embrace were Pavel and Dreissen. Each was trying to grab the other by the neck.

'Stop!' Tom ducked in, and wrestled to separate the two men, dodging past two other heavy-set locals, who danced around them aiming blows where they could. With a sinking feeling, Tom saw that Pavel's nose was already bloody.

He grabbed Dreissen from behind by the neck of his jumper to pull him away.

Dreissen turned and aimed a swipe at him. His garbled expletives were plain enough. Pavel had tried to kiss his daughter.

'*Hoerenjong!*' Dreissen swore, his breath reeking of alcohol. He aimed an inexpert blow at the side of Tom's head. Pavel smacked

Dreissen across the face just as a swarthy man in a cloth cap joined the fray and landed a punch to the side of his jaw.

'Whoa,' Tom shouted, holding up his hands. 'British! RAF!'

Of course he wasn't the British RAF but it made Dreissen pause for a second and stop trying to beat Pavel's brains out with his fists.

No sooner had the two men separated than Liese piled in, all nails and screeching at her father in Dutch.

At her appearance, Pavel backed off, staggering, pressing the back of his hand to a bloodied lip. Dreissen took hold of Liese by the armpits and shouted threats before dragging her protesting around the corner, out of sight. Pavel was panting, and pressing his sleeve to his lip, but his eyes slid towards their retreating backs.

The stupid fool. Liese was too young to mess with. Tom grabbed Pavel's sleeve and took him to one side under the eaves. 'I hope you damn well apologised,' he said. 'You should never shit on your own doorstep, didn't anyone teach you that?'

'Not my fault. She was playing hard to get, and you take it where you can find it these days.' He grinned.

You're despicable. Tom thought it, but didn't say it.

They argued over it for a few more minutes, with Tom trying to persuade Pavel to patch it up with Dreissen, and Pavel scowling and shrugging through Tom's lecture.

Finally Tom sighed. 'Let's go and get our things. It's clear enough going further with Dreissen is a non-starter unless you want to be pulped again.'

But when they got back to the canal the barge was gone. A crowd of children were scavenging in the pile of their things, which had been unceremoniously dumped on the towpath.

'Get outta here!' Pavel shouted, and ran towards them like herding geese. They scattered, dropping the few items of clothing they'd gleaned from their rucksacks.

Tom's stomach turned over at the thought that Dreissen could have taken Pavel's vital equipment with them. It had been idiotic even to leave it unattended for a moment.

'Now what?' Tom said. He was terse. The fact that Pavel could be so stupid as to jeopardise their whole journey had really got to him.

'Same as before. We blag a lift,' Pavel said. 'Pass me the map.'

Thank God the map was still there. They hunkered down on the towpath, blowing on their chilblained hands as they unfolded it.

'We're here,' Pavel said, his voice slurring through his swollen lip. 'And we want to get to here.' He pointed a nicotine-stained finger at the map. 'We might have to hitch a lift, I guess. After that we'll arrive at the border of these marshes.'

Tom looked at the ribbons of water linking the few patches of dry ground. It looked a hell of a long way away and a bigger area than he'd thought, now he saw the scale of things on the ground. 'Come on, then.' He was impatient to get moving before he froze.

They'd just got up and hitched on their bags when a group of men approached. The set of their shoulders boded trouble. At the front of the mob was the man from the tavern, the toothless old chap. He was being followed by what looked like reinforcements, in the form of three other glowering villagers, all big men, older but solid.

'You not pay,' he said. Even to Tom, the Dutch words were clear.

Tom looked around, there was no-one to help them and they were outnumbered. Dreissen already had most of their money, and worse, he'd not only scarpered, but left them with the bill.

'I'll try to talk my way out of it,' Tom said. 'Apologise, say we didn't mean to—'

But it was too late, one of the big men was trying to take Pavel's camera case but Pavel responded by trying to knee him. At the same time, another of the men lunged for Tom to try to take his bag.

Tom was unprepared and took a blow to the side of the head that made him reel. He grappled for a moment, thinking,

'Shit, we're done for.' But then the noise of an engine. The man turned to look and Tom heaved his bag out of the man's grip.

A convoy of army trucks was bumping down the road towards them.

'British!' yelled Tom, leaping into the road and waving an arm in front of the first army truck.

The truck skidded to a stop, just as a solid, sweating farmer made to grip Tom by the arms again.

'Help us!' he shouted again. 'We're British!'

Pavel was on the ground, groaning and curled around his camera box.

Thank heaven, two men jumped down off the back of the truck to help Tom manhandle Pavel and their bags aboard.

Over the growl of the engines, the angry locals yelled insults and tried to land extra punches and kicks at them.

Somehow though, the sight of the armed British soldiers deterred them from attacking again, except for the man who'd been beating Pavel. He continued to curse and try to drag Pavel's box off the truck until it ground away in a spatter of mud and grit.

'Merry Christmas!' shouted the driver. 'What you bleedin' done, then?' the driver yelled. He was a cockney judging by the accent, with ears sticking out like jug handles.

'Lady trouble,' Pavel said. His eye was already half-closed and purpling.

'Gawd, what I'd give for a piece of that! Not seen my missus for nigh on two year. Christmas bloody day and here I am.' He threw both hands off the steering wheel towards the sky.

Christmas Day? Tom was taken aback. He hadn't even noticed. The Dutch celebrated their Christmas early, he remembered. His thoughts went instantly to Nancy. What would she be doing today?

He startled as the cockney lad yelled, 'Where you headed?'

'Biesbos,' Tom said. 'But Den Bosch will do.'

'You're in luck mate.'

Another soldier, his face already grimed with muck, grinned with uneven teeth. 'We're gonna fix the bridge there. Hold tight, it'll be bumpy.'

As they rattled along Tom scanned the barren countryside as his heart slowly eased from pumping like a steam engine.

Bleakly, Tom realised the foolhardiness of what he was trying to do, to get someone out of occupied Holland. He was shocked by the bald flat terrain, by the lack of forest or tree cover. Any kind of mission or illicit activity would be impossible to conceal, and with a sudden flash of insight, he understood now why the Dutch had to become collaborators in their German-controlled land. Sharp spatters of rain stung his eyes as he squinted out at ruined windmills, rusted torn-up railway lines, and wrecks of fighter planes and tanks.

The cockney in the front of the jeep yelled 'Pothole!' every time the truck was about to bounce, like it was great fun, but Tom feared for Pavel's delicate equipment – the box of cameras and lenses.

Outside 's-Hertogenbosch, or Den Bosch as the men called it, they passed through uninhabited villages blighted by more blackened ruins of burned-out cottages.

'My God,' Tom said to Pavel, 'even in the countryside the Germans have left hardly a stone standing.'

Their cockney friend turned, delighted. 'Not the Germans. Us. Our men burned the lot – we had to flush the Nazi bastards from their holes with tanks and flamethrowers.'

An almighty judder. The driver turned to drag the steering wheel back on course. 'A few weeks ago you wouldn't have got down this road at all,' he yelled. 'We're lucky. They mined the road. We had to get flail-tanks to beat 'em and blow 'em up. That's why there's so many bleedin' potholes.'

'Did you get that?' he asked Pavel over the roar of the engine and grinding gears.

'Yep. Sounds bloody.' Pavel wasn't really listening, he was trying to light a cigarette – ridiculous in this knife-like wind.

The bone-rattling journey took three hours, with Tom gleaning as much information as he could from the other four men in the truck about the current lay of the land and positions of the Germans on the other side of the river. With trepidation he learned that the river crossings were all heavily defended with artillery.

By the time they got to the bridge, to Den Bosch, Pavel was lying like an invalid in the bottom of the truck, arm wrapped around his ribs. They were both filthy from the amount of mud and puddle water chucked up out of potholes.

The truck screeched to a stop. Ahead of them, the bridge itself was gone, and chunks of masonry poked out from the brink. A makeshift wooden bridge of flimsy slats had been slung across. Tom got out with the rest to tentatively creep across as the driver manoeuvred the truck onto it. It creaked and moved perilously under their boots as the heavy truck inched across in first gear. Tom didn't dare look down. Beneath him, he heard the river gush by in its winter swell. One false step and he'd be a goner.

On the other side he let out a long breath. Back on board and into the maze of buildings. No house or shop was untouched and bomb craters had turned the roads into death-traps. As they ground past, over chunks of brick and mortar, shattered roof tiles slithered down to fall among the debris of bricks and mud.

Tom glanced at Pavel, who was sitting up now, squinting through his camera lens with the one open eye. *Perhaps he's braver than I am.*

In the town centre they were shoved off the truck and the cockney driver wished them well. He pointed to a crossroads with the sign obliterated by gunshot holes. 'That way. Cross-country to Werkendam and the marshes. It's about a six-day march.'

Six days. Jesus. As they stood by the side of the road, the rest of the convoy trundled by, troops on their way to repair the bridges in the town, ready for more Allied soldiers when another push north would begin.

'I'm not marching,' Pavel said. 'My ribs feel like they've been smashed. Sod that for a game of soldiers.'

Tom couldn't help but laugh at this turn of phrase delivered in a deadpan Dutch accent. 'What then?'

'Go into the town, sweet-talk someone. See if someone will take pity on us, take us by car or cart.'

'You'll be lucky. You don't look too pretty right now.'

'At least they didn't break my nose. Does it look really bad?'

'Like you've been in a fight with Joe Louis.'

They hoisted their packs onto their backs and picked up their cases. In the centre of town a festive market crowded the town square – people had brought out whatever they had to barter or trade. He passed trestle tables with bottled fruit, pickled vegetables and packets of dried beans. An elderly woman in a traditional bonnet sat on an upturned bucket milking a cow, the milk hissing into a pan right there on the street.

The local people stared at them as they passed. They looked odd, Tom realised, walking around in civvies with their mackintoshes and overladen with bags and suitcases, like some sort of mad tourists. Pavel's black eye and limp didn't help.

Pavel stopped at a stall selling second-hand items – a motley collection of bric-a-brac. Tom browsed through the junk – every kind of household thing, many cracked or scorched – salvaged from bombed-out buildings he supposed.

He heard Pavel talking and looked up.

Trust Pavel. The girl behind the table was attractive – poor, her coat was threadbare and her scarf fraying, but her bronze-coloured hair and slant green eyes gave her a certain appeal. How did Pavel do it? Even looking like he'd been in a prize fight, his patter still worked. He must have some sort of magnet!

He saw Pavel give the girl his most charming smile, touch his eye and shrug, and then point to Tom and the luggage.

Tom put down the clock with the cracked face he'd been examining. The fact Pavel was flirting again made Tom think inevitably of Nancy. Every woman paled into insignificance beside his feelings for Nancy. The feeling that his chest might cave in from longing. They'd been apart so long it was almost unbearable.

Meanwhile Pavel had got out his camera and asked the girl to pose. Tom watched with incredulity as she simpered into the camera, and Pavel clicked away – giving her instructions about how to smile, to put one shoulder forwards, or to toss her hair. Sickened, Tom turned his attention back to the table.

'Hey Tom, got us a lift,' Pavel said, sauntering over, grinning. 'Her brother will come to collect her in a van, and they'll take us to Werkendam. Their family farm is there.'

'You were talking to her a long time. What did she say?'

'I told her we were looking to get someone out of the occupied zone and she let slip that she might be able to put us in touch with a line-crosser working across the Biesbosch and the Merwede. Her name's Truus, by the way.'

Well, knock me down with a feather, Tom thought. Perhaps Pavel's womanising was good for something after all.

Tom and Pavel squeezed in the back of the van, a clapped-out thing powered by gas, whilst Truus and her brother were in the front. The brother, introduced as Henk, was a giant of a man with a tinge of redness in his hair. Tom guessed him to be over six feet four tall, even taller than Pavel, and his hulking presence reminded Tom of a Viking. He spoke a little English, which was a relief, and Tom liked him immediately. He listened whilst Tom explained they were journalists who wanted to go into the occupied zone and that they'd travelled from England to do it. To take back pictures and reports to persuade the politicians to act.

'Crossing is not so easy,' Henk said. He pursed his lips and then wiped his forehead with his coat sleeve. 'The winter weather, see? More dangerous in winter – snow, ice. Not impossible, but will need a good plan.' He looked to Truus, and she laughed back at him from the passenger seat in a knowing way.

Could they trust them? They had little choice. He hoped to God that they weren't members of the NSB – the Nazi party of Holland.

The journey was overnight and into the next day along rough roads. Twice they were stopped by Canadian troops at road blocks who made them hand over their papers and insisted on searching the van. Tom hadn't realised the Canadians were part of the Allied force. How little they knew in London of what was actually going on.

As dusk fell again they bumped down a remote track to a farm cottage on the outskirts of a place called Geffen. A pig was rooting in a sty just outside, and chickens, their feathers ruffled because of the cold, scratched in the yard. Beyond the farm a glimmer of marshland stretched away towards the Maas River. Tom shivered – that was it. The divide between free and occupied Holland.

As they arrived, the thin rain turned to sleet, and the landscape of the flood plain grew patchy and white. The thought of going out there was daunting.

They left the stuff in the van and sat on hard chairs in the tiny whitewashed kitchen. A soot-blackened range gave out a small trickle of heat.

'Friday next, Truus is going to make the crossing to the North,' Henk said. 'There is room in the boat then for you. Not before. That is the day she takes medicines. The other days she takes food and there will be no room.'

Tom turned to stare.

'I've made many crossings,' she said in English, her voice defiant. 'Safer to be a woman. I can deliver things unnoticed. And men, they want too much to be in the fight, they don't know how to be quiet.'

She was too young, surely? She must only be about nineteen.

Pavel was open-mouthed.

'We'll be quiet,' Tom said. 'As long as you can get us across.'

She shrugged. 'Is easier now this side is free. Used to be harder. But it's still a dangerous crossing. The boat is only small, a rowing boat, not one with an engine. An engine would be making too much noise. So it takes three hours, longer if there are Germans near the marshes. And it must be done at night. The worst part is if there is ice, so we wait for the weather. Too much ice and we can't go. Okay?'

'Okay,' said Pavel, who was looking embarrassed now his life was in her hands. 'You speak very good English.'

'Because I have to talk to British soldiers,' she said, as if he was stupid. 'Airmen, injured soldiers.' She paused to let her words sink in. 'Remember; if you fall in the water, no-one will save you. You will last only a few minutes and no-one will risk their skin to get you out.'

Henk was nodding. 'She'll be armed. She's a good shot. Our father taught us. He was a member of the *National Knokploeg* – the LKP resistance. Until he got caught doing the crossing. They shot him and we couldn't retrieve his body. He's out there somewhere.' He looked through the darkening glass of the window before adding, 'It's why she still does it.' A pause. 'And why I don't.'

Tom was silent. What could he say?

A sudden thump on the table. 'Don't think Henk does nothing,' Truus said with passion. 'Henk was the one who got our people out of the camp at Vught. Resisters who'd been arrested for sabotage. They tortured them in the Oranjehotel and then sent them here to the camps for more torture.'

'Are there still men in the camps then?' Tom asked.

A huff of outrage. '*Nee.* When the *Moffen* saw the British were advancing, they closed them down. Before anyone could see what went on in there. Hangings, firing squads. Naturally the guards destroyed the archives. The prisoners were taken away. Ravensbrück, we heard. No-one's come back.'

'Did you see much of the fighting?' Pavel asked.

'Plenty. When fighting began here, Henk cycled over to the British in Heeswijk to tell them where the Germans were. Without him, Den Bosch wouldn't be free.'

'Stop it, Truus,' Henk said. 'They don't need to know all that.' He turned to Tom. 'Once you're in the North, things will be harder.'

'When we return, there'll be three of us,' Tom said. 'We're bringing out a British agent.'

Pavel gave a small smile, as if the idea was a joke. It made Tom uncomfortable.

'Where is the person you want to bring over?' Henk asked.

'We suspect Amsterdam. That was where we last heard of her.'

'A woman?' Truus immediately looked more interested.

Tom nodded, aware his face was already reddening.

'Then they will need to get her to a safe house in Arnhem,' Truus said. 'We have hopes Arnhem will be liberated soon, but so far, it is still under Nazi control.'

'Take care,' Henk said. 'The Nazis themselves are not happy about their shrinking resources and the fact they are losing. It makes them – what you say? – bad-tempered.'

'Will you be able to get us all back over the river, if the North is still occupied?'

'The question no-one can answer. Who knows who lives and dies? Three might mean two trips. And life is always a lottery. We can take you one way, but can't guarantee your return.'

Chapter 15

The Hague

Fritz found a memo on his desk from his aide, Dobermann, asking him to call.

As soon as he'd got the day's business under way, he called him. 'Dobermann? Schneider.'

'Ah yes. Your widow friend Danique Koopman. After a month of no activity, she's suddenly closed her account, and emptied her vault.'

'When was this?'

'In Nijmegen, two days ago.'

'In Nijmegen? On Wednesday?' That didn't make sense. He'd had a cosy night in with Danique that night. 'Give me the exact time of the withdrawal.'

'Two-forty-five on Wednesday 27 December.'

Schneider was quiet a moment. How could Danique have got from Nijmegen to The Hague in so short a time, and during the holiday disruption too? It was impossible.

'Tell me again who withdrew the money?'

'Danique Koopman. It was the same clerk. He recognised her.'

'I thought I told you to sack that clerk?'

'Yes, well . . . anyway it was her. No mistake.'

'And you say there's nothing left in the account?'

'No. Cleaned out.'

There was something odd about this withdrawal. Maybe it was some kind of foul play and Danique didn't know her account had been emptied. 'Can you get someone on to it. Get that clerk to give you a statement. From my information Danique Koopman's been in The Hague for the last two months. She can't have made that withdrawal.'

Chapter 16

Nancy had managed to keep Fritz at bay with invented tales of her dead husband Anton, but their relationship was becoming more intimate – Fritz was becoming more inclined to touch her thigh for too long, or look deep into her eyes. She veered between hating him and feeling sorry for him, and the visceral fear she might be unmasked. At Christmas he had wanted to give her a necklace.

'You have a beautiful neck,' he'd said, stroking it with his thumb. 'I'd like to see it adorned with something that sparkles, pearls or diamonds, not this old thing.'

'No,' she'd replied. 'Please, Fritz, not a necklace. I always wear this St Christopher medal for safe travels. It was Anton's and I know it's silly, but I'm rather superstitious about it.' She put a protective hand over it. It was a gift from Tom, the only thing she could safely keep.

'I'm surprised he gave you that,' Fritz said. 'The Führer says most Christian saints are just superstitious nonsense.'

'Perhaps the Führer is not a romantic man.'

He'd let that go, but she could see it displeased him.

So on Christmas Day he'd given her a bracelet encrusted with diamonds, like a shackle.

In return she had had to succumb to a kiss where he thrust his tongue in her mouth. Yet still he hadn't let her accompany him to work. As far as that was concerned, his lips were firmly sealed shut.

She knew it was a long game, this being undercover, to build trust, but this role was becoming unbearable. Some days she wanted to just scream and run away. But now, at last, there was some movement, and a shift she could sense. She'd need to sweet-talk Fritz tonight – for the invitation to an interview from Gottfried Glaser had just arrived, and she guessed he would not be pleased.

She clipped the bracelet onto her wrist, feeling its weight, remembering. Until today, Gottfried had forgotten all about her and his offer of employment. So in desperation, yesterday Nancy had gone to the Bloemen Café and met with Helene, hoping that Helene would tell Gottfried she'd been there, and it would remind him of her existence. She spent a grim day with the NSB women sorting possessions from 'evacuated' Jews, and parcelling them for Germany, a task that made her almost physically ill.

Her strategy must have worked though, because the invitation for an interview with the stores department was in her pigeonhole by lunchtime, couriered over and on official prison notepaper. It included a letter to show to the guards and instruction as to how to get inside the prison.

She twirled the bracelet on her arm and set off to Fritz's.

When she told Fritz, that night at dinner, he was tight-lipped. 'You'll hate it,' he said, 'a woman with an artistic soul like you.'

'So it's dull. Dullness never killed anyone.'

'He'll bully you.'

And you're not? She smiled inwardly.

'What time does he want you?'

'Eleven, Monday next week.'

'Then my man Bakker will drive you there. He'll pick you up twenty minutes before, and bring you straight home again afterwards. It's not a good place to walk around on your own.'

He meant, 'I need to control every single thing you're doing.' But she was grateful; the place was a well-guarded fortress so she knew a private German car was a good idea.

He took hold of her hand. 'Danique, I need to ask you something.' She startled, wondering what was coming. 'Have you transferred all your money out of Nijmegen?'

'Of course,' she answered, relieved it wasn't any other proposal. 'Why?'

'When did you do it?' There was something insistent about his eyes.

'A while ago. Money's not safe there with all the bombing.' *What are you getting at?*

'Last week?'

'No.' She laughed. What was this about? 'No, ages before that.'

He looked thoughtful as he poured himself another drink. 'And who are you banking with now?'

She had no idea who she was supposed to be banking with. 'I can't remember. I've had so many changes. I'll look it up later.' She held out her glass. 'Can you pour me another please?'

He was less open after that, and she knew that something about her finances must have rattled him. Perhaps this bracelet should go in the bank? She'd have to talk to Steef, see what could be done. She had a feeling she'd been caught out, just an instinct, and it made her insides squirm.

Chapter 17

Geffen, Allied Zone
January 1945

Tom and Pavel had been given old trousers, knitted jerseys, and worn-out coats of the sort Dutch farmers might wear. Henk had been scathing about their English clothes. 'The Germans will spot you immediately,' he said. 'Why d'you think we have a second-hand clothes stall? We sell British clothes to the British, and buy Dutch for men like you.'

Tom had been reluctant to give up his book and his English identity papers. It made him feel rootless, as if everything about his previous life was being left behind.

'Take this,' Truus said, thrusting a pistol into Tom's hand. He'd seen her put one in her belt, but now the weight of a gun sat uncomfortably in his coat pocket.

The frozen puddles crunched like glass underfoot as Tom followed Truus's narrow back across the marsh. She had a heavyweight rucksack full of medicinal supplies – bottles of iodine, gauze, aspirin, powdered sulfa, plus a rifle slung over her back as well as the handgun.

She too was wearing men's clothes, the only concession to femininity a knitted pixie hood pulled over her head and ears. She strode easily, knowing instinctively which ground was solid, but Tom had to concentrate to keep up, his breath standing in clouds before him. It mingled with the low-hanging mist wreathing thigh-high over the ground.

Behind, he could hear the sound of Pavel's feet, the suck of mud as he drew his boots up through the thin layer of ice. Despite wearing layers of clothes and a thick woollen jumper, Tom's fingers were numb from carrying Pavel's camera case. Pavel was carrying a bag of ammunition to deliver to the Resistance on the other side. Tom wished he still had his transmitter for he'd had no contact with Nancy or with Neil, nor with his own brother in the civil service somewhere in Cambridge. How far away that seemed. What would they think if they could see him now?

His other pack of a few clothes, maps, comb and shaving equipment was strapped to his back as they wove their way, following exactly in Truus's footprints. She'd warned them that to go their own route would risk them getting stuck in the bogs. Some of the tussocky marsh had been linked by what Truus had called 'fascines' – woven brushwood hurdles laid over the watery gaps to make bridges. They tramped their way from one to the next.

At the edge of the river Tom made out the rowboat, tucked in close to a bank. It was surrounded by reeds, stiff and stark and glinting with frost. A fine skin of ice tinkled as Truus dragged the boat from its wooden mooring post to a solid piece of ground, and after she'd thrown Tom the rope, she unshouldered the rucksack and rifle into the boat then nimbly jumped aboard.

Silence as she gestured to them to hand her all the stuff.

The boat wobbled as Pavel handed the heavy bag of ammo aboard, and another bag of medical supplies.

Tom handed in his rucksack, which also contained a few provisions. Truus had told them food was a priority across the river.

Pavel had lost some of his swagger. He steadied the boat by

tensioning the rope, his hands encased in knitted mitts, a bala-
clava making his head appear small as a pin above the bulk of
his coat. His eye was still swollen and he chewed his sore lip as
he hovered by the boat, his case of cameras by his feet. Tom held
out his arms for it, for him to pass it aboard, but Pavel shook his
head. A moment of irritation that Pavel was suddenly possessive
about his precious case.

'Go on.' Pavel gestured to Tom to get in first. Tom clambered
in and settled himself on the front wooden bench, leaving the
back one for Pavel.

Suddenly something hit Tom in the back, something heavy.
He turned to see Pavel had thrown the rope back into the boat.

'I'm not coming,' he said.

'Don't play games,' Tom said.

'I'm not coming,' Pavel said. 'Sorry.' He backed away.

'You're not serious?'

Truus shot Pavel a glare. 'Now's not a time to argue. We haven't
time if we want to use the dark. Are you getting in, or not?'

A shake of the head.

Tom couldn't take it in. 'Come on.'

'I'm staying here.'

'Pavel . . .?'

'Shut up.' Truus's voice cut through the frosty air. 'You?' she
shot a look to Tom, a look that said, *don't you dare pull out now.*

'I can't leave him behind,' Tom said. 'I can't speak Dutch well
enough.'

Truus's face was mask-like. 'I'm risking my life for you. And
for the injured pilot waiting on the other side of that river.' She
threw a glance towards the shore. 'Leave him.'

'I can't just leave him.'

'Yes, you can. I had the measure of him straight away. He's a
freeloader.' She picked up the oars and gave a strong pull, and
the skin of ice separated, as the boat was eased away from the
shore in a flurry of chinks.

Tom felt himself torn in two with indecision. He couldn't leave Pavel, but then he couldn't leave Nancy in Holland either, not now he'd come this far. He turned his head to look. Pavel was still standing there, motionless, like a strange kind of grey heron. Then Pavel swivelled, and head hunched down, slowly picked his way back through the boggy terrain until his figure was enveloped in mist. Tom had the urge to yell at him, *What the hell d'you think you're doing?*

He gripped the bench, as the boat slid away, too shocked to think.

In a rush, his mind caught up, and thoughts whirled as he tried to make sense of it and suppress his rising panic. Was Pavel more of a coward than Tom thought? Was it something to do with Truus? Had he made a pass at her and been rejected? Too many questions.

When Tom turned back, Truus was still rowing in a steady rhythm, her breath huffing in and out in synchrony with the movement. He was momentarily breathless, as if someone had punched him. It had happened so quickly, the fact he was to do this thing alone. He couldn't take it in.

After a moment he saw Truus's set jaw, white under her woollen hood, and marvelled at her composure. She was so young. He was surprised when his low voice came out normal. 'Shall I take a turn on the oars?'

A shake of the head. 'Not until we're out into the main flow. Here, you need to know the way. We don't want to get stuck, because no-one would come for us, and even now we can be picked off by mortar fire from the other side. Quiet now; we don't want anyone to know we're here.'

He nodded, gripping the freezing side of the boat with one hand, the seat with the other.

This wasn't how it was supposed to be. How could he get by with his rudimentary Dutch? At least his German was passable. But the cold and dread made his teeth begin to chatter. He took

138

a deep breath to calm himself. After about a half-hour of weaving through narrow channels, Truus finally let him take the oars. They had to manoeuvre around each other carefully so as not to capsize. In the distance a crackle and the sky suddenly lit up by gunfire.

'German anti-aircraft,' Truus whispered, then put her finger to her lips.

Tom continued to row, glad to be doing something to keep warm and to tamp down the shoots of adrenalin that kept whooshing up his spine. The river was breathtaking, this large expanse reflecting the sky. Beautiful but deadly. He remembered Truus's father and wondered how she could do this journey knowing he lay beneath.

As they neared the other side of the river she gestured him towards another marshy area, where again the mist drifted over thin slivers of ice. There, they changed places again, and Truus steered her way down the narrowing channels towards a broken-down windmill with no sails, and a few ruined houses, their rafters stark black against the mist. The staccato fire of anti-aircraft guns was louder now, and he saw the silhouettes and lights of planes in the sky. He assumed they were Allied planes, but he couldn't be sure.

'Keep still,' Truus said. She paused in her rowing to listen.

He could hear nothing, after the distant fire, not even the night cry of a bird. But then faintly, like a gentle swish, something moving on the land ahead.

Truus began to row again. Was it Germans? He'd no idea.

The slap and lap of water. But then out of the gloom, three figures emerged, like something out of a Dickens novel, three people wrapped in blankets, two propping up the other one.

One of the men came forwards to reach out to pull the boat ashore. Nobody spoke. The other two were standing waiting now, one leaning on the other, still figures in the mist. Truus gestured at Tom to get out of the boat. Stomach in knots, he stumbled as he clambered out but the man on the shore reached out to grab him. 'Voorzichtig,' a whisper in his ear. Dutch. *Be careful.*

He watched as the others came towards the boat. The man who was being helped was in RAF uniform under the blanket. Close-up Tom could see one arm of his uniform had been burned away and his arm was bandaged. His face too was red and shiny, his eyebrows missing, his eyes gaunt with pain. The tang of burning still hung around his clothes. Obviously he'd been shot down and his plane had gone up in smoke.

The men and Tom unloaded all the bags, before guiding the airman to the boat. Tom smiled and gave him a nod as he was helped silently aboard. 'Good luck,' he whispered.

The man didn't reply, it looked like every movement caused him agony. As the man sat down a groan of anguish escaped his lips.

'Sshh,' Truus hushed him. She passed Tom her rucksack then pushed off with an oar and within moments she was gliding away into the mist.

A sudden grip on his shoulder. The man next to him froze, listening.

'*Was ist los?*' A German voice, loud, from further on shore.

Another reply in German that Tom couldn't make out.

A spatter and flash of gunfire that took his breath.

The man at Tom's side dived on him and brought him to the ground, throwing the blanket over them both. 'Don't move,' he hissed in his ear. The ooze of freezing water seeped into Tom's clothes, the side of his face pressing in the mud. The rucksack must contain tins because it was digging into his chest where he'd landed on it. From one eye, through the reeds, he saw the other one of their friends was also flat on the ground, covered by the blanket.

Another strafe of gunfire. The spatter of it hitting the water just past where they lay. Tom thought his heart might burst, it was throbbing so hard. Had Truus got away? He didn't dare look.

Footsteps approaching to his right. He tensed, shoulders rigid. A hundred yards further down, the ghostly figures of two helmeted

Wehrmacht emerged from the gloom. Both had weapons ready. They trudged slowly up the marshy ground towards them. They looked solid as walls in their greatcoats and boots.

'*Sehen Sie etwas?*' one asked.

'*Nichts,*' said the other.

'*Ich habe da was gehört.*' He thought he heard something.

Now they were so close Tom could hear the metallic sound of their coat buttons scraping against their rifles. One turned away to scan the marsh the way they'd come.

Tom was shivering now, his teeth chattering, the contents of the rucksack pressing painfully. He clamped his jaw together, willing the men to leave. The Resistance man's arm was still over his shoulder pinioning him to the ground.

Without warning, from the mound in front of him, an arm shot out holding a gun aimed directly at one German's back. Two soft *phut* sounds and the Germans lurched and staggered. One dropped his gun and collapsed to his knees. The other let off a round of fire, as he turned to see what had hit him. The bullets sprayed over them and Tom buried his head further in the mud.

When he next looked up the Germans were both on the ground. One was writhing. Suddenly Tom's shoulders were free. His resistance friend ran over to where the German soldier was moving and shot him point blank in the forehead.

There was no noise. Their guns must have silencers.

By the time Tom could sit up, the other men he was with were efficiently unbuttoning the Germans' coats, kicking them over and dragging their flopping arms out of the sleeves.

The taller of his new friends put on the greatcoat and helmet, before the other greatcoat was thrust into his arms and he was gestured to put it on.

Tom was still shaking, but he put on the coat, which was still warm from the German's heat, over his thick jersey. The thought made him feel sick. The helmet was tight on his head. They thrust one of the medical bags and the German's machine gun at him and beckoned him to follow. He wished he could see their faces but it was too dark.

He loaded himself up, still dazed. As he went, he looked back. The Germans were lying in the muddy ground, strangely vulnerable-looking without their coats and helmets, and he saw that their boots had been taken off whilst he was dressing, and now he saw their feet, in knitted grey socks. One of them had a hole in the toe and the flesh glowed pink and rosy beneath it.

Tom staggered forwards to catch up with the other two, one hand on the gun in his pocket, terrified that the gunfire would bring more soldiers. They walked for about twenty minutes through a winding labyrinth of tributaries and wetland bog. The coat weighed heavy on his shoulders, and though it was warm, Tom was still shivering. The men in front had German boots stuffed under their arms. He felt more like a captive than a free man, at the mercy of these two men of the Resistance.

And one image wouldn't leave him. He still saw Pavel in his mind's eye, walking away into the mist.

Now he was reliant on these men, and he'd seen that they had no mercy, and it had shocked him to the core that Nancy could be operating with men like these.

Well, what did you expect? He chided himself. But the stony truth of it was like bile in his guts.

After another interminable trudge through boggy ground, they arrived at a fisherman's hut. It was a wooden structure at the edge of what looked to be drained land, given that there was a regular criss-cross of dikes surrounding it, and it was at the end of a long unmade track of grit and gravel. Light was just paling the horizon. The hut had well-sealed wooden shutters and some canvas-covered mattresses, and hooks from the ceiling beams – for fish, presumably, as the whole place stank of it.

It wasn't luxury, but best of all, there was a kerosene stove for boiling water.

'All right?' The man in the Nazi helmet took it off, and for the first time Tom could see his face. He was a small swarthy man with dark darting eyes. He spoke in Dutch, gesturing to himself. 'You can call me Emil.'

'Tom.' He held out a hand and replied in Dutch, 'Thank you. Will they be searching for us?'

'No. In the marshes our footprints easily get swallowed up,' the other man said in perfect English. 'They won't be able to follow us, and Emil here knows these channels like the back of his hand.'

Tom startled. The voice was somehow familiar. 'You're English?' He couldn't help staring. There was something about that face.

'Yep. I knew you were English as soon as I heard you speak Dutch. Been here a few years now. Helping downed airmen get out. Went AWOL from the Brits though, when I saw what a cock-up they made with agent drops.'

'Good grief . . .' He stared closer, realisation dawning. 'Agent Leapfrog? Don't you know me?'

The man took two steps back. 'What the—? How do you know that?'

'It's Tom – Tom Lockwood. I taught you coding, back in Baker Street. But when we heard nothing, we thought you were dead.'

'Shit. It's you.' He let out a laugh like a donkey's bray. 'No. It can't be.'

It was Leapfrog. No-one else laughed like that. 'Why on earth didn't you contact Baker Street to tell them you'd survived?'

'Beauclerk and that bunch of tossers? Why? Because I didn't want to take their orders. Not when I saw what had happened to the others. I'm not good with following rules. So I decided to be dead. Much easier. What the hell are you doing here?' He didn't wait for an answer, but spoke rapidly to Emil in Dutch with much grinning and gesticulating.

Emil rolled his eyes but got to work putting a battered kettle on the stove.

Tom was still staring, trying to reconcile the image of the mild-mannered man in a suit – the man he'd taught in Baker Street – with this mud-spattered killer in front of him.

'God Almighty. Tom Lockwood,' Leapfrog said, sucking on his teeth. 'That's something I would never have expected in a million years. I thought you'd still be stuck behind a desk in London.'

'I was, until a few weeks ago.'

Leapfrog's face took on a sharp expression. 'Hey, you won't tell them, will you? Won't blow my cover?'

'Who am I going to tell, stuck out here? Besides, I've just seen you shoot two guys. I'm not about to take chances with you.'

He brayed again. 'Guess you're right. Look, we need to stay here until the morning, then an old guy in a fishing truck will come to collect us. When we've warmed up, best to settle down, get some shut-eye. And don't call me Leapfrog, for God's sake. The English and their stupid schoolboy code-names. I'm Burt now to my Dutch friends.'

After a few moments Emil had produced hot bitter coffee in tin mugs, and some cigarettes. Tom didn't usually smoke but he took one to be sociable, and because his clothes were still sodden with icy water and he couldn't stop shivering. He took his glasses from his pocket and put them on so he could see Burt's face as they talked by the light of an old paraffin lamp.

The nicotine made his head swim and made him garrulous. He told Burt about his journey so far, and that he was looking for a woman last heard of in Amsterdam. Last time she'd been dropped she was Agent Ludo.

Burt shrugged. 'No, don't know her. She'll have another code-name by now anyway. Or maybe she's gone solo like me.'

All at once, Tom didn't feel like talking any more. 'Guess I'll get some sleep,' he said, and rolled away from Burt to prop himself against the wall.

Burt's words rang in his head. He hadn't heard from Nancy since coming to Holland because he'd no way of contacting her. What if she'd done the same as Burt, and had gone on the run? He wouldn't put it past her. She'd never liked being told what to do. And now Pavel was gone, Tom thought, his mission had imploded. What would he do if he couldn't find Nancy?

The worm of worry niggled at him as he tried to sleep, but he must have dropped off eventually because the next thing he knew, there was the sound of an engine and Emil and Burt were packing up, stowing their few belongings and rolling up the German overcoats, ready for leaving.

The truck was a battered old thing with the pungent odour of smoked fish. Boxes of herring were stacked where they were sitting. Their weapons and German uniforms had to go in carefully concealed boxes over the wheel hubs, along with the medical supplies and the rucksack, which he discovered contained tinned fruits, margarine and flour along with dried peas.

'We're fishermen, right?' Burt said. 'Just keep quiet and lie down in the back when we get near the checkpoint.'

The old guy driving was a taciturn fellow with a bushy grey moustache and sinewy arms steering the wheel. He drove carefully, navigating the rough track. They passed a couple of concrete bunkers with turret holes aimed back the way they had come, but saw no-one. The fact they did not, made Tom tense.

Emil was in the front, eyes fixed to the window, scanning the landscape and the sky. A box of fish was on his knee.

'It's quiet today. No aerial activity. We're headed for a safe house on the outskirts of Dordrecht,' Burt said. 'We'll get you fixed up there, find any intelligence we can.'

'I want to get to Amsterdam,' Tom said. 'How far is it?'

'Sheesh. A hundred kilometres. Not easy. There are no trains. Transport is hard. The Germans have forbidden the use of the canals for navigation, and we're right in the middle between the two opposing armies. Men can't move easily from place to place, not without being picked up.'

'The man I was travelling with – he ran out on me. He was the one who spoke good Dutch.'

Burt didn't answer. He seemed to be thinking. 'If you're solo, you'll have to watch out for the round-ups – they're after workers for their factories. If they spot you, that'll be it. Second, all the German troops are concentrated now in this small corner. This is why we need German uniforms. Only way to get around, to look like a patrol and hope no-one asks you anything. Shame your buddy's gone. Germans never walk alone – too easy to be a target. Quiet now, and lie flat, we have to go through a checkpoint.' He lay down close behind the bulkhead and covered them both over with a blanket. 'Close as you can,' he whispered, reloading his gun, 'so they won't see us.' The fact he was priming the gun made Tom's spine prickle.

The truck slowed. Next to him, Burt was motionless. It occurred to them it was like the game 'sardines', and he recognised the grim humour of his situation.

Sardines in a fish van. Please God, don't let me die like this, he thought.

Guttural German voices outside. Emil was talking to some men through the window. The door slammed. Emil must have got out. His German must be passable and the men were cordial with each other. The Germans were thanking him.

A reverberating bang as the door shut again and the creak of Emil's weight on the front seat. The old guy driving eased his foot off the clutch and they were bumping forwards again.

'Okay,' Emil said.

Burt sat up. 'He bribed them. They see him almost every week and he offers them fish from his smokehouse to turn a blind eye. Food is scarce here. They'd take our dry foodstuffs from Truus if they knew we had them. Truus does what she can to feed us. She knows the Resistance can't operate on fresh air.'

It was still early and the roads were bleak and deserted as they skirted the edge of Dordrecht and edged their way through bomb-shattered streets. Tom was becoming used to this now, the broken windows and cracked paving stones, the greyness and damp. The fact that he could never seem to get warm.

The safe house was actually a shop for women's clothes and millinery. The rest of the street was quiet. There were a few residential houses, and many other shops in the long row that looked as though they'd been looted or abandoned.

Fransine, the elderly woman who let them in, was obviously expecting Burt, but did a double take when she saw Tom.

She gestured them through to a workshop at the back, one with rolls of dusty fabric, and millinery stuffs, hat blocks and industrial-looking sewing machines with treadles. A large cutting table surrounded by stools dominated the centre of the room and they gathered around it.

'Who's this?' Fransine didn't look pleased to see him.

'Fransine, this is Tom Lockwood. I know him from England.' Tom smiled at her but she gave no response. 'Fransine is our contact here,' Burt said. 'She speaks English, Dutch and German. So she coordinates our activities with the people in Rotterdam and Amsterdam. She is our only link. Too much centralisation and it puts whole networks at risk. Not enough, and we could all be tackling the same thing, meaning we're wasting resources.'

'What do you want?' Fransine pinned her gaze on Tom.

The direct question rattled him. 'To get to Amsterdam.' He explained about finding Nancy.

'So, a fool on a half-baked rescue attempt.' Fransine was unimpressed. 'The agent in question doesn't even know he's here. What are we supposed to do with him?' she asked Burt. 'As soon as he gets out of here, he'll be captured, and then that'll be the rest of us down the pan.'

'I'd hold out,' Tom said. 'Twenty-four hours is what we taught our agents.'

'He's a coding expert,' Burt said. 'Could be useful.'

Fransine looked Tom up and down. Tom knew he looked unpromising, in his glasses and his barely dry crumpled clothes.

'Look, I can vouch for him,' Burt said. 'He's one of the best brains in Baker Street. If it needs solving, Lockwood can do it.'

'If he's so bloody good, what's he doing here, on some sort of suicide mission?'

'I can see it looks crazy,' Tom said. 'But I'll do whatever it takes to get the Netherlands back for its people.'

'Ha! What will you do? Invite the Nazis for afternoon tea and ask them if they'd mind going home now, please?' She laughed scornfully.

'I guess you already tried it then,' Tom said, maintaining eye contact.

She folded her arms. 'The last thing we need. A smart Alec who wants to save the world.'

'You're not being fair.' Burt said.

'Then he'll have to prove he's useful,' she said. She turned to Tom. 'Work with us for a month. If you're still alive then, we'll send you on to our contacts in Amsterdam.'

'What if I refuse?'

'You're the one with the brains. You work it out.'

Chapter 18

Dordrecht, Holland, Occupied Zone

Tom had barely seen any Nazi soldiers because he'd been kept indoors for three weeks, learning essential language, orientation and weapons training. Fransine had to work the statutory fifty-one hours a week to produce cotton vests for Nazi Germany. All control of raw materials was from Berlin, and everything anyone produced was not for the home market but for the Germans.

They had a map out on the cutting table, and Tom was learning the whereabouts and timing of the patrols. They were to sabotage a German factory and he wished it was over. All he wanted to do was to go and find Nancy, but Fransine was tight-lipped and refused to give him any information about Agent Ludo, except that her contacts had told her that she was no longer Ludo and no longer in Amsterdam.

'Then where is she?' he asked. 'There can't be that many Scottish agents in your network.'

'I won't give you anything. Not until you've proved you can operate and keep your mouth shut. A month's training, and then you can go.'

He'd glared at her then, but she'd been adamant.

'Anger won't help. We're all angry,' she said, attacking a cotton vest with a pair of scissors. 'If you'd lived under occupation as long as we have then the anger would be deep in your bones. But we use it to fuel acts of resistance against the Nazis, not each other.'

So now Tom was memorising positions and the order of events for the sabotage of a ball bearing factory. Ball bearings were crucial to the repair of just about anything mechanical – tanks, guns, engines. Taking out this factory would affect German production of just about everything.

Burt explained, timing was everything. They had only a few moments to get in position whilst the guards changed shifts. There would, of course, be more Germans then, but they would also be in disarray and not expecting an attack. It was to be the next night, the time of the darkest moon.

Tom gathered that Burt had been assigned to him as a kind of minder. Tom was secretly glad to have someone English speaking giving him 'the knowledge', though Burt's reliance and obvious attachment to his gun was a worry. At the back of Fransine's shop was a row of sewing machines under wooden covers. Only one of them had a machine in it, the others held stores of explosives – grenades, bottle bombs, and small-scale weapons. He noted that one of them concealed a radio transmitter, and he itched to use it if he could ever escape Fransine's eagle eye.

Burt showed him the grenades like they were the contents of a sweet shop. 'This Bakelite one here's a 69,' he said. 'It shatters without producing fragments like a metal-bodied one would. There's a metal sleeve available for it, to increase the flak. They're expensive and hard to get, so we'll be using this baby – the Mark II.' He ran a hand lovingly over its surface. 'Lethal range: five to ten yards. But the fragments can fly as far as fifty yards. It means you'll have to take cover pretty damn quick.'

'Will we all be issued with these?'

'Four of us, from four corners. You, me, Emil and Jaap.'

Burt told him some of the others who would help, like Emil and Jaap, were working in an illegal shoe factory, along with dozens of other young men in hiding. They scrounged leather from wherever they could, and turned it into shoes. It was the only way the Resistance could keep young, volatile men out of trouble and away from the attention of the Germans or the NSB.

'Follow the drill, right?' Burt said. 'Just like you did in Baker Street, we work as a team.'

'You're the boss,' Tom said.

It was after the eight o'clock curfew. In his hiding place, behind the colonnade at the Post Office, Tom's fingers touched the cool casing of the grenade in his pocket. He gently withdrew his fingers. So much power in such a small thing. It beggared belief.

This was his first taste of the city at war. He glanced behind, but couldn't see Burt, who was around the corner, also armed with a grenade. Few people were about, and he saw only a woman pushing a metal-wheeled cart loaded with wood. She was in the road and had to leap out of the way as a sleek, black car rolled by, carrying Nazi officers in peaked caps.

Further down the road he saw helmeted men cross and go down an alleyway. He found it astonishing to be here, where these men would shoot to kill you. He'd been too long in Baker Street away from the war. Nancy had to live with this every day and it brought a constriction to his throat. He glanced at his watch. Four minutes to go.

He hunkered down to wait, a pulse in his neck told him his heart was beating too fast, and he swallowed to ease his dry mouth. Scrawled on the columns where he was hiding were 'V' graffiti – the free Dutch victory sign. It fired him with courage and resolve. He wasn't alone. Somewhere, Nancy was on the same side. It brought him comfort to feel close to her. Unwittingly, he realised, he'd joined the Resistance.

A click of boots from further down the street. Two Wehrmacht men were walking towards them, in no hurry, strolling comfortably, just leaving the factory. He had to wait for them to pass. They approached with agonising slowness. Tom was sweating even though the night was freezing, and the old jacket they'd given him was too thin to offer any protection from the cold.

He stopped his breath as they passed a few feet from his hiding place, and closed his eyes. The ring of the metal on their boot soles followed by voices talking about what food would be waiting for them at their hotel billet.

As soon as they'd passed, he ran in a half-crouch towards the factory gate and slipped inside. Just behind the hedge, he met up with Burt, who had only his eyes visible under the scarf wrapped over his nose and mouth.

Burt signalled to him to go left, as he went right.

Tom put on his glasses and held his wrist up to his face so he could see his watch. Exactly five past the hour. He dreaded pulling the pin too early. He located the window through which he was supposed to throw the grenade. What if he wasn't strong enough and it bounced back? And what if he was caught on the way out? He knew he had to leave by a different route, one at the back of the building where another agent was supposed to have disabled the guards and opened the gate.

Less than a minute to go.

He felt the cold metal pin between his finger and thumb. Said a prayer. Took one last look to his right, but he couldn't see Burt.

The watch ticked around to the twelve.

Now! He pulled the pin and hurled it with all his might at the window.

To his relief it smashed right through. In the dim light the outline became a black hole of jagged glass, before he realised he had to run.

He shot into motion and had made about two strides when there was a deafening boom followed by another hot on its heels.

The flash lit up the ground in front of his feet making him stumble and have to grab on to the wall. Behind him, the noise of debris falling, running feet and shouts.

His legs thundered forwards as he gasped, amazed at the noise and the crash of glass. Something sharp pieced his shoulder with red-hot pain.

Don't stop! In the dark towards the gate. Breathless. Legs on fire. Another running figure shot by him towards the gate. He had no time to register who, as his arm was jerked back behind him.

A quick look over his shoulder.

A big German had him by the arm. '*Seien Sie ruhig, Schweinehund!*'

Behind him more pounding footsteps.

Something was still falling like rain.

For a moment he struggled to escape. Until with one quick wriggle he slipped out of his jacket and left the German clinging to an empty sleeve.

Never in all his life had he moved so fast. The floor was slippery and with a jolt he realised the ground was running with ball bearings. The man behind him gave a yell and crashed to the ground.

Thank God for his brown jumper, which at least couldn't be seen in the dark. But as he pelted through the gate and onto a waiting bicycle, he remembered his papers. As well as new ones issued by Fransine, in which he was now a man called Jacco, his old ones were still in the inside jacket pocket and clearly stated he was Tom Lockwood, an English journalist from London.

He pedalled as fast as he could, away from there, going down the narrowest alleys and only stopping when he was half a mile from the scene of the event. He pulled up next to the pavement, legs astride the cycle, and bent over to get his breath back.

He felt his shoulder and winced as his hand felt ragged flesh and the stickiness of blood. Shrapnel had gone right through his jumper, and somehow his glasses had got cracked. He took them off, shoved them in his trouser pocket.

The side of the street was quiet. A gibbous moon hung above the rooftops, glistening silver. Just as he watched, he heard air-raid sirens and saw a glint of Allied planes as they flew by.

'Good luck old chaps,' he thought.

Calmer now, he cycled the long way round back to Fransine's. When he arrived, Burt was already there. 'Your shoulder. There's a pad and iodine in the drawer.' Burt pointed. 'We put the mockers on them all right.'

'How much damage did we do?'

'Won't know until tomorrow, but I'm guessing quite a bit.'

Fransine came over to where they were talking. 'We'll have to listen out for the word on the street to find out. We have someone in the post office, they may hear something. The factory's still burning. With luck, it will have destroyed the post office too and all their franking machines and make it harder for them to get word to Germany.'

'So now, am I allowed to know where Agent Ludo is? I kept my part of the bargain.' Tom kept quiet about losing his jacket and his papers.

'He did his bit,' Burt said. 'Followed the instructions exactly.'

Fransine raised her chin. 'We've been at war five years. He's been here less than three weeks. I vote we keep him a little longer.'

Tom bristled. 'That's not fair. You made a bargain with me, and now you're not keeping to your side of it. I refuse to do anything else for you unless you tell me where Agent Ludo is.'

'What, and have you going and disturbing her important work? You've really no idea have you, what maintaining any resistance operation is really like. Holland is full of collaborators. The Germans are concentrated in this one small part of our land and they're hungry for revenge. There are too few of us left to take risks. What if you not only exposed us, but also exposed her? She's working under cover, and it could be her death sentence.'

Tom was silent. He paced the floor, anger mounting. He didn't want to put Nancy at any risk. He could see Fransine's point, but something about her controlling manner made him rebellious.

He took a deep breath. Being in a temper wouldn't help. 'So what do you want me to do?'

'Another month or two with us in the LKP.'

'I could just try to find her on my own.'

'We won't let you do that. You've seen too much about how we work.' Her eyes were unblinking, fixed on his face.

That was why Burt was his minder all the time. Suddenly, instead of him being the one in charge like in Baker Street and Burt being instructed by him, the tables had turned. He had no doubt that Burt would actually kill him if he stepped out of line.

He suppressed a shiver. He was caught. If he wanted any chance of finding Nancy, he'd have to play along.

It was worse now because he had no way to contact anyone. Not even Neil.

Chapter 19

The Hague

On the day of the interview with Glaser at the Oranjehotel, Nancy dressed herself immaculately in dark clothing, as befitting a widow, a fox-fur stole slung around her neck. The dead Anton was a very useful tool to keep predatory men at bay. The day before, braving the freezing fog, she'd been to the public library and looked up some examples of book-keeping techniques, so she could talk comfortably about 'double entry' and 'reconciling the books'. Her brother Neil was the one for proper book-keeping. She hoped she'd never actually have to do any, just take the tour.

As Fritz's car drove her in, she glanced up at the gatehouse, daunted. Guards stood before the entrance, two rows of them. Behind them two enormous crenelated towers loomed over an archway, through which she assumed the *Staatspolitie* or Gestapo would deliver their prisoners. To one side was a smaller door. Both were manned by fully-armed, helmeted Wehrmacht soldiers.

Oh Lord, she'd made a mistake coming here. How foolish to think she could just swan in there as if she were walking into a department store. Not only were the walls forbiddingly high, but the whole area was like a wasteland. No trees, no buildings, just bare road. Armed soldiers waved them through a checkpoint.

She'd been just outside The Hague briefly in 1943 when they moved people from Scheveningen into the city, and watched as relatives tried to fit more people into their already overcrowded houses. She'd heard that a whole district was demolished to make way for defences – to make this fortress Scheveningen, and what the Germans called the Atlantic Wall, a defence against Allied invasion. But she'd never actually been here. Its bare bulk dwarfed her.

At the inner gate of the prison her papers were examined minutely, and the process made her hot and jittery. Bakker drove the car away, and she was escorted by an officious prison guard to Gottfried's office. Inside the prison it was icy, and her heels rang on the slippery flagstones. On the way, she made a note of the route inside the wing, and the position of the courtyard.

Gottfried was dressed in ill-fitting SS uniform and stood to meet her as the guard thrust out an arm in the *Sieg Heil*. Nancy held out a languid hand and Gottfried took it and squeezed it between his damp palms.

He invited her to look over some heavy leather ledgers, which were waiting open on a side table for her attention. 'Here, you see the system we use?' he asked. 'Standard layout.'

She took a pair of spectacles from her bag and scanned over the sections – foodstuffs, clothing, office supplies, transportation, cleaning products. Each page had about six columns, detailing the different items, the supplier, plus the date of purchase or remittance amounts. As she leant over the desk, Gottfried was directly behind her, and as he was short, she could feel his breath on her neck, even though the office was heated by a spirit stove.

'It's all very familiar to me,' she said, leafing through the nearest one. 'It will be no problem. But I will need to see your storerooms and stock if I'm to keep accurate accounts.'

'Of course, of course.' A hot hand rested on her shoulder. 'We will go now.' He turned to the guard. 'Arrange for Frau Steffel to bring coffee to my office in twenty minutes.'

The officer clicked his heels and saluted.

Gottfried took a ring of keys from his desk drawer and set off down the corridor, turning left into another wing. This wing opened in the middle to an echoing loading bay, a covered entrance, where a van was unloading bundles of laundry onto the concrete walkway.

'Prison uniform delivery,' Gottfried said, 'The cloth comes from a factory in France, then to the POW camp to be made up. Afterwards to the laundry to be cleaned. Uniforms from the deceased are also fumigated and re-used. You'll need to log these in and out as required.'

They stood a moment watching the grey bales being unloaded. Nancy made a mental note that the loading bay gates were manned by two guards, and were double sets of gates. It would be hard to disable them enough to get a man out unless they were already open for a delivery.

As she watched, another van drove up, this time a black police van, and two Greens got out and opened the back doors.

The prison guards checked their authorisation papers and then disappeared down the corridor. A metallic noise of clanging doors and keys. Harsh voices reverberating in the draught. A shuffling old man and a woman, bowed and clinging together, made their way towards the van, prodded forwards by the guards.

To her horror, she saw they were people she knew. Karel the ironmonger and his wife Luska. So he hadn't got away from Amsterdam after all. She swallowed back the shock like gristle in her throat.

The couple shambled forwards dragging their feet, the guards' rifles jabbing their backs.

Nancy made to turn away, but not before Karel had seen her. His eyes bored into hers. He recognised her of course, but he gave no sign of it. Their exchanged glance was stuffed with unspoken words.

Karel and Luska were bullied into the van and the doors slammed.

When the van had gone, she was composed enough to ask, 'Where are they taking them?'

'Railway station,' Gottfried said. 'From there to a camp. Damned inconvenient all this transportation of prisoners. And it's not only political prisoners, but Jews too. If they'd only stop using the trains to transport the Jews all over the place, we'd have more chance of getting the armaments and supplies we need. The whole system's clogged up with this ferrying of the Jews hither and thither. Hitler's programme for getting rid of them is a hindrance rather than a help.'

'Do they always get taken by police van? Because that seems a waste of resources too.'

'No, it's usually a car. The vans are only for political prisoners who are to be executed. But I expect the train's about to leave and they wanted to make sure these were on it. After all, they're too old to be any use, and we can't keep them here, taking up precious space like that.'

The laundry was still being unloaded. *Don't let it get to you.* Nancy noted the particulars; the type of van, the registration plate, the look of the two laundry workers. She'd an idea for getting Josef out, if she could only find out the date and time of the trial.

Gottfried was already walking away and she hurried after him as he strode over to a large metal door, unlocking it to reveal an echoing vault filled with boxes and stores. Along the wall stood grey metal shelves, stacked with boxes of files and typewriter ribbons, carbon paper and hole punches. Under that was a shelf of Bakelite ashtrays, and a row of heavy black telephones. On the ground – rows of galvanised buckets, scrubbing brushes, dustpans and brooms.

Gottfried pointed to a tall metal cabinet. 'First Aid cabinet. Sedation mostly, plus anything medical. Only I have the key, and you won't need to have access to that.'

The other side of the room was stacked with food stuffs. Meagre rations for the prisoners they were supposed to be feeding. A few sacks of dried peas, boxes of stock cubes growing mould where they stood on the damp ground. Cans of dried beef, battered crates of hard-looking blackish bread. There was actually more stationery than food.

Gottfried was speaking. 'Once a week, you will come here and do the stock take. An officer will bring the account books on a trolley, so you can count the stores and enter them. When I first came, this was only done every few months, but so much pilfering went on, that I had to instigate a better routine.'

She nodded, 'What about my duties the rest of the week?'

'You will be based in my office. When people are admitted we keep a record of their possessions, which are stored in the adjacent room. Come.' He shepherded her out, locked the door, and opened the one next door.

This room was smaller, but shelved with industrial metal racks. There were piles of clothes there, all with brown labels attached. Near the door was a trolley on which more piles were standing. A woman was there sorting them and removing the labels.

'These belonged to individuals who've been moved on, or are deceased, like those you just saw. These civilian items will be sent to Germany or to the front. If the prisoner's going to trial, we let them have them back for that one day. Usually after that they either go on to execution for their crimes, or to a camp, and we repossess the clothing again. Shoes and boots in particular are required for our men fighting at the front. They'll be cleaned, re-oiled and repurposed.'

The woman who was sorting stood to attention like a stiff soldier, until Gottfried moved away.

'When we bring people in, you will inventory their possessions – any money they might have is to be entered in the book. You will need to be exact and report to me if any of the guards take advantage and pilfer anything for themselves. Everything comes through me, understand?'

She nodded. 'Does every man get the same rations?'

'Yes, unless they're scheduled for trial. Then there's no point feeding them because they cease to be our responsibility. The numbers of the prisoners and the dates when they go to trial are in the registration book in my office.'

She stiffened. She must get a look at that registration book.

After their tour – the staff room, thick with smoke, and an empty canteen – they had coffee in his office, where he showed her the registration book, and told her about the pay. The money was meagre, but Dutch people worked for lower wages than the Germans. After all, as a German occupier, he could force someone to do the work. The only reason he didn't was because this information was more sensitive than making munitions or other factory work.

She was trying to thumb through the book to see when Josef might go to trial.

'So,' he said, reaching over her to shut the book. 'When can you start?'

'May I think about it?' she asked. 'It's not the kind of environment I'm used to.'

'You need have no contact with the prisoners,' he said, 'I can assure you of that.'

'It's a big jump for me. But I know that my Anton would have wanted me to be useful to the Party. Give me twenty-four hours and I will call you.'

He seemed satisfied and wrote down his personal number and handed it to her. 'I do hope you'll join us,' he said. 'The stock taking is due a week on Friday, and it would be excellent if you could start then.'

A knock at the door behind her, and a Gestapo officer strode in. It took a moment for her to recognise that it was Fritz, in his full uniform. The sight of him here, in his low-fitting cap disconcerted her, but he seemed not to notice.

He gave a salute to Gottfried. 'Are you finished with Danique? I thought I'd escort her back to her car.'

'We're almost done,' Gottfried said. She was sure he said this only to maintain control, for as far as she was concerned, the interview was over. 'If you start next week there'll only be one prisoner going for trial on Thursday, a man who won't be returning, so an ideal time to start. You can inventory his things.'

'Josef de Jong, is it?' Fritz scowled. 'About time.'

Thursday. The trial was to be Thursday. Too soon. Nancy ignored the jolt it gave her and treated this information as if it were of no interest to her, and the name meant nothing.

Fritz was continuing. 'Can't be soon enough for my liking. And once he's sentenced it will put another nail in the coffin of the Resistance.'

'Keller tells me you couldn't get anything out of him,' Gottfried needled.

Fritz's tight expression showed it had hit home. 'We got enough,' he snapped.

'I'll be in touch,' she said to Gottfried, hurriedly. 'Give me until tomorrow to consider your offer.'

'The car's waiting at the front.' Fritz put a hand on her arm.

On the way out, Fritz muttered, 'Odious man. You'll turn him down, of course.'

'I haven't decided yet. Whilst I'm here, won't you show me where you work – your office? So I can see what sort of size and shape we can choose for your artworks?'

'Not now. Bakker will be waiting. You've already been more than an hour.'

'Work, work work. Anton used to be the same. Thought the place would fall apart if he wasn't there.' She smiled up at him. 'I've nothing else to do today, and it will help us choose something suitable if we can actually visualise the space.'

'I think you might be good for me, Danique. You're right. There's more to life than work.' But he continued to walk her to the car.

She counted every door they passed until they got to a side entrance where Bakker was waiting. Fritz opened the car door for her and she climbed in the back.

He held the door open, and bent to speak to her. 'Danique, you simply can't work for Gottfried. Work for me instead.'

'For you?' Nancy's stomach gave an uncomfortable flip. 'Doing what?'

She shuffled to the edge of the seat to look up at him.

'A secretary. A personal assistant.'

'Won't that get Gottfried's back up even more?'

'Probably. But he's a pig to work for. Everyone says so.'

'But what would I be doing?'

'I don't know – typing letters, answering calls, arranging my schedule. I used to have a secretary to do that for me, but she left. And now Keller does most of it. It will free Keller to be more use elsewhere.'

'I'm not sure, Fritz, I—'

'Say you will. It's an ideal solution. You'll be able to make my office more comfortable too.'

She didn't want to work for Fritz because she could see distinct advantages for getting Josef out of the Oranjehotel if she worked for Gottfried. She'd have access to the goods delivery entrance, and might perhaps be able to smuggle him out somehow.

She got out of the car and put a hand on his shoulder. 'Look, Fritz, I'll be honest. We're friends, aren't we? And becoming your employee would change all that. We enjoy each other's company now, but how long before that would change? I don't want to be beholden to my friends.'

He blinked, taken aback. Probably astonished that someone who wasn't a German had the temerity to say no. To speak back to him like that.

She maintained a pleading gaze, and finally he shook his head impatiently, and stood up.

'You're right. Of course, you're right. I do want to maintain our friendship.'

She was aware that she was the one now in control, but it was a fine line to tread, one that could easily topple her into a dangerous situation. 'I'll think about Gottfried's position overnight, and whether I accept the position or not, I'll go through the proper channels. Thank you for asking though, Fritz dear. I'm ready to go home now.'

'You'll think about my offer?' His face looked like a small boy begging for sweets.

As Bakker drove her away, she realised she was sweating, and that her heart was hammering harder than the rain.

In the lobby she saw Steef at the desk, but didn't stop. Too many Gestapo were talking by the door.

But once in her apartment, she picked up the internal phone, praying it would be working.

'Reception?' Steef's voice.

'Frau Koopman,' she said. 'There's still a problem with my tap. Can you come? It's urgent.'

'I'll be there as soon as I can.'

Nancy got out a pencil and paper and drew a complete map of everything she'd seen, from Gottfried's office to the loading bay, the storerooms and the cupboards. Then the route through the prison and the cells where the resistance men were held. Aiming for accuracy, her quick mind had assessed the dimensions of everything she saw. Steef arrived just as she was finishing it.

'Josef's trial's next Thursday,' she said.

'Next week?'

'I know. It's all moving too quickly. But I was in the prison today. I've been right round it.' She spread out her drawings on the table. 'Look,' she said. 'It can be done.' She explained what she'd seen and heard and how the laundry van came and went. 'It's not ideal, but it's the only thing I can think of.'

'It's not enough time,' he said. 'Photographing the van, finding paint, the right kind of fabrics for disguise.'

'There is if we get on it right now. Today.'

'To get access to the right kind of van?'

'Come on, Steef. Don't get cold feet on me now. I'm the one risking my neck in that place to get the intelligence. You can damn well do your part.'

'You sure you haven't missed anything?'

'How can I be sure?' she asked, throwing up her hands. 'All I can do is my best.'

'And only two guards? Can we be sure of that?'

'No. We can't be certain, but it seems that way. You were the one who insisted we try. I know it's the biggest risk we've ever taken, but worth it – once the trial is over, Josef'll be executed. They told me. He'll never be going back there.'

She saw Steef's face harden. 'For our men, it's sending them to a death trap. If anything goes wrong there'll be no way out. And next week is barely enough time.' He hesitated a moment.

'You knew that from the beginning.'

'You're right. We've got to go for it. I'll ask Greta for new ID cards, and you must be ready to get Josef away as soon as we get him out. Okay?'

'I'll be ready,' she said. 'Just give us a safe house to go to.'

'You've got it.'

'And Steef?' He turned. 'Schneider was asking me about money. He seemed to think there was a problem with Frau Koopman's bank.'

'How can there be? We haven't touched her money. We just left well alone.'

'I don't know. Can you get someone to check it out? And I need to know where I'm banking now. The cover story didn't tell me, and I'll need an account somewhere in case he runs checks.'

A sigh. 'Okay. But it will have to be after the job.'

'After next Friday, I'll be gone from there.'

'Not necessarily.'

Oh no. 'Now wait a minute. I'm not doing this indefinitely, you said just a few weeks, and it's already been two months.'

'Because we couldn't get anyone in there.' His voice held a hint of accusation.

'Because it's almost impossible,' she flashed. 'Be grateful I even got through the doors.'

'It's a useful plant, someone in there.'

'No. After this, I'm out of it. Understand?'

Chapter 20

When he got home on Friday night, Fritz spread out all the documents on the dining table in front of him, a sinking feeling in the pit of his stomach, which was slowly solidifying into anger and outrage. He'd brought the file home, because he wasn't sure what it meant. Or rather, he feared what it meant.

Dobermann had couriered this to him by motorcycle and the file still stank of petrol fumes. The fact that Dobermann might have read it, and worse, laughed at his stupidity, enraged him.

Grimly, Fritz set the papers precisely in date order. Next to them, he placed his own leather diary. He flipped it open, and saw his own writing, with the initials DK, whenever he was meeting Danique. He remembered the act of writing each one, the thrill as he inked them with a flourish, anticipating each meeting.

He pulled a bank statement towards him. Yet here was the evidence that on the very dates he had seen her, including Wednesday 27 December, Danique Koopman, widow of Anton Koopman, had made withdrawals from her bank in Nijmegen, but not only that, just last week a woman meeting her description and bearing the correct *Ausweis* papers had also made purchases at Arnhem, including railway tickets. The dates of these tickets to The Hague were for next week. How could Danique be in Arnhem?

He shook his head. It was impossible.

But bank statements could not lie. The dates were there of all the withdrawals. Small amounts all through January. He scrutinised each one. He had to face it. Either the Danique he knew, or the one in Arnhem, was an imposter. But which? It would hardly be romantic to ask his Danique to show him her papers. And just when she was softening and forgetting that husband of hers.

This woman downstairs, who even now might be sleeping peacefully in front of his favourite painting, was his Danique. The woman to whom he'd exposed his artistic soul! The woman he could imagine on his arm once this war was over. He thought back over their conversations, and the fact he'd been so considerate to her, so gentlemanly in respect of her bereavement. He'd treated her like she was cut glass – restrained himself, out of honourable feelings for her, and she'd warmed to him, as he hoped she would. He loved the sparkle in her eyes whenever they met.

The fact she was so unattainable made her even more desirable. The waiting was agony, but bliss when he knew it would end in his bed. He was sure she felt the same; she'd told him she just had to wait a decent amount of time, or there would be gossip in the Party.

So far, Dobermann hadn't managed to uncover an address for the Frau Koopman in Arnhem, but he'd asked him to follow her and arrest her for interrogation. The Danique downstairs, well it would do no harm to put her under surveillance too. The closer the better. Perhaps he should monitor her personally – there could be added benefits to that. Naturally, if she was innocent – then he wouldn't want her to know she was being watched, so who better to do it than himself?

Chapter 21

Nancy crouched over the transmitter and fiddled with the aerial but it still wouldn't connect. It wasn't the signal, she was certain, but she couldn't risk more time. She'd been trying to make her weekend transmission to Tom. Though she kept tapping in her call sign, there was no answer. Where was he? He was always there on the end of the line. She thought of German bombs over London and shuddered. It was no use, she couldn't risk longer.

She was just putting the transmitter away when there was knock on the door. Not the doorbell from outside, nor the hard insistence of Fritz. Nor was it a rap like Steef's, but a definite, solid knock. In a panic she closed up the suitcase, stuffing the wires inside and thrust it into the wardrobe. The knock came again.

Warily, she opened the door just an inch.

'Frau Koopman? I am Margarete. Herr Schneider sent me.' The scrag-haired woman on the doorstep was plump, which meant, in these days of deprivation, she was paid by the Nazis. The second thing Nancy saw was that she was carrying a cardboard suitcase, and another large square bag was at her feet. Nancy must have looked blank, for the woman explained helpfully, 'He says you will be working and will be in need of a maid.'

The presumption of the man, not to tell her when she'd be arriving!

She couldn't send her away, that would arouse Fritz's suspicion. At the same time, the idea of a maid living here would make everything more difficult, and she'd come at the most difficult time when Nancy was preparing to leave.

'Oh, yes,' Nancy said. 'He did mention it, but I'm afraid I don't have a room prepared yet, maybe in a few weeks—'

'Oh, never mind that,' Margarete said, stepping towards her so she had no choice but to let her in, 'I'll soon have it sorted out. I have sheets in here.' She pointed to the bag.

With a gnawing feeling in her chest, she showed Margarete to the small box room, feeling at the same time guilty that it was so cramped. But Margarete seemed pleased. 'A good bed,' she said, feeling it with a fleshy hand. 'I will unpack, and then I will make us some supper.'

'I'm afraid I haven't much—'

'No, no. I have ingredients for soup. You mustn't worry. I will take care of it.'

From this it was clear that the woman was intent on taking over her life. It grated. Already she had taken a dislike to the officious manner of Margarete, though she had spoken only a few words. It was the way she treated the apartment, as if she already owned it.

There was little she could do about it.

Her undercover life was closing in round her, making her breathless.

She cursed Gerard, Anna's contact in Amsterdam who had started her on this botch of an assignment. That night she slept restlessly. In the darkness she got up to burn any evidence of her previous life. She agonised over what to do with the transmitter. Margarete would find it, she knew. Taking the bull by the horns, she got up, got dressed and gently removed the case from the wardrobe.

She knocked gently on Steef's door with the 'V' knock. No answer. She had to try three times before he peered out, hiding behind the door in his threadbare pyjamas.

She explained rapidly that she couldn't keep the transmitter in her apartment and why.

'And what am I supposed to do with it?'

'I don't know. They trust you, don't they?'

'It can't stay here. I'll have to take it to the bank.' The bank was now disused, but the cellar beneath was used as an air-raid shelter and there were a series of rooms above – regularly searched by the Gestapo, but one of the rooms was used by the Resistance for meetings, and had been kitted out with under-floor hiding places between the joists and behind a blocked-up chimney breast.

A sigh, but he took it out of her hands.

'Thank you, Steef.' She meant it. She'd always worked solo, but was realising that having allies in The Hague could save your life.

Back upstairs, and Margarete's snores told Nancy she was still sleeping. In her bedroom she searched for anything else that might incriminate her. Reluctantly she took out her one photo of Tom, hidden in a book in her bedside drawer.

His face was smiling out at her. It had been taken on one of their outings up Primrose Hill – two summers ago when she had leave. They'd taken photos of each other with his box brownie. How she longed to go back to that time! A time that had been all the more poignant because she knew she had to return here to Holland.

She took up the inner lining of her shoe and placed the photo there before slipping it back on. That way he would be with her everywhere she went, and Margarete wouldn't be able to ask questions.

She had spent long hours weighing up the advantages of access to Scheveningen, but had decided it was too risky to actually work there. She had a plan in mind to try to get Josef out when the van came to do the laundry drop, and when that happened, she would need to be as far away as possible, as if she worked on the inside, she would certainly be an object of suspicion. Tomorrow she would send Gottfried a message, tell him she had decided not to take the job. She and Steef had so much to do, she had to prioritise getting everything in line by Thursday for the prison raid.

The next morning, she was up and dressed early, and was just about to get pen and paper, when Fritz knocked. Margarete hurried breathlessly to open the door.

'Ah, Margarete,' he said. 'Very good.'

'Good morning, sir,' Margarete said in German.

He turned to Nancy, who had hurried from the bedroom. 'This arrangement will be most satisfactory, eh, Danique? And even more so, since you will be out at work all day.'

'But Fritz, it's Saturday and I was just about to write to Gottfried and tell him—'

'Ah yes, about that. I decided that you will work with me in my office. Not with Gottfried. I thought about it overnight, and it won't affect our friendship, I assure you. I remember you even suggested it once at dinner. So we will travel together, yes?'

'You mean, I am to have an interview? Today?'

'No, no. Of course not. We know each other well enough, and I'm sure you will be absolutely perfect for what I need. It will be good to spend more time together, yes? I have already sent a memo to Gottfried. He will hate it, but it can't be helped.'

She couldn't take it in, what it would mean, both for her and her mission to get Josef out. 'But what will I be doing?'

'We'll discuss that on the way.' The set of his mouth told her it was an order. You couldn't say no to a Nazi.

'Lovely. I'll just collect a few things,' she said, over her shoulder. So he was to dictate every moment of her life. An involuntary shudder, that she masked by walking away.

She felt his eyes on her back, strangely still, as she went.

In the bedroom she picked up a notebook and pen, and slicked on some lipstick. She was doing everything like a puppet. She couldn't believe she was to work with Schneider, the director of the Oranjehotel – the place where so many resistance workers had been tortured or shot. She couldn't think of any excuse that wouldn't blow her cover.

Last until next Thursday, she told herself. *That's all you have to do.*

She put on her jacket and a false air of confidence, and went back into the living room.

'Ah, very nice,' Fritz said, giving her a look of approval. 'I'm sorry I have a weekend shift. You will enjoy working with me, yes?'

There was no answer she could possibly give.

With a small bow, he held the door open for her and she followed him out. It felt even more vulnerable to leave Margarete in her apartment. She hated the idea of Margarete snooping through her things – for she was in no doubt that this was what she'd been tasked to do. In Holland everyone spied on everyone if it could bring them an advantage or be used as a bargaining chip. She had a momentary panic wondering if she'd left anything else incriminating in the apartment, before telling herself sternly, *if you have, it's too late to do anything about it.*

Mesman accompanied them down in the lift, which was actually working for once, and Bakker the uniformed chauffeur stood waiting with the car. As usual Bakker drove, Mesman travelled in the front, and Fritz and Nancy behind.

The car registration was obviously familiar to the guards for they sailed through the gates and into the inner compound with no trouble.

Fritz introduced her to Keller, who was sour-faced, and also to another mouse-like man in the outer office. 'She will be my personal secretary from now on, but Keller, you will have some additional duties, like taking down shorthand.'

'I take it she will have "additional duties" too,' Keller said. 'Like Fraulein Jacobsen.'

His response was met with a glare from Fritz. 'You will treat Frau Koopman with the utmost respect, or you will be looking for a post nearer the Front. Do I make myself clear?'

Keller's expression was stony, but he sat back down and continued to scribble in German on a pad in front of him. The other man in the office, a thin bird-like man with a prominent nose, swallowed and looked uncomfortable as he opened up a file.

Meanwhile, Fritz showed Nancy to a desk on the far wall, which was already set up with a typewriter and what looked to be a wax cylinder recorder, as well as two telephones. She noticed there was a painting of a landscape with a stag in a forest next to the door.

'Oh, Fritz. That does cheer the place up,' she said.

'It's a good choice, you think?' He was staring at her in an odd way, his head on one side.

'Very good.' She kept her jacket on because it was still cold, even in here, but she hung her handbag on the back of the chair.

Fritz turned to her. 'You will find a kettle and a spirit stove in the hospitality room near the door. I like to start my day with a cup of coffee.'

When she got back, Fritz was in his inner office with the door closed, and only Keller was there. She put the coffee tray down on her desk.

'Would you like some?' she asked Keller. 'I brought a spare cup.' She hoped to mend the animosity between them straightaway.

'You won't last long,' he said in a hoarse whisper, glaring at her. 'Inge Jacobsen was his last conquest, but there were several other gold-diggers before you. They're all in camps in the East now.'

'Then I need your help,' she said, going closer to his desk. 'Tell me what I can do to stop that happening to me.'

He was surprised. He hadn't expected her to face it head on. 'Nothing. There's nothing you can do. He treats women like a box of chocolates. Takes the ones he fancies, then discards them to the trash like they're only the wrappers.'

'How soon does he tire of them?' She poured him a cup of coffee.

'A few months, four or five if you're lucky.'

She was relieved. She wouldn't be here that long. 'Then I'll need to keep him sweet, won't I?' She added sugar to his cup and stirred it.

'I know all his habits, all the small deceptions he makes for himself. That's why he keeps me on, even when I get drunk and try to thump him. When we have to torture them, that's when he calls for his secretary.'

He was watching her face, but she was careful to keep it blank.

'Afterwards. To make him forget,' He picked up the coffee and took a gulp. 'Not bad. Make it like this every day, and you might last a few more weeks.' He grinned, but his eyes were cold. 'There are some handwritten memos that need typing, and some lists he needs for this morning. Better get a move on. If Fraulein Jacobsen is anything to go by, barely a few hours goes by without him needing some . . . how shall we say . . . attention.'

She took Fritz his coffee. He was on the telephone so just gestured at her to put it down. Then she went back to her desk, sat down and began to type. The handwritten paper was a memo to another officer about his hours of duty. She mis-typed and had to use the whitener because her mind was racing over what Keller had told her. Was he saying it just to get back at her for choosing Fritz over him, or was Fritz as bad as he said?

She threaded paper and carbon paper into the typewriter, and picked up the next document. A list of detainees and where they were to be sent to. As the words came out on the paper, she couldn't help looking for the names of anyone she knew.

Aachen, Bernhardt
Boogman, Johannes
de Jong, Trude
Klinger, Albrecht
Kossmann, Ernst
Seger, Grietje
Van Hoff, Koos

Nancy made a sharp inhalation. One name jumped out at her immediately. One of her contacts in Amsterdam who had been part of the Obermayer kidnap plan. Koos was going to a place called Herzogenbusch Kamp. There was little she could do to stop the deportation, but all of a sudden she realised she had access to intelligence that could be of immense value, information that would allow people to trace their loved ones. Yet she was to be out of here in little more than a week. The thought made her heart clench.

So what to do? She couldn't memorise all these names, and with Keller there, she couldn't make extra copies. She continued to type, trying to figure out a solution. But before she'd even finished the list, the adjoining door opened and Fritz was there.

'How are you getting along?' he asked. 'Is the first list typed up yet?'

'Almost,' she said. 'On the last few names now.'

'Get it done, and then come into my office please.' She marvelled that after only a few hours, he was already behaving like a boss, rather than her friend. The power dynamic had shifted and it sent a frisson of fear up her spine.

She finished the list and typed the deportation order at the end leaving a space for him to sign. Keller, meanwhile, came and went in the office bringing various files and talking loudly into the phone on his desk, arranging a requisition for more prison uniforms.

She ignored him, and went into Fritz as he'd asked. She couldn't help but feel Keller's gaze on the back of her neck as she went.

As soon as she was inside the door, Fritz slid the bolt across on the inside.

'It's driving me crazy, you being so close,' he whispered. 'We don't want to be disturbed, do we now?' he said.

She swallowed. Here it was, the moment she'd been dreading. She'd have to do what he wanted. *Just until the end of the day, then you'll think of something*, she told herself. She had to close her mind to everything he wanted to do, to lock it away in a separate compartment.

He kissed her sloppily, and pushed her up against the wall. She tried to respond but almost gagged. He had his hands thrust down the back of her skirt when the telephone shrilled. He left it a while, his hands roaming over her underwear, his crotch pressed up against her. 'You want me, don't you?'

'Yes, Fritz,' she attempted a moan of pleasure.

The phone kept on ringing. Finally, with one hand, he reached for it.

Immediately he shot to attention, 'Yes, Herr Direktor,' he said. 'Yes, I'll see to it. *Heil Hitler*. Sorry, my sweet, but duty calls,' he said. 'That was the boss. He's ordered some interrogations. A man's going to trial on Thursday next week. A high-profile case. They want enough information to sink him.'

'Won't it wait?' She tried to look seductive.

'Orders from Berlin. Willem Brant from the *Sicherheitsdienst*, Himmler put him in charge here, but he's away so often that I'm always the one left making decisions. Nothing in this place would ever happen without me. Brant's never here. Now suddenly, he wants things done yesterday.'

He stuck his head out of the door. 'Keller. Get Kruger and Scholz.'

When he came back in Fritz smoothed down his trousers, slicked a stray strand of hair back over his ears. He tilted up her chin to kiss her again, and she complied.

'Who are you interrogating?' she asked. She wrapped her

arms around his waist, around the hard black material of his uniform jacket.

'Same man. He's an assassin from the Resistance. He's guilty, whatever he says. He stank of chloroform when we picked him up. But a smell is inadmissible as evidence. No matter, we have his colleagues as witnesses. They've been happy to spout for us.'

'Do they keep assassins here, in this side of the prison?'

'Don't you worry, you'll be quite safe. Stick to this side of the building, the left wing after the main gate. The right wing is where we house the dangerous prisoners, except for Jews, they're on this side – but then, they're never here long.' He sighed, but his demeanour was a good deal more cheerful than it had been first thing in the morning. 'You're good for me,' he said, smiling. 'But you must stop distracting me like that!'

'I'll get back to my lists, shall I?'

'Yes, get the rest typed up.'

She straightened her clothes and went back to the main office where Keller gave her a 'told you so' look. A few moments later she heard the telephone ring, and Fritz's voice talking to someone, sounding upbeat, before he stuck his head around the door. 'Keller, are those officers available?'

'They're on their way, sir.'

'Tell them to take the man in sixteen to the interrogation room. I'll be there in about fifteen minutes.' Then to her, 'Danique, can you find the index card for Josef de Jong. He's linked to Koos van Hoff who confessed yesterday. Should be in our files – index cards, second drawer down, files in the walk-in cupboard next door. Here's the key to the storeroom.' He handed her a key before he walked over to put a hand on Keller's shoulder to stop him leaving. 'It implicates de Jong, so we can tell him we know it all.'

Nancy went to the cabinet to find a card under 'J'. The card had a number and letters on it, which when she went next door corresponded to box files on a shelf. She scanned the room, surprised at the number of shelves. Some were packed with foolscap files end to end, others had box files stacked on top of each other.

She found Josef's file without difficulty and, with a quick look over her shoulder, opened it to see what sort of things it might contain. Josef had obviously been under surveillance a long time. There were multiple reports of what the Germans called *Deutschfeindlichkeit* or Germanophobia.

She kept one ear to the corridor all the time, in case Fritz should come past, and sifted through the contents. Suddenly, she froze. There was a picture of her there, a photograph of her pass when she'd been Rika, the pass she'd given to that Green policeman Dirk van Meveren. She couldn't leave that in there! What if Fritz were to see it? Yes, it was grainy and not a good likeness, and she'd be out of here by next Friday, but the risk was too great. There was a note paper clipped to it – *Cross-reference with file 216B – Hendrika van Hof*.

She extracted the printed pass as fast as her shaking hands would allow, folded it and shoved it down her brassiere. Just in time, for a voice came from behind – Keller.

'What are you doing? You've been ages. Oberführer Schneider asked me to keep an eye on you.'

'Why?' She kept her voice light.

'Because you're new, why d'you think?'

'Just checking if this is the right file,' she said, slamming down the lid. 'The coding system's new to me. I'll get used to it.'

'I'll take it then.' He grabbed the file from her hands. 'I'll take the key, too.'

Damn, she'd wanted to stay a little longer to find a file with her name on it. *Hendrika van Hof*, her old alias. File 216B. The thought made her insides quake.

She tottered back into the office on shaky legs and put her head in her hands. Both Keller and Fritz were out of the office. Now wasn't the time to do nothing.

Quickly, she searched the desk drawers looking for anything

useful. She glanced through the diary on Keller's desk, memorising when he'd be out and absent from the office.

Tomorrow afternoon he had a meeting with the Kommissar for The Hague – it was entered in the book as 'meeting re new accommodation'. She also repeated all the names she could remember of people who were due for transport. It was vital she should recall them. Her mind slid to Josef with a silent prayer. She knew he was being interrogated by the two SS men.

Keller reappeared in the office before Fritz, just as she was putting another sheet of paper in the typewriter. He didn't speak to her, just opened up a dossier he had under his arm and began to copy information from it into another prisoner's file. She could hear the scratching of his pen as he worked, and the insistent thought that these snippets were being constructed together to lead to someone's execution or deportation numbed her.

She ignored him and got on with her typing. There was a big backlog because the previous secretary hadn't been there for so long. As she was typing, the screams of a man echoed down the corridor. They curdled her blood. Was it Josef? She couldn't tell, even though the shrieks were quite clear and ricocheted all around the building.

She glanced at Keller but he continued to write as if the noise didn't exist.

After an hour, Fritz returned, his face taut and she could see by the set of his shoulders he was tense and angry. He was carrying a briefcase with him and he unlocked the door and threw it open so it banged against the wall. He hurled the briefcase into the room.

'Frau Koopman,' he called from within.

She hurried through to his office, where he promptly shut the door behind her and bolted it.

'He wouldn't talk,' he said. 'What makes these men think they can disobey us? Even when we have proof, they still refuse us. Day after day, with no results. And I must answer to Kommandant Brant.'

'I suppose they have their principles, just as we have ours,' she said.

He shot her an incredulous look. 'They've lost,' he said. 'I can't understand why they don't just accept it. It would be far easier if they faced reality.'

'Poor Fritz. I can see you're stressed,' she said. 'Why don't you just sit down and I'll rub your shoulders.'

'No,' he said, 'Please, take off your blouse.'

'What?'

'Take off your blouse.' He lunged towards her, pushing her back against the desk, his hands fumbling for the buttons.

'Fritz, what is this? Just wait a minute—'

She clasped her arms around her chest. He mustn't find the pass. The corner of the paper with her photograph dug into her skin.

He tried to kiss her neck.

'Let me help you,' she said wrestling away. She'd have to find a way to get rid of it. A shrill bell made her startle. The telephone again. Thank God.

But no, he didn't answer it, but let it ring. He grabbed her again by the back of the neck, and forced one button undone and now his mouth was all over her throat. The corner of the desk was sharp in the small of her back.

He slipped open another button as the noise continued. Desperately with one hand she fumbled for the cradle behind her, snatched up the receiver and put it to her ear. 'Oberführer Schneider's office?' A female voice on the other end announced she was putting the line through to Kommandant Brant. 'It's Brant again,' she said.

Angrily he grabbed the receiver out of her hand, 'Ja?'

She almost collapsed with relief.

Fritz tried to insist he should call back, but Brant obviously wouldn't take no for an answer. Fritz was soon involved in a long conversation about prisoner numbers, and she was able to tidy herself and slip out.

Keller gave her a smile that meant, *I know what goes on in there*, and it made her feel both humiliated and angry. Immediately she hurried to the ladies' room where she tore the pass with Rika's photograph into tiny pieces and flushed it away.

What was the matter with Fritz? He was behaving oddly, quite different from how he'd been before. Something was going on with him and all her protective instincts were on fire. God help her if she had to put up with that every day. The sooner the trial day came, the better.

Chapter 22

Dordrecht, Occupied Zone
February 1945

For the past week Tom and Burt rarely ventured out in the daytime because of the round-ups, but today they were disguised as factory workers, with faces rubbed with engine grease and fuller's earth, wearing the traditional worn caps of the older generation. Fransine had instructed them to stoop, and walk as if they were old. This was it, his way to prove to Fransine he was savvy enough to make contact with Nancy.

They were cycling through the milky fog to await a convoy of food destined for the Luftwaffe out towards Apeldoorn. Tom stood down on the stiff pedals, already out of breath. Everything was an effort because they were hungry, and nothing worked properly – the bikes were clapped out, tyres filled with sand not air, the chains rusted and apt to stick for lack of oil.

Fransine's latest plan was that they were going to intercept the Nazi food convoy for the Resistance. Such a risky and blatant robbery filled Tom with unease. He'd accepted he was a kind of hostage, and in this situation it was better to figure out how to survive, otherwise how could he ever find out where Nancy was? He'd resigned himself to taking life moment by moment.

'Our people will get a square meal for once,' Burt said, swerving off to the side of the road by a burned-out house.

Already hidden in the house were a stash of Wehrmacht uniforms and a cache of German rifles delivered earlier by a female farm worker. Two other men arrived, Piet and Nils, hardened fighters from Fransine's network. They changed efficiently into German uniforms and Tom and Burt did the same.

The effect was chilling. To suddenly be this patrol clad in *feldgrau* – the greyish green of the enemy.

They stowed their civilian clothes with the cycles. The factory overalls would have to be sacrificed when they hijacked the truck.

'Time?' Tom said checking his watch.

'I make it ten-fifteen,' Burt said. 'Should be any minute.'

Piet and Nils were loading their rifles and complaining the uniforms were badly mended, when the thrum of an engine made everyone jump to attention. Tom grabbed his rifle.

'Load up,' said Burt, readying his Sten gun. 'Here she comes.'

Burt leapt into the road, his gun to his shoulder, with Tom a fraction behind.

'No!' Piet's yell was a second too late.

What was rounding the corner was not a truck, but a car. An open-topped BMW Cabriolet, the one favoured by German command. Four men inside, and the one in the back wore the SS officers cap.

'Shit.' They'd have to brazen it out.

Piet yelled at Tom, 'Get the fuck out of the way!' Then stepped calmly into the road waving his arms. What the heck would he say? What excuse could he give the SS for stopping them?

The car slowed an instant, but then, unbelievably, the crack and flash of gunfire.

It took a moment to register. The men in the car were firing on them.

Tom ducked, knees crunched down into the dirt. Why? Something about them must have warned the occupants they weren't real Wehrmacht.

A bullet struck the ground near his face. Without thinking, Tom squinted down the barrel of his rifle, took aim at the driver and fired.

The driver jerked and the car stalled. Piet and Nils ran in towards the car, rifles firing all the way.

Tom took another shot at the man in the back of the car.

A spatter of fire near his feet. One of the men had an automatic weapon. All was confusion. Now he didn't know if the shots were theirs or his, but as quickly as it had begun, the noise fell silent.

The men in the car weren't moving.

'What the blazes . . .?' Burt threw down his rifle.

Nils was on his back in the road. Tom ran over and knelt beside him, felt for a pulse in his neck. Nothing. He shook him gently, but he knew it was no use. His chest was ripped open.

He stood up. The men in the car still hadn't moved. Burt strode towards him but stopped as Tom shook his head.

Piet strode over waving his rifle. 'What the fuck did you think you were doing? Why didn't you wait for the Wehrmacht truck?'

'How were we to know there'd be a car?'

Piet grabbed Burt by the lapel. 'You jumped the gun, you absolute clown. And now look at the mess we're in. Didn't you know there were orders from the SS that no cars were to be stopped by Wehrmacht under any circumstances?'

'What?'

'It's a new rule. They just brought it in a month ago. To stop people like us from assassinating the SS. And you only bloody fell for it.' He pushed Burt hard in the chest. 'Now we've lost Nils.'

Tom turned then to where the car was, its doors flung open. He crept warily towards it. One German was half-hanging over the passenger door.

The man in the back had lost his SS cap, but was motionless. The other two were slumped in the front seats, blood staining the backs of their uniforms.

In the distance another engine.

'That's the truck.' Piet grabbed Burt's arm. 'We've no more ammo. We've got to move.'

'What about Nils?' Tom asked.

'No. Just get your arse out of here!' Burt dragged Tom towards the cycles. Piet was already ahead of them.

Tom somehow managed to clamber into the saddle. Behind him he heard the truck engine die and then shouts, but he didn't dare stop the frantic pumping of his legs.

As soon as they could, they dismounted, shoved their cycles behind a church, and crouched behind the gravestones. They didn't dare look up but heard the truck go by, slowly. He imagined the soldiers scouring the graveyard for them.

Finally they heard it drive away, taking with it their precious cargo of food.

When it had gone, they set off walking back into the town, trying to act like a German patrol. Tom was shaky. Nils' blood was on his cuffs. What if they met another German patrol? He prayed they wouldn't, and took his cue from Burt who was strolling, relaxed, rifle at his shoulder. Tom tried to get into the feeling of being how the Germans usually were – sure of themselves, invulnerable.

Burt seemed impervious to fear. Perhaps he was just used to it. About a mile into the city, Burt led him down a side street and knocked on a door. The woman who opened it stepped back in shock.

'It's alright,' Burt said, holding his hands up in reassurance. 'Not German. Friends. The uniforms are just a disguise. Fetch Lars.'

Tom guessed that must be the husband. The woman let them in, though she was not pleased to see them, he could see that by her manner. She let them into her dining room and then called someone on the telephone.

'What about Piet?' Tom asked

'He'll be okay, he's experienced, he knows where to go.'

An hour later, a van drew up outside her house, and Piet was already in the back.

The driver, Lars, began speaking in rapid Dutch, gesticulating. His accent was not easy to understand, but it was obvious he was saying the operation had been a complete cock up.

Burt translated. 'We've only taken out General Weiter and his aides.'

It meant nothing to Tom.

Burt gave an exasperated sigh. 'Himmler's right-hand man and a big nob in the SS.'

'Then good riddance.'

'We wish. The bastard's still alive. They took him to hospital. But he's ordered a house-to-house search. That's why we've got to get back to Fransine's right now. Warn everyone.'

'Shit. I thought they were all dead. He'll recognise me if he sees me again.'

'No, it was all too quick, and we got him in the head and lungs. Doubt if he got a chance for a proper look. Bastard won't be coming out of hospital for a good while, is my guess. But the Nazis won't let this go, I know that much.'

'What will they do?'

'God only knows. Reprisals, I should think.'

Fransine was raging. She told them in scathing tones that they had put the whole cell at risk.

'You're bad luck, you are,' she said to Tom in her heavily accented English. 'Whoever said you were any use to us wants his head examining.'

He ignored it but couldn't help wondering if it was true.

All night they were on tenterhooks waiting for the search, but the night was eerily quiet.

'I'm going to see what's going on,' Fransine said the next morning.

'I'll buy a paper to see what the report is. You stay here,' she said to Tom. 'You've done enough damage.'

He didn't see how it could all be his fault, but he guessed she had to blame someone.

Piet puffed himself up and went with Fransine, but Tom and Burt were told to lie low, and they waited in the millinery shop for her return.

With Fransine out, it felt like a straitjacket had been removed. Tom took in a deep breath, felt his lungs expand. They waited all day, wondering why Fransine hadn't returned, until Tom realised the time. It was seven, English time. If he was quick, he just had the time to get on the wireless to Neil. If Fransine wasn't there, she'd never know.

Tom was aware of Burt watching his sudden activity as he searched out the radio under the machine cover, but Burt didn't stop him when he unravelled the aerial and hung it from an upstairs window. He merely smoked his foul herbal cigarette, foot tapping, wearing an air of disapproval.

'I have to do this,' Tom said, 'so don't look at me like that.'

Burt pulled the shop blind down. 'You're risking our skins, you know that? And we're already in the shit.'

Tom didn't reply. He had the silk code ready, which he always kept inside the label of his vest. His underwear was the only thing he'd managed to retain, though it was a danger. Burt watched him – the unpicking of the label, the finding of the frequency and the painstaking clicking of the Morse button.

'Yes!' he was elated when he got the okay signal.

'Quick then.' Burt said. 'They could be back at any moment.'

MISSED YOU Neil morsed after he'd given his call sign. The next message told Tom that Neil was now working for Radio Oranje. Tom morsed his congratulations and told Neil that he was 'on holiday' now, and going to look up 'Aunt Vera', their code for him being in the occupied zone searching for Nancy.

GIVE AUNT VERA MY REGARDS came the reply, OVER.

It sounded so simple.

Tom daren't do more in case the Nazi detector vans tracked them down. But he had a momentary flash of Neil's face, sitting in his living room at home in London. He was glad Neil had got his job with Radio Oranje at last. Thinking of him on the other end of the line gave Tom a sharp stab of both euphoria and pain.

'She won't let you go,' Burt said, interrupting his thoughts.

'Who?' Tom was confused.

'She told me. Fransine likes to control everything. But it's how we've survived this long. She's meticulous. She wants you here where she can keep an eye on you. Plus, your Dutch is too poor to risk you going anywhere else.'

'Thanks for nothing. I can understand most things and ask for stuff. I thought I was doing quite well.'

Burt shrugged. 'Maybe it sounds okay to a German. But it's still bad Dutch. Best tell it like it is, mate.'

Tom put the transmitter back under the machine cover and wound in the antenna. 'You won't tell her I've been on?'

'What do you take me for? Nah. Your secret's safe with me.'

The door crashed open and adrenalin shot up Tom's spine. The detector van! Tom grabbed his pistol, ready for the Gestapo.

But no. Standing in the doorway was a woman – hysterical, clutching herself around the waist, eyes streaming under a knitted beret.

'What?' Burt said, taking a step towards her and immediately dropping his pistol to his side. 'Angelique?'

She tried but failed to utter a word, her face contorted with crying.

Tom hurried over to try to comfort her, but she pushed him angrily away.

She pointed an accusing finger at them. Tom made out enough of the words to understand what was happening. 'Fransine's dead,' she said, struggling to speak. 'Shot. In the square.' She gabbled off a lot more in Dutch, wringing her hands and shouting.

'What is it? I didn't catch it all, and who is she?'

'Oh, your expert Dutch failing you now, is it? She's Angelique, one of our couriers. They shot Fransine. With . . . I don't know, thirty others. They brought prisoners from Scheveningen. And took more off the street. Anyone who was watching. Women. Women off the street. Crying for them not to shoot their little children.'

'Fransine?' Tom asked. 'You're sure?'

Angelique's eyes blazed. 'I saw it all. Saw her shout, '*Oranje zal overwinnen.*'

Orange shall overcome.

'What about Piet?' Tom asked urgently. 'Was he with her?'

'It's chaos. They wouldn't let us leave. They rounded him up just before dusk, after the first lot had been shot,' Angelique said bitterly. 'He didn't survive. Reprisals because of the men murdered in Weiter's car.'

Tom didn't dare look at Burt. It was them. They'd been the ones to bring this about. He felt sick.

'And you say they shot prisoners?' he asked in halting Dutch.

'Brought by truck. Two loads. They forced us to watch, corralled us in. When they began pulling more from the crowd, I thought my time was up. One woman wet herself. But they made us watch until they searched them for their papers and there was nothing but blood running in the street. You can't understand the silence after all that shooting. It was thick as snow.' She dashed away her tears.

Tom leant back against a desk; he thought his legs might give way.

Burt rushed to a cupboard and brought out a flask. 'Brandy,' he said. 'Drink it.'

Angelique drank it in gulps, wiping her mouth, rubbing her wet cheeks.

They watched her drink. Tom turned to Burt, and spoke in a low voice. 'Without Fransine, what'll happen to the network?'

Tom asked. Shooting at the wrong car was sending ripples in all directions. He had a sudden sense of everything being out of his control.

'The Nazis will come to take over the shop as soon as they know who she is,' Burt said. 'It seems they don't know she was a member of the Resistance yet. She was just a woman in the wrong place. Which means we've got to get out of here. They'll be coming for us once they see her false papers.' He turned to Angelique and spoke in Dutch. 'Don't come here anymore. There's a man called Karel in Amsterdam, owns a hardware shop. Citroenstraat 10. His wife's called Luska. I think he's still there. Try to find him, it's not safe to stay here.'

'Will you let Fransine's people know?' she asked.

'Of course,' Burt said. 'Rest easy. Go home now and keep undercover until you can get to Karel.'

Within a few moments she'd gone.

'Who else should we contact?' Tom asked. 'Is there a list?'

'No-one.' Burt was already opening and closing drawers. 'We'll keep quiet. Best to get the hell out of it altogether. Check the cupboards and the machine covers will you? Anything useful. We'll leave Dordrecht and head into the country. Too dangerous to contact anyone else in case the *Moffen* have already found them.' He paused. 'What are you waiting for? Grab a holdall and put in anything useful. We'll go across country as much as we can.'

'I'm going nowhere,' Tom said. 'Not until I know where Nancy is. Agent Ludo. I'll go there.'

Burt came close and fixed him with narrowed eyes. 'No, you won't. If you must know, she's in The Hague and it's a hotbed of Nazi bigwigs and Gestapo. More there than anywhere else, all bitter that they're losing and wanting to take it out on men like you. It would be a suicide run. Cities are out.' He turned to open another drawer, shoved a German stick grenade in his belt. 'Small towns are safest.'

'What? You knew where Nancy was all along, and you never said a word?'

No answer.

'For God's sake, Burt!' He was so angry he could barely speak. 'I trusted you. I thought you were on my side.'

'I had orders, that's all.'

'I've had enough. Fuck you. I'm not some kid you can all bully. I'm going to The Hague.'

'You're crazed.'

'No, I'm not. I'm saner than I've ever been. Fransine's not here to stop me. This Resistance cell is finished, so it makes no difference to anyone what the hell I do.'

'They'll eat you alive. You won't last two minutes.'

'Watch me. I'll get there somehow. What does it matter to you anyway?'

'It matters because I still can't get over the fact that you're upper crust Tom Lockwood of the parquet corridors of Baker Street. That you're actually here at all.'

'And I can't get over the fact that you, Agent Leapfrog, the biggest duffer at coding, the one who couldn't even solve the test code to save his life, is . . . still alive.'

Burt looked angry a moment, before his face split into a grin. He began to laugh. 'Don't know why I'm laughing,' he said. 'Go on then, I'll not stop you. If you've got the guts to try it, then good luck to you. But I've got a cover name to help you.'

Tom waited.

'Everyone knows of Agent Ludo, they call her 'the cat with nine lives' – the only woman to last that long. She's had several names, but right now she's going under Danique Koopman. The name of the widow of an industrialist. A Nazi supporter. She's undercover pretending to be the lover of an SS man.'

It was a second or two before Tom could take this in. *The lover of an SS man.* The shock reverberated through him so his pulse began to race. He turned Burt by the shoulder, desperate for answers. 'Do you have an address? Is she okay? Have you—?'

Burt held up his hands to ward off the barrage of questions. 'That's all I know. All Fransine would tell me.'

He grabbed Burt by the sleeve. He didn't want Nancy being anyone else's lover. 'How will I find her?'

Burt shrugged him off and didn't answer, he was too busy rifling through drawers and shoving stuff into a bag.

'Burt?'

Engine noise. A motorcycle. And a flash of light under the crack in the blackout blind. Tom dived to the window and lifted the blind a fraction to peer out.

He dropped it back as if it was red hot. 'Gestapo.'

'This way!' Burt was already on the move.

Tom didn't need to be told twice, he was right on Burt's heels as they careered towards the fire exit at the back.

'No, not the back,' yelled Burt, 'they'll have men there.' He sprinted up the stairs, just as there was banging on the door. Tom hared up after him, into a dark bedroom where Burt grabbed a hooked pole to open the trapdoor in the ceiling.

'What the . . .?'

Burt hooked a wood and rope ladder out of the hole. 'Up!' he hissed.

Tom didn't think, just grabbed the swaying ladder and grappled his way up, reaching his arm down for the holdall.

Below, they heard a window smash and the tinkle of glass.

Burt hoisted himself up and dragged up the ladder. 'It goes right across,' he said. 'Go go go!'

Tom was off then across the attic, crouching so as not to bang his head. He made an almighty racket, but it was matched by the sounds from below of banging doors and breaking glass.

German voices. And then Burt scampering towards him like a fox in a hunt.

An almighty bang and the attic trembled like in an earthquake. The air bloomed with smoke and dust. The stick grenade. Burt must have lobbed it.

One of the attics adjoining had a skylight which let in a faint glimmer of light, and Tom's eyes were adjusting now, so he could make out the dim shapes of joists and roof trusses. They scrambled across three houses before coming to a brick wall at the end of the block and a trapdoor in the floor. Tom scraped it open.

There was no ladder.

'Jump, okay?' Burt said.

The house beneath smelled of mould and decay. Obviously nobody lived there. He shunted to the edge and prepared to jump and roll, the way he had read that parachutists did.

The floor came up to hit him too soon and the roll was more of a flop. A crack as he smacked his elbow on the banisters, which set a ripple of fuzzy pain up his arm. He gasped but was on his feet to get out of the way for Burt.

First the holdall, then Burt's feet landed with a great thump, but in an instant Burt was scrabbling downstairs like a whippet. 'Out the back!'

Tom leapt after him. Through the kitchen – stripped bare, no cupboards, no furniture. *Looted*, Tom thought as he fled after Burt, brought up short, crashing into Burt's back.

Burt was breathless, his panting only matched by Tom's own. Burt peered out of the back door. A broken lock dangled.

'Quick!' Burt struggled out of his shoes and pointed to Tom to do the same. 'We'll make less noise.'

Then he turned, briefly, to give Tom the signal to run.

Tom gripped tight to his shoes and ran. He saw little, only the flash of the icy ground and the burn of it through his socks as his feet slithered painfully down the road, keeping to the shadows, head down, not daring to look. He was dimly aware of a cluster of motorcycles and vehicles parked outside the milliners and dark helmeted figures gathered in the gloom. Smoke pouring from the front door and men yelling. No moon, thank God.

Burt was loping onwards, going at a lick. Tom fixed his eyes on his back. His eyes watered from the pain of running over bomb debris on the frozen ground.

Around the corner, heart thumping so hard he was sure it would burst through the skin. He wanted to stop, the stitch in his side was making him double over, but he daren't lose Burt, who dodged sideways and crouched down behind the wall of one of the houses.

Tom couldn't see what was up, but followed his lead, just as a sleek black car came around the corner, headlights slicing the road. He was just inside the gateway, squatting like an animal, when it roared by, grinding to a halt outside Fransine's shop.

He didn't wait, but as soon as it passed, ran to catch up with Burt.

'Jesus, that was close,' Burt said. 'You okay?'

'How did you know about the attics and the trapdoor?'

'One of Fransine's contingency plans.' He paused a moment. 'She was tough. We're not the only ones who owe her our lives. Christ, what a mess.' He began hurrying away. 'Let's get out of here before they rumble us.'

'Where you headed?' Tom asked.

'The Hague. Or I'll never hear the end of it. Where d'you bloody think?'

Tom grinned. 'Guess I'd better tag along.'

'You damn well will. Come on, let's go find Agent Ludo.'

Chapter 23

The Hague

As she swung in through the lobby doors Nancy was ready to tell Steef what she'd found out at work about the deportations, and Josef's condition. Only a few days remained before the trial and their attempt to get him out.

To her surprise, Steef was already waiting impatiently and approached her as soon as she came through the door. 'Trouble,' he said. 'Come in the back.'

Nazi Wehrmacht men were passing through the lobby, so Nancy waited for them to go, pretending to search her handbag for her key, before she dodged into Steef's small cupboard-like room.

'What?' she asked, her voice low.

'I had an enquiry today from a Frau Koopman. From Arnhem.' He let the words sink in. 'To rent an apartment in this block. A friend of hers already lodges here.'

'What? You told me she was dead. It can't be the same person, surely?'

'It is. The real Danique Koopman's still alive. I asked for ID and she gave me her current address but also the address of her husband's business and their former apartment in Nijmegen. It's her. She told me her husband had died and she's been staying with a friend in Arnhem. No mistake. She's arriving in The Hague on Monday. The six-thirty train in the evening. The only passenger train still running. And she only knows someone here and wants to live in the same building as them! Of course I said I'd meet her and show her the apartment. I couldn't risk her renting elsewhere in The Hague.'

'What shall we do?'

'Get rid of her, of course. It's terrible timing. We can't have two of you, and she'll blow your cover if she comes here. We'll meet her, you'll interview her, find out what you can about her, and then we'll dispose of her.'

'But what about the person she knows? The friend who lives here? Do we know who that is?'

'A man called Ritschel of the SS. He's a hardened Nazi, one in control of overseeing the logistics of the Jewish deportations. He's on the top floor. Apartment four.'

'Shit.'

'I know. The last thing we need, now you're all set up.'

'This Ritschel, I've never set eyes on him, thank God. What will we do about him?'

'We'll have to remove him too somehow. I have a key to the apartment, so we can get in.'

'We? It's not my fault. Who thought this alias was a good idea?'

'It was researched thoroughly, but it's war. Mistakes happen. We weren't to know. We needed someone with impeccable Nazi credentials.'

'And now two people have to die?' She put her hands to her forehead, trying to take it in. 'Is this Ritschel the only one in The Hague who knows her?'

'She gave that impression, we'll have to hope so. When we meet her, we can interrogate her and find out.'

'I can't believe this is happening.'

'Look, we need you to keep your cover. Getting insider information about Scheveningen and getting Josef out is more important than anything else.'

'Janitor?' An impatient voice in German.

Steef thrust a batch of clean linen into Nancy's hands. 'Yes, Frau Koopman,' he said loudly. 'Straightaway, it won't happen again. I'll speak to the launderer.' And he chivvied her out of the door.

Whilst waiting for the lift, clutching her unwanted clean pillowcases, she heard Steef placating the Nazi resident. He'd wanted to send a telegram and was blaming Steef for last night's lack of electricity.

As the lift rose, she clasped her arms around the pillowcases, inhaling the smell of starch, holding herself tight. This was one thing she had never expected. That the real Frau Koopman would turn up. Assassinations were always bad news. And somehow, the killing of her namesake had to be a bad omen.

In the Oranjehotel, Fritz handed a slip of paper to Keller.

'The train comes in at six-thirty, got it?' He passed the slip over with the time and the platform number. 'Make sure you're there, and then follow the woman wherever she goes.'

'What's her name?'

Fritz didn't want to say. 'It's classified. But one of our men, Dobermann, should be following her on the train. I've told him to tell the guards to alert him when her *Ausweis* comes through.'

'How will I know it's him?'

'He'll be wearing his Nazi Party brassard on the wrong arm. So when you see that, you'll know it's the woman he's following. He'll give you the eye. Fall in behind her and see where she goes. I guess she'll try to find a taxi, so detail someone to be ready with a car. Once you have an address, you can report back to me.'

'Should I approach her?'

'No. On no account. And I don't want her to know we're on to her. I just want surveillance for now.'

Chapter 24

'Ready?' Steef asked. He and Nancy were waiting under the canopy at Hollands Spoor Railway Station. 'You'll be doing the interrogation, okay?'

The place was busy with uniformed Nazis waiting for the train, all impatient at having to wade through the glut of refugees from other parts of Holland, people with nowhere else to go. She watched two *Moffen* clear a path through the crowd by shoving them out of the way with the butts of their rifles.

Nancy clutched her handbag to her stomach. The interrogation worried her. She was to quiz Frau Koopman to find out who she knew in The Hague, and to promise her she'd go free if she cooperated. Steef thought this would be better coming from a woman. Afterwards, Frau Koopman would be killed. It was no good pretending otherwise. Nancy swallowed and put this thought to the back of her head.

The train was late. A goods train had come in, and there was confusion over which platform the passenger train would pull in at. Steef and Nancy rushed up the stairs and over the bridge, jostling with the rest of the crowd.

Steef was dressed in a neat suit, an NSB badge on his lapel, and had an umbrella hooked over his arm. He'd told Frau Koopman he'd be carrying one aloft, so she could find him in the crush.

Nancy's stomach was full of butterflies.

In the distance, the rumble of the train and a piercing whistle. The crowd shifted forwards to the edge of the platform. With a belch of steam, the train creaked by them before it clanked to a halt.

Most of the passengers disembarking were men in Wehrmacht uniform, but one woman, an imperious looking woman in a grey hat, made a beeline for Steef, who was holding up the umbrella like a flagpole. But she wasn't alone. A small boy of about seven was clinging to her hand. He was dressed in the Dutch *Nationale Jeugdstorm* uniform of blue shirt and black tie, with the obligatory *Karpoets* – the black wool cap with the seagull badge.

Steef shot Nancy a look. This wasn't in the plan. But he stepped forwards to greet Frau Koopman calmly. She was older than Nancy, with a face that looked as though it was carved from marble, but the boy's eyes were wide, staring around at all the people, taking everything in.

'Herr Brouwer?' she asked.

'Good to meet you, Frau Koopman,' he said. 'And who is this?'

'My nephew, Dex.'

Dex stood to attention. '*Heil Hitler,*' he squeaked.

Nancy acknowledged the greeting, but her stomach dropped. No-one had mentioned a relative, let alone a child. What were they to do?

Steef filled the awkward gap. 'Well, I trust you both had a pleasant journey.'

Frau Koopman gave him a look that said, *you know perfectly well I haven't.* 'Is the apartment far?'

'I'm sorry, but there's been a change of plan,' Steef said to Frau Koopman. 'The apartment you asked about has already been let.

Your friend asks that I drop you at the De Beurs Hotel instead until there's a vacancy.'

What? Nancy tried to work out the new plan. The De Beurs Hotel was a rundown place in the middle of the oldest area of The Hague. A place that housed, as they all did now, German troops and their *Moffenmeiden*, or prostitutes. She couldn't imagine Frau Koopman there, but she knew they couldn't take her back to the apartments either.

'This way,' Steef said. 'Our car is waiting.' He introduced Nancy. 'This is Frau Aisling, my secretary. Just follow us.' *Secretary. That was rich.*

'I need my luggage.' Frau Koopman's eyes had already dismissed Nancy as of no account, as she turned to yell for a porter. Of course there were no porters now. Evidently realising her error, Frau Koopman summoned the train guard who handed down her luggage. There were several suitcases and bags. Nancy wondered what was in them all, fascinated by this woman she was supposed to be impersonating. She steeled herself. The woman was a Nazi party member. One of those that had brought desolation and destruction in its wake.

She followed the little group out of the concourse, trying to get close enough to Steef to ask him what was happening, but he strode resolutely ahead to where Albie, another of their resistance friends, waited with the car. Albie was wearing a chauffeur's cap and looked tidier than usual, his moustache tamed and trimmed.

'De Beurs Hotel,' Steef said, with the air of a man ordering a taxi. Albie startled and turned to catch Nancy's eye with a look that meant, 'What's going on?' He was supposed to drive Frau Koopman to the old bank so they could interrogate and then eliminate her.

Steef cast her a look that said, 'I know what I'm doing,' as they stowed everything into the trunk of the car. Nancy's gaze shifted to the boy. He gave her a shy smile.

She blinked, unable to smile back.

As Frau Koopman chivvied the boy to climb in, Nancy thought she saw Detlef Keller just by the ticket office. She ducked her head and quickly got in the back seat too. She prayed he hadn't seen her. What was he doing here instead of at the prison?

No. She must be imagining it. Albie set the car in motion, with Steef in the front seat.

'We didn't know you were bringing your nephew,' Nancy said.

'His mother wanted him away from enemy lines and the bombs. Safer in The Hague, I think.'

The irony of this statement took Nancy's breath away. The men said nothing. Now Frau Koopman was in the car, no-one wanted to talk. A sheen of sweat was visible on Steef's neck, she noticed, despite the chill. Frau Koopman seemed unconcerned, but stared out of the window, gloved hands clasped in her lap. The nephew sat quietly biting a thumbnail.

When they pulled up at the hotel, Steef got out to help Frau Koopman with her luggage and made to go inside with her and her nephew.

Nancy saw Frau Koopman look up at the rundown façade with disapproval.

As soon as they were out of the car, Albie turned. 'What the hell's he playing at?'

'I don't know!' Nancy said. 'She was supposed to be eliminated. A contact called Erik is waiting at our hideout at the bank for us to bring her back there. He was to do the job and get a car to dispose of the body. But whatever's going on, it puts paid to my cover story.'

They sat in glum silence until Steef came out.

'Just drive,' he said. 'Get us back to our apartments.'

Albie put the car in gear and drove away.

Steef burst out, 'Look, it was the only thing I could think of. I wasn't going to kill the kid, was I? He's like my Rudi. Same age. But I knew she couldn't come back with us, or it would blow your cover. And the Hotel des Indes is impossible – too full of Schneider's friends.'

'But what about Ritschel?' Nancy asked. 'Won't he wonder why his friend hasn't turned up?'

'I'll deliver him a message, saying she's been delayed. Give us time to deal with him before he asks too many questions. Erik's been detailed to do that job too.'

Nancy made a frustrated groan. 'She'll try to contact him tonight, bet you. I would, if I were her. And especially put in that rundown place.'

'It's an unholy mess,' Albie said. 'You should have stuck to the plan. Killed the kid too. Now we're in worse shit.'

'I'll sort it,' Steef snapped. 'Leave it to me.'

'How?' Albie asked. 'How can she pretend to be Frau Koopman now? What's she supposed to do, with this other one walking around The Hague like an unexploded bomb?'

'I've said, I'll fix it, haven't I? So trust me.'

Nancy said nothing. Arguing wasn't going to help. She just looked out of the window watching the darkened city flow by, and wondering if really this time, she had come to the end of the line.

The next morning a note from Steef had been slid under Nancy's door. She opened it and read:

Our visitor from the South will have a friend to show her and her nephew around the city to see who she meets and where she goes. Do your job as usual.

What did that mean? Someone had been assigned to Frau Koopman as a minder? Was it Erik? He was the double agent she'd heard Steef speak of. It made her extra wary. Could they trust him?

Nancy read the message again before burning it. As she did so, the thought 'playing with fire' wouldn't leave her. Erik couldn't be with Frau Koopman twenty-four hours a day, could he?

Nancy got ready for her day with Fritz with even more misgivings. When he arrived to escort her to the car though, she put on a brave face and made a mental note of the last-minute things she needed to find out that day for Josef's rescue mission – the exact time the Dutch police were collecting him from the Oranjehotel and what time his trial was to take place.

She ticked off her mental list. She must remember she'd need to engineer a chance to ring and tell the laundry that they didn't need a delivery this week.

'You're sure it was Herr Bouwer from our apartments?' Fritz asked Keller, as he paced his office.

'Positive. And he was with Danique Koopman, your new secretary. They took the other woman to the De Beurs Hotel. She had a boy with her, her son maybe? I watched them check in from the car. Afterwards Brouwer and Danique came back home to our apartments.'

Schneider frowned, tapped his fist on the desk. A son. Now that was interesting.

'Who is the woman, sir?'

Fritz chewed his lip, unwilling to unveil his suspicion to Keller. 'Arrest Herr Brouwer and bring him in for questioning, okay? Put him in number eight.'

'What about Danique?'

'No. Let's have Herr Brouwer first, see what he can tell us. And Keller,' he pointed a finger at him, 'not a word to Danique. I don't want her to suspect anything. Not yet.'

'What's she done?'

'I don't know. Probably nothing. But I had a tip-off, and I daresay with a bit of persuasion, Herr Brouwer will tell us everything.'

Nancy's day was orderly except for her nerves which meant she'd developed an itchy rash on her inner arm. Stress, she supposed. Fritz Schneider was evidently a man who was used to putting his thoughts into different compartments, because that day there were no further interrogations and she was left to file papers and type deportation lists. In fact, he was curiously absent.

Once, he came in to stare at her as she typed. His eyes held an assessing gaze. A look that made her feel as if a ghost had walked in. He couldn't know about the other Danique, could he? No, she was just overwrought, imagining things.

Keller appeared late in the morning, stuck to her side, even during lunch in the canteen. It made her edgy. Hesitant to get out her notebook, she made copious mental notes and made sure all was ready for Friday's plan.

On the way home in his staff car, Fritz was back to being the polite and charming man who was her friend. The wild-eyed man who had pushed her roughly against his office wall was gone. But she wasn't fooled, she knew the wolf was still there under the sheep's clothing.

He held the door open for her to get out of the car, but didn't make small talk the way he usually did.

In the lobby she looked for Steef but instead there was a new man behind the desk. He had the NSB badge on his lapel.

Fritz approached him and gave him the *Sieg Heil* which was returned. 'Ah, Mulder, good to see you again. I hope you will find everything you need.'

'Yes, sir, of course sir.'

They went to wait for the lift. She was concerned about Steef. 'What happened to Herr Brouwer? Is he retired?'

'We found a transmitter in his cupboard. We took him in for questioning.'

He was watching her reaction with a slight smile. She kept her eyes blank. *No. They'd found her transmitter.* 'How inconvenient,' she said lightly. 'Still, I expect the new man will be better.' Inside, her mind was screaming, *Not Steef. Not my only friend in this building.* Would the plan still go ahead? If only Steef could hold out for long enough.

'You'll dine with me tonight?' Fritz asked, as they went up in the lift, Mesman standing behind them as usual.

'I think not. I'm a little tired. I think I'll have an early night.'

Fritz ignored her refusal. 'I thought my chef could cook something special.'

Hunger made it tempting. *Play carefully.* 'I would have loved to,' she said, 'but I'm feeling a little under the weather, achy, and I feel as if I might have a cold coming on.'

'I hope not,' he said, stepping away from her in the confined space. 'When did it start?'

'Only about an hour ago. I suddenly began to feel chilled, and my throat is sore.'

The lift doors opened and they got out.

'I'm not surprised,' Fritz said as he followed her to her apartment. 'The weather has been terrible the last few weeks. I don't know why it is always so damp here. In Germany we have such crisp clear winters, not this terrible dreary greyness. That's the trouble with this awful low-lying land, all those mists can't be good for the chest. No wonder people get ill. Can I get you anything?'

She paused outside the lift. 'No. It's probably just a cold, but I don't want you to catch it, dear Fritz, and I want to be fit for work tomorrow.'

She could tell by his hard expression Fritz wasn't pleased. She always had to be the perfect friend he imagined, not a real woman subject to colds and troubles as other people were.

'I'll rest up, and I'll see you in the morning,' she said. 'Thank you for the lift.'

He gave her a small bow, and strode away towards the stairs. She breathed a sigh of relief. She knew he would not see her the next day, or ever again. Especially not now they had taken Steef. Their whole cell was at risk. She prayed he could hold out. *Twenty-four hours*, was always the instruction. Against beatings, electrocution, water torture. Hold on for twenty-four hours so the rest had time to run.

She hurried down the corridor fumbling for her key. Even if they got Josef out, she wouldn't be able to stay in this apartment. The SS would realise straight away that the only new person who could have got information about the inside of the prison was Schneider's mysterious female friend, Danique Koopman. She prayed the real Frau Koopman would never escape her minder.

Nancy had forgotten all about Margarete until she found the apartment door unlocked and Margarete cooking in her kitchen.

She cursed under her breath. All she wanted was to be alone. To escape this nightmare of pretence as soon as possible. She went into the bedroom, shut the door and packed only a few things into her small handbag. Everything belonging to Danique Koopman had to stay exactly where it was. She'd already set up the excuse that 'Danique' would be too ill to go to work, and must stay in bed, but the problem was, if she was going to be ill, how would she get out of the apartment without Margarete becoming suspicious?

Chapter 25

Thursday, the day of Josef's trial, and the cold was knife-sharp. A coating of frost had etched the apartment windows with ferns and Nancy couldn't help but shiver. How very convincing, she thought – after all, she was pretending to be ill with a cold. Steef was in the hands of the Stapo and every door slam made her think they were coming for her.

She tottered to the door when she heard Margarete preparing breakfast, and croaked, 'My cold's got worse. Please will you do me a favour? Run over and tell Fritz I am too unwell to come to work.'

Margarete frowned. 'Let me feel your forehead.' She laid a clammy hand on her, and said, 'You are not too hot. Have you any aspirin?'

'No, I don't need anything. Just apologise to Fritz for me and tell him that I'll send him a message when I'm well enough to return.'

'You're not going to work?'

'No. I'm not well enough. My head is throbbing.'

Margarete tutted and kept on staring at her.

'Go and tell him, please, Margarete. He may need to make some arrangements for someone else to cover my duties.'

Margarete was reluctant. No-one wants to be the bearer of bad news; but finally she went.

Nancy rubbed her forehead and cheeks until they were red and grabbed a handkerchief.

It was a good thing she did, for less than ten minutes later, Margarete was back with Fritz frowning at her shoulder.

Fritz examined her from the door. 'A cold is nothing much. You will feel better if you get up.'

'I can't, Fritz. I'm aching all over.'

He was about to step closer, but she held up a hand. 'No! Don't come any nearer,' she croaked. 'I don't want you to catch it.'

He surveyed her with narrowed eyes. Was he suspicious? 'Margarete will fetch you something for it,' he said. 'I know where she can get honey and also something for the headache. I have a small bottle of brandy too in my apartment. Perhaps it's influenza. You must stay in bed and rest.'

'Thank you, Fritz, dear.' She apologised again for being so ill and unable to go to work.

Fritz gave a shrug. 'I could have done with some help today. My men will interrogate Steef Brouwer and it will need typing up.' A pause. 'In case we can find any of his associates.'

He knew. She had a sudden flash of insight and a cold tremor ran through her body. She felt the danger like an icy undercurrent, but was powerless to do anything about it. *Stay calm. Don't react.*

'The Resistance's days are numbered,' Fritz said. 'General Weiter's still in hospital, and though reprisals have taken place, we have reason to believe the perpetrators might flee to The Hague now that their leaders are dead. They won't find much of a network here though. Most of their resistance friends are enjoying our hospitality at what they call the Orangehotel. The SS are combing the city thoroughly though. They won't get away with picking us off like that.'

'Good,' she croaked. 'The resistance men have got away with too much recently.'

'And women,' he said casually. 'Don't forget some of them are women.'

A moment of silence. She filled it with a cough.

'I'll be busy with transfers too. Himmler's sent an urgent telegram requesting more prisoners for public execution. He's determined to prompt anyone sheltering resistance workers to hand them over. It means more paperwork of course.'

She kept her face blank, though the horror of such a request made her freeze inside. 'I'm so sorry, Fritz. Does that mean the trials today won't take place?'

'Of course not. Procedure must always be followed. Those that are to go to trial will still do so. We will supply the firing squads with riff-raff, that's all. People no-one cares about.'

There are no such people.

But thank goodness the trial would still take place. She coughed and apologised yet again. Fritz blinked at her outburst and seemed to soften. 'Ach, it is no fun being ill. You must be careful; chest infections are easily caught in this damp climate.' He turned to Margarete and issued rapid instructions, telling her where to get various cough remedies from Nazi suppliers. Nancy gave an inward sigh of relief. Thank God, Margarete would go out, and whilst she was gone 'Danique' would do her disappearing act.

She heard their muffled conversation in the hall, with Fritz impressing on Margarete that she was to fetch the medicines and then watch over Danique to make sure she took them.

This would be a problem, she couldn't predict exactly what Margarete would do when she came back and discovered 'Danique' had disappeared. Would she just search for her, or tell someone? What would she do? Perhaps she'd telephone Fritz. The thought made Nancy's skin clammy and her pulse race.

As soon as Fritz had gone and she heard the lift doors clang, Margarete appeared at Nancy's bedroom door, her hat jammed down over her ears. She threw an extra quilt on the bed and then told Nancy to try to sleep whilst she was out. She was obviously annoyed at this extra duty of fetching medicines.

When the door banged shut, Nancy leapt out of bed. She bundled the clothes under the quilt in a passable resemblance to a sleeping form, then changed her mind – that would make it look like she'd planned it. Better just to disappear. She swept up her coat.

This was the most dangerous part, getting out of here without being stopped.

She glanced at the clock. She'd have to be quick. She was due to be at the garage, where the van was waiting to rescue Josef, in less than twenty minutes. She tied a headscarf over her hair and pulled it low over her forehead. And now there were these extra prisoners to worry over; the ones going for execution. What could she do about them?

She took one last look at the apartment before she left. It always caught in her throat, this feeling when she had to leave somewhere for the last time, and the hollow feeling of having no identity and nowhere to call home.

She glanced out of the window. Fritz's car was still parked there with his chauffeur, Bakker. She'd have to wait until he left. She drummed her fingers on the sill, willing him to leave.

Fritz was back in his apartment, the telephone clamped to his ear, impatient for Keller to pick up the internal phone. *Come on, come on.*

Was Danique really ill? Fritz wasn't sure. He was torn by indecision, veering first one way then the other. The fact she could be fooling him was something he didn't want to admit to himself.

He shouldn't have been so rough with her in his office. If she was really Danique Koopman of the NSB, then he'd been crass.

Maybe his demands had been too pressing and she was backing off. The thought he might lose her felt like grief, a twisting agony.

No, she wouldn't have betrayed him, not his Danique.

Keller wasn't answering. Curse him. Where was he? Fritz rang off and dialled his number again. Only then did he remember he'd given Keller time off to visit the dentist. Had he already left?

Fritz was about to ring off when Keller picked up. 'Sorry, sir, I was in the bathroom.'

'Listen carefully. I want you to wait outside Danique Koopman's apartment and if she goes out, I want you to follow her and see where she goes.'

'Excuse me, sir, but my tooth . . . you agreed I could take this morning off. I've got a dental appointment at—'

'You'll need a longer appointment if you don't do what I ask.'

Fritz's car pulled away. A turn of the key in the lock, then Nancy headed along the corridor towards the stairs. She was about to go down, when she heard another door behind her bang shut. Involuntarily, she turned at the noise. Keller was striding towards her. There was no doubt he'd seen her, but she had no time to think, she just hurried down the steps, hand skimming the handrail.

'Frau Koopman!' he called. 'Danique! Wait!'

She didn't stop. Maybe he'd think he was mistaken.

She ran now, out of the door and around the corner into an alley, and pressed herself back against a doorway.

He didn't come after her. No doubt he would be going by car to the Oranjehotel. But would he tell Schneider he'd seen her going out? Probably. After all, Fritz would tell Keller she was ill, and wouldn't be in to work and Keller would then tell him he'd seen her going out. Damn, damn, damn.

Too late to do anything about it now. She hurried as fast as she dare, heels skidding, for ice made the pavements slippery. Down the dark back streets where no light fell on the glassy flags, and into a disused motor repair shop used by the Resistance. It was a place they'd broken into, and was empty, except for a few old exhaust pipes and dead batteries, and a van equipped with a gas chamber for fuel.

The men were already there, putting the finishing touches to the sign-written panels. It looked identical to the laundry van she'd described to them. Someone must have gone to photograph it, Erik probably.

'Good job,' she said to Albie, who was to be the driver.

They stood by to be briefed, although all of them already knew their roles. They would be dressed as laundry workers and the laundry van would follow the police car that was to take Josef from the Orangehotel to go to trial. The two vehicles would 'coincidentally' arrive within minutes of each other and therefore be in the loading dock at exactly the same time. Nancy's crew would wait until Josef was taken to the car, and then, using force if necessary, kidnap him from his minders, put him in the laundry van and bring him here.

It sounded easy.

'Here, put this on and get in,' Albie said. He handed her a laundry worker's grey overall coat. It was large on her, but would have to do. It covered all her other clothes and made her look drab. Inside the van, Nancy put on a pair of thick spectacles and a cap and sat down on top of the bale. It wasn't real laundry, but a batch of rags tied together with grey cloth to look like the uniforms.

She glanced over at Dolf and Thierry, two of their men who were also dressed as laundry workers in overalls and caps. They were armed with pistols fitted with silencers. Both men looked white with fear. Dolf was young, his face full of acne, his Adam's apple bobbing as he kept swallowing, whereas Thierry was a former shipyard worker, all brawn and muscle and glowering eyebrows.

They drove out and parked close to the police station where they waited for the black police car to come out of the side street.

213

They had one false alarm, where a van came out and they almost followed it.

'No,' Nancy said. 'Too early. That's a van. We're waiting for a car. The van'll be because they're going to be taking some other prisoners for execution. Schneider told me there are to be reprisals today.'

'Then we have to stop them!' Dolf said.

Albie turned in the driver's seat. 'We stick to the plan. We've had one plan go wrong already. We can't get diverted. We need to get Josef out. Everything else is secondary.'

'How can it be secondary when people will die?'

'People die every day. We have to choose our battles. Stopping executions will be messy. Too many people and not enough plan. We need to survive, and carry out our instructions. It might seem harsh, but there it is.'

Dolf wouldn't let go. 'You wouldn't say that if it was you going to be shot.'

'Just shut up, Dolf,' Albie snapped. 'We know it's bloody. No need to rub it in.'

The silence grew intense while they waited. Nancy knew the Nazis were sticklers for timing. Dolf let out growing sighs of frustration. It was another fifteen minutes before a black car pulled out.

'This is it,' Thierry said, 'Got to be. Fifteen minutes to collection on the dot.'

Albie started up the van. He let the police car get about five minutes in front of him before setting off for the Oranjehotel, aiming to arrive only four minutes after the Nazi Polizei. That would give the prison security guards time to get Josef from his cell.

Timing was everything. Nancy studied her watch – the seconds ticking inexorably round the face.

At the gate to the prison, the guards were used to seeing the laundry van arrive.

214

'You usually come on Fridays,' the guard said.

'The consignment came early,' Albie said, his German for 'consignment' hesitant. Nancy winced.

'And you're not our usual delivery man.'

'No,' Albie said. 'Our usual man got picked up the day before yesterday. He's gone to Germany to do factory work. Only us old ones left now.' He shoved his paperwork through the window, and the guard looked it over.

The guard glanced at it briefly, and then handed it back. He looked bored; he must do several of these checks every day, and the van was identical to the usual van, Albie's uniform identical to the usual man. With a shrug, he waved them through.

On the wooden bench inside the van, Nancy prepared herself. Being inside a Nazi fortress like this without Fritz's protection made her insides tremble, and worse, she was responsible for the plan. She'd thought it through dozens of times, trying to anticipate any failings, and there were too many, but this was their best shot.

Their only shot.

Through the windscreen ahead Nancy had a view of the black doors of the police car, which gaped open, waiting for Josef to be brought out. The green-clad policemen, one tall and wiry, one shorter and stockier, lounged against the concrete pillar, ready to take the prisoner from the prison guards. They rubbed their hands and stamped their boots in the cold air.

Nancy pulled her cloth laundry cap low over her forehead and peered through her disguise of thick spectacles. She clambered out of the back of the van, leaving the doors only slightly ajar to mask the men waiting inside, who were also dressed in factory clothes – caps pulled down, scarves muffled over their jaws.

She dragged the prison uniform bale to the platform and heaved it up by its string. No-one paid her any attention, though her pulse was pounding at her neck, and she could barely catch her breath. Slowly, as if it was a job she did every day, she went back to the van to get a second bale, and as she did, she heard voices and footsteps, the sound of people coming out of the prison. She almost faltered, so strong was her desire to turn, to see if it was Josef. But she didn't dare.

At the van she caught Dolf's eye and gave him an almost imperceptible nod.

The two Greens got ready to take custody of the prisoner, but their guns were still in their holsters; they were expecting a quiet handover.

It was time. She dragged out another bale and loaded it onto the platform. When she returned, with a sudden thrust, she flung the doors open. Two figures in grey leapt from the van and flashed past her.

Too late, she saw that Josef was handcuffed to the guard. Shit. She hadn't thought of that.

Too late because Dolf and Thierry were already shooting, their eyes wild with adrenalin.

One officer, a look of mild surprise on his face, tried to speak, but then fell, a bullet through his neck. The other guard, hand-cuffed to Josef, toppled and fell heavily, dragging Josef down with him, both men collapsing like demolished towers onto the concrete floor.

In a blink, Nancy took in that Josef was weak, thin, his hands broken, one eye already bruised closed. The police were slow to react but now one of them was turning towards her. She dived to crouch behind the doors of the white van, just as Dolf swivelled ready to shoot the taller man.

But Thierry was fractionally quicker and his shot hit home. Both the police fell, but the second one had managed to fire a shot. A muffled grunt from Dolf as he dropped to the ground. The police guns had no silencers and the crack was like a whip. She startled, knowing it would bring every prison guard for miles.

Dolf was groaning now, lying in the road, right in the way of their van. Thierry dragged him to the side, took out a gun and shot him at point-blank range in the forehead.

Nancy was horrified. 'What the hell?'

'We can't take him back with us, and he'd have talked, wouldn't he?' Thierry's words were broken up as he was trying to drag Josef clear of the guard. 'The whole lot of us, we'd be down the pan then.' He stuck out his chin. 'Trust me. He wasn't going to make it.' He wrestled a moment with the handcuffs. 'Don't just stand there! Find the key. We have to get Josef out.'

Nancy leapt in to search the pockets of the two guards for the key, clumsy fingers fumbling in the cold, she shoved her hands into their pockets dragging out anything she could find, cigarette packets, handkerchiefs, fluff.

'Just go,' groaned Josef, now aware of what was happening. He looked into her eyes. 'Do it, Rika,' he insisted. 'Leave me. I'm dead meat anyway.'

'No.' Nancy felt tears prick her eyes. She was still searching, but couldn't find the key. She couldn't accept the idea the plot had failed.

'Out!' Albie yelled through the driver's window. 'Move it! Now.' He was at the wheel, tyres screeching as he reversed out, frantically revving in case more prison guards came and sealed the gates.

'He's right,' Thierry said. 'Let's get out of here. One dead man is enough.'

He grasped Nancy by the arm trying to pull her away. 'No!' she said. 'A few more moments.'

'We can't.'

Thierry grabbed her around the neck, dragged her backwards and threw her bodily to the back of the van as it reversed out.

As they did so, shots rang out and the van window shed a shower of broken glass over them.

Albie drove like a man possessed, wind and glass in his face. They lurched around corners, up side streets, along the edge of the canal, and all the time, Nancy was thinking about Josef, lying there handcuffed to a dead man, and Dolf, shot by their own.

She began to shake violently. At the garage where they'd

217

camouflaged the van, the garage doors were open ready to receive them. As soon as they parked inside, Thierry leapt out immediately to drag the metal garage doors shut.

Inside, a group of people were ready, primed to give Josef a change of clothes, to rip off the van number plates, and take off the laundry stickers from the bodywork.

Albie killed the engine and got out, his face a mass of cuts. 'Bloody disaster,' he cursed.

Nancy followed Thierry, jumping out of the van from the back doors.

'Where's Josef?' someone said.

'We didn't get him. Just don't ask. And we lost Dolf.'

'What d'you mean, lost? Where is he?' Hannie, Dolf's girlfriend, grabbed Thierry by the arm.

'Shot,' Nancy said. 'By the police.' She didn't look at Thierry, or at Hannie, but at the ground.

Everyone began to talk at once. Hannie was shouting, demanding answers. At the same time, a fearful activity began as they hurried to remove the number plates and labels, all the incriminating evidence from the white van.

'The SS won't be far behind us,' Nancy said. 'Leave it. There's no time. We have to get out of here.'

'What about me?' the man who owned the van cried. 'I can't stay here.'

'Go with Albie. But we should scatter now. Meet later at Albie's so we can decide what to do.'

She ripped off her glasses and the laundry overalls, and Thierry did the same.

'Out the back way,' shouted Thierry, grabbing Hannie by the arm and hauling her, still protesting, towards the door.

'No! No. What about Dolf?'

'Shut up,' Thierry said, slapping her. 'D'you want to end up in a camp? Act like we're strolling. D'you understand?'

218

Hannie's face turned to stone, she bit her bottom lip but kept quiet.

Nancy saw the horror of this. That even grieving was to be forbidden. She changed her shoes with shaking hands and put on her coat. She followed them out, turning left where they turned right, her handbag over her arm, acting as if she was simply another woman out to queue for rations, though her chest was thudding and her legs felt limp, as if the tendons had been cut.

The sound of cars arriving at the front of the garage. Nancy ignored them, but as she rounded the corner she could see, reflected in a shop window, that a bunch of SS men were leaping from their cars and hammering on the garage door. That was her ninth life, she was sure.

She walked away, counting her steps to stay calm, curtailing her urge to run. What had they left in the garage? Anything that could lead them to her? Her mind wouldn't work. She'd had one too many close shaves, and her brain was shutting down. It was too exhausting to think.

Chapter 26

That afternoon they met at Albie's house. Nancy was relieved to get indoors after a day of skulking the streets.

'The SS are in a rage about it,' Albie said. 'Erik eliminated one of their top SS men last night. Ritschel of the SS. Slit his throat. Now two of their prison officers are dead, and two of the Greens. A right botch job. Everything that could go wrong, did.'

'And the worst is; they took Josef and he stood trial, if you can call it that. Death sentence, as we thought. But now they've decided to do it without ceremony, on the dunes. They don't want him made into a martyr.' Thierry wrung his big hands in a gesture of defeat. 'And they'll take random civilians unless we hand ourselves in. We're the most unpopular men in The Hague right now. They're saying ten men for every one of theirs. Forty innocent people. I've half a mind to confess.'

Nancy shook her head. 'No. It would do no good. They'd take ten anyway, their bargains are always traps.'

'And we don't know how long Steef will hold out,' Thierry said. 'We're sunk. And there's still no-one to coordinate getting food from the South to us.'

She looked around the room. Everyone looked thin now, their cheekbones jutting from their faces, no flesh on their arms or legs. And they were grey-faced, eyes hollow and defeated.

'Then if we can't get help, we'll have to find a way to do it ourselves,' Nancy said. She felt responsible, her heart ached at the thought of more lives being lost.

'How?' Albie said, with a disdainful laugh. 'Have you got a plan?'

'Not yet, but I'll make one.'

'I'm not trusting any more of your plans.'

'Go on, blame me,' she flashed. 'Nobody could have known about the handcuffs. They didn't use them on the other people I saw.' She looked around the group in appeal. 'What else can we do? Feel sorry for ourselves and do nothing? No. The first thing we have to do is warn people not to gather in large groups. The Nazis could use a crowd as an excuse to pull people out for the retaliations.'

Thierry rolled his eyes. 'People are not stupid. Soon as they heard about it, everyone's already gone to ground. There's barely a soul on the streets.'

Nancy ignored him. 'Nevertheless, it's our duty to warn people. Albie, you can go to Greta and get some leaflets printed to warn people.'

'Talking of Greta, she says there's a food store under the Hotel des Indes,' Thierry said. 'A contact of hers told her. If we could get another van, we could raid it.'

And I think I know who that contact was, thought Nancy bitterly. 'Forget it. We had enough trouble with the last van. We should avoid any grand gestures for a week or two. Lay low. Every SS man in The Hague will be after us. We don't want to do another raid just yet. They'll be on high alert.'

'Then how will we feed our people?' Thierry said. 'Answer me that?'

'We must keep trying to persuade the Royals to put pressure on the British and Americans. We're only a small cell, we can't feed a whole nation. It needs proper organisation.'

'A small cell that's getting smaller all the time,' Albie said.

Thierry sighed deeply. 'People are hungry now. They don't want to wait for some good Samaritan to deign to throw them a crust. The woman next door to me – her husband died. He couldn't go out to scavenge because he was a diver, then she got ill, and the next we knew, she began this unearthly wailing. He'd died in the night. Actual starvation.'

'Two children died last week in my street,' Albie said. 'If there's any chance of food, I say we go for it.'

They were getting nowhere bickering like this. 'What will we do about Josef?' she asked.

'There's nothing we can do.' Albie said. He slapped the palm of his hand on the table and it was like a door shutting.

Silence.

'Except fight back,' Thierry said in a low voice. 'How else? But we're getting weaker. The rations have been cut again. From next week its only four ounces of bread per person.'

'Like I said, we need to contact London.' Nancy stood up and paced. 'But the SS have got my transmitter. Found it in Steef's room.'

'We have to try something,' Thierry insisted.

Albie shook his head. 'No. You must get out of The Hague, Danique. Even if Steef holds out, when you don't go home, Schneider will start looking for you. You'll have to go underground for a while, you most of all.'

'Is there no safe house I can go to?'

Thierry looked uncomfortable. 'Nowhere's a safe house now. And we can't risk billeting you with another resistance member. Too risky for them.'

'So where will I go?'

'There's a tenement flat, used to be in the Jewish Quarter. It's empty and we have a key. But you'll have to keep yourself to yourself. It's on the third floor, the top floor, and there are other tenants living there. Do your best not to bring them trouble, eh?'

'Then shall we go?' She stood up. She was so tired she could barely speak. So much stress and still nowhere to lay her head.

'Papers,' Albie said. 'New papers for us all are here. Greta organised them a few weeks ago.' He opened a drawer.

Nancy walked over to find another identification card with her photo on it. Next to it were more. She spread them out with a finger. Dolf wouldn't be needing his now, nor Josef.

She began to feel sick. She opened the document with her photograph and stared at the name. *Catharina Stuyvel*, supposedly younger than her, supposedly the unmarried daughter of a cigar merchant who was now deceased. She was apparently working at the railway station as a clerk. She stared at it with no recognition. She'd been too many people. She had no idea how to be another one. She'd entirely exhausted her ways of being.

Still, she picked up the card and pocketed it. Carefully she tore up the identity pass of Danique Koopman and left it in the ash tray on the sideboard.

Albie nodded to her and set light to it with a match. The pungent smell of burning cardboard filled the air.

Nancy swallowed. What was the real Danique doing now? The woman she was casting off like a snake sheds its skin? What sort of a woman was she? Instead, she asked, 'What happened to Catharina Stuyvel? Will she suddenly turn up too?'

'No,' Albie said. 'She's pure invention. She will suffice only for a cursory check. But then we are not putting you in an apartment full of the SS this time.'

Pure invention. That was how she felt now. As if nothing any more was real.

She said goodbye to Thierry, her nerves jangling. Then she took Albie's arm.

She was Catharina now, not Danique.

223

Chapter 27

Amsterdam

Tom and Burt were a few miles from The Hague, at an Amsterdam railway station. This was the safest place to be when homeless and stateless, to blend in with other displaced people. It had taken them three days travelling by night to get there. Both were muffled up in old clothes with scarves over their faces. Burt had hold of a newspaper, which they leant against a pillar to read cover to cover. They'd bought a street map of Amsterdam from the station bookstall. It was in German and obviously designed for German troops.

'We're looking for Corellistraat,' said Burt, 'where Gerard lives. He's the head of operations here and in The Hague, but I don't suppose that's his real name. All I know is that it used to be a safe house, and we just have to hope it still is. We haven't got a number for the house.'

Further down the platform a grizzled old man was handing out yellowed sheets of paper. He looked furtive, so Tom held out a hand and took one from him. He read enough of it to see it was called *Ons Volk* and was obviously an anti-Nazi tract. As soon as he realised, he rushed after the old man to take hold of him by the arm.

'Ow. What is it? I haven't done anything.'

'It's all right,' Tom said in Dutch. 'Friend, Okay?'

The old boy stared, uncertain whether to run or stay.

'We just need help,' he said. 'This isn't a safe place for us to stay. Too many Nazis.'

The man shook his head and tried to move off.

'Do you know someone called Gerard? On Corellistraat?' It was a long shot, but worth a try.

The man looked up, suddenly appearing younger. He took in Tom's eager expression. 'What about him?'

'We just need a number,' Tom said. 'We've come from Dordrecht and he's our contact.'

He seemed to make a rapid assessment. 'Nine,' he said. 'But I didn't tell you.' Then he shook off Tom's arm and hurried away.

Tom hurried back to Burt who was still squinting at the map.

'It's nine,' he said. 'And here, a bit of light reading.' He thrust the copy of *Ons Volk* at Burt.

'Put it away,' Burt said, 'D'you want to get us arrested?'

Tom shoved it in his coat pocket and they set off walking, keeping to the smaller roads and tiny alleyways on the map.

They arrived at Corellistraat 9 before curfew when there was still light.

Burt knocked on the door, and Tom saw a shutter open an inch or two. Nobody answered.

'He's in,' Tom said. 'I saw the shutter move. He's watching us. Knock again.'

Burt knocked, and a large dark shadow moved behind the shutter. Tom took out the copy of *Ons Volk* and held it up to the window.

A few moments later and the door opened. 'In quick, don't hang about on the doorstep.' A deep voice in Dutch. Tom guessed this must be Gerard.

They followed him into a cramped sitting room, where the ticking of two competing cuckoo clocks was the only sound.

It was only when they got into the room that Tom realised this huge bear of a man was pointing a gun at them. 'Who are you and what do you want?'

'We're looking for a woman, cover name Danique Koopman,' Burt said in flawless Dutch.

'She's English,' added Tom in his more hesitant Dutch, 'or rather Scottish, and we believe she's working with you.'

Gerard put back his shoulders and looked at Tom with suspicion. 'No. I know of no such person,' he said. He kept the gun pointing at Burt's face.

Tom tried again. 'You're Gerard, I think. I worked with Fransine in Dordrecht. We were hoping you'd have some use for us.'

'Who gave you this address?'

'Fransine, like he said.' Burt refused to be intimidated.

'Listen here. I don't know who you are or what you want but I want you to leave, and right now. I don't know any Fransine, or anyone called Koopman.'

'Just put us in touch with someone else who can help. We need a safe house, anywhere we can spend a few days.'

Gerard clicked the gun to prime it. 'I said get out. And I don't want you anywhere near this house again.'

'Come on,' Tom said. 'Let's go.'

They backed out and heard the door slam behind them.

Tom looked back to see the shutter closing behind the window.

'Well, he was no help,' Burt said.

'He was scared,' Tom said. 'I could see it in his eyes. We just turned up out of the blue. We could be Nazi collaborators. And it's not surprising he's wary given that Fransine's dead and her network scattered.'

'So what do we do now?'

'Guess we just try to get to The Hague.'

'Oh yes, and staying alive might be a good idea too,' Burt said.

226

'You realise we stick out like a sore thumb? Two strapping lads like us. Well, one strapping lad, and one who looks wet behind the ears.'

'You'd better get yourself a towel then,' Tom said.

'Ha, bloody ha.'

It wasn't safe to travel to The Hague by train because Nazi troops would seize on them for factory work if they saw them. So they walked the whole way across country, skirting town and city, through fields and quiet roads, dodging Nazi traffic and patrols. On one occasion they had to pretend to be farm workers digging in a field, as a patrol passed.

But they'd made it, and headed for the railway bar near Hollands Spoor station, an old-fashioned place and a hub for refugees passing through. Burt had heard it was a meeting place for the Resistance, so it seemed like a good enough place to start. Now he was in the same city as Nancy, Tom couldn't help his gaze snapping to the door every time it opened. He kept hoping he'd see her. Though he knew it was total foolishness; she'd never be out in a bar like this. Especially if she was supposed to be some sort of Nazi sympathizer. The thought of her being on the arm of a Nazi enraged him.

There was a woman behind the bar, though, a big blousy woman with blonde sausage-shaped curls and a generous smile.

Tom ordered the beers.

'Sorry, it's not Bavarian,' she said. 'We can't get it. Just fermented barley, and only half-measures. You got coupons?'

Burt handed them over.

'Not working?' she asked Burt.

'Railway workers. We're on strike.'

'Oh, yes? At the central station?' she asked.

Tom saw no reason to lie. 'No. Got stranded. We're from Dordrecht, close to the line, so we walked here.'

'We need a place to stay,' Burt said.

'Ah.' She looked them up and down. 'Dordrecht, you say.' She seemed to assess them. 'Try the old bank. We use it as an air-raid shelter. So they're not too fussy who goes in there. Their basement's bombproof.'

'Sounds good,' Tom said.

'Night-time opening's at 5.30 pm. They say there are rooms to be had above, for special friends. It's only a rumour, mind you.' She gave them a pointed look, and made her fingers into a V on the counter. Tom made the same gesture back. 'And for God's sake get yourselves out of sight, you're like a walking invitation to the Nazis.'

'This bank – how d'you get there?'

'Down the road and left. Then follow your nose until you see the *Maritshuis* roof, then left again. Can't miss it.'

Tom made for the door, but she yelled after him, 'The bank'll wait. Finish your beer, no good wasting it. Who knows when it'll run out?'

As they waited there Tom could see the woman talking on the telephone with her hand over the receiver to muffle her voice. She kept glancing through to them as she was talking. It gave the impression she was talking to someone about them. Tom's instincts made him jumpy.

'Who d'you think she's calling?'

'The brewery probably. Stop being so jumpy.'

'I can't help it. She keeps looking at us.'

'She'll be checking us out. We're taught to do that if strangers turn up on our patch. You'd better call yourself something else, you can't be Tom Lockwood.'

'Then what do you suggest? Lucky Jim?'

'Ha! Jim'll do.'

They finished their drinks, by which time another man had arrived and was sitting on the table next to them, reading a paper. He was a younger nondescript individual – could have been a doctor or a lawyer. He had that vaguely official air about him. He had an NSB badge on his lapel, which made Tom wary.

A sudden wail of a siren.

'Air raid,' said Burt leaping up.

Instantly everyone was on the move. Tom noticed the man by the door grab his overcoat. They ran the few blocks to the old bank. Tom was sure the man was following them, but he said nothing to Burt. It would be natural for everyone to head for the shelter.

The bank basement was crowded and damp, full of unwashed bodies, 90 per cent women and children. Tom squashed himself up against a wall, surprised to see the huge old cast-iron safe still standing there. Presumably it was empty. Burt huddled up next to it.

That man again. Tom noticed the man from the bar had inched his way close to them and was now just on the other side of the safe. He had balding blond hair and protruding eyes. He beckoned Tom over.

'You looking for a room?' the man asked. 'Somewhere to stay?'

'Who's asking?'

'Someone who can see you've not been in The Hague five minutes. Name of Erik. Barb, the woman in the bar, told me to make contact.'

'Jim. And him over there? That's Burt.'

Erik was better dressed than most, in a newish suit and tie, with a smart overcoat. The NSB badge was prominently displayed on his lapel. Tom was wary of the fact he seemed so friendly.

'We need extra bodies,' Erik said. 'I can introduce you both to someone. Someone who can give you a good day's work to do.'

'What kind of work?'

'This and that.'

'For the NSB?'

A splutter of laughter. 'Nah.' Erik tapped the badge and leant towards him. 'That's just for show. There's a man called Albie, might have work for you, but it will have to wait until tomorrow because I'm busy on a job. But I can fix you a room.'

Burt saw them talking and came over.

'What's up?'

'This guy's offered to get us a place to stay. Erik, meet Burt.'

'Soon as the all clear goes, I'll take you up,' Erik said. 'I've got a key.' They gleaned from him that there were also Jews hiding in the building, and that members of the Dutch Royal family also had a suite of rooms somewhere in this vast edifice. 'But I have to be back at the De Beurs Hotel soon as the raid's over,' Erik said. 'I'm staying there, watching some of the residents. They've gone to the German shelter with their Wehrmacht friends. But I didn't fancy popping my clogs with a load of *Moffen*, so I came here.'

For the first time, Tom relaxed a little. The man wasn't a Nazi sympathizer. 'Are they dangerous, the people you're following?'

'Nah. Just a woman and her kid. I'm tailing her – got to detail everyone she meets. So far she's done nothing except order room service like she's in Paris, and take the kid for a walk in the park. Someone at the hotel said she's waiting for an apartment to become vacant for them.'

Tom nodded along.

'She's not a bad looker though, this Frau Koopman. Might fancy my chances if it wasn't for the kid.'

Tom looked at Burt, unable to believe what he was hearing.

'It's her,' Burt said.

Electricity seemed to be coursing in Tom's veins. 'Do you have any idea what her first name is?'

'Danique. Danique Koopman.' He leant closer to whisper in Tom's ear, 'it was supposed to be a hit job, but they called it off. Don't know what she's done, or why I'm supposed to be keeping tabs on her, but hey.'

'What does she look like?'

'Tall, skinny. Brown hair?' he shrugged.

'And she's definitely at the De Beurs Hotel?'

'Her and her nephew.'

Nephew? That didn't sound right. It couldn't be her nephew. Neil had no children yet. 'You're sure that's the name? I'm trying to connect with her.'

'Really? She's a Nazi. I overheard her talking with one of the Wehrmacht officers. I expect that's why I've to keep tabs on her. She walks about like she owns the place.'

'You can get a note to her? This Frau Koopman?'

Erik frowned. 'Not unless I know what it says. First, she was supposed to disappear, now I'm supposed to be keeping her under surveillance. Notes from strangers are exactly the sort of thing I'm supposed to be noting.'

'Look, you can watch me write it if you like. Have you got paper and a pen?'

Erik pulled a notebook from his pocket and tore out a piece of paper.

I am in The Hague, Tom wrote. He paused. *Long story.* 'Is there somewhere private to sit in the hotel?'

'Yes, the lounge bar is quiet. It serves coffee and hot chocolate, or should I say chicory and fake Supercrema.'

Meet me in the lounge bar at 11 am tomorrow and I'll explain. Tom

'You realise I'll have to be there too?'

'She isn't a Nazi, no matter what you think. And I won't keep her, as I know she's doing something important.' He folded it over and wrote *Danique Koopman* on the front of the paper.

Chapter 28

On the way to the safe house, Nancy followed Albie a few paces behind, alert for a patrol, or the sound of marching boots. There was no getting away from it, the raid had been a disaster and The Hague was becoming a ghost town. Today the streets were deserted except for the queue outside the *Gaarkeukens* – the soup kitchen lorry. A crowd of women and children scrabbled in the metal vats used by the council to distribute their watery cabbage and potato soup. Nancy was now too used to these people swarming over these bins, wielding spoons brought to scrape them out.

A child, emaciated under his blue cloth cap, scraped the gunk off the lid of one of them with his nails and sucked his fingers. The sound of it, and the pitiful sight made Nancy's stomach contract, but she put her head down and hurried on. Once she got too far behind Albie, and a Nazi patrol stopped her and quizzed her on where she was going.

She took out her papers.

'Maartensstraat?' the solid-looking German asked.

'Yes. Third floor. It's been emptied of Jews now.'

The address calmed them a little and they let her go, but she had the feeling they were watching her as she walked away. She went slowly, every step one of fear and tension, looking straight ahead.

As soon as she reached the end of the road, she turned sharp right and searched for Albie.

There, at the next junction. She saw him take out a key and open up a rust-coloured door in a house that looked emaciated, as if it had been squeezed between two others.

She heard his rough boots clomp up the stairs, and by the time she reached the third floor she was near the top of the building and the door stood open.

The upstairs room at Maartensstraat had the sour reek of mouldering damp, of a place that hadn't been loved for a long time. Half the floorboards had been ripped up, except for where the bed stood.

'Looters,' Albie said. 'They need the fuel.'

An old drop-leaf table, much scuffed and covered in cup rings, with its two leaves ripped off was shoved to the edge and teetered on the remaining uneven boards. Beside it was a rickety chair with no back, and in the corner an iron bedstead with a plain white chamber pot beneath it.

'Is this it?' What a come down from Fritz and his plush sofas and pristine napkins.

'The neighbours are pleasant people. He's an engineer at the dockyard; the Germans requisitioned their old place and put them here. She takes in sewing and looks after the two children. Sorry. It's only one child now. The eldest one died not long back. You're lucky. Their place is not much bigger than this.'

She didn't want to seem ungrateful, but its greyness, the dilapidated state of it, with its damp patches around the window and on the ceiling, made her shoulders slump.

'With Josef gone,' Albie said, 'there's no hope of coordinating. It's every man for himself now. If I were you, I'd get out of

The Hague somehow. Get your English friends to get you out.'
He said 'English friends' with some scorn.

'Is that what you think? That I'll just up and go when things get tough?'

He didn't answer, but his thin face showed his discomfort.

'I'm not quitting. Not until this war's won.' A pause. 'When will we meet again?'

'How the hell should I know? Everything's in disarray.'

'You're supposed to be coordinating us, aren't you?' Nancy said. 'That's what everyone expects because you've been doing this the longest. Well, do something.'

'With what? We've no ammo. We've no more men. Only Thierry and he's close to the edge. Look what he did to Dolf. Things are bad when you shoot your own friends.'

'Albie, we can't give up.'

'Speak for yourself. We can't even feed ourselves. And the SS'll be looking for us all over The Hague. You especially. Being in touch with you is a risk none of us can afford.'

'With Josef gone we need a plan.'

'There is no plan,' Albie said. Then he passed her a ration card in the name of Catharina Stuyvel and left her.

His boots rang out on the treads as he went downstairs. He couldn't mean it, could he? That he was giving up the fight?

The light from the window drew her there and she tiptoed across the joists to look through the misted glass. Distant cranes of the shipyards, skeletal fingers reaching for the sky now still and silent, and Nazi guns pointing off the rooftops to target British planes. To her left, a ruined building stuck out of the ground like the stump of a bad tooth.

There was nothing to see out there that she didn't already know.

She sat on the bed to think and wished she could have had any of Danique's comforts, but to keep anything was to take too big a risk. Now she was only a worn-out body in the clothes she stood up in, a threadbare skirt and patched jersey. A look around didn't help. The bed was furnished with one grey blanket and no pillow. The fireplace was a bare grate, and she supposed that was all she'd have to cook on, and there was no fuel unless she could burn the furniture.

But years of being an agent had taught her one thing. Waiting for things to improve was never the answer. You'd die if you didn't take your life in your own hands. *Carpe Diem*. You had to seize the day.

She grabbed her handbag and tiptoed over to the other door across the corridor and knocked.

A tired female voice answered warily, 'Who is it?'

'Catharina. I'm your new neighbour. I just wanted to introduce myself.'

The clunk of a lock and a thin, peaky face poked out from the door. 'I'm Ellie,' she said, and this is Rosa.' She joggled the baby on her hip. 'Have you anything to eat?'

'No. nothing.' The woman's face fell. 'I got bombed out,' Nancy improvised. 'I need to barter for a few things. I wondered if you'd let me mind the baby in return for anything you can spare.'

Ellie shook her head. 'We've nothing left. We had to sell most things to buy food on the black market. I'm not sure there's anything I can give you. But come in, I'm just making a hot drink. It's only hot water with a bit of dried catmint and grass. Something green for the vitamins.'

Nancy turned to lock her door and followed the woman inside. The baby began to cry, a croupy high-pitched wail. Ellie gave her a chunk of old, wizened sugar beet to chew on. She shook her head, 'She's hungry and I can't make milk. What can I do?'

Their living area was a single room with a bed curtained off. There was a fire in the grate but it gave off little heat. By it rested a pile of sawn up floorboards.

Ellie saw her looking at them and shrugged. 'We didn't know if anyone would use the room again, and my son was ill. Pneumonia. He died three weeks ago.'

'I'm sorry.'

'There was nothing we could do. No food, no medicine. The least we could do was keep him warm and hold him while he coughed.'

'How old was he?'

'Four.' She choked back a sob. 'He was four.' She turned away and reached for the blackened kettle steaming on the grate and poured hot water onto a few dried leaves in two cups.

When she handed Nancy the cup, her face showed the numb resignation Nancy saw everywhere. To cover her awkwardness Nancy took a sip from the cup. Surprising what a bit of warmth could do. She cupped her hands around the chipped teacup.

'I'm glad it's a woman in there now,' Ellie said. The last one was a diver, and it was terrible when they came for him. They took his mother too, arrested her for hiding him.'

Fierce knocking from below, followed by gruff protests, and then a man's voice shouting, and a woman crying.

'Oh no, not again,' Ellie said.

The noises went on for about ten minutes, growing louder and more insistent. When they looked out of the window, they saw a young man being marched away at gunpoint.

As soon as they had gone, the tightness in her throat eased, but Rosa was still griping, despite the fact that Ellie had picked her up and was dandling her.

'They were searching for divers, not for you.' Ellie said. 'I know you're one of them. The resistance people. Since the last diver went, the room's often empty. When it is used, it's by fly-by-nights, men who work for the resistance. You're one of them. I can always tell. People think we don't know, but the signs are always there. The sudden arrival from nowhere. The lack of possessions. That hunted look deep in the eyes.'

'I hadn't realised it was that obvious.'

'Why d'you think we have so little? Every person who comes in that room comes to us for help, and at first we were generous. But it gets wearing. Look at it!' She gestured around. 'We've nothing left to give you. But you're the first woman. I don't suppose you'll stay long. They never do.'

'We mustn't waste the tea,' Nancy said.

'True. And it's a bit warmer in my place than yours, thanks to your floorboards. And if you want to trade something, I'll need to know what you've got.'

They sat in the two old chairs near the grate. Nancy got out her St Christopher from around her neck. Tom had given her it, as a talisman for safe travels, and she wore it always under her clothes. But now she must sell it, for Fritz had seen it around her neck and noted it. He'd be looking for a woman wearing one like this.

Oh, Tom. I'm sorry. But better to be alive without it than dead.

She unclipped the catch and held it out in her palm. 'It has sentimental value, but I can't keep it. It ties me to an identity I need to be free of.'

Ellie took it and weighed it in her palm. 'Heavy. I haven't seen gold like this in years. It might even feed us. But there are no Jews now to give us a good price. Dani might know of someone. Might buy a few potatoes if there are any to be had, keep Rosa alive a few more days.'

'Help will come, somehow.'

'That's what everyone says.' Ellie thrust the St Christopher back to her. 'Keep it. There's nothing to buy with it, and if it means something special, hold it to your heart. Meaning's important. So much of this war has no meaning. Love is important, we need to keep things to remind us it exists.'

'But how will you feed Rosa?'

'I don't know. I worry she'll go the way of her brother. And then who would I be? I wouldn't be a mother then, would I?'

Nancy reached out to touch her hand. 'You'll always be a mother, no matter what.'

'Put your necklace back on. We all have so little, don't let the Nazis take it all, even our memories.'

Nancy fastened it on and tucked it down under her jumper. Maybe Ellie was right; it did feel good to keep it.

'You know, we keep praying for food,' Ellie said, 'but the rest of the world seems to have forgotten us. It doesn't seem fair that God will feed babies in France but not here in the Netherlands.'

'War's never fair. Not on the men who must fight, though it's not their fight. Not on the women who must endure bombs and bullets. And not on the children who don't understand why it's happening at all.'

Ellie didn't reply. Her blue eyes were candid, and her expression one of acceptance, even though her cardigan was more darn than wool, and the legs poking from her thin print dress and into her wood-soled shoes were chapped with cold. She must have been attractive once, but now there was no water for washing and like Nancy, her blonde hair was tucked under a scarf.

It was good to talk to another woman. Nancy told Ellie about Tom, without giving too much away about her life in Holland. Ellie confessed that she and Dani were like souls waiting for their lives to happen. They were too concerned with feeding Rosa, and keeping warm to have time or energy for anything else.

Ellie was right, in the face of such deprivation, Tom felt like a mirage now, something she'd imagined.

When Ellie's husband Dani came home they were still there talking. Dani was gruff and obviously unhappy to have Nancy, another mouth to feed, in his house, so she took her leave politely and left. There were a few hours before curfew. If Albie would do nothing, then perhaps she could. She could try to get food to Ellie and Rosa. There was food in the Hotel des Indes, and though it was madness to try to go there now, she was determined to try. She was far too restless to stay there.

Chapter 29

Tom looked at the scratched face of his watch. Exactly eleven o'clock. He tried to quiet his apprehension, put his shoulders back and walked into the De Beurs Hotel. The lobby had a few Wehrmacht soldiers hanging around there, but Tom smiled politely at them and acted as though he owned the place. Erik had given him an NSB armband, and besides, no *onderduiker* would dare go in there at all. It seemed to do the trick, for they paid him no attention. He'd smartened himself up as much as he could by rubbing his shoes with water and making a neat knot in his tie, though he was aware he still looked shabby.

Nancy won't care, he thought.

He went to the bar where a young pudding-faced girl was serving coffee and he ordered a cup. At least his Dutch was up to that. The girl stared but made him one and pushed it over the counter. At the edge of the lounge there were a few easy chairs around small teak tables, and Tom sat himself down, stomach twisting in knots as he waited for Nancy to come down.

At the far corner of the lounge, Erik was smoking a cigarette behind the morning copy of the Nazi rag the DNZ – the *Deutsche Zeitung in den Niederlanden*. Erik clocked Tom, and their eyes met, but Erik returned his gaze to the paper.

Tom almost leapt out of his chair at every noise. He was on tenterhooks waiting to see Nancy's reaction when she saw him. She'd recognise his handwriting he knew – she'd seen it so many times during their work together for the SOE in Baker Street. He couldn't wait to see her. His hands wouldn't stay still in his lap, nerves kicking in. What would she make of him being in Holland? The idea he was rescuing her seemed totally ridiculous, yet when he set off that was exactly what he thought he was doing. How little he'd understood.

The door to the lounge opened and closed and a woman stood there. Not Nancy. Tom turned his attention back to his drink.

A moment later she'd come to stand directly in front of him. An overpowering waft of some sort of floral perfume. 'You're Tom?' She spoke in Dutch.

He stood up, confused. 'Yes?' He replied in the same language.

'I'm Danique. You sent me a note?'

Tom reeled. He couldn't take it in. He stared at this woman who was taller and broader than Nancy, with darker hair and a heavier jawline. Her expression was not one of warmth but rather irritation that she'd been interrupted.

'There's been a mistake,' he said, struggling with the Dutch. 'You're not the lady . . . not the lady I expected.'

'The note was addressed to me,' she said, frowning. She held it out in front of him. 'What do you want? Is it money?'

'No, no, I don't want anything. I expected a friend, that's all.'

'You know another woman called Danique Koopman?'

'No . . . I must have got the name wrong.' Tom was floundering, and he knew it.

'I'm not happy with this.' She turned to the girl behind the counter. 'This man's not Dutch, and he's harassing me. Would you fetch the manager for me, please.'

The girl stared over at him before turning to tug a bell pull on the wall behind her.

Tom didn't wait. The disappointment was like a needle. He had to get out of there. 'Sorry,' he said again, and he hurried out, leaping over the threshold, not even looking back at Erik who was listening in the corner.

He headed straight back to the bank, going in the back entrance with the passcode Erik had given them. Burt was surprised to see him back so soon.

'I think I've cocked up,' he said.

'Why? What's up?'

'It's not her. You must have got the name wrong. There was a woman there, but it wasn't Nancy.'

'Hey, don't blame me! That's the right name. I saw it written down, Koopman.' He spelled it out. 'Danique.'

'Then I don't get it. Why would they give her a cover name of someone else?'

'That's crazy.'

'But what I do know is that this Danique Koopman is a Nazi, and worse, she's now deeply suspicious. She got a good look at me, and will probably report me either to the hotel manager or the porter, or both.'

'What about Erik, the man who was following her? He got his instructions from somewhere, didn't he? Didn't he say his boss was called Albie? Well, whoever he is, he must have a vested interest in Danique Koopman. We just need more information. Can you go back and try to have a word with Erik?'

'I daren't go back there. They'll arrest me, she was making a right fuss and palaver.'

'Then it'll have to be me,' Burt said. 'I'll go back, see what else I can find out. You sit tight. And don't answer the door except to the "V" knock, okay?'

* * *

In the Oranjehotel the day after the raid, Fritz put his head on his elbows where they lay on the desk. He was taking deep breaths and pressing his eyes into his sleeves to push away the images that wouldn't leave him be. Why was all anyone could ask him, 'Where is Frau Koopman today?'

And he had to answer through narrow lips, 'She's not well. A cold. She's taking a few days off.'

He should have guessed. As soon as Keller had telephoned him yesterday in a panic to say that Danique Koopman had gone out, but that he'd somehow lost her in the city, the back of his neck began to prickle. But foolishly, he'd ignored it.

He groaned. What would he do if Danique was mixed up in the prison raid? He'd be a laughing stock among his men. The guards said a woman had been there, but a laundry woman? No. Unthinkable. Danique could never stoop so low.

When the alarm siren had wailed its warning, it had made him leap from his chair. Then the unmistakeable crack of gunfire. He'd dashed over to the loading bay expecting to find a prisoner dead, but the dead men on the blood-spattered floor were all uniformed men, except one dead traitor who would be no use to him at all. The sight of them lying there turned his innards to stone. He knew then, something serious had gone wrong. And unthinkably – on his watch.

Why was everyone standing around doing nothing? Incensed, he shouted at the gawping officers, told them to fetch women to mop up the mess. Then he had to send for body bags, and hustle away the gleeful Gottfried and the other ghouls who wanted to come and stare. And they all looked at him, as if to say: 'How can this have happened?'

The only glimmer of satisfaction was the fact the raid had failed. One of the bastard resistance was dead – and they'd flush out the rest. Had to.

Josef de Jong would soon be spattered across the dunes, another corpse for the crows. They'd come for him at dusk and they'd do it without ceremony.

The ache in his chest made him physically sick. Danique had disappeared. When he got home, he had almost guessed it. The housekeeper Margarete was full of excuses and he had her taken away immediately and put on a train East. He could no longer stand the sight of her and her whingeing apologies.

He remembered staring at his favourite picture, the silent misty trees, on the wall of Danique's apartment and then throwing the bottle of cough medicine at it, watching it drip down the wall, brown and sticky.

He'd find her, he vowed. Already he had men stopping every woman of her description.

He was still there, reliving it all, elbows on his desk, head in his arms, when there was a rap at his door.

Keller poked a wary head around the door.

'What?' Fritz snapped.

'They pulled a body out of the river.'

'So?'

'Her papers were in a leather pouch in her pocket and they're still legible. According to those she's Danique Koopman, but we need to do more checks to be sure.'

The name brought an earthquake of emotion to his chest. He stood and turned his back on Keller, breathing hard.

'Description?' He could barely speak. Perhaps he was wrong, perhaps Danique had had an accident.

'Five feet ten inches, size eight feet. Brown hair. Wearing a suit and a string of pearls.'

His heart plummeted. 'No St Christopher?'

'What?'

'Did she have a St Christopher medal around her neck?'

'No. What I said. Pearls.'

It wasn't his Danique. 'Drowned?'

'Shot in the temple.'

Fritz let out a groan. His Danique was alive. But at the same time a rage was rising in him. She'd betrayed him, taken him for a fool. The certainty that the body must be the real Danique Koopman made him slump back into his chair, the hurt in his chest bitter as poison.

A noise in the corridor outside.

The door swung open, and all at once it was filled with black-clad SS men.

The ramrod figure of Kommandant Brant pushed past them all and closed the door. After the obligatory *Sieg Heil*s, Keller made a hurried exit.

Brant sat down and leaned towards Fritz, flanked by two hatchet-faced SS men he didn't know. Brant smiled, as if he was about to deliver good news, but Fritz knew it could only be bad.

'I'm sorry, Oberführer Schneider,' Brant said, 'but I'm relieving you of duty. Goering thinks it better I should be here now, where I'm needed. In case of any more . . . trouble.'

Fritz refused to be cowed. He sat himself up straighter. 'Is that so? Then where does he suggest I will be working, if not here?'

'We thought with the security police,' Brant said, leaning back to cross his long legs. 'Back on the beat. They need more help with the round-ups.'

A demotion. Fritz's bitterness turned into resolve. This was that woman's fault. He could no longer call her Danique. He'd find the traitorous bitch, and then she'd wish she'd never been born. When Brant had gone, he lifted up the phone and yelled orders.

Chapter 30

Nancy had to get the forged authorisation papers from Greta if she were to get into the Hotel des Indes to get food for Ellie and the baby. Travelling in the dusky light was risky, but Nancy hunched herself over to look older, and kept to the back alleyways and small side roads. She was used to having eyes in the back of her head, to being aware of slight movements that might betray someone watching. Every foray was one where she held her breath.

Greta was at home and beckoned her inside with sharp staccato movements of her hands.

'You shouldn't have come here,' she hissed. 'They could be on your tail.'

'That's always been true. So what's different?'

'You know damn well. There's a search out for you. One of Thierry's children ran to tell me with a message. Schneider has issued an order that you are to be found as a matter of urgency. They went to your apartment.'

'So I'm in hiding again. That's nothing new. Did you copy that authorisation I gave you, and the food coupons?'

'Not the coupons. Just the authorisation.'

She's lying, Nancy thought. She'd done the coupons, but had given them to someone else. Years of being betrayed made Nancy suspicious. She knew though, that the authorisation couldn't be faked because 'Danique Koopman' would need to accompany it in person.

Nancy narrowed her eyes. 'Give me the authorisation papers then.'

'They're useless. You're not going there. Not when every last SS officer in the city is out looking for you.'

'If I go now, Karlauf, the store manager at the hotel, might not have heard the news of the raid yet. And his *Moffen* won't think to look for me at a Nazi hotel.'

'You've finally lost your mind.'

'People need food. I've just seen a woman and her child close to starvation. The hotel has plenty. It's worth the risk. Do something good before they find me.'

'There are people like that in every doorway. Besides, they won't let you in. You don't look like Danique Koopman anymore. You look like a wreck.'

'Oh, thank you. You don't look exactly tip-top yourself. More like a scarecrow. You'd be better off in a tulip field scaring the birds.'

Greta laughed, a hoarse laugh like a witch's cackle. 'Might prefer it to being locked in a bomb shelter with a press all day. Well, if you're determined to get yourself killed, maybe I can help you on your way. Wait there.'

She hurried into the back room and came out with a fur coat and a red felt hat.

'Only a loan, you understand. In return, I want half of whatever you get. And don't think to do the dirty on me because I happen to know your new name. I forged the false papers that are in your handbag. One word from me, *Catharina Stuyvel* and it will be –' she mimed a gun to the head. 'It would stand me in good stead you know, the Nazis love a good collaborator.'

It was true. Greta was being pragmatic, as they all were. Nancy knew she had no choice. 'All right. But not half. A third. There is a woman with a baby that needs it more than we do.' She stood her ground, staring Greta down steadily.

Finally Greta threw up her arms. 'What the hell. We'll probably both be dead tomorrow anyway. Take the coat. But if it doesn't come back to me by tomorrow morning, I'll be telling the men in green all I know.'

She thrust the coat towards her and Nancy grabbed hold of its cloudy softness. Hurriedly, she pulled on its heavy warmth over her jumper and skirt, tidied her hair and put on the hat.

'Have you a basket?'

'Anything else, milady? How about a diamond necklace or a tiara?' A grunt of annoyance, as Greta emptied her knitting onto the counter and passed Nancy the basket. Before putting her handbag over her arm, Nancy got out lipstick she had used as Danique and now she slicked it on.

'Now you look like a Nazi trollop,' Greta said, standing back, hands on hips.

'Good. Wish me luck,' Nancy said.

'You don't need luck, you need a bloody miracle.'

The Hotel des Indes was almost deserted. No officers guarded the door as they usually did, and the lobby was hushed. A lone man – an older man that Nancy did not recognise – stood behind the reception desk, polishing the counter with wax polish and a cloth. She asked for Karlauf the store master, said he knew her, and she was told politely to wait whilst he telephoned him.

The man spoke rapidly to Karlauf, his eyes fixed on Nancy. His stare was disconcerting and she pulled her fur collar more closely up around her face and let her gaze range around the foyer, with its plush velvet chairs and heavy drapes.

'He will come up shortly,' the man said, replacing the receiver in its cradle.

'You're very quiet tonight,' she said.

'Yes. There's been a disturbance at the prison and now a round-up. Someone escaped probably. They won't tell us anything, but it's created a lot of extra work.'

Just then, Karlauf appeared. He greeted her pleasantly. 'Good evening, Frau Koopman, how can I help?'

She passed over the forged authentication slip, and he looked it over.

'All in order,' he said, 'though it's rather late for shopping. I trust Oberführer Schneider will be pleased, I have some veal tonight. Very special. You want some?'

'That sounds wonderful. I can't get anything on the black market anymore.'

'The way to a man's heart, eh?'

'Exactly.' She gave a little tinkling laugh.

In the stores she filled her basket, and was treated to a parcel of bloodied brown paper from the cold store, which was under a fly net. She assumed this was the veal. Her mouth was already watering at the thought of food and her stomach kept up a constant rumble.

She tried not to look at Karlauf as she filled her basket, but couldn't help noticing that there were far fewer vegetables and far less bread on the shelves. Sacks full of turnips stood under the window, and some of the shelves were empty.

'Be careful with that veal now,' Karlauf said. 'They have dogs searching for the escaped fugitive, whoever he is. You don't want them sniffing you out!'

She laughed the tinkling laugh again, though her stomach had tightened and a wash of adrenalin rippled up her spine. The thought of dogs tracking her was something she hadn't considered. 'I'll be going straight home,' she said. 'Fritz will be wanting his dinner. He's always hungry if there's been trouble at work.'

She thanked Karlauf and told him she'd give his best regards to Fritz, and, stomach churning, headed for the stairs.

Trying not to run, she climbed back up to the lobby. As she passed down the corridor, two men in SS uniform and high boots, strode past her. She flattened herself to the corridor wall, but they ignored her as they headed towards the dining room at the rear of the hotel.

The fur coat had done its job. She gave a nod to the man at reception, then hurried out into the cold.

Dogs. She hadn't thought of that. They'd take dogs to the SS apartments, and then use them to sniff her out. What was she to do?

She hurried back to the upstairs rooms on Maartensstraat. Truth be told, she didn't relish the idea of going back. But she had been moved by Ellie's plight. The women were struggling in this fight too, even more so, as they were the ones expected to produce food.

In the stark light of day the area looked even more dilapidated. Trees on the pavements were stumps where they'd been hacked down for fuel, and rubble from bombed-out buildings had weeds growing that had been stripped of their leaves. Anything green and edible was gone. There was barely a blade of grass to be seen.

One of the ground-floor apartments in the building had already been looted. The one where the diver had been living. The doors and the floorboards were missing and someone had smashed the windows and even taken the frames. The fireplace was gone, leaving an ugly brick gash, and every shelf had been pulled from the wall. It was as if locusts had swarmed in the minute someone was taken.

Shaken, she climbed the stairs, wondering if even the few things in her billet would be gone. She was about to unlock the door when she saw that the door had already been broken into. There were crowbar marks on the lock and scuff marks and scratches. Warily she pushed it open. The room was as she'd left it, except that the bedding had been thrown on the floor as if someone was searching.

She backed out. She knocked softly on Ellie's door. 'It's Catharina,' she said.

No answer.

She knocked again. 'Ellie, are you there?'

The door opened a crack, and Ellie's face appeared behind it. Her eyes were red and swollen.

Nancy held up the basket. 'I've brought you some food. There's a half-tin of milk powder there too for Rosa.'

The door opened further. 'I didn't recognise you. You look . . .' Ellie shook her head.

Nancy stepped inside. The room looked even less welcoming because the fire was out and the room was so cold there was frost on the inside of the windows.

'They've taken Dani,' Ellie said. 'An SS man came and put him in a car. They're sending him to a factory in Germany. They say they don't want engineers like him in Holland any more. They need them in Koln, wherever that is. Some of the other workers have been taken too. One of the other women came to tell me. They've taken her husband too.'

'Oh, Ellie, that's terrible.'

'I thought he was safe,' she cried. 'That if we kept our heads down and he kept working for them, we'd survive somehow. I don't know what I'll do. His rations meant we could eat, but how am I to manage? I can't do much in the way of work. There are already too many women doing repairs and laundry. Too many women selling themselves on the street to any Nazi that offers them a slice of bread.'

Nancy put the basket on the table and unpacked a loaf of bread and some cheese. 'Here, eat. Feed the baby. Don't think about tomorrow. Eat slow, so you don't make yourself sick. And make it last because I don't know if I can get more.'

Ellie hadn't heard her, she was so distraught. 'He'll be so far away. We used to share his rations because he was working and got more. But he was still so thin. What will he be doing in Germany? They say they never come back.'

'Look, help is coming. The war is already over for the Germans. The Russians are on their way to Berlin. It's only a matter of time.'

'No. They've forgotten us.'

'Then they need reminding. I have friends in England. I'll see what I can do.'

'You can't do anything.'

'I can and I will. Promise. And I'll stay here tonight, so you don't have to be on your own.'

Ellie cast her a disbelieving look. But finally she began to eat.

Chapter 31

Fritz strode after the two SS men who were straining to hold back their beasts by their collars. The dogs, big German Shepherds, had been primed with the scent of Danique. They'd let them roam her apartment, and now, after a few false starts, the dogs were panting, intent on dragging their handlers down a residential street.

'Looks like they've picked something up, sir,' said Braun, the most junior of his men.

Braun was a thug, but stupid. Naturally Schneider hadn't told these officers he'd been sacked. He'd given them the impression that, as a man with a reputation for getting things done, he'd been put there undercover – to supervise them and report back any shoddy behaviour.

Their boot heels echoed on the pavement as the dogs gave out small barks, their breath clouding the cold air. In through a gate to a residential terrace in Bezuidenhout. Braun and his friend Zoll pulled back the dogs on their leashes so Fritz could hammer at the door.

By now the dogs were frantic, barking fit to warn anyone hiding that they were there.

'Control your dogs, can't you?' Fritz snapped.

The door opened and a woman in a nightdress and shawl opened the door, terror in her blue eyes. Fritz pursed his lips. Not Danique.

'You are?' He asked in Dutch.

'Greta van Schelle. *Heil Hitler!*' Her red hair was grey at the roots and mussed from sleep.

'Papers?'

The woman hurried to a drawer, her hands shaking as she withdrew her identity card, and a card that stated she was a member of the NSB. Fritz grabbed the documents from her hand and gave them a cursory glance. Behind him the dogs kept up their incessant barking. He winced and signalled Braun to shut them up.

'You know someone called Danique Koopman?' he asked, over their whining.

She shook her head dumbly.

'Let them loose,' he called to the men.

Immediately the dogs were everywhere, eyes bright and glassy, dragging their handlers from place to place – under the table, into the kitchen, into the bedrooms. Fritz waited, watching the woman's face. She was standing very still, hands clutching her nightdress, as if she were a statue. Just a slight trembling betrayed her fear.

The men and dogs returned to the kitchen. The dogs were overexcited, letting out guttural yaps. '*Nichts*,' said Zoll.

'Search again upstairs, you oaf.' They went.

Schneider suddenly raised a palm and slapped the woman hard across the face.

She gasped and tears sprang.

'Where is Danique Koopman?'

Her hand was on her reddening cheek. 'What is it? I know no-one of that name.'

'Tall, brunette. Wears a St Christopher medal around her neck.'

'No. I don't know her.'

'She's been here. The dogs' noses don't lie.'

'I tell you I don't know her!' She backed away until she was against the wall. 'Wait! There was a woman . . . a week or so ago . . . she just came to deliver some leaflets from the church, that's all. I don't know her name, but that could have been her—'

'What leaflets?'

She scuttled to fetch a printed sheet from the sideboard. 'I kept it only for the stove. I'm not interested in church. I'm a paid-up member of the NSB.'

Fritz squinted at her. Was she telling the truth? Her papers seemed in order, and the NSB membership card was in her name.

Scrabbling of dogs' claws on the floorboards above, before they came leaping down, still pulling at the leads. They'd found nothing. Danique wasn't here. His disappointment made him angry.

'Your dogs are useless,' he railed at Zoll. 'They couldn't find a drunk in a tavern. Get them out of here.'

His men dragged the reluctant dogs away as he took one long last look at Greta van Schelle. He walked over to where she had pressed herself back against the kitchen wall.

'You're sure there is nothing else you want to tell me, Fraulein van Schelle?'

She pulled her shawl closer over her scrawny chest. 'There is nothing more to tell. I hope you find her, whoever she is. But she has nothing to do with me.'

After staying at Maartensstraat, Nancy waited until dark the next day to walk hurriedly back towards Greta's house alongside the canal, heart thumping, breath pumping out a white cloud. At the end of the canal near the bridge, she saw there was a patrol block, so she veered left into an alley next to someone's garden. She knew that this would look extremely suspicious to be skulking in an alley like this, but she couldn't risk meeting a patrol, not dressed in fur and with her new papers that stated she was Catharina Stuyvel, an impoverished worker in a cigar factory.

The thought suddenly occurred to her that she was exactly like a wild animal, clad in fur and looking out for the hunt. It amused her in a grim kind of way, but she was too busy navigating the route to dwell on it.

When Greta answered her knock, she nearly fell inside.

'Thank God. They didn't find you,' Greta said, holding up the oil lamp, an expression of shock on her face. 'There's no-one after you, is there?' She stuck her head out into the street and then bolted the door again. Urgently, she said, 'You can't stay. They've got dogs out searching for you. They came earlier.'

'Are you all right?' Only now did Nancy notice that Greta was trembling, that her eyes were wild and agitated.

'The Nazis and their dogs!' Greta thumped a fist on the table. 'Bloody terrifying. The SS think more of their dogs than human beings. Dogs are more human than the Jews according to them.'

'Did you—?'

'Of course I didn't say anything! What d'you take me for? But what if they come back?'

'Let's hope they don't.' Nancy shrugged out of the fur and the hat and lay them on a chair.

'I'll have to get rid of it,' Greta said. 'What if it smells of you? I don't want them coming here again.'

'Who was it who came?'

'An SS officer and two lackeys with dogs, looking for Danique Koopman.'

'What did he look like, the officer?'

'Tall, blond hair. Thought he was God in his big shiny boots. Ugly, like them all.' Greta was already taking out the things in the basket as she spoke. 'The bread looks OK.'

She tore off a corner and Nancy grasped her wrist.

'Ouch! I could eat the whole loaf. And lard, that's grand. I'll take my half now.'

'Not a half, we agreed a third. I was the one who had to risk my life to get it, all you had to do was sit here and wait.'

'And be attacked by Nazi dogs. Besides, it was my coat. You couldn't have done it at all without that. Please, let's just eat.'

'Look, Greta, let's think of the bigger thing. Not just ourselves. When we couldn't get Josef out, Albie said it's every man for himself. But if we go along with that then our hope goes with it. If being an agent has taught me one thing – it's that we rely on each other. There's only resistance if we have solidarity with each other.'

'But it's hopeless. We're like flies batting against a window. The north of the country is sealed shut. We can't get out, and pretty soon if they don't shoot us, we'll starve and die.'

'No. We can work together. It's our only hope. If we made this veal into a stew, the meat would go further. All our resistance men are weak from undernourishment. We need to think about feeding them as well as ourselves. Set up some sort of helpline for them.'

'But what about us? We worked for it.'

'We'll get our share. Have you a big pot?'

Greta pointed. 'Under there. But I don't want you in my house, not if they're looking for you.'

Nancy winced at that comment, because she knew Greta was right. She was a risk. But she was safer in here than trying to go back to her place at Ellie's. 'I'll be useful, I promise. Let's work out how many portions we can make, and get cooking.'

'But how will we get it to them?'

'We'll think of something.'

It was surprising how working together could dispel the animosity between them. Nancy saw how thin Greta was, and how afraid. She had a bruise coming on her face, her nails were bitten to the quick, and every noise made her jump. Greta was continually watching the door, and checking the windows were shuttered and locked.

'Good idea,' Nancy said. 'We should seal the doors and windows and stuff up the cracks with rags,' Nancy said. 'If anyone smells this, half the neighbourhood will be on your doorstep ready to kill for it.'

'Or the Nazis' dogs.' Greta found rags and old clothes to seal the kitchen.

The veal stew was on the fire now, and the smell was so intoxicating they both had to restrain themselves from eating it even before it was cooked. They'd added a few handfuls of old pearl barley and some dried-up turnip.

Once it was made they stood back, filled with achievement.

'I've had an idea,' Greta said. She hurried down into the basement and came back with two printing ink cans. She put them down on the table. 'I've got five of these,' she said. 'I was saving them because the *Moffen* keep coming round for scrap metal and you have to give them something.'

'Are they clean?'

'Yes. Scrubbed out the best I can. I did it in case they took the pots and pans for armaments. And anyway, a bit of ink won't kill anyone. And I've got a couple of big glass pickle jars with screw-top lids and wooden handles. Empty of course.'

A half-hour later and the portions were in the jars, along with a slice of the bread wrapped in brown paper for each one.

'You realise that if they catch us delivering it, they'll want to know where it came from?' Greta said. 'It has to be tomorrow so it doesn't go bad.'

'I'll call on Thierry; tell him there's something for him to collect. He can call on the next person, and so on. Tell them to leave a good gap between visits.' She ladled some stew into two bowls and carefully measured out a portion of bread each.

'*Bon appetit!*' Nancy said.

They ate as slowly as they could, savouring each small mouthful.

'It was a good idea.' Greta looked up at her and smiled. 'Good to do ordinary things again. Cooking, and eating at the table with friends beside you. What shall I call you? You can't be Danique anymore. Catharina?'

Nancy thought a moment. 'I'm tired of code-names. Tired of never being myself. My real name's as good as any other now. It's Nancy.'

'Well, Nancy, you can stay here. In the bomb shelter with the printing press. I guess they won't come back and if it's safe enough for the press it will be safe enough for you. You needn't tell the others; it can be our secret.'

Nancy took hold of Greta's hand and pressed it. Only friends took such risks. She smiled. 'Next time, I'll bring dessert,' she said.

Greta laughed. 'And Nazi pigs will fly.'

Chapter 32

Thierry was the first to arrive at Greta's to collect his portion. He seemed rather overcome. But then he began making a strategy about how to get in touch with Albie, the next on the list. For the next few days Nancy and Greta delivered the food, which kept well because it was so cold. The temperature barely lifted above freezing. Nancy was aware now that Schneider, and she was convinced it was him, was out searching for her with his tracker dogs, and it made her anxious every time she heard a noise.

She wished she could smoke to relieve the gnawing tension in her belly, but no real cigarettes were available now. Today, the few remaining members of the Resistance were to meet in the old bank, waiting for Erik, the man who was a double agent and worked for both the Gestapo and for them in the Resistance. He was a man they'd dealt with for years. He had a fierce sense of justice and they knew he could be trusted. Erik was useful because he was the only one of them who could walk freely in this city.

The room at the old bank was cramped, but that didn't matter now there were so few of them left in The Hague to be able to do anything. Albie was the last to arrive, shambling in like an old man. 'News from the Oranjehotel,' he said.

They all looked up expectantly, Thierry, Greta, Hannie and herself.

'It's good and bad.'

'Tell us the bad first,' Nancy said.

'Steef's dead. Took his cyanide pill.'

A gasp ran round the room.

Albie sank down onto an old trunk, and leant his elbows on his knees. 'I heard the Nazis talking about it. They weren't pleased, because he wouldn't talk – called it "the easy way out".'

'Easy? To go that way?' Nancy felt tears welling, but blinked them back. 'No. He did it for his family. And for us, in case he cracked. The bloody stupid man!'

'He wouldn't have got out alive anyway. He knew that.' Greta's voice was like flint.

Nancy looked around at the worn-out faces of her friends in the Resistance, at the skin scored by worry lines, at the thin wrists poking out of old darned clothes, and wondered how they could carry on. The cost was just too much.

Thierry, sitting on a spindly chair, and no longer the huge giant, was haggard, and his skin pale and waxy from not seeing enough light.

Having said his piece, Albie leant back now against the wall, agitated, picking bits off his knitted jumper, unable to be still. The women – Greta, Hannie and herself – fidgeted on the remaining hard chairs. Instinctively, they knew, the women were the only people who could do anything now. The only people who could organise any kind of food. All men ran the risk of being picked up.

Nancy looked at her watch. Erik was late. Nobody spoke for a moment or two, they were all watching the door.

'You know they searched your old apartment in Wagenstraat the other day,' Albie said.

'Yes, I know.' Nancy swivelled to face him.

'I pretended to be fixing the lights. I'd gone to get news of Steef. Showed the new janitor my electrician's pass. They turned your apartment upside down. SD men and Gestapo. With dogs. The lift kept breaking down and they kept cursing me – that I hadn't fixed it. I could hear their boots thumping up and down four flights of stairs all morning. Schneider was shouting at your housekeeper, and she was taken away in a black van.'

'Did they find anything?' Thierry asked.

'Who knows? I couldn't stay there in case the real electrician turned up. I just went to get news about Steef.'

Another man gone. Nancy thought of Tom, of London and home. But she pushed those thoughts away. A noise in the corridor outside and they all turned expectantly as the door opened into the room.

Nancy stood so Erik could sit down. He was a man Albie had told her to trust, but she was still uncertain of him – the fact he was a man paid by two masters made her uncomfortable, even though she herself had been in the exact same position. So difficult to know who real friends were in this nightmare world.

Erik sat down, pulled up his trouser legs with an impatient gesture. 'I suggest you tell me about this Frau Koopman now,' he said to Albie. 'It seems you weren't telling me everything. Not only did I have two resistance men from out of town asking after her, but later, I had a call from Oberführer Schneider of the SS, asking me to try to find her.'

'But did you do as I asked?' Albie was leaning forwards in his seat.

'Of course,' Erik said. 'She won't bother us again. Her body's in the canal, been there days.'

'What?' Nancy shot a look of daggers at Albie. 'Why? She's no danger now I've left the Oranjehotel! And I'm not using her name, am I?'

Albie shrugged. 'She'd seen both you and Steef. She was intent on making a fuss. I wasn't to know Steef would top himself, was I? If she were to recognise him, well . . .'

'What about the boy?' Nancy couldn't believe it.

'He's with his own tribe. They'll look after him, won't they? He's one of them.'

'He's a child!'

'Don't stare at me like that. We're so few. We couldn't afford to lose anyone else.'

Erik was frowning. 'I don't understand all this. Are you telling me someone was impersonating this woman?'

'It's a long story,' Nancy said. 'When I took on her name, we thought she was dead.'

'She is now,' Erik said. 'But I don't get it. Why are the SS so concerned about her?'

'Because when I had her name, I was secretary in Scheveningen prison.'

Erik frowned. 'Doesn't explain why these two men I met yesterday were looking for her too. Like Steef said, I was keeping tabs on her. Until I got Albie's message to . . .' He mimed a gun to the head.

'What men?' Nancy was trying to keep up.

'Two from Dordrecht. One calling himself Jim, the other Burt. Probably not real names. Their cell had gone down after a mishap shooting an SS General. A bit odd – one of them arranged to meet Frau Koopman, but then scarpered as soon as he saw her. The Koopman woman was mighty upset and called the manager but by that time he'd gone. One of them came back looking for me, with a confused story about the other one looking for a woman called Agent Ludo.'

The name made Nancy stiffen. *Who could possibly know that alias? Schneider? Surely not.* 'Where are these men now?' she asked.

'Upstairs on the floor above. I said I'd try to link them up with our network, but you might want to check them out first. One of them sounded foreign, maybe English.'

'An airman? What did you think of them? Did they look like you could trust them?' Greta asked.

Erik shrugged. 'They looked like the rest of you. Skinny and scared but putting a brave face on it.'

'Shall I go up and see them?' Albie asked.

'It can wait,' Thierry said. 'Let's decide what we're going to do first.'

'There's not much we can do,' Nancy said. 'We need to radio England for help. If I could get a transmitter, I'd call every hour until they listen. Impress upon them that we're dying here of starvation. That the Dutch people don't care about the war any more. No-one cares who wins what scrap of land as long as we can eat. We can't let children starve.'

'You think they'll listen? They never have before.'

'I'll keep on until they do.'

'Then the Nazis'll pick you up.'

'No, because I'll send from a different place each day. You'll have to help me find the places. I'll need contacts – as many as we can get. And the more contacts we have around the world the better. I'll try to get the message through to Radio Oranje, to the US, to Sweden, to anyone who'll listen. We have to beg. It's all we have left. But we must put all our effort into it, you understand?'

Nobody answered.

She stood up. 'Come on! What's the matter with you all?' They looked at the ground, unwilling to meet her eyes. 'Don't you dare give up. Not now when there's no food coming through at all! Not now the shops have closed their doors.'

'There's not enough of us to fight,' Hannie said. Her eyes were ringed with dark circles. 'The soup for the central kitchen was raided by Germans. They even shot the horse and have taken it for butchery. What chance do we have?'

'None,' Greta said. 'But we have to fight or starve.' She turned to Nancy. 'If you'll risk being picked up, there's a transmitter in the shelter with my printing press.'

'And you never told me?' Nancy was aghast.

'You never asked,' Greta said.

You mean you didn't trust me. 'I'm asking now,' she said tersely. She let her gaze rake round the others. 'We'll broadcast our first Mayday from Greta's house. And I'll ask my friend in London for more contacts; anyone who might help. And Erik, can you make a list of anywhere the Germans are getting food? Any black market businesses that are selling food to them, and whether we can intercept that supply.'

'Yes, okay.'

'And maybe these men from Dordrecht have contacts in the South. Or if one of them is English, maybe they'll have communications with someone.' Nobody else moved. It seemed she was the one in charge. Nancy turned to Erik. 'My English is good. You can take me up now, and I'll talk to them, check them out.'

Chapter 33

Nancy followed Erik up stone steps, worn smooth by generations of clerks. The corridor was mostly storerooms here, but she knew that there were families of Jewish people hiding in these lumber rooms behind the disused filing cabinets and stacks of old desks. She was tired, and even climbing these stairs made her legs weak.

Erik knocked on the door with the 'V' signal.

'Who is it?' A voice in Dutch.

'Erik.'

The door opened a crack and a tall, tense-looking man with a flop of brown hair peered out. On seeing Erik, he held the door open and Nancy went in.

The other man had his back to them looking at a map, but turned as they entered.

Nancy felt something shift inside her, as if her body was two steps ahead of her thoughts. 'Tom?' *No. It couldn't be. She must be losing her mind.*

He just stared. He was thinner, with the nervy look of a

greyhound. His glasses were cracked, she noticed, and his face had more than a few days stubble.

He took a step towards her, then said, 'I'm dreaming, aren't I?'

She gave a choking laugh. 'Were you looking for me?' she asked, though the words she said were not the words she meant.

He took another step forwards and held out his arms.

But she couldn't go into them, not now, not with these other two people watching them. She saw them drop back to his side.

The space between them seemed to solidify, become electrically charged.

'You two know each other?' Burt asked him in a low voice.

'From London,' Tom said, without taking his eyes off her.

Erik said, 'Guess that means they're kosher. I'll go then, before curfew. Get tired of showing my papers to those goons. I'll see what I can find out, and be in touch.'

'Yes, yes, thanks.' Nancy was distracted, she couldn't understand why Tom was here in The Hague when she'd been about to contact him in London. *How the hell did he even get here?*

She only dimly heard Erik go, as Tom whispered urgently to the other man, 'Burt, could you give us a few minutes?'

His friend slipped out, and at last they were alone.

'You're not angry?' he said. 'I had to come.'

'Angry?' What did he mean? She moved towards him and all of a sudden it was a run, and his arms closed around her waist and he held her so tight she thought her ribs might crack. She pressed herself into his embrace until he gently pushed her away so he could look into her eyes. He lifted a tentative finger to stroke her face, and wipe away the tear that was sliding down her cheek.

'What the hell are you doing here?' she asked, the English words thick and clotted with tears. 'Who sent you? The SOE?'

'Nobody sent me. I'm supposed to be a reporter.'

'A reporter? But how long have you been in Holland?'

'Months. First I couldn't get across the river into the North, then I couldn't find you.'

'You should've looked harder.' A ghost of a smile.

He took off his glasses in that familiar gesture she knew so well. His first kiss was gentle, as if she might break.

'You're so thin,' he said.

'And you're so dirty.'

He smiled. 'Still the same old Nancy. God, I've missed you.'

The sound of her name made tears flow again but she scraped them away with her sleeve. They kissed again, this time more deeply.

When she came up for breath, she was full of wonder. 'That you should be here . . . it just doesn't feel real.'

'I thought I'd never find you. I've always been looking for you, from the first moment I landed.'

'Tell me. Tell me all. What are you doing here and who was that, the man you were with?'

'Burt? He's one I trained in coding. From Baker Street. Met him by chance. He got dropped two years ago as an agent but absconded.' He explained about Fransine and Dordrecht. 'But her cell got broken up, so now we're here.'

'You'll work with us?'

'Who's in charge of this network?'

'Nobody. I mean, we just do what needs to be done. Our organiser was called Josef but he was arrested and executed. Now we all muck in. The men don't like it that the women are more in control, but it can't be helped. We're the only ones who can actually do anything.'

'What about Erik?'

'Yes, Erik's all right. He plays both sides, to our advantage. But he can't be seen with any of us in case his Nazi masters get suspicious.'

'I still can't believe I'm talking to you.' He interlaced his fingers in hers. 'Where do you live?'

'With a friend, Greta. She runs a printing press from the bomb shelter in her garden. There won't be room for you though.

Men on that street would look too obvious. The neighbours would start tattling.'

'But I'll see you, won't I?'

'Of course. We're trying to set up some food supplies, and we might need some muscle when we get any response.'

'That's what I was supposed to do. Report back with articles from behind enemy lines. Try to persuade the Allies to get a food charity going. But my transmitter was confiscated immediately and I've only been able to send one message back to Neil since I got here.'

'Neil? You mean my brother? You're actually in touch with my brother?'

'He's with Radio Oranje now. We planned he'd use my material to pull strings at the other end.'

'Good grief. Is he all right, I mean—'

'Yes, he was fine when I last saw him. Both him and Lilli. She's expecting.'

'Really? But I've got access to a transmitter! Can we really get Neil on the other end?'

'Provided the *Moffen* don't get the detectors on us, yes.'

A 'V' knock on the door, and Burt came in. 'We're in trouble. Message from Erik. Gestapo are carrying out another raid tonight. We've to stay where we are until he can get us some German uniforms.'

'When?' Nancy asked.

'After dark.'

'I'd better get moving then.' She reached to embrace Tom, but Burt's words stopped her.

'No. Don't go out there. That's not all. Erik says the Stapo have discovered Frau Koopman's body. The boy alerted them she was missing, and now her name's everywhere, and the fact someone was impersonating her. They're checking every woman for her papers and her *Ausweis*.'

'They won't check us all, surely?'

'Schneider's issued a description of you. The real Frau Koopman was a personal friend of Ritschel, a high-up in the SS, and he's shouting foul play. It's only a matter of time before there'll be reprisals again.'

'Who's Schneider?' Tom wanted to know.

Nancy explained, leaving out the detail of her assignment. 'I need to get to the transmitter. If I don't then more people will die. Greta told me yesterday the hospitals are already full of starving people. They're feeding only those children who will die tomorrow, but tomorrow more will starve. Every day is a death sentence.'

'It's too dangerous for you to go out alone,' Burt said. 'The Wehrmacht are trigger happy because they've heard they're losing.'

'What shall we do then?'

'We wait. And we have to trust Erik will come through and find a way to get us out of here.'

The room was shrouded in darkness. Tom's mind had been ranging over the possibilities of what might happen for hours, and none of the outcomes were good. He let Nancy lean on him, hoping the comforting warmth of his arm around her shoulder might reassure her. In the distance, faint gunshots and shouts. Every time that happened he felt her whole body shudder and it gutted him that he couldn't do more to protect her. Burt paced, in between the furniture, smoking a cigarette that smelled like burning grass.

The noise of boots on the street. The Germans were close. Too close.

When the 'V' knock came, his heart almost leapt from his chest.

Burt reached to unlock the door and Erik burst through.

'You've not much time, they're at the end of the street,' Erik said, panting. 'They even checked my papers.' He dumped a parcel wrapped in an old sheet in front of them. 'Hurry and get out of here.'

Nancy struggled to her feet and tore open the parcel. Grey uniforms of the Dutch Landstorm SS, the collaborators, with the black shoulder straps and collar flashes, and matching field caps. She thrust the black cavalry trousers at Tom, and held out the boots. 'I hope to heaven these fit,' she said.

Tom looked at the pair of boots and said, 'No chance.'

Burt threw his pair to him, 'Here, these are bigger.'

The noise of men shouting and banging doors was nearer now.

Tom frantically did up buttons with fingers that didn't want to work, and ripping off his socks, forced his feet into boots that were two sizes too small.

'I can barely walk,' he said.

A crash and screams from below. Footsteps on the stairs.

'Hurry!' yelled Nancy, frantic.

In the parcel were two rifles, but though they searched, there was no ammunition.

'Ready?' Burt said.

'Take off your glasses!' Nancy said, grabbing Tom's arm. 'Look like you're arresting me.'

'Now!' yelled Burt.

Tom burst out of the door, dragging Nancy by the arm, with Burt following behind. Tom's eyesight meant the stairs were blurred as he crashed down them in the dark, just as more Wehrmacht were on their way up.

They shouted something, some sort of instruction, but Tom just ignored it and kept a good grip on Nancy's wrist. Nancy played her part, shouting and protesting, as if she were being arrested and putting up a good fight.

At the bottom of the stairs he almost barrelled into the back of an old woman who was screaming obscenities at the Germans and earning herself a slap in the face. The hallway seethed with grey-clad troops and bewildered men and women who'd been dragged out from the underground air-raid shelter. Desperately heading for air, Tom shoved his way past, dragging Nancy with him.

He winced as Nancy cried out, for her arm was stuck in the crush, and he feared he might dislocate her arm, so tight was his grip. She'd have bruises there tomorrow, but he couldn't risk losing her.

At last she cannoned free. He hoped he was doing a good impression of a Dutch Stormtrooper with an intent expression on his face. Tom marched Nancy onwards into the lightless street, ignoring the excruciating pain in his feet from the too-small boots, with Burt following right at his shoulder. He was about to drag Nancy around the corner when a stout Wehrmacht commander in a greatcoat and cap shouted out to him. 'Here!'

Shit. What now? Tom ignored him, but the man yelled again, looking annoyed.

Tom and Burt were forced to stop.

'Have you checked her papers?'

Tom hesitated. His Dutch was poor and this was the worst possible question. If he said yes, then he'd have to say they weren't in order. If he said no, then the commander would do it there and then, and he didn't know how good Nancy's papers were.

'Too dark.' He went for the least possible words.

Burt pushed himself forwards. 'She's a whore. She's been over-charging us. We're taking her to teach her a lesson.'

'I don't care what she is. All women between eighteen and thirty are to be taken to the square for SS-Obersturmführer Schneider to check. You can hand her over to me now and search the next street.'

Tom saw Burt's face tighten at the name Schneider. Obviously if they took Nancy to the square it would be the end for her. But it would also let him and Burt off the hook. Tom clung tighter to Nancy. She wasn't going anywhere without him.

'I don't want to go with these men,' Nancy said coolly 'And I'm not a whore.'

What was she playing at? Then he got it; she was acting, trying to sacrifice herself, to let them go free. A clench in his heart.

Tom gripped even more tightly to her arm. 'She's coming with us,' he said thickly in German.

The German frowned at his accent. 'Hey, I don't recognise you. Which unit are you with?'

A fraction of a second pause then Burt lifted his rifle in a sudden movement and struck the German a heavy blow under the chin. He staggered back and fell.

'Run,' Burt yelled.

Tom almost lifted Nancy off her feet as they ran stumbling down the street, with Burt following. Gunshots.

They kept running, heads down, feet echoing on the flagstones, but as they whipped around the corner they came to a bridge over the canal. They crouched low as they ran over it to get behind the stone parapet. It was one of the few canals left and the water was oily black, the bridge festooned in shadow. They dived behind a parapet out of view.

Burt's loping figure was about ten yards behind but one of the Wehrmacht rounded the corner just as he was headed for the bridge and there was a flash of fire.

With a jerk, Burt stumbled. Another flash and crack and he couldn't carry on running. Tom grasped the sleeve of Nancy's jersey, as he felt the shock of the noise reverberate through his chest.

Burt staggered towards the bridge but another burst of fire took him off balance, and there was a loud splash as he fell into the canal. Beside Tom, Nancy was panting, her eyes fixed on the small gap between the parapets.

The Wehrmacht man went to look into the canal.

The few seconds were enough for Tom to drag Nancy over the bridge and into the shadow of its undercroft.

They waited there clinging to each other as they heard the footsteps of the Nazi walking across the bridge above their heads. Tom could only see the whites of Nancy's eyes and hear her shallow breathing. Neither of them dared move.

At the other side, the soldier came to the edge of the canal, so close they could hear him breathe. But they were pressed so far back into the shadow that he didn't see them.

The thud and scrape of his boots walking back across the bridge.

'*Etwas?*' shouted another soldier.

'*Nichts.*'

Tom heard the first one curse and call them resistance scum. But the man walked away to join his friend.

They stayed there another few minutes to be sure they'd gone. Tom stood up from his cramped position. 'I'm going back for Burt,' he whispered.

'No, it's too exposed,' Nancy said.

But he wrestled away from her restraining arm and crept down to the water.

The canal was silent. There was no sign anyone had even been there. The surface was still and dark. He crouched to peer down at it but could see nothing but his own white-faced reflection.

He was tempted to get in there and search, but a part of him knew that was fruitless. No-one could survive that many bullets and a plunge into icy water. He was still there, crouched, when a pair of warm hands rested on his shoulder.

'When they find him, they'll think he was a collaborator,' Tom said. 'And it's not fair. Without him, I'd have been dead four times over.'

'Come on,' Nancy tugged at his arm. 'We have to move. We'll go to Greta's. She won't turn us away.'

Chapter 34

At Greta's Tom found he couldn't speak. He simply took off the cursed boots and let Nancy do the talking, because he knew if he tried to speak he might break down, and he didn't want to look weak in front of these women who might be relying on his strength. The thought of Burt under the cold dark water was haunting him so that he could almost feel that water seeping into his bones.

Burt. Jokey, capable Burt. Who was so much more of a man than he had ever suspected when he first met him in Baker Street. Burt, who'd stuck with him through thick and thin and had saved Tom on so many occasions. Without Burt, he would never have found Nancy. Tom gazed into the blue flame of the single wick floating in a jar of oil – all they had for light. The fact Burt was gone wouldn't sink in. He'd been a friend he could rely on, Tom realised, and now, abruptly, Tom was alone. And it would be up to him to get Nancy out of this hellhole.

Greta was instantly disapproving of Tom and he felt her animosity as soon as he arrived through the door. Partly it was the uniform. Just the sight of the grey Landstorm uniform caused a visceral dislike.

Nancy had gone with her to make tea and he heard the raised voices from the kitchen where the women were gathered around the pot-bellied stove.

'We can't have men here,' he heard her telling Nancy in Dutch.

'It's just for a night or two.'

Tom stood up and found his voice. He went to the doorway. 'Don't fall out over it,' he said in Dutch. 'We'll be leaving soon. I'm taking Nancy back to England.'

Nancy turned. 'What?'

'I'll get you out, the way I came in.'

'No. I'm not leaving. I've a job to do. There are too many people relying on me.'

'Oh, so we're *relying* on you now, are we?' Greta bristled and turned to Nancy. 'So, you're the grand expert? You think we can't do anything without you English interfering? Well, I've news for you. We don't need you, or anybody.'

'I didn't mean that, you know I didn't. We're all in this together. And I'm not leaving until The Hague is free.'

Tom felt his certainties crumble. 'But it could be months.'

'It must come soon, surely,' Nancy said. 'The Allied invasion must come soon.' She swung back to face Greta. 'And in case you didn't know, I'm half Dutch, and that's the half that's staying. Besides, we all need to eat. Tom thinks he can get in touch with my brother in England, who'll help us. He works for Radio Oranje.'

'Help us how? Bomb the city like Nijmegen?'

'Don't be like that. We hope he's someone who can persuade the British to send food aid.'

'Huh. By the time you do that, we'll all be dead. Sweden has promised us relief, and what's happened? They send a few loaves of bread that are snapped up by the Germans.'

'A few days, Greta. While we contact England. That's all.'

275

'We're not feeding him.'

'Ah, so that's what this is all about,' Nancy said. 'It's all right. We'll fend for ourselves. We just need access to the transmitter and the battery.'

'Then he'll have to pedal for it. It's the only way we can get enough charge.'

Tom was worried to see the women fighting, and shocked at how worn out Nancy looked. Greta was still prickly whilst they located the transmitter and got it wired up to the pedal battery in the bomb shelter. In the end, it was Nancy and Greta who did the pedalling, whilst Tom tried to get through to Neil.

Though he kept up with the call signal, he had little hope that Neil would reply. After all, it had been ages since he had managed any sort of call. The first attempt was a complete failure, and that night as they lay bundled in blankets on the floor of the living room, Nancy said the words he didn't want to hear. 'If we can't get through, what then?'

'We have to keep trying,' he said.

'I'm glad you're here, Tom. We've all done too much, have too many things on our consciences to give up now. To tell the truth, we're scared to give up, because if we don't win, we'll remember the awful things we did for the cause.'

It was the first time they had been able to be alone since she had first set eyes on him in the bank.

'I won't leave you,' he said. 'That much I can promise.'

He turned to kiss her. A tender kiss on the lips. He daren't do more, though he longed to. She was still so beautiful, even after all this. There was beauty in her strength and determination, but he sensed that it was a fragile shell and he didn't want to break it. She wound her arms around his neck, and after a few moments her steady breathing told him she was asleep.

Tom lay awake still, staring up at the ceiling. He felt numbed by Burt's death, as if the props of his life had been pulled away.

And now he couldn't contact Neil, he felt useless. And if they couldn't, it wouldn't be long before Greta threw them out onto the streets.

The next morning he woke to the sound of women's voices and groggily hauled himself out of his nest of blankets.

'We need to get civilian clothes for Tom,' Nancy said. 'I'll go out today and see if I can contact Erik.'

Tom went to the kitchen door to watch the women grating beet into a bowl, ready to make porridge and molasses, the only food that was available now. They had to boil and pulp it, straining off the thick liquid.

Afterwards they each had a small bowl of the bitter pulp. He guessed it had little nutrition but at least it filled his stomach. The molasses was for drinking when they got too hungry; it had sugar and some vitamins, Nancy told him. Many people could not get even beets now; the few that were left were wizened and soft.

Tom couldn't shake off his worry. His day was spent indoors, huddled around the stove reading an underground paper, and fretting about Nancy. She'd gone to find him some second-hand clothes. The paper was a two-page bulletin, *Ons Volk*, the illegal news-sheet – Dutch propaganda about how the Allies were on their way. He was sceptical now, they'd heard it too often.

In the bomb shelter, they tried the next night to contact Neil, with Nancy pedalling furiously to supply the power to the battery.

Tom pecked away at the Morse with his call sign. Anything could have happened, he thought. The possibilities ran through his head, maybe Neil had been bombed-out, maybe he'd misremembered the call sign. Maybe there just wasn't enough power in the battery.

At that moment Greta appeared in the doorway.

'I want you out tomorrow. It's a risk. I've already had the tracker dogs here once. I won't get a second chance. The vans will be out looking for anyone transmitting. Once was enough. We're not even allowed a radio, and you know the penalties.'

Nancy tried to placate her. 'I know. Just one more night, let us try one more. If it doesn't work, we'll go.'

'I have no more beet. No bread. Nothing. You can't stay here.'

That night Tom couldn't be still. His nails were bitten raw, and the thought of how Burt had been alive one moment and dead the next, wouldn't leave him. He agonised over what they would do if Greta threw them out. Their chances would be slim, but he and Nancy would have to get back to the river crossing somehow, and they'd be better off in the countryside where there might be food. He couldn't let her starve to death over here.

He looked over at Nancy, who was trying to keep busy unpicking and re-knitting an old sweater, but he could see her mind wasn't on it. She was as restless as he was.

He went over to sit on the pallet where they slept. 'What are you making?'

'Socks. It's all I know how to do. But it keeps my hands busy, stops me being hungry.'

'Talk to me, Nancy. Tell me about what you've been doing since I saw you last,' he said. 'We've so much to catch up on.'

'I can't. I can't say anything about anyone, even to you. It's too much of a risk to them to speak their names. All I can tell you is my own. They know me as Rika or Edda or Danique or Catharina. I've been so many people I can't even remember who I am.'

'I love them all,' Tom said. 'Especially Nancy, my first love.'

'Fool.' She shook her head, but there were tears in her eyes. He took her knitting from her hands and hugged her tight. She was right. He couldn't talk about Pavel or Fransine either. It was all too raw.

In the evening Tom tried Neil again with his call signal. He was about to give up when, through the crackle of static, a burst of Morse. Neil's call sign, he was sure of it. An answer! He nearly whooped with excitement.

Even Nancy heard it and stopped pedalling.

'Keep going!' Tom shouted, throwing on headphones. 'We can't afford to lose battery now!'

Tom sent his message. DESPERATE HERE STARVATION KILLING CHILDREN SEND AID URGENT

The reply came back MESSAGE UNDERSTOOD WILL PULL STRINGS and Tom scribbled it down.

SERIOUS AID NEEDED IMMEDIATELY

OK GOT IT

Nancy was pedalling furiously. Tom thought a moment then tapped out SISTER SENDS LOVE

The reply was almost instant XXXX OVER

Tom took the message to Nancy. 'Will it work?' she asked. 'D'you think he understood?'

'I don't know. It's too hard to explain everything. I'll have to try him again tomorrow.'

'It's good though, isn't it? Let's tell Greta. Maybe she'll let us stay.'

They had only just begun to speak, when there was the low burr of an engine outside. The doors were already locked. Greta immediately extinguished all the lights. Nobody moved.

Engines in your street at night were bad news. Only Nazis and the Landwacht had cars or trucks. If the Germans searched them now, they'd find the transmitter and the bike that powered it.

The tread of boots walking up and down the street. It was the only sound above their heartbeats. Tom looked at Nancy – so still, so composed. 'You are one brave woman,' he thought.

Time seemed to stretch, but then, the slam of doors and the noise of the cars departing.

Greta's hushed voice came out of the dark.

'You leave in the morning, okay?'

Chapter 35

Fritz was unable to sleep. He paced around the clutter in his apartment, still fully dressed in his SS police uniform. Even inside it was cold and the city was silent, as if already dead. He lifted a blackout blind but nothing moved. After so many years of war, of activity, of tension, he couldn't believe it had all been for nothing. That they were going to lose this damned war, and for him there would be no glorious return. No cry of victory.

He caught sight of his grey face in the window, pinched, like the face of a weasel. He had no doubt what would be coming to him if the British or Canadians got hold of him. He knew what he had done. The screams of tortured men echoed deep in his belly like a dark sludge that couldn't be shifted. How had it started?

He wanted to vomit it all up. He thought of it like that, that if he could only purge himself of it, he could still be saved.

Meanwhile, Danique Koopman was still out there somewhere. It was the thread he hung on to, a kind of madness. His men laughed at him now. Today he'd hauled more women in for questioning, insisted that Braun empty a whole row of houses and bring out all the women. None of them had been her.

He turned away from the window and aimed his boot through the nearest canvas. He recognised that he was a man obsessed, but what else could he do? He craved this one small victory. In the daytime he still held on to the faint hope that it was all a mistake, that his Danique would somehow emerge shining from this hellhole of war. At night the fantasies of how he might make her grovel for forgiveness sent him half-insane.

He got out the map of the city. He'd sectioned it into places he'd already searched, and places yet to be scoured. With stabbing motions of his pen he drew a box around another block. Braun and Zoll would roll their eyes, but they could do nothing against his orders, and they had uncovered more *onderduikers* because of his thoroughness. She was here somewhere, and he intended to find her.

He remembered the place he'd once searched with the dogs. How they'd behaved as if Danique had been there. He'd go back again to that house in the Bezuidenhout, interrogate the woman again, see what could be found out.

In Greta's bomb shelter in the Bezuidenhout, the sound of distant sirens woke Nancy where she and Tom lay huddled in blankets, and she leant over to see Tom's watch. Last night they had made love for the first time, and it had been intimate, shattering. The feeling of skin on skin, of naked passion, of being so alive.

Tom's body was lean, his face gaunt, but he was still her Tom. They had been greedy for each other, for touches that were tender not brutal.

The clock on the makeshift shelf of the shelter showed eight o'clock. They had overslept. By now he was stirring too.

'First time I've heard air-raid sirens since London.' Tom said. 'Stay there – I'll go take a look.'

She watched him dress through the piercing wailing, as she

threw on her own clothes, unable to let him go anywhere without her. She dragged one skirt over another for warmth, and because one of the skirts threatened to fall apart it was so thin.

As she put her jumper on, Nancy followed Tom up the stairs towards the front door.

'Probably a false alarm,' Greta shouted from the kitchen. 'As soon as it stops, you leave, Okay?'

Nancy winced. Reality struck home. So Greta hadn't changed her mind. In a way she didn't blame her; she knew housing an Englishman was a risk. Nancy put a hand on Tom's shoulder as she went outside to look towards the city centre, but it was foggy. A thick mantle of mist meant she couldn't see much of the city. What she could see though, were the dark shapes of aircraft through the grey. The wind chill cut through her sleeves making her fold her arms against its bite.

'It's ok, they're British planes,' Tom said, his hand shadowing his eyes.

Just as he said that, they saw a black shape fall from the sky about a hundred yards away, and immediately a searing flash of bright yellow. Moments later, before they could even exclaim, a thunderous bang and hot ball of air almost knocked them off their feet. A plume of black smoke dissipated into the fog.

By now the sky was full of planes, and more of the black shapes were falling.

'Christ Almighty!' Tom grabbed her and covered her head with his arms. The ground erupted like an earthquake. He tried to drag her inside as in front of them buildings crashed to the ground, but Nancy was mesmerised by the sight.

All at once she lurched into motion. 'What the hell? More are coming!' she yelled. Another wave of bombers rose like whales out of the fog.

'Tell Greta – the shelter!' Nancy dragged him back in the house. 'They're bombing us,' she shouted to Greta as they stumbled inside to warn her.

'No,' Greta said. 'What's going on?' She took a step towards the window to look out.

'Don't go near the—'

Another almighty sound, like a cross between a roar and the crump of an explosion. The curtains blew inward with shards of glass.

Greta was on the floor before they could do anything. There seemed to be a lot of blood, but they dragged her out through the back door and down the steps into the bomb shelter just as there was another deafening boom.

They huddled close to the printing press, using it as protection.

Nancy pulled the printing rag from the ink bin and pressed it to Greta's face. The wounds seemed to be surface cuts from broken glass, but Greta's eyes were wide pools of shock. They crouched, immobile as the ground trembled under more thuds and booms, and concrete dust showered down from the ceiling making the air thick and heavy. Finally after what seemed to be endless pummelling, the noise stopped.

Tom brushed the dust from his hair and shoulders. 'You okay?' he asked, holding Nancy tight.

'Fine.' She couldn't actually hear him, her ears were muffled as though stuffed with felt.

Tom eased his way out of the door which was stuck at a strange angle. A chunk of metal had embedded itself in the door frame.

They picked their way past it desperate to breathe some fresh air.

The scene that met them was unrecognizable. An icy wind blew across an empty landscape they didn't know. At first Nancy thought it was snowing. She brushed a few flakes from her shoulders, then turned. Behind her, their end of the street was still intact, but the rest of the houses nearer the centre of Bezuidenhout had been obliterated, as if they'd never existed. People were running, mouths open, screaming. Their voices didn't penetrate her ears, only the look on their faces as they ran. Some couldn't run, but staggered and fell.

Behind them the sky was lit in an unearthly orange glow and palls of black smoke clung to the sky.

Beside her Greta was coughing. The air smelled of cordite and burning, and chunks of ash and soot whirled past them.

A horse and cart came trundling up, with a red cross painted on its side. There was just one woman in it, a grey-haired nurse in a ragged coat with a Red Cross armband thrust over it. She was shouting at the horse and flapping the reins, but the horse was spooked and wouldn't go. Tom rushed out and stood out in the road waving his arms.

'What can we do?' he asked. 'Are ambulances coming?'

She cut off his words with an impatient shake of her head. 'No fuel. No drivers. You look fit enough – come on, we need help getting the wounded on board. I'm Betje.'

'I'll come too,' Nancy said.

'No,' Tom insisted. 'You wait here with Greta, the fire might spread. Help Greta save whatever she can. Get the transmitter and anything that might be useful. Start tearing sheets for bandages. I don't know what the hell's going on, what the English are playing at, but I'll be back as soon as I know.' He grabbed her by the shoulders and planted a kiss on the top of her head.

As he spoke a group of people were struggling towards her, laden down with possessions. They had the blank look of shock that said they had seen something terrible.

'Can I help?' Nancy shouted.

An elderly man, his face and glasses blackened with smoke crumpled as if his legs might give out. He was carrying a blanket bulging with papers and what looked like small pieces of silver, almost too big for him to heave onto his shoulders. He stopped to rest, his head hanging. 'The fire. There's no water. The dikes were bombed. No firemen, all taken to Germany. And the wind has the fire in her teeth. It's raging, all down my street. And so many dead. Whole streets just flattened.' He took a ragged breath.

'Are you on your own?'

A nod. 'The *Moffen* took my son before Christmas. My lodgers have all fled – gone the opposite way, towards the forests, but it's a death trap. The German V2 rockets are there and they're guarded.'

'Rest a while here. We have water and can give you a drink,' Nancy said.

'Will they come back?' He looked anxiously at the sky.

She left Greta to answer that, as she hurried inside, crunching over broken glass until she could get to the tap. She filled a cup and was about to take it to the man outside when she heard a car.

Germans. She hesitated and then took herself upstairs to where she could see out of the window. The car was a sleek German machine, though covered in dust. She recognised the uniforms as that of the German police.

Greta stood up, as did the old man. It was what you had to do with the Nazis, as if they were royalty. Even if you were injured. Greta and the old man looked bedraggled, beaten, next to these tall men in their shiny boots.

'You are Greta van Schelle?' Nancy stiffened. The voice was immediately familiar and set her pulse racing. 'I think you have some information we might need. I ask you to collect your papers and come with us.' Was it Schneider? She tried to lean a little further out to see.

'It might take me a while to find them,' Greta said. 'As you see, we have suffered some bomb damage.' Nancy looked round the room for any way to escape, but there was nowhere. She had to just keep silent and pray.

In the room downstairs she heard Greta opening a drawer and two sets of feet crunching in the room.

Don't come upstairs, she begged.

'Who needs enemies when the Dutch have friends like yours,' the man's voice said. 'They've done the job nicely for us. Our men are on the outskirts with roadblocks, ready to take any *onderduikers.*'

'What do you mean?'

'The British bombs. Too stupid to bomb our rockets and bombed Bezuidenhout instead. The rich part of the city where no doubt all their friends are hiding. But no fear, those who are not already dead will be searched as they leave.'

Nancy put a hand to her mouth. She was certain now it was Fritz's voice. And those bombs were Allied bombs. They'd unwittingly played right into German hands. She felt her nose and throat begin to tickle from the sooty air. She had an intense urge to cough.

Mustn't cough.

A few moments silence below. She wondered if Greta had handed over her papers.

'What's that out there?' Fritz asked.

In their haste they hadn't covered the door to the shelter.

'Okay. You come with us.' It was an order. 'Zoll, take her to the car.'

The front door banged. *Please, Greta. Don't tell them I'm here.*

She watched one of the policeman push Greta into the car, whilst the other got in the driving seat. Fritz didn't even glance up, but she watched him stride around to the side of the house. Definitely him. Thank God for that distraction. She guessed where he was going and tiptoed into the back bedroom to look from the window. Through a chink in the curtain she saw him cross the garden and head towards the stairs into the bunker and disappear in the door.

It was over for Greta. He'd see the printing press and all the plates for the false documents, including the false NSB membership cards they all carried.

She rubbed her palms together; they were sticky with sweat and grit.

Would Greta tell? Would Schneider come back in the house? She had the insane urge to hide under the bed.

Fool. He would certainly find you there, and you would look ridiculous.

To her relief, she heard the engine start up and the car draw away. Adrenaline made her feel dizzy. She sat on the bed, her head pressed into her hands. She knew one thing, if they questioned Greta, she had only about twenty-four hours before they came for her, maybe less. Would Greta give up her contacts? Would she tell them about Tom? Greta's was no longer a safe place – not for her and not for Tom. She should have gone with Tom, she realised.

She took a gulp of water from the cold tap before filling the cup for the old guy.

On the street though, the man had gone, replaced by more people streaming out of the ruins. She looked down the road. A roadblock of Wehrmacht men had been set up there already.

She must find Tom, and quickly. And he mustn't come back here.

A scene from hell; that was all Tom could think. The horse stopped and threw up his head, refusing to go on. Tom was unsurprised for the heat from the fire had reached them now, and the stench of burning. What was worse though was the stream of injured people limping, running, crawling from the ruins. Many were bleeding, body parts missing or bloody, all screaming for help to get their relatives out from under the rubble.

Tom couldn't move from shock. As if his brain had switched off. He merely stared at this catastrophe. The scale of it was too immense to take in. Anything they could do would be so small, like pissing in the wind.

'It's hopeless,' the woman said, despairing. 'We've no telephone or radio to call for help. The Germans have confiscated it all.' She jumped off the cart and was tugging at the reins trying to persuade the horse to go on. But it struggled, rolling its eyes and throwing up its head. Tom couldn't blame the beast, he didn't want to go on either.

Among the survivors, a little girl ran towards him, her mouth open in pain. She was clutching a torn arm, with shrapnel wounds to the face and legs. She was shouting something incoherent. Overwhelmed by her distress he ran to meet her and without ceremony lifted her onto the cart.

'No, no!' she shouted. 'My mama's underneath our house. You have to come!'

'We'll mend your arm first,' he said in Dutch, over the girl's protests. Then to the woman, 'We need to get them to hospital,' he said.

Before long the cart was full of injured people and they turned to take them back towards the city. As they approached though, he saw the roadblock with the grey-green Wehrmacht uniforms.

She turned to him. 'Best get off here. Try to assemble more injured people by that lamp post over there. I'll come back as soon as I can.'

The little girl screamed as he tried to get off, 'No, no!'

But he turned to her and said, 'I'll go back, see if I can find your mama. You go with the nice lady, okay?'

It was the hardest thing watching them go.

Chapter 36

Fritz took Fraulein van Schelle to the police station at Jaaverstraat 28.

'So you have an illegal printing press in your bomb shelter,' he said pleasantly. 'You never told me that, the last time I visited.' She'd been silent in the back of the car, closed in on herself, but he'd soon make her talk.

The police station was busy, with a crowd of handcuffed men waiting to be settled in cells. He asked his men to search her in front of them, right there in the lobby. She was a scrawny-looking woman, all skin and bone. When they searched her, his men laughed and said she was too bony a chicken to mess with.

The search always made the captives understand how serious he was. Something about having people handle you roughly, like a piece of meat. It was a part he enjoyed because it established his power immediately. Her fellow Dutchmen, the ones waiting to be assigned a cell, said nothing but watched the search all the same through furtive sideways glances. It had the desired effect – Greta van Schelle was already quaking when he brought her in for questioning.

Earlier in the day, they'd interrogated a man who'd been hiding Jews. He was in a bad state, in the adjoining cell. His groans could be heard clearly from where he and Greta van Schelle sat, across the table from one another. An ashtray and a clipboard lay in the middle of the table. Zoll stood by the door – standard procedure in case she should run, but Fritz knew immediately she wouldn't. Her body language showed that she was already half won over.

'What do you know about Danique Koopman?' Fritz asked.

She was silent, in a half-hearted attempt not to give anything away. He'd seen this sort of token resistance at the Oranjehotel and it was such a waste of his time. He saw her legs tremble and she pressed both hands down on her knees to stop them.

Suddenly, he was tired of it all. Of this game.

'Take her for a look into room two,' he said to Zoll.

He knew what they'd find. A man strapped to a table, with a back bloody from the whip, and feet scorched black and blistered with burns.

A few moments later Zoll brought her back. Her face had lost all colour.

'You will talk now. Understand me?'

'Yes,' she whispered.

'Danique Koopman. Where is she now?'

'At my house. With her friend, Jim, an Englishman.'

'She's there now, you say?'

He stood, he was so surprised. But he caught Zoll's slight smile and fought the instinct to go straight back to the car.

'And what is her real name?'

'Nancy.'

'Surname?'

'I don't know it. She's a British agent.'

Schneider turned to Zoll with a look of triumph. 'So two British agents in your place.' He leant in towards the woman whose eyes were now leaking tears. 'You've been very busy, haven't you, Fraulein van Schelle? You will tell us everything.

All your contacts. If you do that then perhaps I will send you to a camp instead of beating you or executing you as a traitor, hey?' He took hold of the clipboard. 'Zoll, you will take down details of everything this woman says, then put her in cell three. Any trouble, cell two.'

He stood up tall, put his cap back on his head, and strode out. 'Braun, come with me.' He was going back to Bezuidenhout.

Nancy was throwing clothes in to a bag, Tom's spare kit and her own. Coughing, she grabbed the suitcase transmitter and set off towards the still-blazing ruins of Bezuidenhout. She was the only person going in that direction, and she searched every building, every group of people for Tom. Frantic, she called for him, 'Tom?'

But she was not the only one searching. She realised she had to ignore the other people looking for their lost loved ones in this city of carnage. She clung to one thing, Tom mustn't go back there, to Maystraat. They had to leave Greta's and leave straightaway.

The fire raged ahead of her like a huge hot wave. The whole of the area of Louise de Colignystraat seemed to be one ball of flame. *Please let him not be in there*, she prayed.

Streams of people were running from the blaze. As she hurried nearer she saw people flinging their possessions into the road lest the fire should burn down their houses. Still, she ran frantically like a waif from ruined house to ruined house, calling for Tom.

She'd almost given up when she spotted a horse and cart waiting by a lamp-post amid a group of injured people. Some were amputees dying where they lay, some blinded, with rags tied around their eyes. The nurse Betje that she'd seen earlier was crouching over them with a flask of water.

Nancy ran towards her, her voice a croak. 'Where's Tom?' she asked. 'The man you were with earlier?'

Betje pointed to two men carrying a makeshift stretcher made out of a ladder.

291

Nancy almost wept. Tom was dragging his feet, and his clothes were covered in stains of dark red blood. She waited until he'd loaded the man onto the cart which was bound for Bronovo Hospital, a mile away in the Benoordenhout district.

Immediately Tom saw her there with the transmitter, he said, 'What's the matter?'

She moved closer so she could look into his eyes. 'They've taken Greta. The Gestapo.'

'Shit.'

'And they found the printing press and the bunker.'

'Then she's sunk. I don't suppose there's anything we can do?'

She couldn't even form an answer.

He understood. 'Is there another safe house we can get to?'

'Not that I can think of. And it will be hard to get past the roadblocks carrying this.' She lifted up the transmitter.

'Dump it,' Tom said. 'God, what an unholy mess. What shall we do?'

'Go further in. It's all we can do. Hope that we can find somewhere standing that we can hide in. The place is full of refugees, maybe we won't stand out too much.'

'Let's get ourselves as far from Greta's as we can. We should head for Arnhem. Erik thinks that's where the Allies are planning their next offensive. We can meet them there. But I don't understand why they're bombing us here – some sort of diversionary tactic?'

'I told you. I'm keeping the transmitter and I'm not going back to London. Not yet.'

'We have to. Arnhem's the best choice. The Allies might invade there at any time. They'll be needing people in the Resistance to help the invasion force when they get there, particularly interpreters like you.'

'I don't know . . .'

'I'll help Betje get these people on board and then let's move away from where the Gestapo might find us.'

* * *

Fritz was not foolish enough to go into the house in Bezuidenhout alone. He took Braun, and told him to wait outside whilst he went in.

Braun looked disgruntled, but stood outside. 'See if you can find any food,' he said.

Fritz ignored him; he suspected Braun thought his search for Danique was a waste of time. In the hallway, ridiculously, he called out her name, 'Danique?' It sounded plaintive and foolish.

He chastised himself. His Danique was not Dutch at all, but English. And her name was not even Danique, but Nancy. A name he felt no affinity for at all. Perhaps it was another cover name. He couldn't believe she had felt nothing for him; that a woman could cheat him that way. And who was the man she was with? The thought of another man made him grind his teeth.

The house was silent except for a clock ticking in the hall. In the distance he could hear falling masonry, running feet. He went in the kitchen and sat down there. Had Danique eaten here? He imagined her, the neat way she placed her napkin on her lap, as she had sat opposite him at his own table.

Had another man sat opposite her, the way he had?

Enough. Desperate to escape these thoughts, he got up to cross into the living room and then strode up the stairs into the bedrooms. The hall swam with dust from the bombings. Shafts of light bloomed across the walls. A quick search revealed nothing – empty rooms shivering with dust. He opened a few drawers hoping to find a trace of her there, but there was nothing he recognised, none of the clothes were hers, not even a whiff of her perfume. Instead, the stench of burning rasped his throat.

He took off his officer's cap and sat down on the bed, with a creak of worn-out springs. Unaccountably, this sad, bare room seemed to conjure up the loss of her. The loss of everything, his job, the war, any friends he'd had. Stupidly, he'd hoped she was here to somehow comfort him.

An intense desire to weep made him let out a strangled moan, but he stiffened his spine. SS officers never cried. They remained true to their outer shell of grit and efficiency. But in this room he could have a moment to stop pretending.

It was over. It was only a matter of time before they would have to admit they'd lost. The Russians were on their way to Berlin, it was the whisper everyone heard, but no-one dared speak aloud. He'd given himself completely to the war, to this whole ideal of Nazism.

He remembered how it had started – the young men shining with health – women would kiss them on the street, so loved were they by everyone, these golden boys and girls. All of Germany was intoxicated by the idea of the glorious future lifting over the horizon like a sunrise. Yet now, outside this house, when he looked around, all he saw was carnage; men grey with hunger, cities unfit for habitation, fine buildings razed to the ground. And hardest of all, the fact that everywhere he looked the eyes reflected back hate and fear. Even his own side now dished out cruel mockery because they could no longer bear what they had become.

Fritz sat in silence a few more minutes, exhaustion seeping into his bones. Then he stood up, and jammed his cap back on. She couldn't have gone back the way he'd come because he'd checked the patrol. He'd move them closer in, like a noose. Go to every patrol point, every route out of Bezuindenhout until he found her. It was all he had left to do. One small gleam of triumph. Nothing else was worth living for.

He checked the pantry. Empty except for the wizened end of a beet. He picked it up, and as he went out, thrust it into Braun's hands.

Tom and Nancy had hidden in the ruins for a week now, and were growing weaker by the day. Scavenging had given them little sustenance; the bottom of a jar of pickles, a scraping of oats from the bottom of a sack, and a few mouldy sprouting potatoes.

The fire had burned the whole of the central residential area of Bezuidenhout into a hollow ruin. There were few people on the streets because the stench of death was everywhere. Nazi patrols no longer came along these streets, only Betje and her small team of Red Cross nurses.

The day after the bombing, leaflets were dropped by the RAF telling the population it had been a navigation error and they were sorry. They'd been aiming for the German V2 rocket bases in the forest nearby. Surprisingly this didn't make Nancy angry. She was too numb for anger, and it was reassuring to know that someone out there cared for the fate of Holland.

They were sheltering in a house that had been ripped in half by a shell. The fact it looked so precarious meant it hadn't been searched by the Nazis or other looters. They'd found a quilt that was half-burned away, and a soot-stained blanket to try to keep off the chill as they squatted in the downstairs room. They daren't light a fire in case it attracted attention, now the big fire was out. All the bedrooms were open to the rain and wind and when birds dared to land, chunks of roof tiles rattled down into the ruins of the chimneys. The place was bereft of furnishings. The previous owners had taken anything salvageable, leaving only smoke-damaged debris and charred furniture.

'They must come soon,' Tom said. Nancy knew he must mean the Allies.

She nestled against his shoulder. 'I feel so useless. All I can think about is food.'

'At least we're together,' he said. 'But it's frustrating having so little charge for the battery. It's on its last legs. If only we could get through to Neil.'

'It seems so odd to think of him in London, whilst we're here. That the red buses will still be running, and he'll have Sunday lunch as usual.'

'Don't.' He pulled her closer in to keep her warm. Survival meant they had less and less of importance to say. Just an embrace was enough. She knew that inside his head he had his own land-scape running, his own interior world, one filled with his own fears, his own images of bombs and blood.

That night he hung up the wire and tapped frantically away, despite the risk the transmission would be traced. She watched his face, taut with concentration, knowing how impossible it was to convey anything in a few short syllables. Whenever Tom came off the air, he was stoic, and tried not to show how much England's lack of comprehension hurt.

Finally the battery for the transmitter gave out and the thing went dead. Nancy felt like weeping.

They watched each day for Betje's cart coming in to collect first the living, then the dead. She always had a few provisions for them, as a thank you to Tom for his help in evacuating the injured. The Red Cross had access to a little food for the sick, dried meat, and dehydration solution in glass bottles.

The next time she came, Betje told them she was going to stop coming; one more day, then her work there was done. They'd have to leave the ruins of this place or starve.

Tom broke the bad news. 'We can just about look like survivors now, because people are still coming and going for their belong-ings, but soon no-one else will come out of here and we'll just look too obvious. We'll have to get out – try to act injured, like Betje's survivors.'

'Have you got papers? Some sort of ID?' Nancy asked him.

He shook his head. 'Left them when I had to dress as a Landstorm officer.'

She bit her lip, it didn't bode well.

Betje was dubious about getting them out. 'There's only one way it might work. Find more corpses and put you both under-neath them. Perhaps then, the guards on the roadblock won't look too closely. We can take some goods too, but we'll be searched; we always are. The suitcase is a big risk. But I'm willing to try it if you are.'

They looked at her lined face, her grey hairs escaping from her nurse's cap. They were awed at the fact she was willing to risk death for herself, in order to help them.

'You don't have to help us,' Nancy said.

'I know I don't have to. But I want to. Every single person I can save is one more to testify against them when that time comes.'

Nancy feared for Tom more than herself. 'Is that the only way to get past the patrols?'

'Without papers, and with a young man like him? Yes.'

'It's a chance,' Tom said, 'and if it doesn't work, Betje will have two more corpses to deliver to the hospital.'

Nancy summoned a smile.

Over the next few days Tom managed to find some blood-stained rags, and he and Betje had located two corpses that looked possible. Nancy didn't want to look until the last possible moment.

Before they got ready, Tom took Nancy in his arms for a tight hug. He ran a forefinger tenderly down her cheek, his eyes troubled. He spoke to her in English, not Dutch. 'If I get caught, you stay quiet, right? You act dead and then try to get the hell out of here. Okay?'

'Then you have to agree the same,' she said. 'If I'm caught, you just try to survive. Get home to Neil. Tell my family I love them.'

'It won't come to that. I'll see you on the other side, at the hospital.'

They loaded the transmitter and put it under a pile of rags, and a blackened rug. Tom gave Nancy a copy of the silk code he'd agreed with Neil, written out on a piece of paper.

'You remember how to use it?' he asked.

A nod. The thought of it, of how they'd invented it together back in Baker Street, made her emotional. She gathered herself together. 'Shall we swap call signs so Neil knows who's calling?'

Tom seemed to read her and held her in a tight embrace. 'We'll make it,' he whispered. 'Chin up.'

Nancy hugged him back and stowed the slips of copied paper in her brassiere.

They'd found two corpses, a woman and a man from the same bombed-out house. The woman was barely recognizable for burns and it revolted Nancy to look at her. The man was heavy and took all of them to drag the body to the cart, even though he was thin. They were all weak from malnourishment. One of the man's legs was missing, and just the sight made Nancy want to heave. She steeled herself as they thrust him aboard, she apologised to the couple as if they were alive. His papers were still in his jacket pocket and though the photo looked nothing like Tom, Tom took them all the same and memorised the name of Frans Veldekens, a railwayman and member of the NSB.

'Though I don't agree with his allegiances, I'll find their relatives if I can,' Betje said. 'If they have any left.'

Nancy tied an old blood-stained shirt around her head like a bandage to cover most of her face. With difficulty they arranged themselves under the weight of the dead man and his wife.

Betje had suggested they bring the charred quilt and blanket from the house, and Betje now covered them over. 'Sleep well,' she said in Dutch.

Under the stinking blanket Tom took hold of Nancy's hand and squeezed it.

'This is it,' he said. She felt him cross his fingers before re-grasping her hand.

Nancy was curled on her left side half-covered by the man's corpse, and her heart thudded against the wooden boards of the cart.

The cart shifted under them and began to rumble forwards. Betje drove the cart towards the checkpoint. The journey was only about half a mile, but time seemed to have stretched. Every jolt made Nancy want to run. But she stayed motionless, her fingers wound into Tom's warm grip.

'Halt!'

The cart lurched to a stop.

'What have you there?' A soldier's voice asked in German.

Betje replied, her voice calm and steady. 'The usual. No survivors now. I'll take these to the morgue at the hospital.'

Footsteps crunching on the hard ground, getting closer. Tom slowly released Nancy's hand.

Nancy held her breath, praying her heart was not making as much noise as she thought. She kept her eyes closed under the bandage but felt a sudden draught and flash of brightness as the blanket was shifted away.

'Stinks,' the man said.

Then she felt a hand by her throat. 'What's this?'

Oh, no. Her St Christopher. It had fallen out of the neck of her jumper.

A tug as a hand tried to wrestle it from her throat. Then he let go with a gasp of alarm. 'Hey! This one's still warm.'

A sudden sharp pain in her side, as something stabbed into her. A gun? What?

She couldn't help but make an involuntary movement. It happened before she had any control over it.

A grip came around her arm and started to pull. 'Here! Over here!'

More running feet. She knew then it was all over. Betje yelled at the horse to move, but her continued shouts made her realise it was shying in its traces.

Nancy's arm was being wrenched from its socket. *Should have attacked first.* But with no weapon, she had nothing to fight with. A flashback to her training at Arisaig. From the one un-bandaged eye she glimpsed three uniformed men.

Divert them from Tom. That instant she decided to run. Tom's arm tugged at her from beneath the blanket. She scrambled up and tried to make a mad leap, but one of the soldiers threw his weight onto her and she crashed back.

Betje shouted again at the horse.

A man's eyes under a metal helmet glared into hers. *Knee to the groin*. She jerked her knee up, but he swore, punched her in the face and pinned her down. A rough hand ripped off the bandage. He was pressing her throat until she gasped for breath. In the harsh bright light of day his face loomed over her.

At the same time she heard Tom's yell of 'Leave her alone!'

No. You fool! Our agreement! Don't tell them you're there.

Tom's words were in English. Shit. Nancy twisted and writhed to try to get up, but Tom had already leapt off the cart to come to help her.

From the side of her eye she glimpsed Betje flicking the reins and yelling obscenities at the horse to get it to move on. The horse shot away just as she managed to sit up, and one of the soldiers fired at it as it passed. The bullet zipped past her ear but the horse, spooked, broke into a wild canter. She tried to call out to Tom but the horse swerved to avoid a pothole and she lost balance and fell back, cracking her head on the side of the cart.

By the time she looked up, she couldn't see Tom. He was completely pressed to the ground by armed men.

Chapter 37

'Up! Up!' A pistol was at Tom's throat, but he couldn't move for the soldier's weight on his hips. German words and ragged English came thick and fast. 'Pretend to be dead, would you? Who was that woman?' The questions came too rapidly for him to answer and besides his mouth was full of dirt.

The other Wehrmacht man crouched by his head and dangled the St Christopher medal in front of Tom's face, swinging it by its broken chain. 'Who is she? Why is Schneider looking for her?' He was a man with bad breath and a chin that had been shaved completely smooth, eyes shadowed by his helmet.

Tom kept still, didn't react, his mind working to try to fathom what to do.

'What do you mean, Schneider's looking for her?' The man turned his attention to his friend and the gold chain but kept Tom pinned.

'He's searching for a woman with a gold necklace, a St Christopher medal like this one. Zoll told me he's obsessed with her. This bastard might know where she'd go.'

'You mean take him in?' Pistol man kept the gun to Tom's head, though Tom could feel it vibrating as if the soldier couldn't wait to pull the trigger. 'Why? We could kill him now. Just keep the gold.'

'Better not. Schneider's a devil. If he ever found out, we'd be shipped to the Eastern Front before we could even say *Heil*. This woman's on the SS "Wanted" list, I'm sure of it.'

'So? He won't know.'

'Could mean promotion, a commendation at the least.'

'Shove him in the truck then, and we'll take him in. He's got to be worth a pip or two.'

Nancy was dizzy. She'd hit the back of her head on the edge of the cart and now nausea overtook her. She could only think of one fact. They'd got Tom, and she dreaded what might happen to him. As the cart bounced over the potholed road, she put her sore head in her hands and cursed herself. It was her necklace that had got them into this mess.

Betje drove like fury, the horse clattering down empty streets. Nobody stopped them, for everyone was conserving precious energy by staying indoors. After a while, when no-one seemed to be coming after them, the horse slowed, blowing and panting. Betje turned back to shout, 'The police station is on Jaaverstraat. That's where Schneider works and where he'll have taken him,' Betje said.

'There? I thought he worked at the prison?'

'Not any more,' Betje said.

They pulled up shortly afterwards at the hospital. Betje turned to face her, her lips quivering. 'He's no hope of getting out.'

'If he doesn't talk?'

'Execution if he's lucky. Or, there's a prisoner transport leaving in two days for Westerbork.'

Nancy put a hand on her shoulder. 'What about you?'

'They'll come for me too. Can't pretend they won't. They know me too well, and where I work.'

'Can't you get out of here?'

'What do you think?' Her answer meant no. 'This is my city,' she said.

Nancy helped Betje unload the bodies from the cart, wrap them in the blankets and take them to the morgue. The place was already full, and stank of putrefaction. Betje labelled the couple with their address, writing it on their arms in pen.

She looked up from her grisly task and pointed to the transmitter suitcase now grey with ash. 'There are men from the resistance hiding on the top floor. Ward 8. If a Nazi comes they go into the laundry storerooms or the operating theatres. We keep NSB people out of those rooms – nobody goes there except men working for the resistance, and a few Jews. We save the lives we can.' She stood upright and stretched her back. 'Head for the top floor and ask for a man called Gerard. He's taken charge of this network now, as well as the one in Amsterdam. I must go and help now with the injured from Bezuidenhout.'

Gerard. Oh no. Nancy didn't hold out much hope of help if it was him. He was the one who had given her this doomed assignment in the first place. Wearily, she picked up the wireless case and clinging to the banister, hauled herself up the stairs and along the corridor to Ward 8.

Her head throbbed and her mouth was dry. But worse, the wretchedness of losing Tom ate into her heart. The thought of him being in Schneider's hands made her hot with rage and futility as she blundered down the corridors. This hospital was not a quiet place of calm and refuge like a hospital in peacetime. Every inch of floor space in the corridor was covered by a body, many groaning or crying out. Blood and dust; that was her main impression. And too few nurses, but those she saw went from man to man giving whatever comfort they could. None of them had complete uniforms – some just an armband or a cap, some an apron. All of them had hunger-riven faces and blood-stained hands.

Ward 8 was no better. Men lounged against the walls, or slept actually underneath the hospital beds. It stank of filth and ammonia, and hands reached out to her for help as she passed along.

'Has anyone seen a man called Gerard?' she asked.

A lad stood up. 'What do you want from him?' He was young, face full of freckles, he looked about thirteen. He had no visible injury, except the haunted look shared by everyone else.

Nancy took a chance he was a resistance courier. 'I need help to get one of my friends out of a difficult situation. He's an agent, an English agent.'

'You're in the right place, Miss.' The lad stuck out a thumb to indicate she should follow as he wove through the ward. Nancy lugged the case after him. This floor seemed to be all people with head injuries. The end bed was occupied by a man with a bandage over his face. He was lying on his side, sleeping.

The boy prodded him hard on the shoulder. 'Hey, Gerard, someone to see you.'

Gerard sat up and looked at Nancy through one eye before pulling off the bandage. The big bear-like man scowled at her, only now he was unshaven and his eyes sunk in wrinkles.

'You again,' he said. 'You still here? Thought you'd gone under-ground.'

'I need help. They've arrested my friend and I need to get him out.'

'If he's been caught, we can't do anything.'

'He's from Fransine's cell in Dordrecht. A friend of Burt. They called him Jim. He's English.'

Now Gerard sat up, his eyes penetrating. 'Who told you all these names?'

'He did. He's been taken to the police station on Jaaverstraat.' She gave a brief update on how they'd come to be arrested, whilst the others in the neighbouring beds listened to the story.

'Who else does he know?' one man asked. 'All those people are dead.'

'Thierry, Albie, me. But I know him, and he won't talk,' Nancy said, 'but better to get him out quickly. He's going to be useful to you once the Allies break through.'

Gerard clapped his hands and several men clustered around the bed. They all had head wounds, but it soon became apparent they were fake, and the bandages a way of concealing their faces and identity should the Nazis come snooping.

'Does he know someone called Erik?' Gerard asked.

'Yes. Erik sorted out a Landstorm uniform for him during a raid.'

'Then we're in trouble, he might give Erik away. Best get Erik in, have a word.' Gerard immediately sent the young freckle-faced boy to find Erik, reeling off a list of instructions. 'Tell him to see what he can find out from Schneider about the man held in there – the Englishman that came from the Bezuidenhout.' He turned to Nancy, who was still clutching the transmitter. 'Is that case what I think it is?'

'My transmitter.'

'Yes, I know. I supplied it. Gave it to Steef, who passed it to you at the apartment in Waagenstraat. Have you got contacts in England?'

She explained how Tom was negotiating with Neil, to try to get food aid dropped into Holland.

'Then you'd better get on with it.'

'What about my friend?' She could think of nothing but Tom.

'We'll wait for intelligence from Erik, then see.'

She had to be content with that. Meanwhile, Nancy had to wait in the hospital. A nurse gave her a nurses' cap, but Nancy wasn't convinced it would be enough if the Nazis came.

In a police cell at Jaaverstraat Tom had become calm. They'd searched him and removed his coat and shoes, but thank God hadn't found the code sewn under the label of his vest. But he knew the only way out of here was going to be the hard way. He was just glad Nancy had got away.

Where was she now? His chest heaved with emotion.

The cell was painted an institutional mushroom colour and was bare except for a latrine bucket. The emptiness made his mind suddenly clear. He was just a bare-footed body in this blank space. For now, he could hear his breath as it flowed in and out. But this would be the end, he was sure, and truth be told, he'd been lucky to make it so far.

If only the British would come. They'd all been months waiting, and still Holland was crushed under the anvil of the Nazis. His thoughts were interrupted by the clang of the door opening, and two Greens who took him roughly by the arm and propelled him down a corridor.

Here it comes, he thought. He was thrust into an interrogation room with a rough-wood table and two chairs. A man in black SS uniform had his back to him. This must be Schneider, the man the soldiers mentioned, the one Nancy was supposed to be spying on.

The man turned and looked him up and down. He had a pale pinched face under his black cap, with its Totenkopf skull emblem. 'They tell me you're English. An English officer.'

Tom said nothing, appraising the other man. He couldn't imagine Nancy on this man's arm.

'Name?' It was barked out in English.

Hold out. That was what Burt had told him. Hold out for twenty-four hours. Give Nancy time. Time to get the hell out of Holland.

Schneider placed the St Christopher on the table in front of him. It settled there with a metallic clink. Of course he recognised it, but he tried to show nothing on his face.

'This belongs to your friend, Nancy. Also known as Danique Koopman. Did she tell you we were lovers?'

Tom felt his lips tighten. He was lying. Just saying those things to rile him.

'She was not bad at warming my bed,' he said with a tight smile 'Quite a voracious little fox. But we'd like to know where she is now.'

Say nothing.

He sighed. 'So that's how you want to play it, is it, Mr Englishman,' Schneider said softly. He stood up and turned away. 'Braun. Zoll. Take him to Room Two. Give him the usual.'

Chapter 38

Later that evening, Nancy made a transmission to Neil using Tom's call sign and code and electric power from the hospital, though she simply couldn't face telling her brother what had happened to Tom. It was all too much to bear. Instead, she concentrated on keeping the Morse steady. She was nervous because she was surrounded by men from the Resistance, all curious to see the outcome of this transmission.

Neil's reply was succinct.

DROP WILL BE SOON STOP YPENBURG AIRPORT
ARRANGE DISTRIBUTION TRANSPORT NETWORK TO
STAND BY OVER

Nancy was just scribbling this down when there was a commotion and shots outside. The men rushed to the windows.

'Gestapo,' Gerard yelled. 'Get to your places.'

Instantly men leapt into beds, others disappeared into the operating rooms, scurrying down the stairs like rats.

Nancy dragged the wire from the window where she'd been transmitting and stuffed everything back in the suitcase.

Two nurses came running in, just as Nancy wondered where the hell she was going to hide. One of the nurses grabbed the transmitter from her hand and shoved it into a laundry basket along with a heap of blankets. Another fit young man jumped in on top and the nurses rushed to cover him over with bloodied sheets.

'Quick,' one of the nurses said, 'curl up under there and don't move.' She pointed to the end of Gerard's bed. Nancy clambered up, squeezing her legs up to her chest as a large cage contraption draped with a blue sheet was lowered over her.

She could see nothing, except Gerard's stinking feet were hitched up next to her nose.

Moments later heavy boots thumped along the corridor. She guessed at four or five men. Even the blood in her veins seemed to freeze.

The men in the ward immediately started moaning, as if in pain.

'Quiet!' shouted a voice in German. 'All the nurses are to line up with their papers, so I can look at them.'

A shuffle of feet. Nancy held her breath as she heard boots walking up and down the centre of the ward. From the thin sliver of gap between the sheet and the bed she saw the SS man go along the line of nurses. He pulled one of them from the line and she began to weep as she was hustled away by an aide.

Moments later they were at the bed next to hers. She daren't twitch the cloth down lower.

'What's wrong with this man?' the voice asked.

'Head injury, sir,' the nurse replied. 'Not fit to fight.'

'Stand up.' The order came sharp and clear.

The noise of the man in the next bed groaning and getting up, the creak of the wheels on the bed. He was one of theirs, a man Nancy knew to be a resistance man.

'See, he can barely stand,' the nurse said.

'We'll see about that. Take him down.'

The noise of feet moving. She saw the black-clad legs of the SS men moving away with a pair of bare feet and pyjama-clad legs between them. One pair of SS legs remained, and she watched the boots turn towards Gerard's bed where she was tucked into a breathless ball.

'What about this one?'

Gerard was still, as if dead. Nancy screwed her eyes shut.

'Leg amputation, sir, a right mess. Bombed in Bezuidenhout. We had to cut off at the knee; saw right through the bone, hence the cage.'

The legs took a step back. 'He's no use to us. Will he die?'

'Probably, sir.'

Nancy flicked her eyes open as the boots stepped further away and she saw their shiny blackness retreat.

'Search all the cupboards,' came the order.

Nancy gripped the sheets. She'd no idea where the rest of the SS were, whether they were behind them, and Gerard was completely still. More noises of doors opening and closing, the click of cupboard latches, the dragging noise of laundry baskets on the floor.

A sudden yell, as a man was found and caught. The nurses' protested that they had no idea anyone was there.

Nancy felt like a foetus, holding on to a thin thread of life.

Finally the footsteps retreated, and a nurse called, 'All clear.'

Nancy could no longer move. She shook with the effort of staying so still. Her legs were numb, and her head fuzzy from lack of breath.

A nurse flipped open the sheet and helped her out as Gerard ripped off his bandage and shook his head at the empty bed next to him.

'Shit. They took Danny,' he said.

'And Giles,' one of the nurses said. 'But they didn't get the transmitter. They were looking for men, not luggage. But they've arrested Betje. They came for her first, downstairs. We all knew it was only a matter of time for her. She took too many risks.' A heavy sigh. 'I don't know what we'll do without her.'

Nancy folded her arms as if to protect herself from the news. For her to survive, she had to tread over so many others. Greta, Betje. And now Tom. Guilt washed over her.

A grind of gears and splutter of engines as the convoy of cars and trucks drove away.

'We should have done something,' Nancy said.

'Like what?' Gerard said. And Nancy knew that to answer was futile. 'What did the message from England say?'

She got it out of her pocket, where she'd stuffed it, and read it to him.

Immediately Gerard swung out of bed. 'Thank God. At last. We need to get on to this straight away.' He beckoned his men over. 'Hey, we've got news. Good news.'

The ward gradually refilled with people all anxious to hear this good news in the teeth of the bad.

Gerard tapped the paper. 'We've to arrange distribution chains for food and supplies as a matter of urgency. Anyone with any kind of vehicle must be able to stand by. Find out what happened to Betje's wagon, notify anyone who can get any kind of barge or water transport.'

'What about Jim?'

'Who?'

'My friend. The agent at the police station. You said you'd help get him out.'

'It's not a priority right now. This is.' He waved the paper again. 'It could save thousands from starvation. We haven't time to worry about one man.'

'Now just wait a minute,' Nancy snapped. 'Without him setting it up, we'd have no contact. Without him contacting my brother in England there'd be no intelligence about this. And you're telling me we're just going to leave him there to rot?'

'We lose agents all the time. You saw for yourself. They just took three of ours. Think yourself lucky. It could have been you. We can't dwell on losses or we'd do nothing useful.' He turned away and began instructing his men about who was to cover which area.

'No,' Nancy said. She grabbed Gerard by the shoulder to swing him round. 'I've done everything you asked of me. I've been central in this network for over a year and I say we get him out. Then we worry about the food drops.'

Gerard shoved her hard in the chest, and immediately Nancy was surrounded by other men. One of them had a pistol pointed at her face.

Gerard loomed over her, his face threatening. 'Think you can tell me what to do? I'm in control of this network now. And in this game you're either with us, or you're against us. Which is it?'

Nancy said nothing. She didn't want to climb down, but nor did she want to spark a fight and divide the few of them that remained.

Gerard acted as if she had answered. 'So, she'll keep in touch with England by wireless.' It seemed there was to be little choice. 'Let the lady do her job. She's on our side, after all, isn't she? Just needs a bit of education.'

The men laughed, and it made Nancy seethe.

'We'll wait and see what Erik tells us, eh?' Gerard said, with a self-satisfied smile. 'Could be we'll do something for your English friend, but could be, we won't.'

Chapter 39

Fritz had not slept. Seeing the Englishman had unsettled him and brought up a rush of emotion. She'd actually turned him down for that bastard. How dare she? He felt like a beggar at the gate, looking for scraps. He'd planned on leaving his wife once the war was over and the fact Danique would choose that haggard-looking man over a life with him was something he couldn't begin to fathom.

The man was handsome, all right. Even dirt and hunger couldn't disguise that. And with that supercilious air of all Englishmen. He hoped Braun and Zoll had broken his bloody nose.

Fritz staggered around his apartment, tripping over the paintings left in piles, over yesterday's clothes, reliving the conversation, trying to make it end differently. He shaved with shaking hands and nicked himself with the razor, so blood trickled down his neck onto his vest. It had all been a sham. Danique had been a phantom. She'd never cared.

He couldn't interrogate the Englishman himself because he'd an instinct the Englishman had sensed his resolve, and no matter how much he beat him, he was terrified it would end in another failure. That the Englishman would get the better of him again. So now he just wanted him out of here. Out of sight. Away from Danique. Deportation; that was the answer.

On the way downstairs he saw there was a letter for him from Germany. He recognised the handwriting straightaway and it filled him with annoyance. From Stella, his wife. He had barely thought of her at all, he realised. Their lives were separate. At first, he had written weekly as duty demanded. Then as life got busier it dwindled. But since Danique . . . well, he hadn't been inclined to even think of Stella.

Fritz Schneider in Holland was not the hen-pecked man he'd been in Arnstadt. He didn't want to go back to Stella, to a provincial life where he had no importance at all, where he was a nobody. What did she want now? He used a finger to slit the envelope open. It was brief, and he had to read it twice before he understood what it meant.

As I have heard from you so infrequently and you have showed no interest in me or the children, I have let our house and moved back to my mother's. I have no wish to see you again when this whole fiasco is over, not now your friend Gottfried Glaser has just returned to Germany and told me of your frequent infidelities. It's over, and I shall be seeking a divorce on the grounds of desertion.
Stella

Gottfried had run too? And worse, the toad had gone bleating to Stella.

Immediately, his thoughts about her changed. How dare she? Stella was his wife. The thought that there were strangers, even now, sitting at his table, in his house, made him full of fear. When it was over, where would he go?

He felt his power diminishing. At the prison he'd been in

314

charge of fifty men, a chauffeur drove him everywhere. He had a bodyguard and men saluting everywhere he went. Now he'd no car, and he'd been left with just Braun and Zoll who showed him scant respect. It made him shaky, as if an earthquake was happening deep in his bones.

He got two Greens to drive him to his office, and thumbed through his diary to look at the schedule and at his meetings for the week. The pages had degenerated into scribblings and crossings out. Everything seemed to be in flux. Thursday. There was a transport on Thursday afternoon.

Later in the morning, Braun knocked and told him Erik Neumann was there to see him. Erik was an old friend of the *Sicherheitsdienst*. An informer who'd given the police many good leads about *onderduikers* and the resistance cells in The Hague. Erik had his fingers in all sorts of pies. As usual Erik was able to offer a real cigarette and not just strands of dried grass rolled up in cigarette paper. Fritz lit up, suddenly in need of nicotine, though he'd always thought smoking to be a weakness.

'You know it's over?' Erik leant back and blew out a puff of smoke. 'British and American troops have just crossed the Rhine. There are men pulling out everywhere, desperate to get back to their families. It seems the Rhine was some sort of symbol of the holding back of the enemy, and now that's breached . . . well, it's a stampede. Who knows what the English will do to us when they get there? When they hear what we have done? The whole damn mess of it?'

Fritz considered his wife, Stella. He hoped an Englishman would give her what she deserved, the bitch. He stubbed out his half-smoked cigarette with venom. Defeat stared him in the face from all sides.

'Now's the time to go,' Erik said. 'And I'm arranging transport for those that want to go home to Germany before the shit hits the fan.'

'I'm not leaving,' Fritz said.

'You could walk out of here right now. Men are giving up their commands everywhere I look. Hitler's lost his grip on Europe, everyone knows it.'

'That's what Braun and Zoll keep saying, but they have no sense of duty or loyalty. Besides, we have prisoners in the cells here that need dealing with.'

'Surely they don't matter. They could rot there, couldn't they?'

'No. I want to make sure one of them gets on the transport to Westerbork. And the next transport of Jews isn't until Thursday. Perhaps after that I might consider it.'

'You're concerned about a Jew?'

'No. A British agent.'

'Why haven't you just executed him?'

It was a good question and he didn't answer immediately. Because he wanted him to be sorry. Because he wanted him to feel pain. To be betrayed the way he had been by Danique. By Stella. By everyone.

Finally he said, 'I want him to have plenty of time to think. I intend to make sure he gets on that train, the train that takes a long slow journey to nowhere.'

At the hospital, Nancy scrutinised every visitor, but it was much later in the day by the time the boy returned with Erik.

Erik looked smart and well-fed as usual.

'News?' Nancy asked, sitting up on Gerard's hospital bed.

'Your man hasn't cracked. But the *Moffen* are all spooked by the fact they're losing the war. There's a last transport out of The Hague the day after tomorrow to Westerbork. Schneider tells me he's going to put your agent on it. That's if he hasn't killed him by then. They're somewhat unpredictable now.'

Gerard and the others, who'd been plotting in a corner, gathered around the bed as Erik was speaking.

'In that case,' Gerard said, 'we can't do anything. It's a death trap to intercept. Far too risky, and we can't spare the men.'

Nancy was definite. 'I'll take the risk. What's the route from Jaaverstraat to the station?'

'How will we do it? Grenades, what?' The freckle-faced boy was keen.

'We're not doing it at all,' Gerard snapped. 'We're focussing on the transport for the food drops and we're minimising risk. We need every man alive to think of the hungry population, and not waste their time on heroics. Got it?'

'But the safety of this agent is paramount,' insisted Nancy. 'He's one of the best brains in Britain. A personal friend of Beauclerk of the SOE. He can speak German, Dutch and English. The Allies will need him if we can possibly get him out of this.'

'The food drop's more important.'

'Then I'll do it alone.'

Gerard tightened his lips, and then threw up his hands. 'Looks like the Tommy's got himself a heartthrob – and she's got herself a death wish.'

The men laughed again, but Erik frowned. 'I've met him, this man. She's right. If he was trained by Fransine, he's an asset. I say it's worth a shot.'

'Another sucker for romance. Well, if you want to get yourself killed, you can go with her.'

More laughter. The rest of the men retreated back to the corner to discuss plans for the food transport.

A moment later Gerard turned back to Nancy. 'Use your head. A whole population's at stake. You want to see more children starve? No? Then you'll carry on here and keep on transmitting for us.'

Nancy closed her eyes for a moment, torn in two. Gerard was right and it hurt. It was what she had come here to do. She should focus on the food drops. But she couldn't just leave Tom there. No way.

A hand on her arm. The freckle-faced lad looked up at her. 'I don't mind helping rescue the Tommy,' he said. 'Sounds better than working out maps.'

'You're too young,' Nancy said.

'I'm fifteen.'

Nancy shook her head and laughed.

'All right, all right. I'm thirteen. But I'm strong, and I know how to shoot.'

'What's your name?'

'They call me Pim.'

'All right, Pim. You can be lookout, okay?'

Pim gave a whoop. Erik rolled his eyes and whispered, 'You've saddled us with a baby. Have you got any sort of plan? We can't just shoot our way in.'

'No, but I can see it's not made me popular. I need a friend I can rely on. Can you get back into the police station and get a message to Tom? You're the only one I can trust.'

Erik blinked. He looked rather flattered. 'I can try. But we haven't much time.'

Tom had been alone in his cell for two days, and since the first beating nobody had come near. He was still suffering the bruises, especially to his kidneys and ribs, which he suspected were broken, and they throbbed like the devil. But the men had been half-hearted, and halfway through started discussing how they'd get home to Germany, and when to run if the Allies came. It could have been worse, and he dreaded them coming back to finish the job.

Yesterday, a hard hunk of bread and a tin cup of water was shoved at him through a hatch, but the face that appeared was not Schneider, but a young Green whose face he didn't know.

Tom tried to talk to him, but the man slammed the hatch shut, so it caught the ends of his fingers. Surprising, how painful that was in comparison with having broken ribs. He nursed his pulsing hand and every time a door clanged, he caught his breath, expecting Schneider to appear again or another beating. Despite his pain, the waiting was the worst thing. Were these his

318

last days? Would he be taken somewhere and shot? Where was Nancy? Was Betje keeping her safe?

On the third day he heard keys jangling and voices. Schneider and the familiar smooth voice of their agent Erik. He put an ear to the door, so he could hear what they were saying. Schneider was asking Erik if he could arrange a car for Thursday from the central *Sicherheitsdienst* office. 'Of course I can slip you a few extra coupons if you can. It's unofficial business.'

'Should be possible,' he heard Erik say. 'How many prisoners?'

'Just one. But I'll need a chauffeur and two men. Braun and Zoll have gone absent without leave. Didn't come in for work this morning, so now it's only me.'

'Told you. There's food in Germany and the rats are leaving the sinking ship. Have you told the chief at the *Reichskommissariat* yet?'

'No. They'd blame me. It's always someone else's fault.'

A shrill ring interrupted their talk. The telephone in the office. 'Excuse me,' said Schneider, 'I'd better get that. Could be news from Braun. Perhaps there's been trouble.'

Schneider's footsteps moved away and the phone stopped ringing. 'Ja?'

Schneider's office door clicked shut and Tom heard his muffled voice agreeing with the caller.

But then, as he was about to move away from the door, a whisper from the corridor right outside his cell. 'Jim? It's me Erik.'

'Yes, I'm here,' Tom said. He'd forgotten he was Jim.

'Message from Nancy. Look under the door. Read it, then eat it. Do as it says. Good luck.'

A sliver of thin white paper appeared under the door and Tom bent to pick it up.

His heart leapt. So she was still alive, and obviously still here in The Hague. *Thank you, thank you.*

Erik's feet moved away and Tom heard Schneider's voice calling for him.

Tom kept his ear to the door a moment longer, staring down at the miracle of the paper.

'That was head office,' Schneider's voice. 'Did you know the English and the Americans are planning a food drop?'

'Oh, that. Yes, I haven't any details yet,' Erik replied smoothly, 'but my contacts are talking about preparing to distribute any aid if it comes. Personally, I don't think they've a hope in hell. Not with our guns on the ground.'

'Head office want to deploy every policeman,' Schneider said. 'In case it's a cover for an attack and the British are intending to drop men or troops.'

'Sounds possible, but I don't know. I'll have to ask around. If I find out anything more, I'll let you know.'

'Good. Either way. We'll shoot down the planes, or if it's really food aid, we need to intercept it and stockpile the food. Hunger's what's driving too many of our men back to Germany.'

Tom gripped the paper. So the food drop was happening at last. Elation warred with concern. It was happening, but the Germans might sabotage it. Perhaps that was what Nancy had to say. Tom unfolded the message.

He took the paper to the light and read the few words over and over, pondering what they could mean.

When they take you to the car, go quietly.

Schneider had mentioned a car. For Thursday.

Stay calm no matter what, there will be people there to help you. I love you. N x

Nancy and Erik were making plans, leaning against the wall in the hospital corridor, out of earshot of Gerard. Pim was cross-legged beside them, eager to be in on the action.

'They'll be taking him on this route,' Erik said, drawing out a map on the back of an NSB leaflet. 'They wouldn't let me requisition a car, so there'll be a Green driving it. It's straightforward enough, but once we get closer to the station there are a lot more

320

troops, and there'll be queues of Jews, gypsies and other prisoners going to the transport. I can't believe they're still sending them, not with the Allies so close. Once we get to here,' he stabbed down his pencil, 'there'll be too many troops and no chance of getting to the car.'

'So we'll have to go for it here at the police station, as soon as they get him out of the cell.' Nancy put her finger on the place. 'Where can we wait?'

'There's an alleyway,' Erik said, pointing, 'though it's a dead end. There's an empty shop opposite – we've used it before for surveillance. But one of us can be on the roof here. Easy access up and down via the fire escape.'

'Me!' Pim said. 'I'll be up there.'

Erik sighed. 'It's not a bad idea. A kid is less suspicious. Whoever is up there must cut that wire – the one going to the police station. We cut that wire, it'll stop Schneider calling for reinforcements.'

'Gotcha,' Pim said.

'The only trouble is guns and ammo,' Erik said. 'Gerard's locked all small arms in the instruments cupboard in the operating theatre, in case the Nazis search the place, and the cupboard's always locked.'

'Except when they're operating,' Pim said. 'Which is nearly all the time.'

Nancy sighed. 'We can't go in during an operation.'

'Why not?' Pim asked. 'I do it all the time. I like to watch. I'm going to be a doctor one day.'

Nancy turned to Erik and raised her eyebrows. 'It's a chance, isn't it?'

Erik made a face. But then he turned to Pim. 'Listen, if we make a list, can you try and smuggle out some weapons and ammunition? And make sure they match.'

'What do you think I am, stupid? I'll have to wait until they're very busy, then do it bit by bit, so they don't see me.'

Nancy turned to Erik. 'D'you think it's possible?'

Erik shrugged. 'No idea. But if the kid says he can do it, then I guess we'd better believe him. Worst thing that could happen is he gets Gerard's back up for pilfering.'

'What are our chances of getting Tom out?'

'About one per cent above zero. Getting out – possible. Getting away? Questionable. But I'll concentrate on disabling the driver, because you'll need me to drive, and we need to have a route planned that goes through the minimum of checkpoints.'

The following day Tom heard a commotion in the corridor and the clank of the keys. He shot to his feet. When the door opened a shoe hit him hard in the chest, followed by the other.

'*Raus!*' a uniformed Green yelled. '*Raus!*'

He'd barely time to shove his shoes on his feet before they yelled at him again to move. They were Dutch police, ones he'd never seen before. Both were armed and prodded him out of the cell and down the corridor. The shock made his heart thump in his chest as if it was trying to get out. Was this it, the interrogation he'd feared?

But to his confusion, they bullied him out of the front of the building to a car pulled up directly outside. A car. Nancy had said there'd be a car.

He had a frantic look around but could see nobody, just the glint of sun on a nearby fire escape and the flap of the red Nazi banner that hung on the front of the police station.

The Greens were about to push him into the back seat of the car, when he heard the ringing of feet on metal, and a scrawny figure rushed down the fire escape opposite. Everyone turned their heads to look. Tom pulled, trying to break free.

An almighty bang as the boy fired a gun directly at them. His arm jerked and the shot went wide, skimming the bonnet of the car with a metallic screech. The driver crouched and shot out of the side of the car, just as the man gripping Tom's arm thrust at his shoulders to cram Tom into the back, but Tom clung to the sides of the door frame.

Another shot followed but by now the Green on his other side had got out his pistol and was firing back.

The lad was on the pavement now, red-faced, backing away, still firing what seemed like random shots. Tom saw he was only young, wide-eyed and jumpy, his freckles standing out over his nose. He kept firing but every shot made his arm recoil and the shots went to the sky. The last shot was a mere click.

Out of ammunition. The lad looked at his gun in horror, as if it had let him down. Instantly, his face took on a look of fear and he began shrinking away. One of the Greens followed him, took careful aim and fired. The boy's chest caved in but he took a few more tottering steps backwards, empty gun wavering. From nowhere, a woman thrust herself in front of the boy.

'Don't fire!' she yelled in Dutch.

Nancy! The fool! What was she doing? Behind her the boy whimpered and held his bleeding chest as he crumpled slowly to the ground.

The Green took aim again.

No you don't, you bastard. Tom lunged to knock the gun out of his hand, but only hit his forearm and the shot went wide.

Meanwhile the gunfire had brought Schneider striding out from the station, his pistol in both hands extended to arm's length.

Tom twisted hard, just in time to see Erik shoot the driver at point blank range. Where had Erik come from? It was enough distraction for Tom to knee his captor in the groin. The Green staggered, fell to his knees and dropped his pistol. Tom scrabbled to grab it from the ground.

As he stood up, he glimpsed Erik grab the keys to the car and thrust them in his pocket, and Tom leapt towards Nancy. But before he had time to think, Erik's arm around his neck brought him up short, and dragged him down behind the car.

'Leave it,' Erik hissed. 'Unless you want a gun battle with the whole of the Wehrmacht. Let them think we've gone.'

'But what about Nancy?'

'It's a dead end. D'you want to get shot?' Erik yanked on his arm to drag him across the road. They went round the back into a filthy yard and in through a broken window of a disused shop. Nothing inside except the smell of damp and the scuttle of spiders on the empty shelves.

They peered out through the side of the blind. The Green on the ground had recovered and was running to the alley. Moments later, Schneider strode out, ahead of the two Greens who had Nancy struggling between them.

A few moments later they'd taken her into the police station, and the big black door closed. There was no sign of the lad. Tom guessed he was dead.

His worst nightmare. He was free, but now they'd got Nancy. He punched hard on the brick wall feeling the pain radiate up his arm, but it didn't stop the feeling of wanting to scream.

'We've got about half an hour,' Erik said. 'After that amount of fire, they'll be sending soldiers to search these buildings. We have to wait until one of the men goes for reinforcements.'

'Won't he just telephone?'

'No. If Pim did his job, he cut the wires.'

'I need to go get her out.'

'No. Our best chance is to stay watchful, wait for the best moment. Now, calm down and check that gun's loaded.'

Chapter 40

Nancy had stopped struggling. It was against her dignity. The Greens took her into a bare room where Schneider was gazing out of the barred window.

'Sit down,' Fritz said, without turning.

She didn't sit. She wouldn't obey any command from him.

When he didn't hear a noise, he turned, eyes narrowed.

She put her chin up and returned his stare. It had been a reflex reaction to smile because she knew him, but she'd swallowed it. He was thin. His face was gaunt, and he had dark shadows under his bloodshot eyes, which were flickering, as if some other film was running in his head.

He licked his chapped lips. 'So Danique, you should have given me written notice if you wanted to leave my employment. And we never did get another dinner date. I wonder why that was? Could it have been because your name is not really Danique?'

Nancy folded her arms but wouldn't give him the satisfaction of answering.

'I'm informed by your friend Greta van Schelle that your name is Nancy. And you are English.'

'Not English,' she answered with a touch of defiance, 'Scottish.'

'So? No difference. We will need all your history. Of course we will. But for now, I would like to see Danique again.' He turned to the man by the door. 'Get this woman soap and water and some good clothes. You will find a suitcase of women's clothes in the wardrobe at my apartment. A good suit and shoes. Bring them and dress her.'

He brought out a key from his inside pocket and put it on the table.

The Green frowned. 'But sir, isn't it a little irregular—'

'Just do it.' The man backed away.

'I refuse,' Nancy said. 'I won't be manhandled by your men.'

Fritz smiled but it was only a fraction of a smile. 'You either do it conscious or unconscious. Your choice.'

She had no choice, she thought bitterly. But agreeing might give her a chance to escape.

'And don't think to escape,' he said as if to read her thoughts. 'Two men are to accompany you at all times.' He turned to them. 'Stay armed, and make sure she never gets a chance to run.'

'Yes, sir.'

'Take her away and bring her back to me when she's presentable. And you,' he jabbed a finger at the other Green, 'our telephone's not working. Get it fixed. And when your colleague returns, take a message to head office to bring a detachment of men to search the area. An English agent, and maybe an accomplice, escaped onto Jaaverstraat. *Schnell!*'

Every moment Nancy was looking for a means to escape, but it never arose. One of the men, the skinny nervous one, brought a basin of cold water to her cell and insisted she wash.

Courage, she thought. Nancy closed her mind to the indignities of washing with a man squinting at her through the hatch, and the fear that made her have all-over goosebumps.

'Everywhere,' the man said.

The cold water made her mind sharp. All the time she was running through possibilities. Tom had got away; she should be thankful for small mercies. She tried to concentrate on one thing at a time. The feel of the soap, the sting of it in her eyes. She tried not to think of her own situation or the fact that they would certainly kill her soon.

She hadn't had good soap for so long. The silky feel of it made her want to cry. But she pressed her lips together and washed as the man watched through the hatch like she was a peepshow. At least he hadn't tried to touch her. Too scared of Schneider probably.

By the time he'd thrown in a rough towel, the other had arrived with a bag of clothes. He pointed to the cloth bag as he lobbed it through the door. 'Dress. Hurry,' he said waving his gun at her.

She dried herself hastily, anxious to get covered. When she pulled out the clothes, the underwear smelled of jasmine, a perfume she never wore. She wondered what woman had worn these last. A Jewess, or a rich Parisian? Until she unbuttoned the blouse and saw an embroidered name tape: *D. Koopman.*

A shiver. What was Fritz up to? Had he lost his mind, or was this some macabre game he was playing? She dragged out the lace-trimmed slip, anxious to cover her underwear. Her legs were shockingly thin and white.

She was shivering because her skin was still damp. The suit had been made in Paris, but the jacket and skirt, which were beautifully cut, were a little on the large side. There were even shoes. Too big. Lace-ups with a heel. She'd no choice but to put them on and pray for a moment to escape.

'I need to use the toilet,' she said, to the man breathing through the hatch, hoping to get some privacy, figure out how to get away.

He opened the door. 'No. Now you come,' he said in accented Dutch. 'SS-Obersturmführer Schneider is waiting.'

* * *

327

Nancy took a deep breath and sat down in the unfamiliar clothes, pulling the skirt down over her knees. The interrogation room was the same but Fritz had taken off his cap, so his wiry hair was oiled flat against his head, making his cheekbones stand out even more sharply under his skin.

'Very nice,' he said, looking her up and down. A bottle of Dutch brandy was on the bare wood table, almost drained. 'Drink, Danique?' He pushed the bottle towards her.

She shook her head and kept her voice low. 'What do you want, Fritz?'

'I'm afraid we won't have our dinner tonight,' Fritz said, 'unless you choose to cooperate. I need to ask you some questions. I trust that is all right with you?'

His false politeness stuck in her craw. Was he drunk? His hand was shaking.

She watched as he drew a file towards him, opened it and uncapped a pen. Surely he wasn't going to sit there and pretend she was Danique?

He leaned back and took another swig of brandy. 'Now. It seems to me you have only two choices. You can continue to keep me company as Danique, just the way you used to, and give me the name and whereabouts of the other contacts working for the British.'

No. She would never betray them.

He tapped the pen lid on the desk. 'Think about it. My friends in the SS intelligence service are looking for a woman like you who has good contacts with the British. If you do that and work for us, then your life will be very pleasant. Good food, fine clothes.'

'And no self-respect.'

'We will find your friends anyway. The other choice is that my men will beat it out of you. And as I still have fondness for you Danique, I strongly advise you to take the former path.'

'You talk of fondness, but only when you want something. I know who my real friends are.' She looked up and fixed him with

328

an icy gaze. 'What would you do in my position, Fritz? Would you betray your friends?'

She saw him wince, as though she had struck him a blow. 'This is the last time I will ask. Will you—'

'Save your breath.' She stood up, defiant. 'You'll get nothing from me.'

Chapter 41

From the window of the shop, Tom watched one of the Greens come out of the heavy black door of the station. He cast a wary glance up and down the street before strolling around the Nazi car, which was parked right outside.

'He's checking the car,' Tom said.

Erik went to look over his shoulder. 'He can't move it, because I've got the key.'

The Green shrugged and walked briskly away.

By this time the other Green had appeared on the doorstep, heavily armed, a German machine gun over his shoulder.

'We can't get in,' said Erik. 'Not with him standing there.'

'Take a pot shot at him from here?'

'If we miss, it'll give away where we are. No, we wait. Wait for the right moment.'

'What if it never comes?'

Erik didn't answer but kept his eyes glued to the thin crack between blind and window.

Tom couldn't be still. The words that Schneider had told him, about how he was Nancy's lover, needled him. What would he do to her? He crouched behind Erik. 'What's going on now?'

'Patience. We wait until the man on the doorstep gets bored and goes back inside. Take him by surprise.'

Another torture of waiting. Tom wished he had his watch but Schneider had confiscated it when he took his shoes and it had never been returned. 'What time is it now?'

'He's still there. Oh, wait, the other guy's back. He's got a parcel with him.'

Tom leapt to the window.

'He's gone in. The other man too. Now's our chance. We get into that alley and wait, okay?'

Tom's heart lurched. He was ahead of Erik, scrambling out of the back window and into the fresh air. A quick look left and right, then a wild dash across the street until breathlessly they ducked into the alley. The young lad's body was still there, eyes staring up into the blue; blood a dark mess on the front of his shirt.

'Poor sod,' said Erik.

'Who is he?'

'Pim. His parents were resistance members.' A soft shake of the head. 'Lad's gone the same place as they have now, God rest him.' He peered out of the alley. 'Damn, the Green's back on the doorstep.'

They waited there, out of sight, nerves tingling, dreading that more police would come. Every now and then, one of them would risk poking a nose out to look.

At last Tom saw someone coming out. 'The one with the parcel. He's come out again and gone up the road. The other one's gone inside.'

Erik pushed past him to look. 'You ready? We don't want to join Pim.'

'I'm shitting myself,' Tom said.

'Join the club. You take out the guard, I'll go find Schneider.

He knows me, so it might give us a bit more time. Then this is what we do when we get in there.' He outlined the plan.

Tom held out his left hand, the one that wasn't holding the gun.

Erik laughed. 'Ever the Englishman.' But he took it and clasped it all the same. 'Good luck,' he said.

The next few moments were a blur. Tom burst through the door but saw no-one. Then to his left an open door. He put his head around the corner just in time to see the Green get up from a chair. He didn't think, just pulled the trigger. A single shot, and the man fell. Tom gaped; he was astonished it was so easy. But there could be more men, so he crept along the corridor until he came to a sharp right turn.

The passage was empty. Along here were the cells. The first two were vacant, but then in the last one he opened the hatch to see a well-dressed woman, just walking away from the door. Could it be? He knocked gently on the hatch.

Nancy startled and turned.

He knocked again. She stared a moment with eyes wide and then put her face up close.

'Tom?' he saw her mouth move but couldn't hear her.

He pressed two fingers to his lips and then to the glass. 'I'm going to get you out,' he mouthed.

Fritz put his head in his hands. He had drunk the rest of the brandy and now the walls of the room were swaying. He'd thought Danique would see sense. How could she not? It shocked him that she'd choose death, rather than to live with him. He'd stumbled back to his office to decide what to do, when he heard a shot outside.

The reinforcements. He got unsteadily to his feet, and tried to get out another round of bullets from his desk drawer. Some of them scattered from the box as he loaded his gun. He leant to peer out of the window onto the street. Everything looked quiet at this side of the building.

A knock at his door. The knock was reassuring. This would be his men now. He went to open it.

Erik Neumann was in the corridor. Fritz held the door open for him to come in and put his gun on the table as he sat back down at his desk. 'I heard a shot. What's all the fuss,' he asked blearily. 'Have they found anyone?'

'No.' Erik reached over and swiped the gun towards him. 'And I don't think they will. But on the other hand, you, like many of my race, will be getting on the train to Westerbork.'

What was he talking about? 'You're . . .?'

'Yes. I'm a Jew, though I've spent nine years hiding it from men like you.'

A click. Erik was pointing the gun right at him. The reality of what was happening sobered him instantly like a blow to the head. 'You bastard,' he said.

'No-one will come. Your man is dead,' Erik said. 'Put your hands up.'

Schneider's eyes grew wide. 'You. You scum. How much are they paying you?'

'Nothing. We can't all be bought. I do it for love,' Erik said.

How dare he? Fritz got to his feet. Just then another figure appeared in the doorway. The Englishman.

Fritz's mind could not process it quickly enough. He knew the Englishman shouldn't be there, but it wouldn't sink in. After that everything happened too fast for him to react. Before he knew it, Erik was pressing a gun to his temple and the Englishman had one pointed at his heart.

'Keys,' the Englishman said, keeping the gun trained on him.

He wouldn't surrender them. But then he felt the cold nose of the pistol next to his ear. 'In the desk drawer,' he said, in a gasp.

The Englishman tugged the drawer open and grabbed the keys and hurried out.

'Undress,' Erik said, nosing him with the gun.

'No.' Fritz couldn't move. He thought his heart might give out. He was aware he was panting now, like a dog.

A few moments later the Englishman and Danique were both in the room. The sight of her gave him a thread of hope.

But Danique was pointing a gun at him and regarding him with a cold expression he'd never seen before, her eyes hard and dark. 'You heard him. Two can play at dress up. Now take off your clothes.'

Chapter 42

'What will we do with him?' Nancy asked Erik, who was now dressed in Schneider's uniform, whilst Schneider was dressed in Erik's trousers and braces over his vest, but no shirt or coat.

'Keep him, then hand him to the British,' Tom said. 'Geneva Convention.'

'No,' Erik said, looking surprisingly convincing as an SS officer. 'They might be weeks getting here. We turn him over to his own. The transport leaves soon. They won't know who he is.'

'No,' Schneider said. 'Please. I'm just obeying orders. I haven't done anything wrong.'

Nancy shook her head at this total fabrication. How could he lie when he'd tortured so many men? Without his uniform he suddenly seemed smaller; she couldn't get over the wrinkled skin of his bare arms, the pallid pink of his chest.

Just then the noise of an engine outside and German voices exclaiming. Tom who was near the door, hurried to hide in a cell, but Nancy wasn't quick enough before the first of two Wehrmacht officers appeared at the door. Thinking quickly, she shoved the gun in a drawer, tried to look calm, like an officer's wife.

Erik, dressed in Schneider's uniform, strode towards them.

The Germans saluted him with a *Sieg Heil*.

'*Heil Hitler*! I'm SS-Obersturmführer Schneider,' Erik said calmly in perfect German, 'and this is . . .' He glanced at her. 'My wife.'

Would they buy it? The men nodded deferentially to Nancy, and she nodded, but inside she was rigid.

Schneider tried to walk forwards but Erik still had a gun pointed at him. 'This prisoner was trying to escape the transportation. He shot one of our men, but I apprehended him and disarmed him.'

Schneider's eyes were wild. 'Don't believe him. He's lying. I'm the officer. He changed clothes with me.'

The Wehrmacht grinned at each other and rolled their eyes, as if to say, a likely tale. 'Empty your pockets.'

Schneider protested. 'They're not my clothes, I keep telling you—'

'*Stumm!*' One man aimed his machine gun at Schneider, whilst the other went through his pockets. Nancy glanced to Erik.

They withdrew papers from his pockets, and opened them. 'You are Heinrich Volkstadt. An Austrian Jew. It says so right here.'

Nancy felt shock ripple through her. Were those Erik's papers?

'No. This is ridiculous,' Schneider insisted. 'I'm Fritz Schneider of the *Kriminalpolizei*, fetch anyone from head office to—'

But the Wehrmacht soldier struck him hard across the face with the machine gun, making him stagger. '*Hande hoch!*' Hands up!

'Wait,' groaned Schneider, 'get the Englishman, he's the one you want.'

'There's no Englishman,' Nancy said in German. 'The Jew talks nonsense.'

'Now move.' The other soldier grabbed Schneider by the arm to pull him forwards.

'Don't worry, sir, we'll deal with him,' said the other.

Nancy and Erik followed them out, past the outer office where a man's body was splayed on the grey linoleum. Nancy was aware of Tom hiding somewhere in the building. *Stay there*, she prayed, *don't come out.*

The truck was waiting at the kerb but Schneider made a sudden twist. He dodged out of the soldiers' grip and sprinted away.

A stutter of machine-gun fire. The staccato fire was deafening and made Nancy tremble. Schneider didn't stop running. A second burst.

Now he fell, and in the silence the soldiers slapped each other on the shoulders.

Erik and Nancy went to look. The German truck was parked behind the car, but Schneider was on the ground in the middle of the road.

Nancy's hand went to her mouth. He wasn't dead. He was trying to get up and crawl away, but the strafe of machine-gun fire had mangled his legs. He was her enemy but she looked away. It was too much to bear to watch another man die.

'One less for the wagons then,' one of the Germans said, 'he'll die here.'

'We'll move him for you, sir,' said the other to Erik, 'so you can get your car out.'

Nancy winced as the men kicked and dragged Schneider to the side of the road out of the way of the traffic. From windows all around she could see pale faces staring down at them.

It isn't what you think, she thought. They're not shooting a civilian.

'Do you need a lift anywhere, sir?' one of the Germans asked Erik cheerfully.

'No, no. I'm going back to *Kriminalpolizei* Headquarters. I'll drive myself there. You may go.'

'*Heil Hitler!*' Two voices. Then the grind of the starter motor and the truck drove away, leaving Schneider in the gutter.

Tom emerged from the front door of the police station, white-faced. 'I heard gunfire. Are you all right?'

She gulped back tears. 'Schneider tried to run.'

'He knew where the transport was going,' Erik said.

'But we can't just leave him there,' Nancy set off towards him.

'Nancy, don't!' Tom shouted.

Schneider was lying in a twisted coil of arms and legs, blood seeping out from the wounds in his legs and back. Pity filled her heart. She crouched next to him and gently turned him over.

'I'm going to die, Danique,' he said.

'Yes,' she said. 'I'm afraid so.'

'I deserve it. Should have stayed . . . stayed in Arnstadt. Now I'll never go home.'

'Tell me your wife's name?'

'Stella. It's Stella.' He was barely conscious, eyes full of pain and a kind of knowing.

'When the war is over, I'll let her know.'

She cocked her pistol and placed it in his right hand.

'You know what to do,' she said, walking away. She turned to see him pointing the gun at her and she had a moment of dread. But then he turned it towards his heart.

A single shot rang out. Fritz Schneider let out his last breath into the cold damp air. It hung there a moment and then dissolved into nothing.

Chapter 43

April 1945

Erik delivered them all back to the hospital in the Nazi car wearing Schneider's SS uniform before abandoning both in a side street. Gerard was angry that they'd gone against his decision, but could say little when Nancy and Tom were standing right in front of him. When Nancy told him about the loss of Pim, it sobered them all.

Gerard was keen that Tom should get on the wire to England about the food aid, and finally Tom managed to get through to Neil. His scribbled Morse revealed a message that made Nancy and Tom leap up and down and hug each other in a frenzied dance.

FOOD DROP 29 4 YPENBURG AIRFIELD ASSIST IF POSS
JERRY AGREED CEASEFIRE

'Do you think it's true?' Nancy asked. That the Nazis will stand by and let it happen?

'I've no idea,' Tom said. 'It's possible. The Germans have run out of food too, the whole country's on its last legs.'

'So what do we do?'

'Twenty-ninth of April. We've got three days. Gather the troops and go and meet it, I suppose.'

Gerard assigned everyone roles; some to go to the north, some to the south, to prepare any transport they could get. Erik was to check the Nazis' positions, and Thierry and Albie to try to get through to farmers in the vicinity who might have wagons.

Nancy and Tom, still wary of being picked up, travelled by night, skirting the city suburbs and heading south-east towards the airport. On the way they passed more convoys of *hongerlopers* – the hunger walkers out in search of food. The fact that she and Tom were together buoyed Nancy's spirits for the roads were full of trudging people. He took firm hold of her hand and the simple warm pressure of his palm made such a difference.

Occasionally she'd see a bicycle, or a handcart, but these were few as Germans had requisitioned them all. No livestock grazed in the fields – not a cow, a pig or a goose. Even the birds seemed wary of landing. But there were fewer patrols, and they didn't see a single German truck.

'Will the landing strip be guarded?' Tom asked her.

'I expect so. The Germans took over Ypenburg, but they haven't done much with it. They don't use it as a base; it's a small airfield, mostly used before the war for civilian flying training. Or so Steef told me. We just have to hope that the powers that be arranged a safe passage.'

At the airfield there were no patrols, but Tom pointed wordlessly to the far side of the field.

There, the stark barrels of artillery guns pointed up towards the sky like black needles. Nancy could see they were manned by Germans, as even from here, their helmets caught the light.

'What if it's just a trap?' Nancy said with a shiver. 'D'you think they'll shoot the planes down?'

'I don't know,' Tom said. 'Neil seemed to think a ceasefire was in operation.'

'Then what are the Wehrmacht doing there?'

Tom didn't answer, because there was no answer to give, and they were both breathless from walking. The rutted road to the airfield was littered with potholes no-one had bothered to fix, and the actual terminal building was splintered by shelling. It had once been a white Art Deco building, all smooth curves and glass, but now it was ruined, with the woodwork ripped out for fuel. Broken glass winked from the air traffic control tower. As they got closer though, they saw an old, wizened man with a dray horse, and two women with handcarts.

'Is it true?' asked one of the women. Her face was pinched, her face scabbed. 'Are they really going to drop food?'

'We heard the same,' Nancy said. 'But it doesn't look a big enough airfield for anything to land.'

The man looked up at the empty sky. 'Guess it's just another rumour. But better waiting here for food than at the soup kitchen. Nothing's getting through to them anymore, not even slop.'

'Imagine if it's true!' The other woman, younger but shrunken, eyes huge in her bony face, sat down on the edge of her cart and hugged her arms around her thin chest.

The sky was as grey as an old blanket. 'Look!' the older woman pointed.

The Germans were moving, getting into position. A sudden burst of activity.

'What is it?' Nancy asked. And then she heard it. The low guttural drone of an aircraft. Across the other side of the field, a truck with a red cross painted on it drove bumpily to the side of the airport building. A few people got out and looked up towards the sky, hands shielding their eyes.

'Red Cross!' Tom couldn't keep the excitement from his voice.

Like albatrosses, two Lancaster bombers, huge, their enormous wingspans painting shadows on the ground, crossed directly overhead. They were so low, they could almost touch them.

Nancy gasped. 'They'll never land here.'

They watched their silhouettes turn and slow even more. The sight filled Nancy with awe. The bellies of the planes cracked open and in a flurry, things were falling from the sky. Parcels floating on parachutes, heavy sacks dropping like stones. The Red Cross people had to scurry and duck.

Directly in front of them a heavy sack thudded to the ground, and another. One split open and flour blew like smoke across the weed-strewn tarmac.

The women had no hesitation, they were on it like lightning, grabbing up anything they could carry. The old man was still standing, amazed. 'I thought it was a fairy story. I never thought it was true,' he said. Then with tears in his rheumy eyes, he hobbled as fast as his legs would go, to drag the sacks to his horse.

At the far end of the field more people had appeared, just as the second plane came in.

Nancy pulled off her coat and waved it. Tom leapt up and down cheering. To her amazement not a single shot came from the Germans, though their guns swung ominously towards the planes. The ceasefire was holding! *Thank you, thank you.*

Inside the hull of the planes, she could actually see men throwing out the packages. Cheers from the other end of the airfield.

Nancy and Tom rushed forwards to collect up what they could. Nancy ran back clutching a leaking sack of flour to her chest when she saw a German car followed by a truck jolting up the road towards them.

'*Moffen!*' she yelled. Elation turned to panic.

The women scrabbled to drag their booty onto their carts while Tom helped the old chap and horse. The car had stopped in the lane, blocking their exit. Oh, no.

Three Landwacht soldiers got out of the truck. Nancy swallowed. They were armed with Mausers, deadly bolt-action rifles.

The women shrank back, afraid.

The car door opened and to her shock she saw it was Mesman, Schneider's old bodyguard. So he was in the Landwacht now.

There was nowhere to hide. He strode towards them, but she turned away from him to busy herself loading the flour onto the man's dray.

'Hey, you.'

She turned.

'I know you, don't I? Frau Koopman?'

'That's not my name.'

'I know,' Mesman said. 'I've always known. Watching and listening tells you a lot. You've got nerves of steel.'

'We'll take these parcels now,' a Landwacht soldier said, signalling the men to surround the woman's cart.

'No,' Tom was protesting in awkward Dutch. 'This is food sent as aid to the Dutch population. You have no right to take it. It has all been agreed by your government.'

'You don't understand,' Mesman said, holding up his hand. 'We're here to help you. The men have orders not to allow looting. It all has to go to the area depot for distribution.'

So the Landwacht had abandoned the Führer and remembered they were Dutch after all, Nancy thought. It heartened her.

They helped Mesman and his men load the truck and the old man load the dray and take it to the old mill. Thierry and Albie and many others they recognised were already there.

Gerard came up to them as they were unloading, his smile making his face instantly younger. 'Did you see the planes? Bloody magic!'

Nancy grinned and passed him one of the parcels to stack, their animosity instantly dissolved.

They worked until it was all carefully labelled and sorted. Not a single crumb would be wasted. Someone set up a table in the corner, and Nancy helped another woman boil up celebratory coffee.

There were no Germans in sight, only the Dutch. She looked around at the small band of resistance brothers that were left, and was filled with pride. It was good to see their faces bright with hope. It was as if by allowing this to happen, the Germans had admitted it was all over. They'd realised they could no longer starve the Dutch people, and with food in their bellies, the Dutch had already begun to feel life returning. The best thing was the children, hanging around the warehouse doors, watching their parents and looking for the first time on the wonder of real white bread.

Tom turned to Nancy. 'I never thought this was possible,' he said.

'It wouldn't have been,' she said, 'if Jim hadn't joined my resistance cell.'

'Who's Jim?' he asked.

'You are, you chump. You'll have to do better at remembering your aliases if you want to carry on as an agent in Holland.'

'But I don't,' he said. 'I want to take you home to England and marry you.'

'Is that a proposal?' Nancy asked, feeling her heart flutter.

'Do you want it to be?'

She paused. 'Let's give it time, Tom. I don't know what I want any more. Except for someone to shoot Hitler.'

Chapter 44

May 1945

On Saturday 5 May the news that the Germans had finally surrendered filled the streets with jubilant crowds and many tears of relief. In the Dutch countryside, emotional crowds greeted their British and Canadian liberators with cheers, hugs and kisses as they restored their shattered towns to Dutch control.

For Nancy it was like releasing a valve of tension, as if her whole being deflated. Exhaustion made her limbs shake and she found herself wracked by guilt that she couldn't have done more for all her friends who had lost their lives in the fight.

When the Nazis left, the hotels became suddenly empty, and Tom and Nancy took a room in a small two-star hotel, unable to bear the idea of going back to the De Beurs or the Hotel des Indes. There they slept for days in each other's arms. When they finally got up, they watched from the window as the streets emptied of Germans and filled with flag-waving British troops and drunk locals who had somehow found their way to the German wine cellars.

Recriminations against Nazi sympathisers were not long in coming and anyone deemed to have been a collaborator was harassed or beaten in the street. Nancy watched from the window in horror as two girls with shaved heads were paraded down the street by a jeering mob; and from that moment she lived in fear of meeting someone who had seen her dressed as Danique Koopman.

Similarly, every person emerging from their dark hiding holes now claimed to have been an active member of the Resistance.

'I can't bear it,' she told Tom, after witnessing the man in the food distribution centre boasting of his exploits. 'Where were all these people when we needed them?'

'It's not like you to be bitter,' Tom said when they got back to the hotel. As they sat on the bed he hugged her tightly as if to hold her together. 'It's only human nature to want to shift the blame, or to claim a part of the victory.'

'I know, but it feels unfair to those who have given their lives, those tortured or shot on the dunes, when men like him can come out of their safe spaces and claim the glory.'

'We can't know what sort of war he had. Maybe he had hardships we can't see. Appearances can be deceptive. The main thing is, Holland is free at last and that's all that matters.'

'My wise Tom.' She wound her arms around his neck. 'What would I do without you? Of course you're right. And looking around, I can see it's no longer my fight. Dutch people are already rebuilding their lives. Bulbs are being planted in the fields, people are clearing the rubble and sweeping the streets. I saw a public bus yesterday with a notice tacked to the front saying 'Amsterdam'. She paused and looked up at him. 'How would you feel about leaving?'

'Leave?' He couldn't keep the hope from his voice. 'You mean, go back home to England?'

She had resisted it until this moment, but now her homesickness was overwhelming. 'I need my family. Someone who knows Nancy, the Nancy from before. A place where I don't have to pretend to be anyone else, where I'll just be accepted without any questions about who or what I am.'

'You know you were incredibly brave, don't you?'

'Brave or foolish, not sure which.' She grasped his hand and squeezed it. 'We need one more cover story, and it will be the hardest, because we'll never be able to talk about what we did here, or tell anyone. Official Secrets Act and all that.'

'"I met a beautiful nurse at a dance in Birmingham," you mean?'

'That's the one.' Nancy couldn't help but smile. 'And we'll have to live a perfectly mundane life, in a boring little house, where you'll mow the lawn, and I'll scrub the front step—'

'Steady on! I might begin to like the sound of it.'

'Fool.' She pushed him playfully on the shoulder.

'So I take it we'll be living together in this boring little house you describe.'

'Life with you could never be boring. Let's go home, Tom. It looks like I've got a wedding to plan.'

'Are you saying yes?' Tom's face had gone pink.

She stilled him by taking hold of his shoulders. 'The biggest yes you can imagine.'

Anxious for a taste of normality, Nancy and Tom managed to get a boat out of Holland soon after the liberation, and take a train north to Scotland, not for a wedding but for a christening. Neil and Lilli's baby was already two months old, and they'd been waiting for Tom and Nancy to get home. Nancy couldn't wait to see Neil and the new baby, so when they drove into the village she jumped straight out of the car, almost hopping with excitement.

'Sis!' Neil was running towards her as fast as his bad leg would allow. He threw his arms around her in a bear hug. 'Gosh, it's good to see you.' He turned to Tom who was locking the car. 'Looking after her, are you?'

'Chance would be a fine thing,' Tom replied, laughing. 'More like she's looking after me!'

'Oh, give over, the pair of you,' Nancy said.

'You look . . . different,' Neil said frowning.

'Nursing does that to you,' she said with a wink.

Neil grinned. 'Here's Lilli now,' he said, as a tall dark-haired woman approached with a baby in her arms.

'Nancy! I've heard such a lot about you,' Lilli said.

'Oh, let me look!' Nancy peered down at the baby, entranced by his tiny eyelashes and miniature fingers. 'He's gorgeous,' she said.

The bells began to chime for the service so Nancy walked arm in arm with Tom as they followed Neil and Lilli down the lane towards the kirk. Nancy was wearing her best Sunday outfit from before the war – an old-fashioned suit and felt hat. Striding out in her good leather shoes, saved for her carefully by her mother, was like stepping back into a familiar lost world.

The small village of Glenkyle was just as she remembered it, as if it had been locked in time. The mountain backdrop, the big expanse of scree and sky. She breathed in lungfuls of highland air, enjoying the breeze on her face.

Ahead of them, Lilli was carrying baby Harry Thomas in her arms as if he might break, his long lace christening gown trailing almost to her knees. Neil had a protective arm against her back, as if to shepherd them along. Dear Neil, he looked older than she remembered. Nancy glanced up to the sky, a pale duck-egg blue and empty of planes. The sun was already sharp and bright and, as they passed, the hedgerows were full of chittering sparrows.

Behind them, Nancy's mother grabbed her for another embrace, before she was chivvied away to talk to her neighbours about the new tractor in a local farmer's barn. Nancy smiled. The conversation was just the same; her mother talking about the Women's Institute and how she enjoyed seeing the cheerful red tractor out ploughing behind the manse.

She glanced at Tom. He was still underweight, with the shadowy look of someone not quite at home in his body. He'd surprised her, she realised, this man of hers. She'd thought him to be a man of intellect not action.

I love you. The thought that ambushed her from nowhere made her squeeze his arm as they went in through the lych gate and under the lintel into the dark of the kirk. She was surprised to see that the pews were full, with neighbours and well-wishers, all anxious to see the baby christened.

Lilli was striking in her wartime utility suit and Nancy was warmed to see how protective Neil was to her and the baby. They must have decided to bring him up as a Christian not a Jew. Hardly surprising, given what Lilli's father had been through. When they'd phoned Neil, he'd told them that Lilli's father had survived the war by the good grace of a Polish farmer, who hid him along with six others who had escaped the Warsaw ghetto in Poland. But he was frail now and too ill to travel, and still recuperating in a Red Cross hospital.

Nancy paused as Tom was stopped by a man seated to his left, his hat pressed to his knees. Tall and broad with a wide face, he stood immediately, put down the hat and shot out his hand to Tom.

'Pavel!' Tom said, as his hand was pumped up and down. 'Didn't expect to see you here.'

'Official photographer,' Pavel said. He seemed to hesitate as if he wanted to say something else but couldn't think what. 'You look well.'

This was so manifestly untrue that Nancy almost laughed. Pavel was the man Tom told her had abandoned him on the crossing to the North, and she was prepared to dislike him. But Tom's face had softened. 'It's good to see another friend made it through,' he said.

Pavel's face reddened. 'Maybe catch you for a pint later?'

Tom put a hand on his arm. 'Glad to.' Then they moved off down the aisle towards Neil,

who'd paused to wait for their mother.

'You look lovely, Ma,' Nancy gave her mother another brief tight hug. She was putting in the effort, Nancy saw, for Father had died in this church, and the memories must still be hard to bear.

Tom stood aside to let her go ahead, and they followed the rest of the family towards the front, Nancy's heels clacking on the old flag floor. To Nancy the fact that her father was gone had still not quite become real. So many things had been lost in the war, and she was still trying to find a foothold in this new world away from Holland.

It was an odd feeling too, to think she was aunt to the small scrap in Lilli's arms, and that she and Tom were to be his godparents. Little Harry was to be named for her father, and his middle name for Tom.

In the pew Nancy sank gratefully to her knees when invited to pray. The coming home had been far more gruelling than she expected, for she still suffered bouts of intense exhaustion and panic. The outside bruises had gone, but the inner ones remained. Letting go of Holland was hard. But today she was determined to surrender herself to Scotland, to the familiar words of the service, and the light streaming in through the clear windows.

The new vicar was elderly and enthusiastic. Nancy's throat tightened with emotion as Neil and Lilli vowed to keep the baby safe from all harm and bring him up in peace and love. She glanced to Tom, and saw him get out his handkerchief to wipe his eyes.

When the baby had been anointed with oil, water was poured over his head, to his obvious indignation, judging by his outraged cries. At two months old he was sturdy, and taking an interest in everything. As he let out a lusty wail, the congregation let out an audible sigh of satisfaction.

'Takes after his mother with that voice,' whispered Tom.

The vicar smiled at Lilli as she dandled Harry proudly before them all. 'May God's joy be in your heart,' he said, 'and God's love surround your living, each day and night and wherever you go. May you know God's presence, in growing and learning, in joy and sorrow, in friendship and solitude, in beginnings and endings – may God keep you and bless you all the days of your life.'

Tom turned to Nancy and his wet eyes mirrored her own.

Beginnings and endings. That was what life was after all. She had seen too many of the latter.

Once they were outside in the fresh May sunshine they lined up to have their photographs taken. Pavel marshalled them all into rows, and Tom pulled Nancy in next to him as they shuffled in the back row just behind Lilli and Neil.

'I never thought we'd have a day like this,' Tom said.

'What a blessing,' Nancy replied. 'I hadn't realised what a privilege it is, just to be alive in a place that's not at war.'

'The baptism was special, but it's the ordinary things that matter more. Like seeing the way you wear your hat at just such a jaunty angle. Like watching the neighbours bicker over who should sit where. Like watching the postman whistle as he delivers the mail. Things where it doesn't matter, where it can all go on, and nobody's going to die.'

'We all have to die sometime,' she said, turning to face the camera.

'But not yet,' he whispered, grabbing her around the waist. 'Not until we're oh . . . sixty or something.'

'Only sixty?' She grinned up at him. 'Then you'll be going without me. I planned to be eighty at least,' she said.

'Eighty it is, then. And keep that hat. You might want to be buried in it.'

She punched him on the arm, just as the camera clicked.

A Letter from Deborah Swift

Thank you so much for choosing to read *Operation Tulip*. I hope you enjoyed it. If you did and would like to get a free story and be the first to know about my new releases, you can sign up to my mailing list: https://dl.bookfunnel.com/e6izwznl1e

If you loved *Operation Tulip* I would be so grateful if you would leave a review. I always love to hear what readers thought, and it helps new readers discover my books too.

Thanks,

Deborah

Twitter: https://twitter.com/swiftstory

Website: https://deborahswift.com/

The Silk Code

**Based on the true story of 'Englandspiel',
one woman must race against the clock to uncover a traitor,
even if it means losing the man she loves.**

England, 1943: Deciding to throw herself into war
work, **Nancy Callaghan** joins the Special Operations Executive
in Baker Street. There, she begins solving 'indecipherables' –
scrambled messages from agents in the field.

Then Nancy meets **Tom Lockwood**, a quiet genius when
it comes to coding. Together they come up with the idea
of printing codes on silk, so agents can hide them in their
clothing to avoid detection by the enemy. Nancy and Tom
grow close, and soon she is hopelessly in love.

But there is a traitor in Baker Street, and suspicions turn
towards Tom. When Nancy is asked to spy on Tom, she must
make the ultimate sacrifice and complete a near impossible
mission. Could the man she love be the enemy?

The Shadow Network

One woman must sacrifice everything to uncover the truth in this enthralling historical novel, inspired by the true World War Two campaign Radio Aspidistra . . .

England, 1942: Having fled Germany after her father was captured by the Nazis, **Lilli Bergen** is desperate to do something proactive for the Allies. So when she's approached by the Political Warfare Executive, Lilli jumps at the chance. She's recruited as a singer for a radio station broadcasting propaganda to German soldiers – a shadow network.

But Lilli's world is flipped upside down when her ex-boyfriend, **Bren Murphy**, appears at her workplace; the very man she thinks betrayed her father to the Nazis. Lilli always thought Bren was a Nazi sympathiser – so what is he doing in England supposedly working against the Germans?

Lilli knows Bren is up to something, and must put aside a blossoming new relationship in order to discover the truth. **Can Lilli expose him, before it's too late?**

Historical Note

The Dutch Resistance

The Dutch Resistance was by no means a unified whole. The earliest resistance movement was the Netherlands Communist Party, who arranged the first general strike in response to the deportation of Jews from Amsterdam.

On the same day that this strike was called, a Haarlem-born teacher produced the first leaflet encouraging the population to resist. Unfortunately, the fledgling organisation was soon infiltrated by Nazi sympathisers and shut down. In the Netherlands, being so close to Germany, there were many who agreed with the Nazi regime, and it was not uncommon for people to be betrayed by neighbours and friends, particularly if the friend thought they could gain a benefit from doing so.

In fact, there were over thirty recognised resistance organisations over the course of the war. Most of the women in these various groups worked as couriers or wireless operators, but there were a few who carried out actual assassinations. The Haarlem RVV group (*Raad van Verzet* – Council of Resistance) included three sisters – The Oversteegens, who not only housed fugitive Jews or Allied airmen, but also made a number of attacks on prominent Nazis. Of the three sisters, Truus, Freddie and Hannie, only the first two survived. Hannie was executed on the sand dunes just outside Haarlem shortly before the end of the war.

All the Resistance activities in the book are taken from real events, as is the accidental bombing of Bezuidenhout. In some cases I have changed the names to make them easier for non-Dutch people to pronounce, or to avoid confusion with other people in the book. For example, in the first scene the Nazi Oelschlägel becomes Obermayer, and the real-life General Rauter in the SS truck filled with food destined for the Luftwaffe, became General Weiter.

Operation Tulip as a name is fictional, invented by my characters, although there was a real-life operation after the war to deport all Germans from the Netherlands, and this was called Operation Black Tulip.

The Oranjehotel

The Oranjehotel was the name the Dutch gave to the Scheveningen prison during the Second World War, Orange being the national Dutch colour. Inside this fortress the Germans held more than 25,000 people for interrogation. People imprisoned there included members of the Resistance, but also Jews and Jehovah's Witnesses, as well as people detained for anti-German activities or dealing on the black market. One of the best-known people imprisoned there was Corrie ten Boom, who survived the war to tell people about Ravensbrück concentration camp. Many like her were tortured during interrogation then sent on to other prisons or camps, or executed on the nearby plain, the Waalsdorpervlakte.

The Hunger Winter

In the Spring of 1940 Germany invaded the Netherlands and the Nazi regime began to crush the Dutch population. During the occupation, the deportation of more than a hundred thousand

Jews to the extermination camps is well documented, and the Dutch people saw the worst of this atrocity with more of their Jewish population murdered than any other country.

What few people have heard about though is the fate of the Dutch after the Battle of Arnhem in 1944, when the remaining Dutch people north of the Rhine were cut off from food and fuel supplies and many starved to death. To the Dutch, this period is known as *De Hongerwinter* or The Hunger Winter.

It came about because of the failure of Operation Market Garden, the mission to create an Allied invasion route into German territory with a bridge over the Lower Rhine. The attack was doomed right from the beginning when British tanks got bogged down in the waterlogged Dutch soil, and at the same time two SS German Panzer divisions had hidden themselves in the woods. Airborne troops that were parachuted in met a battery of artillery fire and soon had to withdraw. This mission was immortalised in the film *A Bridge Too Far*.

The failure of Operation Market Garden left the north of Holland cut off from supplies in the south, and in addition, the country was still occupied by the Nazis, who had yet another opportunity to purloin food stocks, to destroy the ports, and to further terrorise the civilians or enslave any remaining Dutch men in German factories or camps.

In addition, large swathes of the land had been flooded or otherwise taken for defence by the Germans, many trade barges had been seized, and there was no fuel for transport by lorry. In some provinces food was so scarce there was nothing left to eat but tulip bulbs and the beets used for feeding cattle. Civilians cycled vast distances in the hope of bringing home food from distant farms. More than 18,000 Dutch civilians starved to death, including many elderly people and young children, with a further 980,000 classed as malnourished.

Relief was provided by British and American airmen, who made humanitarian air drops, the first ever in the history of this type of aid. The air drop featured in this novel was called *Operation Manna* after the miraculous food in the Bible, 'Manna from Heaven'.

Operation Manna as featured in this book began in April 1945, when British Lancaster bombers dropped 530 tons of food, and this continued with the American *Operation Chowhund*, until 7,000 tons of food had been delivered to the Netherlands. These air drops had a massive impact on Dutch morale as they gave a chance of survival to millions of people, and came at the darkest time in the war when the Dutch thought they had been forgotten. To this day, many people treasure an old food sack, or a rusty ration tin as a memento of the day that food dropped from the sky.

Selected Further Reading

SOE in the Low Counties by MRD Foot
The SS Officers Armchair by Daniel Lee
The Dutch Resistance 1940-45 by Michel Wentling LLM and Klaas Castelein
The Ministry of Ungentlemanly Warfare by Giles Milton
The Hunger Winter by Henri A Van der Zee
The Dutch Resistance Revealed by Joss Sharrer
Special Operations Executive Manual – How to be an Agent in Occupied Europe – Reproduction by HarperCollins

Acknowledgements

My thanks must go first of all to my editor Audrey Linton for her insightful feedback on the manuscript, and to the team at HQ Digital for bringing this series to you the reader. Thank you to Anneliese Jansen from the Netherlands who read through *Operation Tulip* in draft form to check for errors and gave me some great feedback. No novelist works alone and I'd particularly like to thank my Mill House writer friends Carol, Charlotte, Liz and Jenny for our writing retreat discussions and problem-solving for this book and the others in the series. As always I'm massively grateful to my husband John who provides the support that underpins my writing, and listens patiently to my morning lectures on obscure aspects of WW2 history.

Dear Reader,

We hope you enjoyed reading this book. If you did, we'd be so appreciative if you left a review. It really helps us and the author to bring more books like this to you.

Here at HQ Digital we are dedicated to publishing fiction that will keep you turning the pages into the early hours. Don't want to miss a thing? To find out more about our books, promotions, discover exclusive content and enter competitions you can keep in touch in the following ways:

JOIN OUR COMMUNITY:

Sign up to our new email newsletter: http://smarturl.it/SignUpHQ

Read our new blog www.hqstories.co.uk

https://twitter.com/HQStories

www.facebook.com/HQStories

BUDDING WRITER?

We're also looking for authors to join the HQ Digital family!
Find out more here:

https://www.hqstories.co.uk/want-to-write-for-us/

Thanks for reading, from the HQ Digital team